TRAVELER

Book One of the Druid Chronicles

J. Paige Dunn

Steel & Magic
5 Elements Press
Jonesboro, AR

Traveler: Book One of the Druid Chronicles
www.druidchronicles.com

This book is manufactured in the United States of America.

Steel & Magic
a division of 5 Elements Press
Jonesboro, AR 72403

Quantity discounts available to organizations, schools, and libraries.
Contact: 5elementspress@gmail.com

Editions ISBN
Print: 978-1-940882-01-7
eBook: 978-1-940882-02-4

Library of Congress Control Number: 2013954688

Dunn, J. Paige
Traveler: book one of the druid chronicles

Cover design by Leah Kay Suttle
www.leahsuttle.com

Model: Jason Aaron Baca
Photographer: Portia Shao
http://jasonaaronbaca.deviantart.com/

"Rules of Gunfighting"
used with permission from Dean Speir,
who collected them from various contributors,
both living and immortal.
You can find them in their original magnificence at:
www.thegunzone.com/gunfighting.html

Dedication

To my husband, who is always thrilled to see me writing, and who never complains when the house is messy.

To my kids, who think it's pretty awesome to have a geek mom that writes books and plays video games.

To my parents, who have always been encouraging, and my siblings, who have never once thought it strange that I wanted to be a writer.

To my friends, who forgive me when I neglect them in favor of spending time with my imaginary ones.

Thanks for believing in me.
Here it is, the first of many.

Chapter 1 – A Girl Alone in the World

Rules of Gunfighting #1:
Have a gun.

I met her in the springtime, on a road in the middle of nowhere. There's a lot more nowhere than somewhere these days, thanks to the massive earthquakes that brought civilization to its knees just over a hundred years ago. From our ancestors' stories - both written and spoken - it had simply come to be known as the Fracture. For some people, however, it was a beginning.

The young woman stood in the middle of the ancient, broken roadway with an expectant air about her, as though she was waiting for something. I would not ordinarily have come this close to a stranger in the wilderness, but a curve in the road and the thick trees on either side had obscured her presence.

As I was alone, I stopped and looked her over carefully. A backpack was at her feet and a single knife hung from the sheath at her belt. No other weapons were in evidence. I had lived twenty summers and estimated that she was about the same age. Dark brown hair sprung around her face in curls; her skin was the color of rich caramel. She was simply dressed in a light sleeveless blouse that showed off her arms and a blue skirt that stopped below the knee, revealing booted legs and feet.

On one hand, she looked adequately dressed for Travel. On the other hand, she had a woeful lack of weaponry. It was

1

remarkable that she was alone, and even more amazing that she was clean. Outside of town, nobody wastes potable water on bathing unless there is a nearby stream or lake. For that matter, nobody leaves a girl to run around alone.

In my world, that of the Traveler, only one other rational possibility remained – a trap. I checked my machete, making sure it was loose in its sheath. I wiggled my right ankle to feel the reassuring presence of the dagger in my boot. The tomahawks I wore on each hip were secure and could be pulled and thrown at a moment's notice. If necessary, I could also draw the knife tucked into a sheath attached to the machete's scabbard. If things really got hairy, there was always the shotgun in its leather holster strapped to my back.

Trainer always said that a weapon should never leave your hand. I doubted that his aim had ever been as good as mine. I had found that a good 'hawk would split someone's skull and save me a shotgun shell or two. My father said that sometimes a threat is as good as an attack. Often as not, people backed off as soon as I pulled one out and drew back to throw it. When they assumed that I was going to hit whatever I was aiming at, they assumed correctly.

It was obvious that the young woman was expecting to see me – or at least somebody – come around the bend in the road. It bothered me that someone had been watching without my knowledge. Ordinarily I have a sixth sense about these things; an awareness of the world that helped to keep me from being surprised by the unexpected. My special sense was suspiciously silent, so my other five senses went on high alert.

Almost as if she were reading my thoughts, she raised her hand in greeting. I neither waved nor moved closer; it was an obvious ploy to make me let down my guard. The instant I did, her posse was sure to come tearing after me. I was not about to give anyone the satisfaction of catching me unawares.

My response to her greeting was to draw the shotgun. The firearm was at least a century old, being manufactured before the Fracture, but its previous owners had taken meticulous care of it, ensuring its continued function. It had belonged to me for a little over two years, and I took care of it with just as much care and concern. A weapon with this kind of power was too volcanic not to cherish.

People could still make firearms, but it was a time-consuming, labor-intensive process, which meant that the price of the finished piece was prohibitively expensive. I had obtained mine in true Traveler fashion – by doing a dangerous favor for someone.

The shotgun, an Ithaca Model 37, had saved my skin more than once. The black metal finish on its twenty-inch barrel made it easy to conceal in the dark. The pistol grip made it ideal for quick use, but the slam fire capability was what really made it fast. All I had to do was hold the trigger down and slam the pump action for a rapid-fire effect. It held seven twelve-gauge shells plus one in the chamber. I had never had to empty the entire thing to end a fight, and I had ended plenty of fights.

It was unlikely that the group of people who were using this pretty girl as bait would let me kill her. Ideally, they would come into the open so I could kill them before they killed me, but that wasn't likely. Alternatively, I could back off and return the way I had come. There was no need for me to travel this particular road. There were many more for me to explore, and I would just as soon avoid a major conflict.

That was when the girl made her move. She picked up her bag, slung it over her shoulder, and started to walk over to me.

"Stop where you are." I chambered a shell and held the weapon ready to fire. The loud schick-schick echoed off the trees; several birds took flight.

She stopped.

"Nobody has to die today," I said. "You and whoever is with you can just turn around and go back the way you came." I didn't want to kill a woman. Call me old-fashioned, but my parents had raised me to respect women and to never hit or hurt one. I had been forced to kill women twice in self-defense, and I loathed the idea of doing it again.

"There's no one with me," she replied.

She was far too calm for someone with a very large gun pointed at her. It was almost as if she'd never seen one before.

"Right." I continued to scan the tree line, then cast a quick

3

glance behind me. I wasn't about to let them flank me, and I wasn't willing to wait to be attacked from the front. Still keeping my aim, I began walking backward the way I had come. Her head tipped to the side and a puzzled expression crossed her face, followed by one of surprise.

From my past experience with this type of situation, I knew that the best way to get out of it was to walk away. Unfortunately, on a few occasions that had not been a viable option. After one brief firefight in which only a terrified woman and I were left standing, I had learned she had been a prisoner in need of rescue, as well as an unwilling participant in the ambush. I had helped her make it to a nearby town. In return, she had given me a wealth of information, along with the understanding that bait was threatened with beatings and starvation if the prey escaped. Since then, I had tried to rescue trapped individuals when I could.

This was not going to be one of those times. There was too much cover in which enemies could hide. I hated to do it, but I would be abandoning this one.

Part of my brain thought it was strange that she looked surprised rather than alarmed or afraid. She frowned, starting to look put out. I wondered if she was a bandit herself, posing as an innocent. I had run into that before, too.

"Where are you going?" she asked.

"Away from you."

She looked indignant. "I told you there's no one with me. All I want to do is talk to you."

"I'm not much of a conversationalist."

Quakes, was she really going to follow me?

She was. She slipped both arms into her pack and moved toward me again, a determined look on her face. It was insanity, really, if she truly was alone – which she couldn't be. The young woman did not advance past a certain point, however, merely matching my speed.

I stopped; she followed suit. The situation was ridiculous. I couldn't walk backwards forever.

"What do you want?"

"Just to talk."

4

"Nobody just wants to talk out here. They either want to trade, steal, or kill."

She was silent a moment.

"Fine, then. Trade."

"Trade what?"

"Words?"

Oh, for the love of all that was green and good in the world! Did she really think I was going to fall for that? I couldn't help but feel a little annoyed that she was insisting on keeping up her façade of innocence.

"Look, I know what this is about," I said, glancing about. "Your posse sends you out to get my attention, and then rushes out to kill me and steal my stuff."

"I don't have a posse," she insisted. "I'm alone."

"That's ridiculous. Girls don't go anywhere alone."

Somehow, she had moved closer to me without my noticing. I examined her carefully, noting the earnest expression and relaxed posture. I had to admit that it would be quite unusual for a bandit to wear a skirt. I barely looked at her face, continuing to scan the area. After a quick check of my back trail, I turned back to face her once more. Again she had moved forward a few steps.

How was it that she could move so quietly on the road that I could not hear her?

"Are you expecting someone?" she asked. She sounded almost hopeful.

No, correct that. She did sound hopeful.

"No," I said.

"Oh." She appeared crestfallen.

This was, without a doubt, the strangest encounter I had ever had. I wondered if my sixth sense had truly failed me or there really was no danger.

My instincts had never been wrong before.

It seemed like an attack would have come by now, if there was going to be one.

Was it possible that she really was alone?

I lowered the shotgun.

She smiled.

I scowled, and the smile faltered.

"What are you doing out here?" I asked. Impatience had finally gotten the better of me. Trainer had always chewed me out for my lack of patience.

The smile returned. "Waiting for you."

My reflexes took over and I stepped back and away, bringing the shotgun to bear, sweeping the barrel in all directions... at nothing but the singing of birds and the scampering of squirrels in the primal forest. I could have sworn that her words sounded like a signal to attack.

"What the hell...?" I muttered to myself.

"You're a little jumpy." She eyed me as though she might be questioning my sanity. That irritated me. Trainer had also berated me for my temper.

"Look," I said. "Girls don't come out here alone. Girls don't go anywhere without a whole group of men to protect them. And nobody is clean out here."

She opened her mouth to speak but I cut her off. "You just expect me to believe you're out here alone? For all I know, you're supposed to lead me into an ambush."

"That would be pointless, since you're out here alone anyway. Anybody could jump you any time they felt like it."

"You're really alone?"

A doubtful look crossed her face. "Maybe you're not the one I was waiting for," she said. "I rather expected someone more intelligent."

That burned my leather. "Hey, I'm plenty smart. I've been Traveling for two years now, and I haven't survived by being stupid. Or careless."

"Cautious, then." Her expression brightened. "That's understandable."

I searched her face, finally believing the light of truth in her green eyes. All I could read in them was honesty and earnestness, with a hint of desire. Those dramatic eyes gripped me. They were like no green eyes I had ever seen - soft milky green with a dark forest border.

Cursing myself for an idiot, I re-holstered the shotgun. I comforted myself with the thought that I could draw it more

6

quickly than anyone could approach.

"What's your name?" she asked.

"Davis."

"That sounds like a last name."

"It is."

"What's your first name?"

"Why would you be waiting for someone whose name you don't even know?"

The corner of her mouth quirked upward.

"So you believe me?"

"Not yet."

"I'm Angie." She stuck out her hand.

If I shook hands, she could slow down my draw.

What the hell. I had plenty of weapons and was tired of waiting. I shook her hand.

Nothing happened.

"It is my utmost pleasure to make your acquaintance," she said, beaming.

She had a beautiful smile. Her dark skin made her green eyes stand out dramatically. She was, quite possibly, the prettiest woman I had ever seen.

"Nice to meet you," I said, feeling awkward. It was bizarre in the extreme to be introducing myself to her after holding her in my sights for several minutes. Now that we stood within a few feet of each other, I could see the interesting details of her person. Her sleeveless blouse was tucked into a long split skirt with elaborate embroidery at the hem. Large gold hoop earrings hung with beads dangled from her ears and matching bracelets adorned her wrists. The dark, corkscrew curls brushing the tops of her shoulders were ornamented with a variety of feathers and strings of beads. In all my travels, I had never seen anyone like her.

I glanced at Angie's feet, noting with approval the sturdy boots there. My own boots, a gift from my mother, had lasted me two years on the road, with yearly resoling. They were heavy and steel-toed, with metal shin guards that buckled around the back. Best of all, there were no annoying laces. I loved them almost as much as the shotgun.

I tried to think logically in an attempt to understand this

situation. I had come upon a beautiful young woman, dressed for Travel, in the middle of the road. She had no protection and she wasn't an unwilling accomplice in an ambush. Not only that, but she was waiting for me. I tried to wrap my mind around the facts as she had presented them without success.

I shook my head. "This does not make any sense."

"It really does," she said. "And it will, after I explain it."

"There is no possible way for you to be waiting for me," I said. "You don't even know me."

"That's... sort of true."

I raised an eyebrow. My father had always said that no one could split hairs like a woman.

"I mean... I did know you'd be here."

"That's not possible," I said. "Even I didn't know I'd be here until this morning." In fact, I hadn't known exactly where I would be. I had only just chosen my path after breakfast.

"It's possible. Really it is," she replied, looking a bit anxious.

"I'm waiting."

She squirmed. I had the feeling that she wanted to accompany me, and there was no way I was Traveling with anyone without knowing their motives.

"Have you been tracking me?"

She squirmed some more. "Sort of?"

"Are you a Tracker?"

"No. I mean, I can track, but I'm not a tracker by profession."

I had the distinct impression that we were speaking different languages.

"How long have you been tracking me?"

"I've journeyed over two hundred miles," she said. "But I've only been waiting here a couple of days."

"You've been waiting here for two days, in this spot, where I didn't know I'd be until... oh, about two minutes ago?"

She blushed. "Well, no. I had to move around some. It was important to stay ahead of you." She seemed annoyed that I was not just going to lose my mind at the sight of a pretty face and do whatever she wanted just because she smiled and batted her eyes

8

at me.

"I mean, it's not like I could have come up behind you," she added. "You'd probably shoot first and ask questions later."

That was an accurate statement. It made me a little more comfortable, knowing that she understood.

She shook her head, curls bouncing. "This is not how things are supposed to go," she said, almost pouting.

"This is not how what is supposed to go?"

"Oh, fine!" she snapped. "Be that way."

"You do realize that I am giving over quite a bit of trust in even allowing you this close. A little honesty would be appreciated." I paused. "It's important for me to know why you've been waiting for me and how you knew I'd be here."

Angie looked uncertain, and let out her breath in a huff. "You'll just think I'm crazy."

"Try me," I said.

"I tracked you with a fetch."

"Is that some kind of dog?"

"No, actually it was a cat."

"You tracked me with a cat?"

"No!" She stomped her foot. "The fetch is a magical creature bound to my spirit."

She was right. She did sound crazy. Even if I did think she was insane – and I didn't – I wouldn't have made a judgement based solely on her words. I had encountered enough peculiar things and people over the past couple of years that I was willing to entertain the idea of magic. I had met a holy man who could walk barefoot on hot coals. There were stories of shamans who could speak to the dead. I had been to towns who highly revered their village healers because they were so adept at treating wounds and curing illnesses. Who was I to say that magic did not exist?

"Some people would say there's no such thing as magic," I said.

"They just say that because they've never seen it before." There was the light of hope in those dramatic green eyes, now that she had realized I wasn't running away.

"I'm not sure I'm seeing it now."

9

"Yes, you are." Her eyes sparkled with mischief.

"Really?"

"You said so yourself... I'm alone, in a place where girls are never alone. And, I'm clean."

She smiled again, and it crossed my mind that if anything was magic, it was her lovely smile. I shook myself. What was I thinking?

"Maybe it's just your face that's clean," I said, determined not to be distracted by the aforementioned pretty face.

She leaned in closer. With the heat of the day, the stink should have knocked me flat on the cracked concrete. She smelled like wildflowers – honeysuckle, to be exact. It was too early in the season for honeysuckle to be blooming. I decided she was telling the truth about the magic. After all, who knows what changes have come about since the Fracture? At the very least, she believed she possessed magic. So maybe she really did.

Either way, it didn't mean I had to do anything. It was merely a new and interesting experience in a long line of them. Just because she wanted something, it didn't mean I was obligated to fulfill her desires. I was happy with my life as a Traveler, seeing new sights, meeting new people, avoiding my hometown, and being an eternal disappointment to my mother.

However, she was female, innocent, and alone in the wilderness. I had to at least offer her my protection until she was in a safe locale. My conscience would plague me for the rest of my life if I left her to fend for herself. I sighed.

"Look. Angie. Honestly, I don't even know which question to ask first. So, why don't we walk a ways, and you can tell me about yourself."

"Really?"

I nodded. "It's not safe for you to be out here alone. At the very least, I can walk you to the nearest town."

She cocked one hip and put her hand on it, her green eyes flashing. "I am a druid, in a long line of powerful magic users," she said firmly. "I don't need to be walked anywhere."

I shrugged. "Suit yourself," I said. I went around her and continued onward as I had originally intended, leaving her standing in the middle of the road.

Chapter 2 – Man in the Wilderness

Rules of Gunfighting #16:
Flank your adversary when possible.
Protect your own flank.

I wasn't entirely comfortable with walking away from Angie, but if she didn't want me to accompany her to safety, I wasn't going to force her. I had been Traveling long enough to know that sometimes people made stupid decisions that I could do nothing about.

In the beginning, I had tried to save a few people from themselves. It never actually helped them and nearly got me killed, more often than not. There was nothing more frustrating than risking my neck to save someone, only to watch them turn around and plunge into an identical situation thinking it would turn out better.

In the old days, after the Fracture, Travelers were held in high esteem, possessing a near-legendary status. They went where no one else dared to go, bringing news and sometimes precious finds from uncovered caches. They were the ones who broke trails to provide safe paths that others eventually followed. They built little shelters or hung signposts beside places where clean water could be obtained. People sought their advice on how to keep predators and animals from stealing their livestock. Sometimes they were hired to do away with the most dangerous creatures. They were solitary people, keeping to themselves. They were independent and innovative. They were wild and untamed, even in the middle of civilization.

The legends were exaggerated, to a certain extent, and altered quite a bit for the consumption of children. I had realized that after my first journey, and it had made me wonder whether the world had become more violent or if my childhood heroes had been liars. With a return of trade routes and protected caravans, people claimed that Travelers were merely an outdated curiosity of another time.

Even so, I was not sorry to have chosen this lifestyle. Initially I had set out with something to prove, both to my parents and to my hometown. I had been disgraced after Trainer had beaten me the last time, in full view of the whole town. Not one person had stepped in to help me. When my father arrived, he had gotten Trainer off me, and then had pummeled the man until he was crawling in the dust.

I was sixteen.

The townsfolk had forgiven my father because he was doing the right thing in defending his son. I was not forgiven; people were convinced that my big mouth and bad attitude had most likely provoked Trainer into a rage. Once I recovered, people avoided me, even to the point of crossing the street with their daughters when I walked by.

I stopped going into town, and no amount of pleading, cajoling or threatening by my mother would move me. Nor would I disclose the reason why. My parents were respected members of Jonesboro, and they would have been heartbroken to know how I was being treated by the town to which they had given so much.

Part of me agreed that I had deserved a beating. Not for the reasons everyone else believed, but for having been such an idiot to think a beautiful girl with honey-blond hair would prefer me over one of the most powerful men in town.

Since I would not leave our property on the outskirts of Jonesboro, my father put me to work. He might have thought that I would get sick of the difficult labor, but I didn't. It was a relief to have something to do – to work my body so hard that I fell asleep instantly every night, relieved of the parade of thoughts and memories that had given me insomnia for weeks while I had been healing.

Once I had regained my strength, he put me to work of a different kind – teaching me to fight. It was vastly different from what Trainer had taught. In fact, I wondered if the man had really known anything, or if he had just pretended to teach me, so he could knock me around and mock me for being inept.

My father began by training me to defend myself, which included blocking blows and the proper way to take a punch. Afterward, I learned to fight without weapons: the correct way to throw a punch, aim a forceful kick, and choke out an opponent. Next came fighting with daggers and tomahawks, practicing throwing both until I could hit multiple moving targets, one after the other. After that, he taught me to use the machete; first dull, then sharpened to a finely-honed edge.

Once he had deemed my training finished, he tried to teach me the family business. Why he had ever thought I would be interested in farming after learning to fight was beyond me. True, I learned what I needed to know about the running of our farm and the management of its gardens and orchards. When it came to working for others, however, his efforts met with total failure. I was dead set against leaving our property. I suppose he had thought that after training me to defend myself, I would be willing to venture out into the main part of Jonesboro again. He seemed to be acting on the assumption that I was afraid of being assaulted again.

I wasn't afraid, especially not after all the time my father had invested in teaching me combat techniques. I just didn't like the way people had looked at me after the incident with Trainer. They acted like I had raped a girl, instead of just kissing her. What really bothered me was that she had asked for the kiss and had not bothered to set the record straight afterward.

My mother got tired of waiting for me to get over it. My father had an infinite amount of patience, and likely would have let things continue as they had been. She, however, finally succumbed to frustration. We had a terrible fight, where she yelled and threatened and demanded to know why I could not be a good son and go help my father in his work. I told her I would do anything they needed around the homestead, but that they could leave me out of anything where the town proper was concerned. She became full of rage, saying she would have no cowardly son under her roof. She always did have a fearsome and fiery temper.

I left the very next day and did not return to their home until early winter, when the first frost made the grass crackle beneath my boots. My mother was full of tearful apologies and threw her arms around me when I returned. My father accepted my return with the same calm demeanor with which he seemed to accept everything in life.

I had acquired the shotgun on that first trip. When I came home with it, he had frowned at it, but said nothing. It wasn't that I didn't value his training. I did value it; it had saved my life before I had the shotgun, and on several occasions afterward when I had been short on ammunition. It also kept me a lot cleaner, as it gave me the ability to kill my enemies before they came within arm's reach. It was easy to clean blood off my black leather pants. My shirts, however, tended to end up torn, dirty and bloodied. The shotgun saved many a shirt for me, frequently ending a fight before it got started. My father could frown at my ancient technology all he wanted, but I was keeping it.

The road again beckoned to me in the springtime. My mother had been dropping hints, like my father being glad of my help while working for Mr. Farmer when the weather warmed. As the ground thawed and my resolve did not, her temper was sure to flare, so I departed my home once again. It didn't keep her from shouting at me, but as I was already on my way out the door, it was of little concern.

For the most part, I was welcomed wherever I went. When I had nothing of value to trade, I did odd jobs for people in exchange for room and board. Sometimes, people hired me to take care of things that they either lacked the capability of doing or shied away from because they didn't want to dirty their own hands.

I never needed to work for anyone. I did it because I wanted to be like the Travelers that had come before me. I had a wealth of herbal lore that my father had taught me and I was skilled at foraging for nuts and berries. I could trap or hunt animals for meat and fur. Feeding myself was never a problem.

Spending less than half my time in towns, I tended to keep to myself. While I was courteous to everyone, I doubted anyone could call me friend. There was such a thing as being alone too much, however; sometimes I needed simple human contact. After acquiring the shotgun, I began to hire out as a caravan guard. It was an ideal situation for me, allowing me to spend time with people and still give in to my roaming spirit.

After riding along with one such caravan to deliver goods from Jonesboro to Brookland, I had set out on my own to wander a bit further north along the foot of Crowley's Mountain Range. I was making my way to Kingston on a relatively well-traveled road when Angie had come across my path. I had heard that there was a caravan headed to Hardy leaving from there. It was quite a long distance and far too dangerous to walk alone on a first trip; I was hoping to hire on with the caravan.

Unlike my previous years of Travel, this time I had a destination and a goal. I had heard that Hardy was a place where a hard-working individual might apprentice himself and learn a profession. There, one could learn pottery, carpentry, leather craft, book-binding, candle-making, weaving, blacksmithing, and even gun craft. Granted, most people my age were already working at a trade, but I reasoned that a blacksmith might be willing to take me on simply because I had the strength to do the work already. It seemed likely that I would be content to spend my days in the heat of a forge, creating tools and weapons. The tools would make me a valued member of society; the weapons would make me wealthy.

After only two years on the road, I begrudgingly understood what my father had meant when he said I wouldn't be able to Travel forever. I truly loved the walking and the quiet, but at some point, I might want to marry, settle down and raise a family. There was no way I was going to settle in Jonesboro and put my children through the kind of grief to which I had been subjected. I also thought that if I did settle in one place, with a family, my parents just might be inclined to join me there.

However, before I chose a place to settle, I wanted to see more of the world. Most people were in the same town in which they were born, never venturing out beyond its borders to see what lay beyond. I wasn't like most people. I didn't like where I had come from, and if I was to settle down, I wanted it to be a place where people were more open-minded and accepting of the differences of others.

* * *

That evening I chose a likely campsite and shrugged out of my backpack. I stretched my arms and shoulders to loosen the tension that always resulted after a long day. I figured it would only be about five more miles to Kingston, but the sun was setting. Traveling at night was never a good idea.

Since the cataclysm that had destroyed any semblance of government or organized civilization, most of the surviving people had recreated new communities out of those destroyed during the Fracture. They had worked together to rebuild their lives from the rubble, helping one another to survive. Sometimes these gathered peoples had laws and re-created governments like the ones that had existed before. Others, usually the smaller ones, had a council of respected members who made decisions for the good of all.

There were still those lawless individuals who resisted the regimen of law and order, however. Just as before the Fracture, those on the fringe made a living by taking advantage of others. Bandits and highwaymen were always a danger, preying on the unwary at all times, but especially at night. As the visibility dropped, the risk increased.

It was better to spend the night in a safe location; even with some shelter, camping outdoors wasn't exactly secure. I usually relied on my sixth sense to wake me if danger was imminent. I paused, thinking back to when it had failed me that afternoon. Scowling into my pack, I dug deeply into the bottom of it and pulled out a roll of twine and a small leather pouch that contained a handful of small silver bells. They were way down in the bottom because I hadn't used them in a long time. I had only kept them because I never knew when I might need them – like now.

In the beginning of my time as a Traveler, I had hung the tiny bells on twine that I strung around my campsite, wrapped around bushes or trees at ankle height, to warn me of approaching enemies. One small jingle, and I would be up and scanning for the threat. Halfway through my first summer on the road, I realized that I had been awakening on my own, before anyone had even reached the bells. I hadn't used them since, but it looked like I was going to need them now. It was not a comfortable thought.

I stretched the twine in as big of a circle as I could around my bedroll, and then hung the little bells. There was no satisfaction in doing this; I was proud of my sixth sense. It would bother me greatly for it to become sporadic. It would be even worse to lose it permanently.

Using flint and steel, I made a small fire and started thinking. Perhaps I was just tired. The caravan ride had been no picnic. It wasn't bandits that had made the journey so taxing; it was the caravan owner's daughter. The girl couldn't have been more than sixteen, but had repeatedly tried to lure me somewhere alone. She had even tricked me into walking away from the wagons with the ruse of having lost a bracelet. As soon as we were out of sight of the others, she had thrown her arms around my neck and tried to kiss me.

Well aware of how protective the caravan master was of her, and having no desire for a repeat of what had happened in Jonesboro, I had immediately pulled her off, marching her back to the wagons and delivering her to her father. I suggested that she not be allowed to wander off alone because she might end up losing something more important than her bracelet. Fortunately, he took my meaning and from then on, she was required to stay close to one of her parents. As a result, I was the recipient of many venomous looks for the remainder of the trip.

It hadn't bothered me in the least.

When the fire was going well, I grabbed a couple of potatoes from an external pocket of my pack and tucked them into the ashes to cook. A leather pouch hanging from the outside contained a rabbit that I had snared the night before. That morning, I had paunched and gutted it so that it wouldn't spoil during the day. I skinned it and poked a stick through the carcass, holding it over the dancing flames to roast.

I thought again of the green-eyed young woman, wondering what she was really doing in the wilderness by herself. I had met several women who were just as skilled at hunting and woodcraft as any man. She hadn't seemed like one of those. Then again, since she was supposedly waiting for me, I wondered if she really could take care of herself. I felt a guilty prick of conscience. I could have stayed a bit longer to listen to her story, or could have talked her into allowing me to escort her to the nearest town. On the other hand, I had been pretty disturbed at the loss of my extra-sensory awareness, so I couldn't be blamed for wanting to take the extra precaution of leaving the area quickly.

So, while it had troubled me somewhat to leave her behind, she was a rational, healthy adult who was fully capable of taking responsibility for herself. I had no interest in arguing with her, and hoisting her over my shoulder and forcing her to come with me was out of the question. I could hardly carry her to Kingston or Green Country with me, no matter how close they were. If, in fact, she had traveled nearly two hundred miles alone as she had claimed, then I needn't have worried about her at all. I tried to put her out of my mind.

When the rabbit was done, I jammed the stick into the soft earth to allow it time to cool. The potatoes needed to be turned, after which I let them bake a few minutes more. I often ate dried meat, fruit, and nuts in order to avoid such attention, but I was unwilling to pass up fresh meat for supper. While they finished cooking, I realized that my fire had attracted someone's attention.

Pretending that I hadn't a care in the world, I rose and stretched, faking a huge yawn. I fiddled with my pants and walked away from the fire, as though intent on taking a piss. Once I was out of the range of the firelight, I quietly slipped the shotgun from its holster and circled back. Two men stood looking at something – probably my rabbit.

Ordinarily, I would invite a hungry person to share whatever I had to eat. However, these two had not hailed me or announced their presence.

That meant they weren't friendly.

Standing roughly fifteen feet behind them, I chambered a round. Even after a hundred-plus years, with shotguns becoming scarcer, everyone still reacted to that particular noise.

Everyone.

The one on the left was foolish enough to go for his weapon, an antique revolver. Some highwaymen fancied themselves gunslingers. Very often, they challenged each other, both in towns and on the road. Townspeople had little tolerance for that sort of thing and ran them out fairly quickly. On the road, however, it was every man for himself. There was no law, sheriff, or town council to intervene.

Pistols were useless against someone like me. As the first man turned to fire, the scattershot from my weapon ripped his chest apart. His buddy had a revolver in his hand but the muzzle flash from the shotgun had blinded him. I shot him, too, then moved lateral to my original position in case anyone else was with them. The night was deathly quiet after the roar of the shotgun, and I crouched in the stillness for long minutes.

None of my senses could detect another living soul, so I went back and searched the bodies. First, I collected the pistols and ammunition so I could either sell or trade them. Weapons were heavy and only valuable to me for resale value. Neither man had anything else of value.

Of course not. That's why they had been after my stuff.

Unfortunately, now that there were dead bodies lying around, there would soon be scavengers as well. The scent of blood would soon draw predators such as wolves, lions and black bears. I walked back to break camp and heard a jingle as my leg brushed the twine. Realizing that I had not been alerted by the bells, but by my sixth sense, I breathed a sigh of relief. I reloaded my weapon, stuffed my belongings back into my pack, and took down the bells and twine. After slinging the pack on my shoulders once again, I picked up my rabbit, now cooled to the perfect temperature. Stabbing the potatoes with my knife, I lifted them away from the fire and covered it over with dirt, making sure it was completely extinguished.

I started down the road again, munching on my rabbit. It was delicious.

Chapter 3 – Perseverance

Rules #23 of Gunfighting:
Be courteous to everyone. Friendly to no one.

I was roused by the bright morning sun, in a surround of bushes several hundred feet from the road. Usually I woke with the first grey light of dawn, but moving my campsite at a late hour had meant a late bedtime. Before going to bed, I had taken my ball of twine with its tiny bells and wrapped it around the thin stalks of the bushes. I still wasn't sure if my extra sense would warn me adequately, so I did it just to be on the safe side. Sure, it had done so when I was awake, but would it when I was sleeping?

I awoke looking into her green eyes. Angie was sitting cross-legged in my camp, looking at me calmly. I was not so calm, immediately rolling out of my blanket with the shogun and aiming at her.

"If I was going to kill you, I'd have done it already," she said with a smirk.

I scowled at her and lowered the weapon.

"What do you want?"

"The same thing I wanted yesterday. You."

I snorted, then rose and stamped my feet into my boots. I began untying and rolling up the incredibly useless pieces of twine with its stupid little silver bells that had done absolutely no

21

good at all. She was right; she could have killed me.

"It must be pretty important to you, to keep you following me for three days."

"Months."

"What?"

"I've been looking for you for three months."

"I'm not important enough for anybody to follow for three months, much less a pretty druid girl with magical powers," I said, stuffing the twine into my backpack.

"I know otherwise." She smiled, and then I realized I had called her pretty. Quakes, now she'd never leave.

"Then I guess you know something I don't."

"Obviously." Her smile widened.

Ignoring her, I buckled the tomahawk belt low on my hips. Over that, I wrapped a second belt, this one with the machete in its scabbard. Last, I slipped the shotgun scabbard over my shoulder, buckling it over my chest. I packed the rest of my belongings into the backpack and slung it over my shoulders, making sure that it was properly positioned to allow me to draw the shotgun smoothly. I stepped away from my small shelter and headed for the road.

"Where are you going?" she asked, jogging to catch up to me.

"North. Same as the first time we met."

"Why won't you listen to me?"

"You're talking, and I hear you. What more do you want?"

"For starters, to be treated with some respect."

I stopped and looked at her. "Respect? For what?"

She drew herself up proudly. "I am a druid in a–"

"–Long line of powerful magic users. Right, I got that yesterday," I said. "I might be inclined to respect them, since they actually use their magic."

"Magic is not to be wasted on frivolous things." She crossed her arms over her chest and let out a disdainful sniff.

I decided not to mention the fact that she smelled like flowers. Females had entirely different ideas on what was frivolous and what wasn't.

"Right," I said. "Here's the deal. I have plans for a long

caravan trip after the next couple of towns. However, I am willing to accompany you to Kingston, if you want to go."

"I'm not going north." She frowned. "Does it mean nothing that I have been waiting for you?"

I raised an eyebrow. "Should it?"

"Yes!"

"Why?"

"Because you're special."

"I think you have the wrong man." If there was anything of which the world had convinced me, it was that I was most definitely not special.

"That's not possible," she said.

"Believe me; anything in this world is possible."

"Then, it's possible that I have found the right man."

I gave her a quick glance, and had to concede that she had won the battle. I was determined to get rid of her and win the war.

"Just for the sake of argument, say I am the person you have been looking for. What am I supposed to do with that information? Fall to my knees and thank you for recognizing my specialness?"

She blushed furiously, but plowed on with determination. "I'm here for one reason, and one reason only. A druid always needs a warrior for protection. You, Davis, are mine."

"Girl, I belong to one person, and one person only. Me." I turned on my heel and started walking again.

I could hear her trotting after me. "I didn't mean it like that. We are meant to be partners in the old tradition."

"What old tradition?"

"The druidic tradition."

I shrugged. "I've never heard of druids, so that doesn't really mean anything to me."

"Never?"

"Never." It did seem a little bit odd to me then, that my parents had given me such a thorough education in so many subjects. I supposed then that they had neglected the esoteric subjects of magic and miracles because they had wanted me grounded in reality. Of course, that piqued my curiosity, which

23

tended to be insatiable even on a good, sensible day. Trainer used to smack me around for my constant questioning. My father had encouraged it.

I've often wondered if he ever regretted it.

"We aren't supposed to reveal too much of ourselves to outsiders," she said.

"That's convenient."

Angie bristled. "It's for safety reasons."

"Right, because wandering around alone is so very safe."

She ignored this. "I can tell you a few things, though."

"Wonderful."

"Why do you have to be so rude?"

"Because I want you to go away and leave me alone?"

"I've come too far to give up now!"

I tried to ignore her hurt tone. I told myself that it didn't matter what she was saying now because women were fickle. She would change her mind about me soon enough – like when someone bigger, stronger, wealthier, or more powerful came along.

"Suit yourself."

She was quiet for a few moments, but unfortunately, it didn't last long.

"I suppose druids have been around since the beginning of human existence," she said. "We thrived among the nature-loving peoples of the world, which were pushed into marginality more and more by technology and greed. Our Mother grew restless, giving warnings to Her children by occasionally shaking the earth and venting Her irritation with sporadic volcanoes. Even Her attempts to cleanse herself with hurricanes were ignored."

"You mean the time before The Fracture." In spite of my best intentions, she had captured my attention with her storytelling.

"We call it the beginning. The Rebirth," she said, with a mysterious smile. "The Mother rose up in protest of the way humans destroyed Her forests and poisoned Her waters. She was tired of the ravages inflicted by Her human children, and so rose up in a tremendous rage. Her holy body shook with umbrage, creating great cracks and greater upheaval. Her passion burst forth from giant mountains, spewing lava and snowing ash. Tidal waves washed clean the shores of every continent. Old islands died and new ones were born.

"When she settled back into sleep, the human population that had so abused her was reduced to a mere fraction of what it had been. The Mother saw that although they were no longer able to significantly ruin Her, they were also insufficient to repair the damage they had wrought.

"And so, She and all the other gods came together and decided that certain of Her human children should be given gifts – gifts that would allow them to destroy the remnants of the old world, and begin the reformation of the new one. We druids were given the powers to tear down the artifices of the old world, and rejuvenate the new world. This is the origin of our magic."

It was a good story. I compared her words to what my parents had taught me about the end of the old world, using the oral tradition they themselves had learned, as well as the few books that remained from that era.

The end of the old – or the beginning of the new, as Angie would have it – had begun with the New Madrid earthquake, along a fault line that had lain dormant for over two centuries. It had flexed the earth's crust so violently that the earthquakes had been felt thousands of miles away. The southern portion of the San Andreas fault slipped sharply after lying dormant for over three hundred years. The central and northern portions, ever unstable, followed suit shortly afterward. In the following years, powerful aftershocks from various faults had caused cities large and small all across the continent to either collapse or burn to the ground. It went like dominoes from there, one massive earthquake after another, each one destabilizing the fault lines of the next region, all around the world. What had not been annihilated by monstrous events of nature rapidly fell to rampant fires that burned out of control. Earthquake liquefaction caused giant sinkholes and landslides.

The tsunamis continued what the shaking earth had begun. Giant waves born from the shifting tectonic plates poured over every continent. Long-dormant volcanoes violently burst forth from the earth's weakened crust, filling the air with a poisonous fume. Smoking mountains erupted in places where volcanism had been thought impossible.

So much lava pouring into the oceans and seas caused the polar ice caps to melt, flooding every continent for miles inland. Even the billions of tons of melting ice did little to cool the oceans, making conditions ripe for the birth of a hurricane. Not only one hurricane was spawned, but over a hundred, churning across the surfaces of the world's oceans and wreaking havoc upon the newly created shores that had never before experienced such a thing. Much of what had survived the tsunamis, died in the maelstrom. Powerful tornados spun off each hurricane and typhoon, causing further destruction inland.

Their lava-filled bellies emptied, the still-smoking volcanoes filled the air with ash and aerosol chemicals rich in sulfur, dramatically cooling the earth's temperature. It finished what the hurricane activity had begun, decreasing the average temperature to that of the last Ice Age. It was beneficial in that the reforming polar ice caps caused the ocean to recede, but devastating because the seasons warm enough to grow crops had shortened drastically. The genetically modified plant life upon which humans had come to rely wilted and died without adequate sunlight. As the food chain began to collapse, the remaining herds of livestock – cows, sheep, goats, and pigs – were slaughtered en masse to keep people alive. Many species went extinct in heavily populated areas.

The collapse of governments and infrastructure brought humanity to its knees, returning it to the dark ages of primitive living. It truly was an age of darkness, not of ignorance, but of severely reduced sunlight. Sewage and overflow from the oceans poisoned the inland water supply. Famine and disease ravaged humanity; few people knew how to grow their own food or treat even the simplest illnesses. They turned on one another like rabid dogs, snarling and fighting over the scraps of their civilization.

There were even fewer books that covered the time following the cataclysm. Most were handwritten diaries kept by individuals who could only relate the events local to them. My father had acquired most of these during his own travels. One book, written by an ancient inhabitant of Jonesboro, stated that after the original city had been destroyed by earthquakes and flooded by the ocean, the survivors had moved upland "to the ridge." They had rebuilt on the higher, more solid ground, and the world gradually returned to calm within a decade or two, or so people remembered. In sharp contrast to the pre-Fracture era, few written records of any kind remained. Most were in private libraries that were carefully hoarded, or in rare diaries kept by those who had lived to tell the tale and passed onto the younger generations.

The air cleared, as did some of the springs, rivers and lakes. The volcanic activity ceased along with the temblors, the world cooled again, and the seas receded. It was assumed that the polar ice caps had reformed, allowing the seas to return to their pre-cataclysmic boundaries. So much of the surface water had been contaminated, by both man-made pollution and the invading ocean, that care still had to be taken when trying a new water source. By and large, though, there was plenty of fresh water to drink. There were also frequent earthquakes in the area, but they were minor and usually went unnoticed.

There were areas around Jonesboro that had survived because they were on an elevated ridge that had somewhat resisted the earthquakes. In fact, with the flexing and shifting of the tectonic plate, the area had risen considerably, creating Crowley's Mountain Range. It was well above sea level and many people had relocated to its elevations to escape the ocean flood. I had heard that there were towns out west that had survived nicely because they were in the mountains. Unfortunately for them, the Fracture had created other problems with which they had been forced to deal - radiation poisoning, mutant animals, and infertility.

"Your magic is from the gods, hunh?" I tried to sound skeptical.

"Didn't your parents raise you to know the gods?"

I looked at her. "What would you do if I told you my parents raised me to be Triune?"

"That's not possible!"

"Isn't it?" I smirked, enjoying her discomfiture.

She stopped in her tracks, looking dismayed and confused. "Thanks for the story!" I called over my shoulder.

* * *

I arrived in the township of Kingston late that afternoon. The community was a strange dichotomy: it was either eerily quiet or complete pandemonium. There seemed to be no middle ground. The quiet was merely the calm before the storm, as if the people who lived there could not endure the thought of living a peaceful existence. If the townsfolk weren't giving out dirty looks, they were snarling at each other. If they weren't snarling, they were yelling. If they weren't yelling, they were throwing punches. If they weren't throwing punches, they were knifing each other. When all else was exhausted, out came the guns.

It was here, coincidentally, that I had done the favor that had earned me the Ithaca 37 shotgun. A man had hired me to help out on his sheep farm, but before it was all over I was involved in protecting his family and property from the neighbors. The home and family had survived, but the man did not. Neither had his neighbors. I suppose you could say that I had acquired the weapon, rather than earning it. However, I did put in quite a bit of work for it. That man's neighbors were mean, but they did have good taste in firearms.

I strolled down the main street, noting that nothing much had changed since last year. There were outlying farms and ranches, but the town proper consisted of one main road that ran through the center of town and two lesser roads that intersected perpendicular to the main. The main road was a dirt strip bordered by small buildings, none more than two stories high, and those were few. Small temblors were common in the area, and tall buildings rarely survived intact. People built both homes and businesses using log construction, as they seemed to weather the unstable earth better than any other type. People even built their barns in the log style.

Hitching posts and watering troughs for horses stood before each building. At each structure's corner stood barrels to catch the rainwater from downspouts. There was a nearby spring, but it ran through the Hayworth property. Mrs. Hayworth charged people for the privilege of drinking her water; or rather, she charged them for having her sons haul it to town. It amounted to pretty much the same thing.

I couldn't blame her for wanting to protect the best source of clean water around. It was a steady source of income for her, in addition to the sheep farm she ran with her sons. Since the gunfight that had taken her husband's life, she needed that income. I usually stopped by and did chores for her when I was in town. She let me share meals with her ranch hands. I slept in the bunkhouse when there was room and in the barn when there wasn't.

There wouldn't be time to visit this trip; I had just enough money to stay at the local saloon, have a hot supper and a cold beer. Maybe even a hot breakfast in the morning, if I was lucky. I stopped by the general store, sold them the few rabbit pelts I had acquired in the past week, and earned a few silvers of the local currency. I kept the pistols and ammunition that I had acquired from the bandits to trade another time; the last thing these people needed were more guns.

I entered the saloon, ordered supper, and sat in the back corner by the fireplace. The barkeep's skinny assistant brought me a deep bowl of venison stew and a small loaf of dark bread. Large chunks of meat, carrots, and other vegetables were bathed in thick gravy. I had water with my meal, preferring to save the beer for afterward.

Saloon regulars began to fill the chairs, as I sopped up the gravy with the last of my bread. My bowl was taken away and replaced with a large mug of beer. If there was anything Kingston did well, it was brew a good beer.

Maybe that accounted for all the fights.

Every time the door opened, I glanced up out of habit. It was a good habit, because sometimes people came into the saloon with guns drawn, and they didn't much care if innocent bystanders came between them and their targets. I noted when a couple of farmers entered, then a group of farmhands. The green grocer and the miller entered, discussing business in low tones. Several more men came and took seats, around tables and at the bar, all tired from work and wanting a drink. I nursed my beer in the back corner, watching them all.

The sky was growing dark when the door opened again. I glanced up and did a double take.

It was Angie.

I knew in an instant that it was going to cause trouble. The farmhands had switched to whiskey after downing a few beers, and had already begun to get rowdy. The rest were well on their way. The more respectable men in town, like the miller, the blacksmith, and the baker, tipped their hats to her as they departed the premises.

She stood in the doorway looking over the place, until the bartender yelled at her.

"In or out, missy!" he barked. She jumped forward and then yelped when the door banged her in the rump. During the raucous laughter that followed, I shifted in my chair, reaching down for my shotgun. I slid it out of its holster and laid it in my lap.

There wasn't anyone who needed to be shot at the moment, but this was Kingston, and that could change in the blink of an eye. So far, they were limiting themselves to cat calls and rude comments that made Angie blush. She stepped up to the bar and spoke with the barkeep. I couldn't hear, due to the noise. It was clear what she had asked, however, because he turned and nodded in my direction. She spotted me and wove her way to my table, only getting pinched in the rear once. Her yelp caused more harsh laughing and ribald comments to erupt in the bar. This was no place for women. It's why they rarely came to town after dark. They certainly never came to the saloon.

Angie stopped before me. "Do you mind if I join you?" she asked. I almost told her I was leaving, but I hadn't finished my beer and wasn't ready to go.

"Be my guest," I said, gesturing to the chair across from mine. Some days I wished my mother hadn't insisted I learn to be polite. I shoved her chair back with the toe of my boot. That was about as mannerly as I was going to be.

With an uncertain smile, she took her seat and scooted up to the table.

"Hi," she said.

"Hello."

"I guess you're wondering what I'm doing here."

I'd have to be an idiot not to know what she wanted, since she'd already told me twice. In the interests of civility, however, I asked her the question she expected.

"What are you doing here?" I asked. I didn't tell her that this place was dangerous, because I'd had my fill of hearing about her all-powerful druidness. I took a swig of my beer.

"I wanted to apologize," she said. "I don't think I explained myself very well, and I'm afraid that we got off on the wrong foot."

The bartender was giving me the hairy eyeball, probably because I had not ordered a drink for the lady. I had enough money for another beer, or breakfast in the morning. I sighed inwardly, thinking that there was no way this would be worth the pancakes and bacon I would be giving up.

"Would you like a drink?" I asked.

Her expression brightened. "Please."

I gestured to the bartender, holding up one finger. The portly man brought a second mug of the golden liquid. I paid him, and he set it before Angie. She smiled and thanked him.

When he was safely away, she turned back to me and whispered, "What is it?"

"Beer."

She took a sip. I half expected her to spit it out, or at least make a face. She did neither, savoring its flavor instead.

"It's good beer," she said. "It's different from what I'm used to, but still good. Thank you."

"You're welcome."

"Honestly, I'm surprised you bought me one. I thought you'd just get up and leave."

"The thought did cross my mind."

Her eyes lifted from the beer to meet mine. "Then I'm glad you didn't."

We looked at each other in silence for several long moments. It should have been strange, or uncomfortable, but it wasn't. I didn't know what to make of it.

31

"You wanted to tell me something?" I said, breaking the silence.

"Oh, right." She glanced around. "I'd prefer to go somewhere more private, if you don't mind."

She was smart to hold off on discussing magic and druids and the gods in this place. Most of the places where I had Traveled were Triune, and most of them still believed that witches and other pagans were evil devil-worshipers. Some actually carried out the archaic behest to burn them at the stake. I didn't know which kind Kingston was, and I didn't want to find out.

"I wish you'd said that before I ordered your beer." I thought she might take offense to this, but instead she smiled.

"I can think of worse ways to spend my time than having a drink with you." Her green eyes glowed with pleasure, captivating me. No other woman had ever looked at me in quite that way. The girl with the honey blonde hair had given me teasing, shy, or beckoning looks, but those paled in comparison to this. I sat back in my chair and tried to shrug the feeling off.

"So... you're still following me?" I asked.

"Yes."

"May I ask why?"

She hesitated, casting another quick look at the other patrons. "Well... for the same reasons I mentioned earlier."

"Haven't we established that I am entirely unsuitable to your purpose?"

Angie shook her head. "No. My guide would not have led me astray." Her tone was full of conviction. A part of me admired that in her. I couldn't say that I had ever felt that strongly about anything.

"I admit that what you said earlier threw me off track." There was a slightly reproachful tone to her voice. "But then I realized that you hadn't actually denied it." She looked down at her beer, drawing aimless patterns in the condensation on the mug with her thumbs.

"Are you sure?" I said, holding back a smile. She was smart, I had to give her that. She must have heard something in my tone, for she looked sharply at me.

"You're teasing me!"

I nearly laughed at her pouty expression. "No, of course not. It would be foolish to tease such a powerful... woman her quest to find the perfect companion." I had almost said druid.

"Now you're making fun of me."

"Maybe." This time I grinned. She looked as though she couldn't decide whether to be offended or to think it was funny. I was half-hoping she would get angry and leave, but she surprised me by choosing the latter. There was another long silence, during which I felt like she was trying to see inside my mind. I fixed a cocky expression on my face and met her gaze evenly.

"I suppose I have been a little full of myself," Angie said.

"Do you think?" I was again surprised, this time by her admission.

"I expected things to go differently when we met," she said. "Perhaps I've read too many books."

"What were you expecting?"

"In the old tradition, a pair of... people would come together and instantly know they were meant to be partners."

"Yep, sounds like something from a book."

"Yes, except these are histories," Angie said.

"Note the word 'story' in history."

"You're very cynical."

I shrugged. She regarded me for a few moments, brow furrowing slightly. I found I much preferred her smile. It bothered me, because I shouldn't have preferred anything about her. I should have been sending her on her way.

"I'm finished with my beer," she said. "Would you like to go for a walk?"

I looked at my mug, which had somehow emptied itself. "Sure," said my mouth, before my brain had time to think about it. Like she had said, I could do worse than have a drink and stroll with a pretty girl. I tucked the shotgun back into its holster and slung it over my shoulder. The rest of my belongings had been stowed into the tiny room I had rented in the boarding house at the far end of the street.

As we crossed the room, I ignored the looks the locals were giving me. Having an attractive female walk into a bar and choose to join the only outsider didn't sit too well with them. I would have preferred it if she had chosen someone else with whom to keep company and have a quiet evening to myself, but neither of my desires were to be fulfilled that night.

One of the cowboys tried to trip me. It was a clumsy maneuver that I easily sidestepped. His friends sniggered; during the distraction, another one of them grabbed Angie around the waist and pulled her into his lap. She struggled to free herself; he pulled her closer, mocking her futile efforts.

I turned to face him, putting my hands on my hips. While I didn't have my backpack, I still retained every weapon in my little arsenal.

"Let her go," I said. I was not in the habit of giving second chances. After the first one, action was required or no one would take me seriously. On the road, it was very important to be taken seriously. In fact, if we were on the road, I'd probably have killed him already. However, this was town, and as lawless as Kingston was, it still had its own set of rules that had to be observed – by outsiders, if not by its citizens.

"What are you going to do about it, Traveler?" He sneered at me and planted a sloppy kiss on Angie's neck. She grimaced in disgust and struggled harder.

I looked over their heads at the bartender. "Would you like to fix this situation, or shall I?" I asked him. A look of understanding passed between us, and he pulled out a rifle.

"Let the girl go," he said.

"You gonna shoot her, too?" snarled the ruffian.

"What I'm going to do is count to three," replied the bartender. "One. Two…"

The cowboy turned Angie loose, and shoved her away from him. I caught and steadied her, then eased her behind me as we backed out of the saloon.

"You just watch yourself, Traveler!" shouted one of the cowboys. "We'll be watching you!"

"That's what they all say," I muttered as the saloon doors closed behind us. I continued to support Angie as we walked quickly down the street toward the boarding house. Once I was certain that no one was following, I removed my arm from her shoulders.

"Are you all right?" I asked. It was too dark to see her face, so I led her to a nearby gas lamp, mounted on pole in front of the general store.

"I'm fine," she whispered. She was crying.

"You're hurt?"

She shook her head. "No, I'm just... Scared."

"I'm sorry," I said, for lack of anything better to say.

"Thank you for helping me."

"I couldn't just leave you there."

She looked up at me, and the firelight brought out the gold glints in her eyes. "I should go," she said.

"Go? Where?"

"Don't you want me to go away?" she asked, her voice still choked with tears.

"No," I said.

"No?"

"It's night and it's not safe," I said. "Where would you go?"

"I have a camp," she said.

I couldn't imagine anything less safe than a woman alone in a campsite outside of Kingston.

"I don't think so," I said. "Come with me."

Chapter 4 – Bloodbath

Rules of Gunfighting #20
Decide to be aggressive enough, quickly enough.

The next day found me on the road heading north for Green Country. It had rained lightly the night before, leaving the world sweet-smelling and new. Forest animals scampered about in the undergrowth. Queen Anne's lace lined the road on tall green stalks bowed by the weight of heavy-headed white flowers. Breezes pushed through the branches of the trees, causing leaves to spatter drops of water onto my head and shoulders. Birds sang and fluttered about overhead. White puffy clouds floated above, with plenty of blue sky between them, just enough to keep the temperature cool. It was spring at its finest and a good day to be a Traveler.

I was in an exceptionally good mood. I had slept like a baby, even though I had ended up staying in the hayloft of the stable. The couple who ran the boarding house and stable had offered me that space, as I had given my room to Angie and did not have any more money for other accommodations. I was also feeling pretty good about myself for having done a good deed.

As they say, no good deed goes unpunished.

The lovely druid with the arresting green eyes caught up with me around mid-morning. I figured she must have run most of the way, because I had set a fairly brisk pace. In addition, her hair was a mess and her face was flushed and sweaty.

She was also furious.

"I cannot believe you!" was the first thing Angie shouted at me. There were a great many other things she shouted, referencing my selfishness and general lack of manners. She even made reference to the possible illegitimacy of my lineage before she calmed somewhat. By that time she had run out of breath, because I had not stopped to listen to her rant.

"How could you do such a thing?" she demanded. "You left me alone in a strange town, after leading me to believe that you cared about me?"

"You're welcome," I said drily.

"I'm not thanking you! What on earth would I have to be thankful to you for?"

"Obviously nothing. Forgive me, your Highness, for failing to meet your expectations. If you make it clearer next time, I might possibly have a chance of living up to them."

Her jaw dropped, and then she made a noise of outrage.

"How dare you!"

I whirled about and took two threatening steps toward her. She tripped over her own feet backing up. I grabbed both her arms above the elbow and saved her from falling.

"How dare I?" I snapped, jerking her close to me until we were nose to nose. "How dare you, you spoiled little princess? Who the hell do you think you are?"

Her eyes were like round saucers, she was so shocked.

"I... I..." she squeaked, and burst into tears.

I released her, angry and disgusted. She collapsed into a skirted heap on the road, burying her face in her hands. She cried in great heaving gasps, as though heartbroken. I remembered my mother crying that way a few times, after an explosion of rage. My father had always held her and stroked her hair until she calmed.

This woman was not mine to hold and console. Not like that. Still, I couldn't leave her like this. She was too vulnerable. I looked at her, feeling the anger drain away. Taking a deep breath and remembering all the times my father had apologized for things that he had not done wrong, I squatted beside her.

"Angie," I said, and laid my hand on her shoulder. "I'm sorry you were upset – Oof!"

She threw her arms around my neck, nearly knocking me backwards. Somehow managing to correct our balance, I held steady while she proceeded to cry on my shoulder. I had no idea what to do next and settled on awkwardly patting her back. Her bawling quieted somewhat, until she was merely weeping.

It was a relief to hear the storm abate, and I pulled back to a safe distance. Gods forbid that someone should come upon us like this. They might get the wrong idea and shoot me in the back.

"Are you all right?" I asked.

She sniffled, then cried some more, then sniffled again and nodded.

"You want to tell me what that was all about?"

"I'm sorry, I was just so scared when you left me behind," she sniffled.

"Scared? You, the mighty, magic-wielding druid of immense gods-bestowed cosmic power?"

"You're making fun of me again." She sounded miserable.

"Isn't it true? You can take care of yourself, or had you forgotten the two hundred-plus miles you had to travel to find me?"

"I wasn't on my own then!" Her eyes widened, and she slapped both hands on her mouth, too late to stop the words.

Ah. There it was, the truth at last.

"You've been abandoned?" I could feel a touch of righteous anger at the very idea.

"No." A guilty light came into her tear-filled eyes. "I told them it was okay to leave me. I thought we were... that you had..."

"You thought that because I helped you out last night, that I had agreed to your proposal," I said. She nodded and burst into tears all over again. I waited patiently until she had calmed herself again.

"Why didn't you just follow them, instead of running after me?"

She shook her head. "That is not an option," she said.

"Besides, they have horses."

"Not an option?"

"You don't understand how important this is! I will look like an absolute fool if I go back without–" Her jaw snapped shut, and she looked away.

"Without...?"

Her voice dropped to a whisper. "Without my chosen warrior."

"Why is it that's so important for it to be me? Can't you find somebody else?

"No!"

"Why not?" Noting her incredulous look, I said, "Why don't you pretend that I'm some strange guy you met on the road, with no idea about your traditions, and explain it to me?"

A look of confusion crossed her puffy features. "But you are..." Understanding replaced confusion. "Oh," she said in a small voice.

I took a small washcloth from my pocket, wetted it with canteen water, and handed it to Angie. After she had washed her face of tear stains, she handed it back to me. I tossed it onto my shoulder, rose, and offered her my hand. Looking up at me uncertainly, she took my hand and allowed me to help her rise.

"I feel like such a stupid little girl," she said angrily.

"We all have our moments," I replied.

She let out a harsh half-laugh, looking down at her feet.

"Have you eaten?" I asked.

She shook her head. "When I found out you were gone, I just grabbed everything and ran out of town."

"Why don't we sit and eat, and I'll let you explain things to me."

Angie looked up, hope glimmering in her green eyes.

"I am only promising to listen," I said, holding up a finger. "Nothing more."

She nodded and followed me to the side of the road. I moved through the trees until we reached a small clearing, just large enough for the two of us. I shucked the pack and stretched my shoulders. Angie dropped hers amongst the tree roots and sat beside it. I dug around in my bag until I came up with two packets of Travel food – nuts, dried fruit, and jerky. I handed one to Angie, along with a cup of water. It was my only cup, a small tin thing that barely held a few swallows. I rarely used it and didn't even know why I had kept it.

We ate in silence, and I allowed her the time to collect her thoughts. Ordinarily I wouldn't have given anyone this much time and attention, but she had been persistent. It was obvious that this quest was very important to her, and I decided it was only fair to hear her out. I told myself that it wouldn't hurt to do so. When she had had her say, I would gently refuse and offer to accompany her someplace she could pick up a caravan to take her home.

"Where were we?" I asked when she had finished eating.

"I'm not..." She shook her head. "I don't even know where to start."

"I think we were discussing the druid version of history," I said. "The beginning of the new age?"

She regarded me with somber eyes. "You were listening."

"I'm told it's polite." I shrugged. One never knew what useful information could be gleaned from the experiences of others. I had made a habit of hearing what other people had to say. You never knew what might keep you alive.

"I think you were telling me why you felt it necessary to travel so far, following a magical animal? Spirit guide? The fetch?" There was uncertainty in her eyes. The confidence – the faith – that I had seen in her eyes before was now warring with doubt. "I think you mentioned histories?" I said, hoping to prompt her.

"We study the histories," she said at last. "With the idea being that we should continue our traditions, and not repeat the errors of the past."

"That's a good reason." Not that it had ever done anybody any good, as far as I could tell from my own studies. History was full of repetitive errors. I figured the druids were no different from any other people, magically inclined or not.

"Only, in the quest to avoid errors, we seem to be rejecting our better traditions," Angie said, her determination beginning to return. She was quite a woman, to deal with disappointment

40

three times over now and still continue onward. I found myself admiring her spirit.

"One of those traditions is that of the seeking, when a druid – usually female – sends out her fetch to find her partner."

"Why doesn't she just go find some guy she likes and partner up with him?"

"Because the intellect, that which sees on the outside, does not always see what is on the inside," she said. "Sometimes we don't always know what is best for us. The spirit, the deep darkness within where the gods dwell within all of us... that is the part that knows what is best."

It sounded a lot like what my mother used to tell me when I was young – the still small voice of my conscience. When I was a child, it was supposed to tell me when to stay out of the cookies. Later, as I matured, my father taught me that it was the gut feeling that people get, telling them whether a choice was right or wrong for them. It had kept me out of trouble many times; I believed it to be connected to the sixth sense that warned me of the presence of others.

"So, how do you send out a... fetch?" I couldn't believe I was having this conversation. Entertaining the idea that magic might be real was one thing; discussing it like it was something you could see and touch was something else.

She gave me an apologetic look. "Sorry, not allowed to talk about it. Not yet anyway."

"I should have guessed."

"I mean, I can tell you it involves a ritual, but that's about it."

I envisioned a ritual complete with sweat, smoke, and plenty of herbs, weeds, or mushrooms. I wasn't against mind-altering substances as a matter of course; I just knew that a clear head was the best way to stay alive. Besides, Angie was her own person and could do as she wished. Maybe that's why druids needed protection, because much of their time was spent high as a kite. I changed the subject.

"So, in the event that you found me, what was supposed to come next?"

It was a rhetorical question. I had no intention of

abandoning my own dreams to follow hers. She was a virtual stranger, after all. Even so, a fierce light appeared in her green eyes.

"We would travel south," Angie answered. "I was told that if I could find you and bring you back, they would train you."

"I've had plenty of training," I said. Hence my success in the world outside city walls. Success meaning that I had all my limbs and both my eyes still intact. I had lost my shirt (and pants) on one occasion, but since I had gotten to keep my vital organs inside my body, I figured it had been a rather inexpensive lesson.

"Sword training," she said. "Druid warriors fight with swords. You need a sword, and if you don't know how to use one, you'll need the training to go with it."

"But of course." The conversation was becoming more ridiculous by the moment. What use were swords against guns?

I was not terribly interested in learning to wield a sword, but I did give in to curiosity. "So, in these histories, what is that pair of druids supposed to do?"

She looked astonished that I would even have to ask.

"Heal the world, of course. To bring it back into balance."

It was the first thing she had said that actually meant something to me.

"How?"

"Using the magic that was given to us by the gods. It is the only purpose of possessing such a gift. It would be blasphemy not to use it to heal the earth."

"I don't have magic," I reminded her.

"That isn't a requirement anymore," she said, and I detected a sense of sadness about her. "Only women are required to use magic. Their men just have to protect them, as warriors."

"That doesn't sound fair. Or balanced."

"It isn't."

I waited for her to continue, but she changed the subject instead. "You weren't raised Triune, were you?"

"No, I wasn't. Around here, however, that is not something we freely admit," I said. "It'll get you killed in some places."

"That's terrible!" she said.

"Many terrible things have been done in the name of God," I replied.

She nodded. "And in the names of the gods, as well."

I decided that I liked her. It helped that she had come down off her high horse.

Angie gave me a tentative look. "I still believe you are my warrior."

"Ha! I'm no warrior."

"You act like one."

"How do you know?"

"My father is a warrior."

My father was a gardener, but I didn't mention it.

"Do you realize what you are asking, Angie?" I asked seriously. "Do you really expect me to drop everything in my life for a total stranger?"

"But we aren't strangers," she protested. "Not really."

"How do you figure?"

"Because my fetch came to you," she said. I shook my head at her circular logic. It all came back to the magic, the gods, and a mysterious spirit animal that I had never seen.

"I want you to come with me," she said. "I need you."

I studied her for several seconds, looking deep into her exotic green eyes. I could see determination there, and enthusiasm. Most of all, I saw hope.

How long had it been since I had truly hoped for anything of consequence? True, I was hoping for good things out of my trip to Hardy: a profession, a home, perhaps a wife and family. I wondered if I felt half as strongly about my dreams as she did about hers. I wondered what that would feel like, to have such a passion.

"For how long?" I asked.

"Forever," she replied, as if it were the most obvious thing in the world.

It took me a moment to respond. "Forever? You mean like 'for the rest of my life' kind of forever?"

"Yes!" She might as well have said of course!

"Please tell me you know how this sounds."

"Oh, Davis, it will be worth it, I promise!"

"Angie, I can't even imagine what that sort of life will be like, but I'm sure that it's nothing like what I have planned."

"I guarantee that it will be vastly better than anything you have planned," she said. "What do you have to look forward to in a life without magic? Build a house, work the land, and try to eke out a simple existence while dealing with whatever the world throws at you?"

Her words came dangerously close to the truth.

"What if I find someone and want to get married? What if I want to settle down and have a family? What if you do? I don't care how much magic you have, you can't raise children while you're out wandering in the wilderness!" I shook my head. "I'm sorry, Angie. I just can't give you forever."

She bit her lips and looked down at her hands, then nodded. "I understand," she said softly. When she raised her head, I could see the disappointment through the bright sheen of tears. It hit me right in the gut, that place where my conscience was supposed to be. Against all logic, I felt like I had made the wrong decision.

"I suppose I should be going, then." She rose and smoothed her skirts before picking up her backpack.

"What? Where?" I asked, surprised that she was giving up already. My brain rejoiced, but my gut churned with some unpleasant emotion that was related to thinking my brain was wrong. It was the most uncomfortable feeling.

"I have a long way to go to get home," she said. "I might as well get started."

"Now? Alone?"

"I don't see any reason to wait. If I hurry, I might be able to catch up to..." She cleared her throat. "Thank you for listening to me, Davis. The blessings of Mother Oya and Father Shango be upon you."

"Wait a minute, you said they had horses. There's no way you'll catch up to them."

"I'll have to do the best I can without them, then."

"Look," I said. "Sunset isn't far off, and it'll be dark soon. Why don't you stay here tonight? Tomorrow will be soon enough for Travel."

She looked uncertain, hesitated a few moments, then nodded again. We weren't far from the road, and the trees weren't as thick as I'd have liked, but it was a decent spot and the ground was dry. There was a nearby grouping of large boulders that would provide some shelter. As my protective sixth sense was still lying quiet, I might even be able to light a fire. Overall, I was cautious with fires, and made sure to always carry food that did not need to be cooked. Even a small fire could be seen from a mile away on a clear night.

When the light began to fail, Angie had produced a slingshot and slipped away into the trees with it. It was a weapon I had not initially noticed, because she kept it tucked into the belt at the small of her back when not in use. I wondered what other potentially deadly items she might have on her person.

She returned with two fat rabbits. The prospect of fresh meat roasted over a hot fire was too much to resist. Angie skinned and cleaned the rabbits while I collected wood for the fire. I was impressed by how quickly and neatly she did the job. I retrieved the small tinderbox from my pack, and used flint and steel to strike sparks onto the tiny pile of tinder. A delicate curl of smoke rose into the air. I gently blew on the tinder and was rewarded with a flicker of flame. I fed it with a few matchstick-sized pieces of wood, which it ate greedily. In a matter of minutes, it was burning brightly.

"I've never seen anyone light a fire that quickly," she said. "Not without magic, anyway."

I ducked my head to avoid seeing the admiration in her eyes. I didn't need any entanglements, and especially not with someone with whom I would be parting company in the morning. My stomach clenched at the thought. My brain told me to ignore it.

From somewhere in her pack, Angie produced two small sweet potatoes and tucked them into the edges of the campfire. Not to be outdone, I added a handful of chestnuts. We sat in silence, listening to the emerging calls of night birds, and the hissing sound of greasy juice dripping into the crackling fire. After the rabbit was done, I blew on the small pieces of meat, trying not to burn myself. Angie set hers aside to cool, pulled forth a small cauldron full of water, and stirred in some herbs.

45

That done, she sat back and ate her own rabbit, then the potato and chestnuts. I had already wolfed down my share.

"Where did you get the water?" I asked. I had not passed even the smallest pond or creek where a canteen could be filled.

"Magic."

Of course she'd say that. How stupid of me to even ask. I wanted to roll my eyes at her. She probably had a full water skin or canteen in her backpack. As the water warmed, the air filled with the aroma of blended herbs. The soup smelled wonderful. I couldn't wait to taste it, and I told her so. She laughed.

"It's not soup," she said. "It's your bath."

I smirked at her. "It's a little small for me to fit."

She produced a cloth and waved it at me. "You dip this in, then rub it all over your body. Repeatedly."

"Are you serious?"

"I'm sorry, Davis, but you stink. I've put up with it all evening, but I just can't tolerate it when we'll be sleeping together."

"We are not sleeping together," I said. "I don't sleep with strangers."

She rolled her eyes. "I don't mean that. However, we'll be sleeping near each other, and there's no breeze to blow away your stench. When did you bathe last, anyway?"

My stench? Quakes, she had a lot of nerve, following me all over, begging me to come with her, and then telling me that I smelled bad. I slung my pack over my shoulder and picked up the shotgun before grabbing the thin pot handle, stomping away toward a clump of bushes.

"Where are you going?" She sounded worried.

"Over here, where you won't be offended by my stench," I retorted. Once behind the scrubs, I shrugged out of my vest and peeled off my shirt, inadvertently getting a whiff of my own pits. So she had a point. It wasn't necessary to be rude about it, though. I scrubbed my face, neck, arms and chest. I had just wet my hair when I got that funny feeling that told me someone was coming. More than one, in fact. It was a good thing I still had on my pants and boots, with attendant tomahawks, knives, and machete. I dropped the cloth into the pot and picked up my shotgun. I crept through the darkness, circling our camp to seek out the danger.

Three men stood before the little campfire, looking at Angie. She looked scared, but not panicked. I gave their gear a quick glance and decided that they were little more than thugs. Not bandits. Bandits were typically very well armed, quite vicious, and difficult to kill. I rose up behind them and cocked the shotgun. The three men turned around, nervous at first, but then... not. They didn't even hold up their hands.

Why weren't they holding up their hands?

Then the one in the middle grinned, as I realized my mistake with a stunning clarity. They were between me and Angie, and if I fired, I would hit her as well. I holstered the shotgun and pulled out one tomahawk and the machete. I didn't like killing, but hesitation often meant the wrong person ended up dead. I preferred not to be that person.

The man in the middle laughed and gestured to his companions, an invitation to attack me. I threw the tomahawk at the one farthest from Angie, to my left. It flashed toward him in a spinning silver blur and buried itself in his neck. As he staggered, trying to yank it free, the middle one rushed me with a long knife while the third turned to grab Angie.

Dodging his attempt to stab me, I sidestepped and slashed the machete through his midsection. Blood and guts burbled forth from his belly to land in a slimy heap. Howling, he dropped to his knees and grabbed at his entrails, trying to put them back. I turned away and drew the shotgun, thinking that perhaps now it would be of use.

It wasn't. The third man was standing behind Angie, holding a knife to her throat.

"Let her go," I said, aiming the shotgun at him.

"You won't shoot," he spat. "That big gun will tear her apart."

He was right, of course. I kept the Ithaca aimed at him to keep his attention diverted while I pulled out my second tomahawk. It had been a while since I had thrown anything left-handed, but I didn't have a lot of options at this point.

I could let him take her away.

47

I could watch him cut her throat.

Or, I could throw the 'hawk.

Angie's eyes widened when I raised my arm, then squeezed shut when I threw it. To her credit, she never moved a muscle or gave away my intentions. The angular blade bit deeply into his arm, and he dropped the knife with a hoarse scream. Angie dove away from him and bolted into the darkness. That meant I could finish things quickly. I pulled the trigger, and the scattershot went a bit wild, punching holes in his chest, neck and face. I turned to scan for further threats. The one with the tomahawk in his neck was lying on the ground, twitching. The other was sobbing over his dirt-covered intestines. I re-holstered the shotgun and slit his throat with my boot knife.

Turning to look in the direction Angie had run, I was unable to see her. There was no use searching, either; I'd never find her in the dark. Calling for her would only alert any other enemies that might be lurking in the night. I cleaned the boot knife and machete and sheathed them once again. Next, I retrieved both tomahawks, cleaned them and put them back in their proper places. I crouched by the fire, packing the few things we had left out during supper, and kicked dirt over the fire.

There was a noise behind me, and I spun about and drew the shotgun. Angie froze, looking terrified. I let out a huff of breath.

"Don't sneak up behind me," I said. "Usually I just turn and fire."

"Are you... Are you hurt?" She seemed barely able to get the words out.

"No." It was then that I noticed the blood spattered across my chest. "It's not my blood." Now I definitely needed a bath, Angie's delicate sensibilities aside.

She took a deep breath. "Oh, thank the gods."

"Isn't this what you wanted me for?"

She didn't answer. I mentally kicked myself for even bringing it up. It was bad enough that she had been at risk of losing her life. On top of that, I figured that she had never seen anyone kill before, at least not as messily as I had done it. I would have preferred to avoid the confrontation, if only to avoid the mess and dealing with corpses. Scavenger animals – and some predators – would be lured by the smell, and might also end up in our camp. The last thing I wanted to deal with was a pack of wild dogs. Lions weren't common, but not unheard of, either.

"Are you okay?" I asked Angie.

"Yes." Her face was pale, but at least she wasn't crying.

"Let me see," I said, touching her chin. She lifted it, and I could see only a small line of blood where the knife had scored a shallow cut.

"We'll need to clean that."

"It can wait," she replied.

I led the way to the scrub bushes. Retrieving my backpack, I then picked up my clothes and stuffed them inside. We walked a few miles until I found a spot I liked. I dumped everything on the ground and picked up the little cauldron, its water now only lukewarm.

Taking out a cloth, I dipped it into the cauldron and washed the wound on Angie's neck. Afterward I applied a protective balm. At the very least, it would keep out the dirt until the wound began to heal. Finished with that task, I rose to walk away, but Angie grabbed my arm.

"Where are you going?"

"You'll be safe here. Just don't light a fire." I gave her a smile that was probably more ironic than reassuring and went off to finish my bath.

Chapter 5 – Water Magic

Rules of Gunfighting #2:
Anything worth shooting is worth shooting twice.
Ammo is cheap. Life is expensive.

I slept terribly that night. I tossed and turned, rolling around in my blankets. If there wasn't a rock under me, there was a root. If there wasn't a root or a rock, there was a strange noise in the bushes. My conscience pummeled me unmercifully, letting me know I would be the worst kind of man – no, I was no man at all if I let this helpless young woman journey home alone without protection. I finally gave up an hour or two before dawn, and spent the remaining time thinking and watching Angie sleep.

After she woke and attended to whatever it was that women did first thing in the morning, we shared breakfast in silence.

"I've been thinking..." I said, when she again reached for her pack. She paused, looking at me. The light in her eyes that had looked so hopeful yesterday was gone. Now she merely looked resigned. My gut tightened, as if to inform me that I was responsible for her emotional state – which I wasn't.

After all, I had not asked her to travel for a season to find me. So she had left her home when the earth was barely thawed from winter, braving rainy and frequently freezing springtime weather. I was under no obligation to fulfill her desires. In fact, had I known about it in advance, I would have told her not to bother.

"Traveling alone is a bad idea. I don't think you appreciate just how dangerous it will be – magic or no magic."

"What exactly do you expect me to do, Davis? You have made your decision and I cannot stay here. I have duties. Responsibilities. My family will be waiting for me back home. It's bad enough that I have wasted so much time on a failed mission. I have no choice."

"There's always a choice," I said. Gods, I sounded like my father. I wondered what he would do in this situation. No, I knew what he would do. I just didn't want to do it.

"Tell me again how long of a trip that is?"

"It won't take forever to get there, but I'm sure it's still longer than you want to be with me," she said.

"How long, Angie?"

"Three months, two weeks, and four days," she said, shaking her head in disgust. "I will have wasted half a year on this fruitless quest. How people will laugh."

I didn't care about her pride. If she made it home alive, she would be grateful for even the spiteful behavior of others. Traveling alone on the road would virtually guarantee that she never made it home at all. In fact, she probably wouldn't even make it past Kingston. I calculated the time it would take to accompany her home and make the trip back. If we walked quickly, and if there were no delays, I might make it back by Samhain. From a more realistic perspective, I would probably arrive around Yule. In a worst-case scenario, I would be forced to stay in Angie's hometown until spring, when it was warm enough to Travel without risk of frostbite and starvation.

"I think... I should come with you," I said, quickly adding: "To see you safely home. Nothing more." The churning in my stomach eased a little.

"Are you...?" She looked as though she couldn't believe her ears. "Are you sure?"

Hardy would still be there next year, I told myself.

"I'm sure."

* * *

51

We traveled together along the same stretch of road which we had walked separately the day before. This time, however, it was in the opposite direction – south. After the attack last night, it was a relief to know I could count on my instincts warning me of danger. I felt that I could once again rely on that extra sense, as it had only failed me twice in two years. It occurred to me that Angie had been present at both times it had happened.

I glanced sidelong at her. Then again, maybe her supposed druid magic was causing a problem with my instincts. Of course, if I started thinking that way, I would have to admit that I believed in said druid magic, and I wasn't quite ready for that.

"You look like something is bothering you," Angie said.

"It's nothing."

Her mouth twisted to one side, and I could tell she didn't believe me.

I gave in. "It bothers me that you have approached me twice without me knowing."

"How could you have known? Until you actually saw me, that is."

I shook my head, unsure how to explain. "I can just… tell… when people are… around." I sounded like an idiot.

"Sounds like magic."

"It isn't magic. It's just a skill."

"Skills are something you develop. Magic just is."

I shook my head. "I think of it as a sixth sense. Or, it's my other senses working together to give me a clearer picture of what's around me. It's only failed me twice," I said. "The first two times we met."

"What do you mean?" She frowned.

"I've never had a problem with it until I came upon you in the road. Ordinarily I would have known you were there before I even saw you."

"Are you saying it's my fault?"

I shrugged. "Maybe your magic is interfering."

"I haven't been using any magic." Her frown deepened, and I thought I saw a flicker of understanding. It was gone in an instant, so I wasn't sure I had seen it at all.

"Right. Not wasting it on frivolous things."

"You're mocking me again."

"Nope, just reminding myself of the rules."

"There aren't any rules, Davis."

"If there is one thing I have learned, it's that there are always rules. You may not be aware of them, but they definitely exist."

"How very esoteric of you."

"Now who's mocking?" I gave her a sly look. Angie looked back at me and didn't crack a smile.

"Are you always this serious?" I asked.

"Why shouldn't I be? You are."

"The only time I'm truly serious is when I have a fight on my hands," I responded. "The rest of the time, I usually enjoy myself."

"You never look like you're enjoying yourself."

"It would have been awfully hard to get rid of you if I was smiling and cheerful."

She shot me a look. "You were being rude just so I would leave you alone?"

"Pretty much." I think it was Oscar Wilde who said that gentleman was never unintentionally rude. He must have been a clever fellow, coming up with that one.

"Why didn't you say something?"

"I did say something. You weren't listening."

Angie feel silent, and we walked half a mile before she spoke again.

"You're right," she said. "I wasn't."

"I suppose I can forgive that," I replied. "I wasn't exactly listening to you, either."

She gave me a surprised look. I pretended not to notice.

"Either way," I continued. "If you're going to be so somber all the time, this is going to be a long, boring trip."

Little did I know, our journey together would be anything but boring.

* * *

We avoided the main town of Kingston and headed for the Hayworth farm. We needed to stock up on supplies. At the very least, we needed enough to get back to Jonesboro. There, I could get everything for the rest of the trip from my folks' place. I figured the Hayworth homestead might have some work for me to do, as well as being able to pay me in supplies. In addition, I could safely trade the pistols and ammo to them without having to worry about a gunfight starting immediately thereafter. The Hayworths were good people.

"Let me do the talking," I said. When we neared their property, I noticed Mrs. Hayworth and her sons standing around, looking at the spring that was their livelihood. I hailed them and they waved me over. Mrs. Hayworth was a tall, rawboned woman with dark hair streaked with grey and penetrating brown eyes that could either give the warmest welcome or freeze you on the spot. Her sons had inherited her height, as well as her dark hair and eyes. If I looked hard enough, I could see some of their father's imprint upon them as well. He had been a brave man, taking on a rival farm with only his rifle, his oldest son, and a Traveler still wet behind the ears.

"I heard you had already left town," said the Missus, reaching out to shake my hand. "I'm glad the rumor wasn't true."

I took her hand, then shook hands with each of her two sons, Jacob and Joseph. They wore serious expressions, standing there frowning at the water.

"I see you've brought a friend," she said.

"This is Angie," I said. "We met on the road. She had some crazy idea about traveling to Jonesboro alone." The heir to the all-powerful druid magic shot me an irate look.

"That's a dangerous business," said Jacob, the oldest. "A young lady like her should be settling down with a husband and a home, where she'd be safe." I caught the appreciative but respectful glance he sent her way.

Angie opened her mouth to speak, but I jumped in before she could answer. "That's what she's after. Some Traveler passed through Oak Grove and caught her fancy. Said he was going to settle in Jonesboro." I leaned in closer to murmur: "I think he broke her heart. Might have made some promises that he didn't mean to keep." I pretended not to notice her indignant

54

expression.

"Well, that's too bad," said Mrs. Hayworth to the young woman. "Not every man is as honorable as Davis, here. Good as gold, this one is. Has the heart of a lion, and a spine like steel. If it weren't for him, I wouldn't have my land or my boys. You stick with him, and he'll see you safely where you're headed. You won't have to worry about any improper behavior from him, neither." Angie's look of ire changed to one of barely disguised interest.

I was at a loss for words for a moment or two. I had never heard her say anything half that complimentary toward her own sons. "Thank you, Missus, but I really didn't do all that much. Your husband was the brave one," I finally managed to say, before changing the subject. "Is something wrong with the stream?"

"Water's bad," said Jacob, spitting into it as if to emphasize that fact. "Joseph hauled in a barrel for the Isaacsons, and their three little'uns are laid up sick with the collywobbles."

Bad water could destroy a town as completely as any tornado or earthquake. Other than rainwater, this was the biggest source of fresh water near Kingston. The whole town depended on it.

"What's wrong with it?" I asked, watching Angie wander to the stream and look it over. "Maybe a dead animal upstream?"

Joseph shook his head. "We went upstream all the way to the waterfall. No carcasses were even near the bank."

Angie knelt on the bank and dipped her hand into the stream. She lifted a handful to her face and sniffed it.

"Don't drink that, honey," said Mrs. Hayworth. "You don't want to get sick."

"Looks like the source has maybe gone bad," said Jacob.

"It'll be the end of Kingston if it is," his brother replied. "There hasn't been enough rain to fill the town's water barrels."

"It's poisoned," said Angie, rising and wiping her hands on her skirt.

"I beg your pardon?" said Mrs. Hayworth, turning suspicious. "And just how would you know that?"

"She's a water witch," I said. Angie gave me a dirty look. What she didn't know was that in these parts, a water witch wasn't really a witch, but a person who was good at dowsing for water. It wouldn't be too great a leap for the locals to believe that someone who could find water would also be able to tell whether it was fresh or not.

"Oh," said Mrs. Hayworth, visibly relaxing. "That's all right, then." She looked at Angie. "Is there anything you can do about it?"

"I can try," she replied. Turning to me, she said, "Why don't we go look upstream?"

Taking our leave of Mrs. Hayworth, we walked along the streambed, hiking steadily farther up into the ridge.

When we were out of earshot of the Hayworths, Angie spoke in a low voice. "It may not be a dead animal, but it's certainly something foul."

"What do you think it is?"

"Something worse than animal offal."

"Such as?"

"Human offal."

"You think someone is fouling the stream with shit?"

"Really, Davis, your language!" She shook her head. "That's exactly what I think. Maybe some animal dung is mixed in with it, but it's definitely human."

"Wouldn't there have to be a lot of it to cause an illness?"

"Just because it's improbable doesn't mean it's impossible," she said.

* * *

We made it to the waterfall, climbing up the rocks and continuing onward, hiking up the small mountain. We reached a point in the stream where it curved around a massive boulder. An area had been cleared of trees and brush along the opposite bank. There seemed to be some sort of path leading from the muddy area into the woods, down the mountain. We jumped across, our boots squishing wetly in the mud.

"Here," said Angie, pointing. I squatted to study the muddy tracks, and quickly rose again.

"That's not just mud," I said, making a face.

"I can smell it from here." She wrinkled her nose. "I wonder…" She trailed off, noticing that I had raised my hand.

"Someone's coming," I said. We leapt back across the stream and hid behind the boulder.

A mule in harness pulling a sledge appeared. Four men were with the mule: one held the reins and carried a whip. The other three walked alongside the sledge, making sure the barrel on it stayed upright. They were skinny, weasel-faced individuals who appeared to be related to one another; perhaps too closely related. Their clothes were filthy and in poor condition, and their skin was grimy. Among the four of them, they had maybe a full set of teeth. I was grateful that I wasn't close enough to smell them.

They halted the mule near the water, then rolled the barrel off the sledge. Using a crowbar, one man pried the top open, and tipped it over the bubbling stream. I could hear Angie's outraged gasp when the contents came spilling out: brownish-black water with hunks of fecal matter splashed into the pristine crystal water. It looked like a month's worth of chamber pot contents, possibly mixed with pig manure.

Angie darted out from behind our rock. I made a grab for her and missed.

"You stop that right now!" she cried.

The four jumped in startlement, then relaxed and hooted at the lone small woman who challenged them. The man with the barrel jerked it upright, let go of it, and waved to the others. The four men lazily pulled out knives and clubs, starting toward her with jagged, evil smiles. I charged after Angie, whipping the shotgun over my shoulder. I worked the pump action and chambered a round. The telltale sound was lost in the wash of the stream and Angie's raised voice.

"Are you crazy?! This is the only clean water around for miles!" she shouted. "You have no right! You've poisoned children!"

I just managed to come between them, shoving her behind me. "That's far enough," I said, aiming the weapon. I didn't shout, because I didn't have to. My voice carried clearly over the water, but even if it hadn't, the shotgun would have told them all they needed to know. The four froze in the middle of the stream.

"Who are you?" I demanded.

"That's none of your concern!" The leader spat.

"Missus Hayworth says otherwise." Their cocky expressions changed to stubborn anger and they shifted nervously. "You leave the barrel and the mule, and get off this mountain right now."

"This is a free land!" said another. "We don't take no orders from no Traveler!"

"Today you do," I said, pointing the barrel directly at him.

That was when one of them showed extremely poor judgement by drawing back to throw his knife at me. It didn't matter that he wasn't likely to hit. Habit and instinct took over; pivoting in place, I brought the shotgun to bear and peppered his torso. Red spots blossomed all over his shirt, and he fell backwards into the water with a splash.

Because it was scattershot, it also ripped apart the arm of the man beside him. He ran screaming into the woods, blood pumping from the severed artery. Without thinking, I rapidly turned toward the remaining two and fired twice, killing them both. The stream filled with blood, churning a foamy dark pink along its banks.

Great. Now I had fouled the stream even more. I holstered the shotgun and splashed through the bloody water. I slammed the lid back down on the barrel and hammered it with the hilt of my knife, holding my breath to keep out the disgusting odor. Next, I muscled the barrel back onto the sledge and turned to the bloody, ripped-up bodies. One at a time, I dragged the bodies from the stream, dumping them on the sledge behind the barrel. The mule's nostrils flared at the scent of blood, and it danced nervously in its harness. I grabbed its bridle, turned it to face the way it had come and slapped its rump. It reared slightly, then heaved the sledge forward until both it and the bodies were out of sight.

I looked back behind me at Angie, who was still crouched down holding her ears with her eyes squeezed shut. I cleaned the blood off my hands and crossed the stream again, irritated that my boots had gotten water in them. Taking them off, I dumped the water out, and put them back on. My socks were soaked, and it made a squelching sound with every step. I would be lucky if I didn't get blisters on the way back down the mountain.

"Hey," I said, touching her shoulder. "It's over."

She looked at me with wild, wide eyes. "You killed all of them," she whispered.

It wasn't what I had expected her to say. "Did you want me to let them hurt you? Or, maybe I should have let them poison the stream?"

She shook her head. "I told you that you're a warrior."

"I just do what needs to be done," I replied, shaking my head. "Quakes, I made a bigger mess than there already was. Can you fix it?"

"What?"

"Can you clean the water? Can the damage be repaired?"

She looked doubtful. "I don't know."

I scowled at her. It was time for her to put up or shut up. "Either you're a druid with magic who heals the earth or you're not."

Angie's chin rose, and she fixed me with a defiant look. "The stream will cleanse itself in time."

"How long is that going to take? Days? Weeks?" I shook my head. "Those people down there don't have that kind of time. They need that water."

I could see that I had convinced her. She looked at the red-tinged water thoughtfully. It was already clearing on its own in this spot.

"Let's go a little farther upstream," she said. "It'll be easier if I'm away from this filth."

The area did stink, so I made no argument. We trudged through the forest for a few hundred yards, until we came to another waterfall.

"This is a good spot," Angie said. "It would be better if we were at the origin, but there's no telling how far we'd have to go to find it." She removed her boots and socks, then tucked her skirt up into her belt until she was bare to the middle of her sleek, rounded thighs. I averted my eyes, more or less successfully. Next, she waded into the water and plunged both hands into it. She closed her eyes, and I waited for something amazing to happen.

I sat on a nearby rock, watching her pretend to work magic. Irritatingly long and boring moments passed, and I was about to tell her to knock it off when I noticed the stream's natural noise had become slightly louder. As I paid closer attention, I saw that the water level had also risen, from mid-calf to just below her knee. It began rushing far more rapidly, accompanied by a dramatic increase volume.

"Angie?"

I could hear the approach of a low roar, and swiftly the water was over her knees. I jumped into the stream, grabbed her by the waist, and hauled her out. I collapsed a few feet from the bank, with her on top of me.

"No!" she cried, struggling. "I almost had it, Davis! I almost–"

We both froze as the roar reached a frightening crescendo, and a huge torrent of spring water poured over the waterfall to come crashing down where she had been standing only moments before. The furious gush of water rose at an alarming rate, pouring over the banks in under a minute.

"Move!" I yelled, shoving her to her feet. "Climb!"

She grabbed her boots and we raced uphill as fast as we were able, then stopped at a relatively safe place so she could put them back on. We jogged until we were at the top of the waterfall. My chest heaved as I tried to catch my breath. I stared at the rush of churning water just beyond our feet.

"Now do you believe me?" Angie stood with her hands on her hips and a grin on her face. There was no mistaking the pride in her eyes.

Without question, there was no rational explanation for this. It had been a dry spring, with only occasional cloudbursts like the one a couple of nights before. There had been no precipitation anywhere that could have caused this nearly instantaneous flood.

"Yes," I said, looking back at the water. "I think I do."

* * *

Eventually the huge rush of water subsided, and the stream

became a trickle that barely covered its bed.

"People aren't going to like that," I pointed out to Angie.

"It'll come back," she said. I raised an eyebrow.

She shrugged helplessly. "The water had to come from somewhere. I just made it go faster."

"So you didn't create the water."

"Water can't be created. It can only be controlled."

"So that's your gift? Controlling water?" I asked.

"Yes." There was a noticeable pause before she answered. I had the feeling that she was being evasive, but she had a right to her privacy. I let it go.

"That's a pretty good gift to have," I said, staring at the nearly empty streambed.

"Do you really think so?"

"Absolutely. You can't survive without water." I looked at her. "I owe you an apology. I didn't believe you when you said you used magic to fill your little pot."

She let out a modest laugh. "I know you didn't, but that's all right. Asking someone who's never seen magic to believe in it is like trying to describe the sky to someone who's only lived underground."

It was a good comparison. It also sounded like it was out of a book. Possibly a book I had also read. Plato, maybe?

We made good time down the mountain, arriving at the Hayworth ranch a little after sunset. Rifle in hand, Jacob opened the door when we knocked, looking startled to see us.

"Ma, Davis is back," he called over his shoulder.

"Don't just stand there staring like a deadheaded mule," she shouted from somewhere in the house. "Invite him in!"

Jacob colored and cleared his throat. I looked down, as though removing my boots and socks took all of my concentration. They were wet, muddy, and covered in an unidentifiable smelly slime. Angie also took off her boots, leaving her socks on. We entered the cabin, and Missus Hayworth made her appearance.

"We heard the shooting all the way down here," she said, placing her hands on my shoulders. "Sit down, the two of you. I'll fix you some of the leftovers from supper."

61

I thanked her, and after washing our hands, we joined the Hayworths at the wooden table. Their mother told them not to pester us for answers until we had eaten. She served us lamp chops, greens, and cornbread. I hadn't realized how hungry I was until the delicious-smelling food was in front of me. I wolfed it down and had a second helping of cornbread. I noticed with some amusement that Angie did likewise, only she had seconds of everything.

"What happened?" asked Jacob. "Joseph and I saw the stream run like a raging river. Now it's not running much at all."

"There was a dam," I lied.

"We had to clean it out," Angie said, and explained what had happened.

"What did those fellers look like?" Joseph asked. I told him. He leaned back in his chair, rubbing his chin.

"Sounds like those Thomas boys," said the Missus. "Nasty bunch, the lot of them. They have less brains than teeth. Their elderly parents died of the 'flu last winter, God rest their souls, and they've been fending for themselves."

"They won't have to do that anymore," Angie said primly. She looked at me.

"I was just going to chase them off," I said. "You ran out and yelled at them, and when they went after you, I didn't have much choice."

The Missus looked Angie over. "That was brave of you, honey. Foolish, mind you, but brave." She smiled to soften her words.

Angie played with her food. "They were about to dump that entire barrel in the water," she said. "All I could think about was how everybody down here was going to get sick. Especially the children."

"We should probably get over to the Thomas place in the morning and check on that mule," said Joseph. "Maybe see what else they had going on." Jacob nodded.

"If it's all the same to you, I'd just as soon keep my name out of it until I'm gone," I said. I didn't know if the Thomas "boys" had any kin or not, but in many places, vengeance was the order of the day. An outsider always made for a convenient scapegoat. If somebody wanted revenge, I'd just as soon be away from here before they came around.

"I hear there's a caravan leaving out first thing tomorrow morning," said the Missus. "They might need an extra pair of hands."

"I'll look into it, thank you. Thanks for supper, too."

"No need to thank me. There's always a place at my table for you, Davis. I imagine you'll want to be turning in?" I took the hint. It was late for them, and they had ranch chores that started with the sunrise.

"You can stay in the bunkhouse. Boys, you stay out there with him." She turned to Angie. "Young lady, you may stay in the house with me."

Trust Missus Hayworth to keep everything prim and proper.

Chapter 6 – Caravan

Rules of Gunfighting #10:
Use a gun that works every time.

The next morning, Jacob and Joseph hitched up their wagon and headed out to check on the lone surviving member of the Thomas party – the mule. They gave Angie and me a ride to town in the back of their buckboard wagon. It was bumpy and bouncy, but she seemed to enjoy it. Every time we hit a hard bump, she bounced up and down and giggled. You'd think she'd never ridden in a wagon before.

Anyway, it was nice to see her looking happy, instead of being sad and serious. Not that it was any of my concern. I cast several sidewise looks at her, thinking of how she had disregarded her own safety to stop the Thomases from polluting the stream. It wasn't worth dying over, but I didn't really think she had thought it through beforehand. She had just acted according to her conscience. I admired that.

I reminded myself that I did not want to be her protector. I especially did not want the job if she was going to go running around half-cocked and get herself into all kinds of sticky situations from which I would be responsible for extracting her. I had to admit, though… I did feel good about what we had done yesterday.

The Hayworths dropped us off at the livery stable, where a

man and his wife stood glowering at the train of horses, mules, and wagons. I recognized them as the owners of the caravan I had joined in Jonesboro. I had thought they were headed for Oak Grove when we parted company. It seemed that their plans had changed.

"Heya," I said. The wagon master, Tom Michaelson, turned and scowled, then greeted me. Having known him to be a man of fair temper, I wondered what had turned his mood sour.

"Mornin'," he grunted.

"I heard you were headed back to Jonesboro," I said. "I'm looking for passage south for two." I indicated Angie.

"I have all the protection I need," Michaelson replied. "Anyways, we're not going anywhere until I get another mule driver. The last one done ran off with my daughter."

It figured that the horny little wench had found somebody to tickle her fancy. It was too bad that it had put her parents in such a bind.

"I can drive mules," said Angie.

"You can?" I asked.

"You can?" the master echoed, looking doubtful.

"I sure can," she replied with a smile.

"Them's some feisty mules. I'm not sure a little lady like you could handle 'em," he said, with a rueful shake of his head.

"Which ones are they?" she asked.

"The red ones, all the way in the back. We have to keep 'em back there, or they'll fight and fuss, and throw the whole caravan into an uproar." Looking delighted, Angie marched straight for the mules.

"Be careful, they bite!" said the caravan master, hurrying after her. Seeming to disregard him completely, she stepped right up to the mules. The pair of them bared their teeth at her and stomped their hooves. She pulled out a carrot, broke it in half, and fed a piece to each of them. They settled immediately, relaxing their necks and lowering their heads so that she could pet them.

"Well, I'll be." The master removed his hat and scratched his balding head. "Don't think I have any gloves that'll fit ya, though."

"I have driving gloves," she said, thrusting her hand into her skirt pocket. She put them on and wiggled her fingers at him.

"Where'd you get those?" I asked.

"Were you thinking I wouldn't know how to drive mules just because I'm a woman?"

I opened my mouth to answer, then closed it. I really didn't know what to think. I barely knew Angie, so why would this news be surprising? On the surface, it might seem a little strange that she possessed such rugged gloves. They could be used for many different purposes, though. I myself carried several small items that were only useful on certain occasions. Finally, I shrugged.

"I've seen women drive wagons before," I said.

I looked at the caravan master. He scratched his head, then slapped his hat back down over his bald pate.

"Looks like you got yourself a job, missy," Michaelson said. He looked at me. "I suppose you'll want passage for the both of you."

"He is handy with the shotgun," Angie said, stroking the nose of the nearest mule. "And he's really strong." I looked askance at her, wondering how she had come to that conclusion. "Well, you are," she said, almost defensively. Deciding to pursue that conversation at a later date, I turned back to the caravan master.

"Food might be a problem," he said. I figured he was being honest, rather than trying to get rid of me, since he already knew we were Traveling together.

"We can set snares," Angie said quickly. "I'm pretty good with a slingshot, too."

"We'll feed ourselves," I said, noting his still-uncertain expression. "You won't have to worry about us." Missus Hayworth had given each of us a loaf of bread and some lamb jerky for the journey. It was early summer and the only things ripe in her garden were strawberries, tomatoes, and a variety of greens. She generously told us we could pick whatever we needed from her garden. I was happy to have the fresh produce.

"Very well, then," he said, nodding and looking relieved. We'll be leaving within the hour." He hastened off to finish

66

preparations to depart.

Angie looked at me with a pleased smile.

"Not bad," I said with a small smile of my own. "Not bad at all."

"We work well together," she said.

I knew what she was hinting at, and I still wasn't convinced. Yesterday may have been rewarding – and perhaps a little fun – but it didn't mean I wanted to devote the rest of my life to her quest. On the other hand, it was nice to be admired, even just a little bit. Since we had met, she had given me multiple compliments. I reminded myself that she had also called me stupid and paranoid, had screamed at me, and had made several sarcastic comments in between.

"Come on, Miss Mule Driver, let's stow our gear."

* * *

For the first few days, the miles rolled by uneventfully and the mules behaved themselves. Angie named them Mule One and Mule Two; they were virtually identical and we could only tell them apart because Mule Two had a notch in his left ear. No bandits or thieves attacked us, probably because we were only a short distance from Kingston. It could also change at any minute, so I kept my eyes open, my senses on alert, and my shotgun on my lap. The master hadn't needed another guard, but since he had taken me along with Angie, I was determined to earn my keep.

"It's kind of nice to ride for a while," Angie said. "Do you work caravans often?"

"It depends."

"On what?"

"On whether I feel like it."

She gave me a funny look. "You just decide to go on a caravan on a whim?"

"Sometimes I want the money, or sometimes a caravan is going to a place I've never been. It's usually safer than Traveling alone."

"What about companionship?"

"That, too."

"I'm surprised you admit to needing other people," she said.

I shrugged. "All humans need some sort of companion-ship, even if it's just with a dog. People go crazy without it."

"Still," she said. "You seem really determined to stay alone."

"Not at all," I replied. "I was heading north to settle down. I was hoping to catch a caravan going to Hardy."

"You'd stop Traveling? To do what?"

"Hopefully to learn a trade." It felt strange to be talking about my plans. I had never discussed them with anyone, not even my parents. Until now, no one had asked. Perhaps they had just assumed I was happy on the road, and had no further goals beyond it.

"Anything in particular?"

I shrugged. "Maybe blacksmithing."

She snorted.

"What?" I said, feeling defensive.

"I just think you could do better. What could you possibly get out of a blacksmith's life?"

"Respect," I said.

"Is that so important?"

"When you live in a town it is. If you learn a profession and you're good at it, and honest in your business dealings, people respect that. It's easier to make a home, settle down, and raise a family."

"Is that important to you?"

"Yes."

"Which part?"

I glanced at her. She was studiously guiding the mules with her hands on the reins and her eyes on the road.

"Being respected," I admitted.

"And, all those other things are is just a way to gain respect?"

"It might be nice to have a family someday."

"You act like you think that a woman would only want you for your ability to support her."

"It seems to be a big part of the thought process," I said, thinking of the girl with hair like honey.

"So, around here if you don't have status, you can't marry who you want?"

"It would be difficult."

"You sound very sure of yourself."

I didn't answer. I knew it from experience, but I wasn't willing to share that information.

"I should think you'd be able to have any woman you want."

I chuckled at her naïveté. It had a bitter sound to it. "I can assure you, without the shadow of a doubt, that this is not the case."

Angie met my gaze evenly. "She must have been quite a fool."

I couldn't imagine where she got these ideas, and it made me chuckle again. "I don't think you know me well enough to make that judgement."

"I shall have to respectfully disagree," she said with a lofty air. I stifled the laugh, but couldn't manage the keep the smile from spreading over my lips. She had some pretty silly ideas sometimes, but I enjoyed her frank way of speaking.

"Being warrior to a druid is a very respectable position," she said.

"I bet it's not as respectable as being a druid."

Her shoulders slumped slightly. "No."

"That's hardly fair."

"It's no more unfair than needing a noble profession to gain someone's affection."

I had to admit she had a point, but I wasn't about to concede the argument.

"I still wouldn't be able to settle down and have a family."

"You could have a life of adventure and magic, but you'd rather spend it sweating in a hot smithy pounding on iron and going home to a tired wife and ten screaming brats."

"Hey, blacksmiths make those swords your warriors carry."

"No, they don't."

"Of course they do, how else would they–" I stopped short. "They use magic, don't they?"

She nodded, wearing a pleasant expression of pride. I added that information to what I already knew about druids. They could use water, and if they could make weapons, their magic could also manipulate metal and fire. I doubted they were doing any serious mining, so magic seemed a logical choice for obtaining the necessary materials. Her people were powerful; there was no doubt about that.

"It seems to me that it would be a better idea for magic users to be paired up together," I said. "I mean, I think I'd feel pretty inadequate after a while, knowing you had this extremely powerful ability to control water, and all I could do was wave around a pointy piece of metal."

The smile faded.

"Was it something I said?"

"It wasn't always this way."

I waited for her to say more, but she held her tongue. I changed the subject.

"All joking aside, Angie, what about you? Do you not want to get married and have children?"

"Druids don't always get married. Even if they do, some women have a different father for every child. It's a way to instill different types of magic in different children."

This time, I was taken aback by her frankness. I didn't know whether to address the issue of breeding for magical ability, or having multiple lovers. Feeling awkward, I steered the conversation in a slightly different direction.

"Who raises the children?"

"The mothers. Sometimes the fathers help. Sometimes the babies are given to be raised by others, so the druids can continue their work. It's a grove, Davis. Everybody works together."

"What about your parents?"

"My mother died when I was a baby. My father has never..." She trailed off, looking at her hands. "He never found anyone else."

"I'm sorry."

She gave a stiff nod, eyes once again on the mules and the road.

"So your father raised you, instead of wandering off and leaving you in the care of others."

She was quiet for a few moments. "I think he lost his

enthusiasm for the work after my mother was gone."

"He must have loved her very much," I ventured. Her features relaxed, and again, she nodded.

"So how do you feel about finding someone like that for yourself?"

Her head turned sharply toward me, and there was a curious mix of emotions in her eyes – grief and anger among them. There was something more, but I couldn't identify it among the others.

"The partnership between druid and warrior is more important," she replied in clipped tones. "Healing the earth is more important. Doing the work of the gods is more important."

"More important than being happy?"

She looked away, but not before I caught a glimpse of sadness in her eyes.

"Sometimes things don't work out the way we want them to," she said softly.

Three days south of Kingston, we made camp for the night on a narrow stretch of the road closely bordered by trees. The sun's rays still shone brightly in the west, but the forest surrounding the road cast long shadows over the wagons. The reduced visibility made me antsy, and I continually scanned the tree line for signs of movement. As all caravans did, we parked the wagons in the open, depending on numbers and firepower to deter anyone from trying to steal the supplies they carried.

The other mule drivers set the brakes and began to scurry about setting up bedrolls beneath the wagon bodies. Angie took her blanket and settled down near the caravan leader and his wife, as she had for the past few nights. Presumably it was to preserve her honor. I didn't think anything of it, as there were a couple of married women traveling to meet their husbands who would also be sleeping there. I figured that she was as safe there as she was with me, so I stayed with our wagon. I also needed some time alone to think.

Looking around at the line, it seemed to me that it would have been a better idea to organize the wagons into a circle. True, it would have taken an hour of strenuous effort to organize everyone and maneuver the wagons in the narrow space, but it would have made the camp easier to defend. It would also be more difficult for someone to steal a mule team and wagon. As it was, we were parked in the middle of the road where anyone could find us.

When evening came, both drivers and passengers were sitting about a large campfire eating, drinking, and talking. I was last to join the group, as I had taken a little time to scout the perimeter. I also set multiple snares for rabbits or whatever other small critter might venture into them. As I walked, I ate a tomato and some jerky.

While I was fairly certain that Caravan Master Michaelson would invite Angie to sup with the ladies, I was not so certain that I would be equally welcome. After all, it was Angie who was driving the mules. My stomach rumbled for more, but until I saw my catch in the morning, I would have to carefully ration my food. It wouldn't kill me to have short rations for a few days. After all, I wasn't using the same amount of energy that I did when walking all day.

Upon my return, I took a quick peek at Angie to make sure she was fine, and then bedded down inside our wagon. There were a mostly barrels and boxes in it, but there were also several sacks of grain, flour, and rice that made for decent bedding. Kicking off my boots, I lay on the blanket with my hands behind my head. The night was warm, a precursor to the coming heat of summer. Thousands of stars sparkled in the midnight blue of Nyx's glorious raiment as she covered the earth in darkness.

I studied the night sky, picking out the constellations I knew so well from my mother's lessons. Ursa Major and Minor were always the most easily found, and from there, it was simple to locate Draco's slithery form coiling about the heavens. Halfway down, directly below the dragon's head, flew the Kite. When I was small, I had imagined it to be the lost plaything of some celestial child god, ever drifting across the galaxy. Below the Kite reclined Virgo, with Leo stalking beside her. Having been born under the star sign of Leo, the lion had always been my favorite constellation.

My drowsy mind brought up a memory of a stray cat that had stayed with my family on and off over the past few years. I had named her Leona, in honor of the great cat in the sky. She was tan with dark brown spots and a striped tail and legs. I thought it was funny that she stood on her tiptoes to be petted. She never made any noise that I recalled. I feel asleep thinking of her face, round and sweet with large green eyes like Angie's.

* * *

The attack came in the early morning hours, when the barest grey was in the sky and men are at their sleepiest. A dog barked vociferously, warning of danger. It was followed by gunfire and I was jerked from a sound sleep. I recognized it as pistol shots, yanked on my boots, and checked the load on the Ithaca. I slipped over the tailgate of the wagon, glad that I had left it down. Crouching to take a look around, I saw the one of the guards at the rear was lying dead on the ground.

The back of the line was relatively quiet, but that didn't mean no one was there. I crept to the front, ducking reflexively at any weapons fire that sounded too close. Upon reaching the site of the previous night's fire, I was gratified to note that it had been extinguished. There was no need to worry about silhouetting myself or losing my night vision. The caravan guards seemed somewhat evenly spaced at the front, positioned prone at various points beneath the first two wagons. With the dog barking so loudly, I hardly needed to walk softly.

In the distance, I could see several shadowy figures moving about in an attempt at stealth. Carefully creeping over the side of the lead wagon, I relied on the distracting fire of the guards to cover my movements. Whoever was attacking us – bandits, most likely – would not be expecting anyone to be so utterly insane as to attack from the top of an open wagon.

I fired three rounds in quick succession before flattening myself against the wagon bed, relying on the scattershot to draw the first blood. There were several cries, and I dared another few shots, this time with little effect. The farther away a target, the less damage the scattershot would inflict. I reloaded my shotgun and moved smoothly back over the side of the wagon, moving laterally and diagonally as I sought the cover of the trees. There

73

was no sense in staying with the wagons; for the bandits, killing the caravan guards would be like shooting fish in a barrel.

Maneuvering around the trees and using my ears to guide me, I hunted for a good place to draw a bead on the bandits. The rest of the caravan guards kept the attention of the attackers, firing so frequently that I didn't need to concern myself with trying to be quiet. This was the one thing I hated about Traveling with a large group of people; my sixth sense wasn't finely honed enough to determine friend from foe. It was best if I stayed off to the side where I might get a better sense of things.

The caravan master started yelling to attract attention. The guards abandoned their stand and crawled back to the middle of the wagon train as quickly as they could. I crouched by an oak and watched them, puzzled. There was no time to ponder this new development, however.

Emboldened by the departure of the guards, the bandits had left the cover of the trees. In the pale light of dawn, I could easily see them moving forward. It was then that I saw the dog, racing low to the ground toward them. The huge animal remained silent until just before its attack, when a violent, guttural growl escaped its throat, mingling with the screams of its bandit prey.

I saw a muzzle flash across the road, and another bandit fell. Before the body had even hit the dirt, I was up and firing rapidly from cover, taking advantage of having another shooter to catch them in the crossfire. I reloaded on the run, changing my position before they figured out where I was. I knelt and fired again, taking down three more. My opposite number had taken down five or six. It was an impressive number, and I decided he must have a rifle. The dog took down two more and raced back to where I had last seen a muzzle flash. Correction: he had a rifle and a dog. It was a huge dog, at that.

With the frontal attack disrupted and the survivors fleeing for the safety of the forest, I trotted back to find out what Master Michaelson had been shouting about. Grim faces met me on my arrival.

"What's going on?" I asked.

"Oh, Davis, I'm so sorry," cried Missus Michaelson. "They

done took your girl!"

A chill raced down my spine, as I thought of Angie in the hands of the bandits. They would abuse her, passing her around for entertainment until they tired of her, then sell her into slavery.

"Which way did they go?" I demanded.

"You'll never find her in time," said her husband. "We're getting out of here now."

"I think it was that way," said the Missus, pointing. Following the nagging sensation in my gut, I ignored the cries of the others to wait, and raced off the road and into the trees. I had to find her. I had promised to see her home safely; I had to get her back. What little daylight there was soon vanished beneath the canopy overhead. I crashed through the undergrowth, heedless of the attention I might attract. Time was of the essence. I had to get to them before they went to ground in some secret hideaway. If that happened, I would never find her.

There was a flash to my right, and something whined by my ear. Without stopping, I swung my arm in an arc and fired the shotgun. The thunderous boom nearly drowned out a sharp cry and the thump of a body into dried leaves. Now that I was away from the caravan, my sixth sense came to the fore. I detected another person, this one a few yards ahead of me. I fired again. There was an answering yell and another stray bullet, this one over my head.

I slipped a tomahawk free of the straps on my left thigh, and headed in the direction of the cry. A bandit was leaning against the trunk of a tree, favoring one leg. Distracted by the pain and blood, he looked up just in time to see me sink the curved blade into his neck.

Two down. Gods knew how many more were out there. I murmured a quick prayer to the Morrigan and plowed onward. I followed my instincts, charging up the forested hill and firing here and there, occasionally hitting someone with the scattershot. They were literally shots in the dark, intended more to make the enemy cautions than to actually kill. I wanted them to keep their heads down. The fewer enemies I encountered, the faster I would reach Angie.

My intellect told me that I was an absolute fool for running about the woods like a crazed maniac, and that there was no hope of finding her in this fashion. My instinct, however, pulled me forward, convinced that I could still arrive in time to save her from whatever evil plans the bandits had in store for her.

I fired the shotgun three more times, hearing one cry of pain. In the silence that followed, I heard Angie's voice, calling out to me. She recognized the timbre of the Ithaca's lethal voice and knew I was coming for her. I willed for her to keep struggling, to resist being taken beyond my reach.

I stopped for a few precious seconds to reload. A pistol shot nearly did me in, as a burning sensation streaked across my left shoulder. I whipped the shotgun around and fired again; there was a sharp scream, then burbling, then silence. I heard the druid yell again and guessed she was only yards away. I could see a faint glow ahead and felt hope surge in my chest.

Forcing myself to run faster, I came upon Angie, held at gunpoint by a female bandit. There was a small torch stuck in the fork of a tree, casting just enough light to see clearly. The bandit stood behind the druid, one arm holding her around the throat. In her opposite hand, she held a pistol to her temple. Angie was gripping the entrapping arm with both hands, eyes squeezed shut and teeth bared.

"Let her go and I won't kill you," I said. Angie opened her eyes, fear and determination warring in them. She wore a look of serious intensity, like the day when she had called the water to clean the Kingston stream.

"You won't shoot me," the bandit woman said. "You'll kill her, too."

"Don't bet on it."

I meant every word, whether she believed it or not. I could tell she did believe me, though. From the moment I appeared, she had begun sweating profusely. In fact, her hair was already completely wet, and sweat dripped from her bangs. Runnels of perspiration ran down her face and dripped from her nose and chin. Her neck and shoulders were shiny with it, and her shirt was rapidly becoming soaked.

"I don't believe you," she said between labored breaths. "You wouldn't have risked... your own life... if you didn't...

76

care for her."

"I care enough to kill her myself before I let her suffer at your hands."

The bandit woman swayed a bit, clutching at Angie more tightly. It seemed all she could do to stay upright. Without warning, her right eyeball popped out of her skull with a sickening wet sound. She screamed, dropping the pistol to clutch at her face. The druid wriggled free, but continued to hold the bandit woman's arm. It was then that I noticed how heavily Angie was perspiring. Tears ran in unceasing rivers down her cheeks, and her blouse was soaked through. The bandit fell to her knees, gasping for breath and weaving drunkenly.

"Angie!" I said, and the druid released her. The bandit dropped onto all fours and tried to crawl away. Her breaths came in big, sobbing burbles that sounded like air traveling through mud. Finally, she collapsed onto the forest floor. Angie turned away and vomited what looked like a gallon of water. She vomited twice more before staggering back a few steps. I ran forward to catch her.

"Angie, what–?" I couldn't wrap my mind around what I had seen. She threw her arms around my neck, and I felt the drag of her weight as her knees buckled.

"I killed her," she said in a choked sob. "I killed her."

"It's okay," I said, wrapping my left around her waist. I scanned the area constantly for other attackers, but none had appeared – yet.

"Mother Oya forgive me," she sobbed.

"You had to," I said. She only cried harder. "Angie." I shook her a little. "We have to get out of here. Can you walk?"

She nodded, still sniffling. I turned us around, mindful of my tracks. It was too dark to follow them for long, but I could see the footprints I had made within the circle of firelight. When I was certain that I was pointed in the right direction, I led her forward, holding her hand. Even if we weren't going the right way, at least we were headed down the slope. We would eventually come upon the road again, or a stream. Failing that, the sun would rise and allow us to find our way.

We walked until Angie was exhausted, both from the mental

strain of having been abducted, as well as from the physical strain of being forced to march up and back down the hill over uneven footing in the dark.

"I can't... I need a rest," she whispered.

"It's not much farther," I said.

"I think... we went... in the wrong direction." She fell to her knees in the damp leaves.

I took a deep breath and decided we could spare the time for a rest. I squatted beside her and took the opportunity to reload again while scanning for threats. There was neither sight or sound of anyone else present. My sixth sense was quiet, as was that peculiar nagging sensation in my belly. It had vanished as soon as I had laid eyes on Angie.

"We'll stay here for now," I murmured into her ear. "Ten minutes, no more." I felt her hair brush my face as she nodded. Easing down to sit against a tree, I held the shotgun in my right hand, propped up against my thigh. I pulled Angie close with my left hand, trying not to think about what I had witnessed.

The more I tried not to think about it, the more I was plagued by the image of the bandit's dangling eyeball, and how she had dragged herself away in a vain attempt to escape. The druid may have believed that her magic's purpose was to heal the earth and restore balance, but it was clear to me that it could also be very, very lethal.

Chapter 7 – A Fellow Traveler

Rules of Gunfighting #7:
If you can choose what to bring to a gunfight, bring a long gun...
And a friend with a long gun.

Angie and I arrived back at the caravan just after the sun broke over the horizon. We were sweaty, dirty, and hungry, but we had not been as far off-track as it had originally seemed. The druid had an excellent sense of direction, and she guided us back to the road without mishap. No bandits dared show themselves. As we approached, the man who drove the wagon just in front of us stared as I led Angie back to our wagon. The rest of the caravan had harnessed their mules and oxen, ready to go.

"How in the devil did you find her?"

"Just lucky," I said, keeping Angie close. She didn't seem to mind. I helped her up onto the front bench and began to harness Mule One. He tolerated my handling surprisingly well after the chaos that had greeted the new day.

"Not a single soul saw them take her," he continued. "But you never hesitated. You just charged into the woods like you knew exactly where they was headed."

"The Missus pointed out the way," I said, not liking the direction this conversation was taking. I watched a few of the guards come our way, along with the caravan master. The rest of the drivers turned on their benches to see what he was carrying on about.

"That ain't enough to find your way through dark woods full of bandits and rescue somebody." A couple of the guards nodded in agreement.

"I'm a Traveler," I said. "It's not my first time in the woods." I finished the first mule and started on Mule Two. He tried to bite me and I slapped his muzzle lightly. After that, he settled down and let me harness him. I forced myself to stay relaxed and look unconcerned, taking my time with the leather straps. The man looked over his shoulder at the gathered onlookers, which included the newly arrived caravan master.

"Just seems mighty peculiar to me. We lose three good men and a wagonload of goods, but you come back from chasing them bandits with your girl, and neither of you have so much as a scratch."

I showed him my left shoulder, where my shirt was stained with blood. "You don't call this a scratch?"

"That ain't nothin'," he said. "You oughtn't even be standing here right now."

Michaelson scratched his bald head and fingered his own weapon. "I'd like to know, too. It was a one-in-a-million chance that you could find her at all."

Finished with the mules, I turned toward him again, pulling out the Ithaca and making a show of checking its load. I chambered one and held it with the barrel pointed to the sky, ready to use it. I could almost hear them collectively draw a breath and hold it. I turned my head slightly, toward Angie, without taking my eyes off them.

"Get our packs," I said. "We're leaving." She hastened to comply, slipping her arms into her own pack and then jumping off the wagon with mine.

"Wait," said Michaelson, looking a panicked. "Where are you going?"

"I don't appreciate having to suffer the baseless suspicions of others. You've known me long enough to judge what kind of man I am. I'm no thief and I'm no liar. Either you trust me, or you don't. Obviously you don't, so we'll be on our way."

"My apologies, Davis, we meant no harm. I was just

80

curious, is all. Of course I trust you."

"Thank you for that, sir," I said. "I hope we'll meet again sometime." I hoisted my pack on my left shoulder, trying not to wince as the strap slid over the bullet graze.

"Surely you're not still going?" he sputtered. "I need a driver for that wagon!"

I looked him in the eye.

"I will not, under any circumstances, Travel with a group of people who think ill of me," I said. "I don't like to leave you in the lurch, but I'm not staying around for someone to try and cut my throat in the middle of the night because they are under the mistaken belief that I am conspiring with bandits."

A new voice spoke up: "After all, if he wanted to kill you nitwits, he sure as hell wouldn't have been running around the woods shooting bandits. He'd have been picking off all the guards who were lying under the wagons."

I allowed my gaze to flicker over to this new speaker. I had seen her before, as I had noticed all the caravan members. She was tall and slender, with dark brown hair that flowed from beneath a wide-brimmed hat. She wore deerskin breeches, leather boots, and a sleeveless tunic. She carried a hunting rifle, with a holstered pistol slung low on her hip. She never rode in any of the wagons that I had noticed, and seemed to prefer the company of a large, rangy hound to that of any human. In the heat of the battle, I had forgotten who the big dog had belonged to.

The guards shifted uncomfortably, murmuring to each other and nodding. One clapped another on the shoulder, and they turned to walk away. I turned a hard gaze on the caravan master.

"Oh, no, Davis, I'm sure nobody thought nothin' like that. We was just curious, is all."

I looked over the rest of them, standing there looking sheepish.

"I'm sure you were, Master Michaelson," said the woman. "Just as I'm sure that everyone else here will agree they were also merely curious."

There were mutters of assent from the rest of the onlookers, who wasted no time in slinking away. The woman with the rifle nodded in satisfaction and turned her eyes toward me.

I glared at the mule driver who had accused me in the first place.

"Sure, yeah," he said. "I was just curious. It does seem right peculiar, though, you out there alone against a bunch of bandits with only one gun."

"Get out of my face," I said in a low voice. "Or I'll show you just how peculiar I can be with this gun." He started to snarl at me before he remembered said shotgun pointing at his chest. Then, he raised his hands in mock surrender, sneered, and returned to his wagon.

Master Michaelson turned to me, wringing his hands. "Everything all right now?" he asked.

"Yes, sir, it is," I said. "Especially since I'll be riding behind that bastard, and his back will make an easy target if he decides to start throwing around accusations again."

The caravan master blanched and hurried away. Still angry, I stood there taking long slow breaths. It wouldn't do to upset the mules. The rest of them could wait on my pleasure, since nobody was generous enough to help with them. I glanced at Angie to see how she was doing, and saw her watching me with huge eyes.

"Would you really have killed them?" she asked.

"If it's them or me, I'll pick me every time," I replied shortly. "I won't lose a moment's sleep over it, either."

"Nor should you," said the woman with the rifle. I turned toward her to see her holding out a hand for me to shake. I took it, feeling the calluses there, and looked into her dark brown eyes.

"Thank you for your help," I said.

"My pleasure, for a fellow Traveler." The corner of her mouth curled up in a half-smile.

"That was you this morning, wasn't it? Firing from the other side of the road."

"Yes, it was."

"It's funny, I was just wishing for someone to help me create a cross-fire. And just a second later, there you were, picking them off one by one."

"I've had a little practice."

I chuckled, finally relaxing. "I'm Davis."

"Kam Stone," she said, then turned her gaze upon the druid beside me. "And, who is your lucky friend?"

"Angie," said the druid. Her tone was a little cool, and I noticed that she was no longer trembling, but holding her head up and her shoulders straight. I was impressed that she had recovered from her frightening experience so quickly.

At a shout from the caravan master at the head of the line, Kam turned to look over her shoulder.

"Looks like we're leaving," I said.

"Indeed," said Kam. "What about your shoulder?"

The bleeding had stopped and I shrugged. "It'll keep."

She nodded.

"Would you like to ride with us?" I asked. I don't know what impulse had compelled me to issue such an invitation. Maybe it was her eyes, or hair, or her tanned and freckled skin. Mostly, I think it was because it had been a long time since I had spent time in the company of another Traveler. I couldn't believe that I hadn't recognized it before.

"Thank you, no," she demurred. "Tuiren and I prefer to walk." She gestured to the dog, who barked once, as if in agreement.

"However," she continued. "I have no objections to walking with you. It's not often that one meets a fellow Traveler. Something tells me that your stories are going to be quite entertaining." Her dark eyes sparkled.

"I don't know about 'entertaining'," I said, helping Angie back up into the wagon. "But things sure have been interesting." Angie settled herself and gathered the reins.

"Are you walking?" she asked, when she noticed I wasn't climbing up after her.

"For a while," I said. "Just to stretch my legs."

She nodded once, a little sharply I thought, and clucked to the mules.

"What happened up in the woods?" asked Kam, as we paced ourselves to match the wagon's speed.

"Well, I know they don't believe it, but I really was lucky," I said.

"How did you find her?"

I shrugged. "Just followed my instincts."

"Following your instincts enabled you to find Angie and avoid the bandits?"

"Not exactly," I admitted. "The shotgun helped me avoid the bandits. Angie saved herself."

Angie snapped her head around and gave me a furious look. She didn't need to worry; I wasn't going to tell Kam how she had done it.

"Do we have to talk about this now?" she said, with a pointed look at Kam. Then she let out a huff and her shoulders slumped. Her brow furrowed as she chewed on her lower lip.

"Maybe you should talk about it," said Kam. "Maybe it will help."

"I can't see how either of you would understand," Angie said. "Especially seeing as how neither of you minds blowing the brains out of anyone who crosses you."

I couldn't believe she had even said such a thing. If not for my promise to protect her, I wouldn't have had to kill half the people I had over the past few days.

"Davis was just trying to protect you, and now you're going to rebuke him for his methods? That's hardly fair." Kam shook her head.

Angie's green eyes widened, and she immediately looked at me with regret. I could tell that she hadn't really meant what she said.

"It's okay," I said. "You don't have to talk about it if you don't want to." I always hated it when my mother kept nagging me to tell her all my thoughts and feelings. Angie was an adult, and she would talk about it whenever she was ready. I changed the subject.

"What kind of dog is that?" I asked.

"Tuiren is an Irish wolfhound," Kam responded. "My family breeds them. They're primarily used for hunting, but back in the days when people fought with swords and shields, they were used to knock knights from their horses so they were vulnerable to attack."

As I examined the dog's long legs and lean form, I could well imagine her being capable of such actions. Bandits on foot had certainly given her no trouble.

"Impressive."

"I raised her from a pup. From the time she was weaned, she's been at my side. I wouldn't be able to Travel without her. She has guarded and protected me more times than I can count."

"It's never occurred to me to get a dog," I said. "Maybe I should."

"My parents are pretty picky about who they sell their hounds to," she said. "And they don't come cheap."

"Where are your folks, anyway?"

"Harrisburg."

"That's not too far from home." Harrisburg was the closest town to Jonesboro, traveling southeast. I had never been there, as my Travels had always taken me to the north and west.

"Really, where are you from?" she asked.

"Jonesboro."

"We're practically neighbors, then." She smiled at me from beneath the brim of her hat. A bright intelligence shone in her eyes, and her smile held a touch of sardonic humor.

"So, how did you start Traveling?" I asked, leaving out the obvious There aren't many women out here, so why are you? She had probably heard that a thousand times already.

"Curiosity, mostly. You spend your whole life in one place, and eventually you start wondering what else is out there. Take my sister and her husband, for example." Kam gestured toward a couple riding in a heavily laden wagon. It seemed to contain all of their worldly possessions, and the woman held a baby securely in her arms.

"He wanted to leave Harrisburg and see the world. She decided she couldn't live without him, so she left, too. They've been gone about five years, wandering up all the way to Hardy. So, I decided that if she could Travel, I could do it, too."

The mention of Hardy piqued my interest. "I was thinking of riding a caravan there, maybe settling down."

"I don't know if I'd recommend that," Kam said. "Well, I suppose you'd be all right so long as you worship the only god in existence, if you get my meaning."

"So much for that idea," I said. Interestingly enough, I

85

wasn't really all that disappointed. Maybe Angie's opinions on the matter had changed my mind. Maybe this Traveler woman with the wide smile and honest face was turning my mind to other things.

"I figured as much." She chuckled.

"Oh?"

"She most certainly is not Triune," Kam said with a meaningful look at Angie. "So it stands to reason that neither are you."

"I guess it's kind of obvious." Angie's wild curls, liberally decorated with beads and feathers, certainly set her apart from everyone else. She was exotic and untamed, and it was no wonder that the Triune people looked at her with suspicion.

"That might be why they weren't so eager to have you go after her. And maybe why they weren't so happy to see ya'll come back, either."

I frowned. That hadn't even occurred to me. It seemed that no matter how many times I had been hated, despised, or merely discriminated against for my beliefs, one more slight could always surprise me.

"And you?" I asked.

"According to our histories, Harrisburg went a little differently than most places after the Fracture," said Kam. "My ancestors were successful organic farmers who also happened to raise Irish wolfhounds. After all the destruction, they were the only ones who had anything to eat, and their loyal hounds helped defend their lands.

"Fortunately for everyone else – well, those who survived, and there weren't many – the Stone clan deeply believes in giving back to the world as we have been blessed. So, when beforehand they were regarded with distrust and suspicion, afterward people couldn't wait to make friends."

"It's amazing what a hungry belly will do for one's moral stance," I said.

"Indeed."

I didn't ask what gods her family worshiped. It wasn't polite. Within my own small family, we discussed it with ease. Out in the community, we didn't mention it at all. Such was the joy of living in Jonesboro, and one of the many reasons I had chosen to leave.

"So, what happened to your sister and brother-in-law in Hardy?"

"They settled, built a house, began farming, and started raising wolfhounds," Kam said. "When people there invited them to church and they declined with an explanation of their beliefs, things got ugly. They stayed a while, thinking that it was better to stand up to ignorance and prejudice than to give in to it. I happened to be home when my folks received a letter about the baby coming, so I decided to wander on up and see if I could help out.

"I was shocked at how hateful people were to them. When the baby was born, the local midwife refused to come. I delivered her myself. Things only got worse after that. I tried to help, but I couldn't stay on guard twenty-four hours a day. We started finding mutilated animals on their front porch. Then someone burned their crops. After all their hounds were poisoned, we packed up their wagon and left in the dead of night. Luckily I had Tuiren in the house with me."

"I'm sorry," I said after a few moments of silence. It occurred to me that if Angie had not shown up when she had, and if I had not offered to take her home, I would be on my way to an extremely inhospitable place. I considered it a bullet dodged and chalked it up to luck.

"We're all safe and sound, and that's what matters," she replied. "You can replace things. You can even replace a hunting hound. But you can't replace people."

I nodded agreement.

"So tell me about yourself, Davis. Why would a successful Traveler like you be interested in settling down?

"Looking toward the future, I suppose," I said. "I figure it's time to learn a profession, anyway."

She raised her eyebrows. "Most people do that in their teens."

I shrugged. "I don't want to do what my father does."

"Really? Why not?"

"I'm just not interested in farming."

"Farming is a worthy occupation," said Kam. "There is no shame in feeding people." I could hear a touch of reproach in her voice.

"You're right," I said. "But, if I work with my father, then I would end up spending my life in Jonesboro." Alone, I did not add.

"You don't want to raise a family there."

I shook my head. "No." I couldn't help but glance at Kam's sister's wagon, and she couldn't help but notice.

"That bad, hunh?"

"No, but it could be."

"Well, Harrisburg is a nice place to live, if you ever have the time to stop by and visit." She smiled.

"Thanks," I said, touched. "I just might do that."

"I think I'll rejoin my sister and her husband," said Kam, as the caravan stopped for the midday meal. She gave Angie a quick glance and murmured, "I think your friend is feeling deprived of your company."

"She did have a rough morning," I said, feeling a little guilty for leaving her to ride in the wagon alone.

"In spite of what she says, I really think she does want to talk about it," Kam said.

I frowned. "Then why didn't she?"

"Because she didn't want to talk about it with me around," Kam said with a knowing smile. "Nice talking with you, Davis."

Angie and I ate our lunch in silence. She barely even looked at me the whole time. I got tired of sitting, and began walking around the camp perimeter until it was time to leave. We bumped along in silence for the remainder of the day, each of us quiet for different reasons. I assumed that Angie was still upset over using her magic to harm another human being. She spent the ride fiddling with the reins and generally looking miserable.

I, on the other hand, was occupied with more pleasant thoughts. I had greatly enjoyed Kam's company. While she lacked Angie's dramatic beauty, she was pretty and had a good sense of humor. There were few Travelers left in the world, and even fewer of them were female. She might even be the only one. I was intrigued at the possibility of taking a trip to

Harrisburg and meeting her people. I wondered what it would be like to be with someone like her, Traveling and discovering new places and meeting new people. We'd probably get into tons of trouble, if my trip with Angie were any indication of what wandering with a woman was like. On the other hand, Kam could handle both a rifle and a pistol. Doubtless she was competent at foraging, and her dog Tuiren would alert us to danger.

Lost in thought, I daydreamed about spending my days walking the road with Kam Stone and her dog. We would share our thoughts, or simply companionable silence, or perhaps throw sticks for Tuiren to fetch. We could join caravans for a change of pace, sharing the watches and knowing that someone else was also awake and alert for danger. At night, we would share our blankets and bodies, alone in the night beneath the watchful eyes of the gods.

I was jarred by the thought that the life I was imagining was very similar to what Angie had described to me, with the exception of sharing blankets. Granted, with Kam, I would never have to worry about watching her back in addition to my own. Then again, now that I knew more about Angie's magical capability, would I have to worry so much about watching over her? I wondered what else she could do.

It gave me pause. If I set aside my reluctance to commit to following her around forever, were my imaginings any different from Angie's proposal? After all, Kam had in no way suggested she was interested in spending any length of time with me. Sure, she had suggested that I consider her hometown as a place to visit and maybe settle, but that was hardly an invitation to share her life. Angie, however, had expressed such an interest. In addition, Angie had let me know time and again that she found me worthy of companionship. I glanced at her from the corner of my eye. Just how far would such a relationship go?

These musings ran round and round in circles in my mind. I pondered how I had so quickly rejected the druid, but had accepted the Traveler with the same ease and speed. I could come up with no better explanation than the fact that the way Angie had approached me had been presumptive and annoying.

Oh, and that she expected it to be for the rest of my life. I liked my freedom.

What was more important, getting what I wanted, or serving the gods? Would I put a priority on my own personal desires, or healing the world?

We stopped for the night at an open place in the road. Wide grasslands spread out on both sides with forests far in the distance. It would be difficult for anyone to sneak up on us this night. I cleaned and oiled my shotgun before reloading it to full capacity. As we were feeding and grooming Mule One and Mule Two, Missus Michaelson brought over two large bowls of stew with equally large hunks of bread. She set them on the tailgate of the wagon and faced Angie and me.

"I brought you some supper," she said. "I want to apologize for the behavior of them jack-fools this morning. What you did was very brave, Davis. The good Lord above knows, they were all just put out because you showed them for the cowards they are."

"Thank you, Missus Michaelson," I said. "I appreciate your generosity."

"You earned your keep, just like you always do. From now on, you two come get your supper along with everybody else. Anybody says anything to you about it, you send them to me and I'll set them straight."

"Yes, ma'am. Thank you."

She looked at Angie. "I'm glad you're okay, honey," she said softly, and went back to her cook fire.

"How about that," I said to Angie.

"That was really nice of her." Her eyes filled with tears, and for a minute, I thought she was going to cry. She did not, however, merely sniffling a couple of times. We finished taking care of the mules and sat down to eat. Angie ate a couple of bites and then poked around the bowl with her spoon.

I ate my stew and mopped the bowl clean with the bread. Watching the druid mope over her food made me glad we were at the back of the line, for it gave us a lot of privacy. We needed it, considering the conversations we tended to have.

"Would you tell me exactly what happened this morning?"

Perhaps if I understood what had happened with the bandit woman in the woods, then maybe I would understand Angie's continuing misery.

"I took her water."

"You said that before, but what does it mean?"

"Do we have to discuss this now?" Her tone was plaintive.

"I think it might make you feel better."

She sighed and looked away. "I used my magic to siphon the water from her body. It's like how I take it from the air, only... it doesn't go into a canteen."

"Where does it go?"

"First, I tried to make her sweat it out, but it wasn't working fast enough. So I took it into myself. That's why I was sweating and my eyes were tearing, because my body was trying to compensate. The human body is made up of a high percentage of water, but it can only hold so much. I was starting to injure myself with all the extra water, so I put it back into her body. Only... I made it go into her lungs." She turned away, buried her face in her hands

"Oh, Ang." I put my arm around her shoulders and pulled her close. It just felt like the right thing to do.

"I used my gift to kill!" she whispered against my chest. "That is not what it is for! Oh, Mother Oya, forgive me!" Her entire body shook with grief. I waited for the storm to subside before easing away so I could see her face.

"You did what you had to do to save your life."

"I should not have—"

I laid my finger on her lips to still them. "Shh. Listen. I understand. Your gift is for bringing light and healing to the world. I get that. But Angie, if the gods didn't want you to use it for self-defense, then you would not be able to do what you did today."

"They give us many other gifts as well, along with the free will to use them as we wish," she protested. "This gift is no different."

"Yes, it is different," I argued. "If it wasn't any different, then anybody could use it. It seems to me that it was put into the hands of those people who would not abuse it. Like you."

She heaved a great sigh. "I only wish that were so," she said. "It used to be that way, when the magic was first given to us."

"You can't carry this guilt around forever," I said. "She was going to kill you. You defended yourself in the only way you could."

"I could have trusted the gods to save me."

"The gods help those who help themselves."

"The gods help those who have faith," Angie replied stubbornly.

I stifled a sigh, willing myself to patience. If I looked at things from her point of view, I imagine that life was a major earthquake right now. I didn't know what to say to her. I suppose that in the beginning of my Travels, I regretted my kills. After a few months, I rationalized it within my own mind. While I never enjoyed taking a life, I accepted that sometimes I would have to kill in self-defense. If only one person in a conflict was going to survive, I wanted it to be me. That didn't help me think of a way to comfort Angie. Then I remembered a story my father had once told me, and decided to tell it to her.

"At the end of the old world, during the time of the great floods, there was a man who got trapped on the roof of his house. He called upon Hermes, asking for the gift of winged shoes, that he might fly to safety. A few hours later, two men in a canoe floated by and offered him a ride. It would have been a tight squeeze, but they reckoned they could squeeze him in. He refused. 'The gods will save me,' he said, and they left. Later, as the waters rose further, he prayed to Poseidon to send the great winged horse Pegasus to save him. Another two men came by, this time in a much larger boat. They tossed him a rope to pull them close so he could join them, but he refused. 'The gods will save me,' he said, and they left. The water continued to rise, and the man was forced to climb farther and farther up his roof, until he had only just enough room to stand, up on the chimney. He prayed for Apollo to swoop down in his fiery chariot and rescue him. Along came a great flying vehicle, which hovered overhead and dropped a basket for him to sit in so that they could pull him up. He waved them away, telling them that the gods would save him.

"The water kept rising, and the man drowned. He awoke in the Underworld, and standing before him was the god Hades. The man became very angry, and demanded to know why none of the other gods had saved him, after he had demonstrated such great faith. Hades just shook his head, and said, "They sent you two boats and a flying machine, what more did you want?""

Angie gave me a blank look with teary eyes. This time I did sigh, and rather heavily at that.

"The gods did save you, Ang. They gave you your gift."

After several minutes, she set her bowl aside and bowed her head. "I understand what you're saying," she said. "But I still feel terrible."

"How many evil things do you think that woman did in her life?"

Angie gave me a funny look. "I don't know. A lot?"

I nodded. "Probably. My father says that the gods use our hands to work their will upon the earth," I said.

"I would rather not have been the gods' instrument for that woman," she said.

"I know. But I'm glad that you didn't let her kill you. I don't think I could have forgiven myself."

"Why would you have to forgive yourself? It wasn't your fault."

"It was my fault for letting the master talk me into having you sleep with the other women. It was my fault for letting you out of my sight."

"I didn't know you felt that strongly about... that sort of thing."

"I take my word very seriously," I said. "I promised to see you home safe, and I meant it."

Angie opened her mouth to speak, but I held up a hand, noticing the caravan master approaching. He halted before us, looking uncertain.

"Sorry for disturbing you two, but I was thinking that it would be more appropriate for the young miss to stay with the other women this night."

"No, thank you, sir," said Angie. "I'm more comfortable

here, if it's all the same to you."

"Now, miss, you don't want to be doing that. Think of your honor, and the young man waiting for you in Jonesboro. You wouldn't want him to hear anything bad about you."

Angie jumped to her feet and rounded on him with balled-up fists. "No!" she shouted. Her sudden vehemence startled me. "I will stay right here, where I know I will be safe and protected, and that no one will abandon me to the tender mercies of bandits!"

The caravan master practically fled from her display of temper. I was surprised, for I had not mentioned to her that the others had tried to talk me out of following her.

"Why did you say that to him?"

"I'm not an idiot, Davis," she said. "I noticed everybody saddling their horses and readying their wagons when we got back. You were the only one who came after me, and nobody else troubled themselves to help you. It's like Kam said. They were hoping we weren't coming back."

I winced.

"And then there was all that nonsense about you making it back because you were in league with the bandits!" She made an aggravated noise.

"They were just afraid, Angie."

"The Missus is right. They're cowards, the lot of them."

"They're not really cowards. It takes a lot of courage to travel long roads, never knowing if bandits are going to attack, or if there will be a storm, or a tornado."

"They didn't have enough courage to try and rescue me."

I stifled another sigh. "Honestly, in that type of situation, it's best to run away so you can save as many people as possible."

"At least a couple of the guards could have helped you."

"Not everybody's cut out to be a—" the words died on my lips, as I realized what I had been about to say.

Not everybody's cut out to be a warrior.

Quakes.

"What were you going to say?"

"Nothing." I busied myself with unrolling our blankets and lying them side-by-side under our wagon. When I paused to see what else needed to be done, I noticed her regarding me curiously. Her eyes revealed her thoughts, and I guessed that she was running my last words over in her mind. I saw them light up the moment she figured out what I had not wanted her to hear. A slow smile spread over her lips, and she looked just a little bit smug. At least she wasn't depressed and grouchy any more. Then her expression changed, to one of puzzlement.

"How did you know where to find me?" she asked.

I shrugged and didn't answer. I kicked off my boots and stripped the shotgun holster harness from my shoulders, then lay down. The druid curled up in her own blanket, propped up on one elbow, looking at me expectantly, but I continued to ignore her. She waited a few moments, then frowned and turned her back to me with an indignant huff.

In the quiet of the camp, those still awake murmured to one another in low voices. Mules stamped and snorted. Angie tossed restlessly in her blankets, and the question whirled around and around in my mind.

How had I found her?

I simply had no answer.

Chapter 8 – Jonesboro

Rules of Gunfighting #25:
Carry the same gun in the same place all the time.

We arrived in Jonesboro without further mishap. Kam Stone walked beside our wagon for at least an hour each day, telling stories of her travels with Tuiren. Some were sad; some were exciting. They were all entertaining. It wasn't so much that the events themselves were interesting; it was the way she told the tales that captured the imagination.

I had never told stories of my "adventures" to anyone but my father, having quickly discovered that they were generally too violent and gory for children. My experiences on the road had made me disillusioned toward the heroes of my childhood. After listening to Kam's tales, it occurred to me that perhaps my role models had been equally gifted storytellers, rather than out-and-out liars.

Angie walked beside Kam as often as I did, and we took turns driving the mules. The two women seemed to enjoy each other's company. By the end of the trip, I think Angie was as sorry to part company with Kam as I was. While they had walked and talked, I had spent the time driving the mules and thinking. I had some decisions to make about my life and Angie's proposition, and I felt that I should make them before we got to Jonesboro. If I was going to perform the insanely crazy action of accepting her offer and becoming her protector, my parents would definitely want to know.

My brain kept telling me that making this choice was stupid, if not downright suicidal, but I couldn't help but feel that perhaps this is what I was meant to do with my life. My father had frequently reminded me throughout my youth that life was a gift from the gods, and that dedicating one's life and work to them was be the greatest sign of respect that a person could show. I still wasn't sure what the right thing to do was. Following Angie in her quest to heal the world sounded like absolute foolishness... but it felt like the right thing to do.

We parted company with the caravan around midday, when it made a brief stop at the trading post. The caravan master only needed to make a couple of quick deliveries and pickups before setting out again. We took leave of the caravan master and paid our respects to his wife before leaving. Last, we bade Kam goodbye.

"I hope we'll see you again sometime," said Angie.

"Maybe I'll wander down south," Kam said. "You say your home is by the big river?"

Angie nodded.

Kam grinned. "How hard can that be to find?" She and Angie embraced like sisters, and then she turned to me. I held out my hand for her to shake and she batted it away and hugged me, too.

"Take care of yourself, Davis," she said.

"You too, Kam. Be safe."

Angie and I gathered our things, and I led the way to my parents' home. It was a short walk, relatively speaking, as it was on the southwest side of Jonesboro.

"She's really nice," Angie said.

"Who, Kam? Yes, she is."

"And she's pretty." I could feel her watching to gauge my reaction.

"I suppose."

"Do you think she's prettier than I am?"

I couldn't help but smile and laugh a little. There was absolutely no way that Angie's comely face and rich complexion could be overshadowed by anyone. From her alluring green eyes to her rich dark curls, she was simply enchanting.

"No," I said. "She's not." Even though she tried to hide it, I could tell she was pleased by my statement. We walked along a few miles more in silence, and soon I could see the roof of our house. It was the only three-story structure in Jonesboro. Heck, it was probably the only three-story structure in the world. As far as I knew, however, it had never suffered even the slightest earthquake damage.

"For a while I thought you might go to Harrisburg," Angie said, breaking the silence.

"I thought about it."

"And?"

"I made you a promise."

We reached the front gate, and I opened it for her.

Angie did not go through, but simply looked at me.

"If you really want to go, I won't hold you to your promise," she said. "I've been thinking about things, and if I don't show up back home, they will come looking for me."

"Why are you saying this now?"

"Because she likes you."

I couldn't help but glance back the way we had come. Kam had told Angie she liked me? I thought about that for a few moments, waiting for the rush of joy, of excitement, of I-don't-know-what that I expected. It never came. I turned back to Angie.

"I've been thinking about things, too," I said. "Come on. I want you to meet my parents."

* * *

"Heya," I said, opening the kitchen door. Startled, my mother dropped the bowl in her hands. I lunged forward and caught it before it could hit the floor. I placed the bowl back on the kitchen counter and dumped my pack beside the door.

"Oh, you gave me a scare!" she said, embracing me and kissing my cheeks. I hugged her back, soaking in the feeling of warmth and security. My mother was tall and willowy, with dark eyes that seemed to know everything. Hair black as a raven's wing flowed down her back. It was a striking contrast to her coppery skin. I had inherited both my hair color and complexion from her.

"You should lock the door."

"This is town," she said. "Not that wilderness you haunt." My parents' house was actually on the outskirts of Jonesboro, with at least two miles of land between their house and the next one. I grinned and let it drop. My mother hated my Traveling; sometimes it was fun to tease her about it. Not that she would have noticed, because that's when Angie came through the door. My mother's jaw dropped, and then quickly snapped shut. She slapped my arm with the back of her hand, apparently thinking me rude for not introducing her already. I suppose she would have preferred the bowl to shatter on the floor.

"Oh, my!" she exclaimed, holding out a hand to Angie, who smiled and took it. "Hello!"

"Hello, Mrs. Davis," she said. "I'm Angie."

I half expected her to tell my mother she was a druid.

"Oh, goodness, call me Nita."

"I will, thank you." Angie's smile widened.

"Have you eaten lunch?"

"No," I said. "The caravan just got into town and we came straight here."

"A caravan?" Her eyes widened, and she smiled broadly. "You brought Angie here in a wagon?"

It was common practice for people to travel to other places to find a spouse. Understandably, they usually made the journey with a wagon in a caravan, since they often had to transport a large load of goods with which to set up housekeeping.

I had never mentioned working on caravans to either of my parents, and realized that she was going to get the wrong idea. My mother had been ready for me to settle down and get married since I was about twelve. Unless I set her straight, she would think that I had returned on a caravan with intentions of marriage and settling down.

"Lunch would be wonderful," Angie said, rescuing me. "May I help?"

"No, no, no…" my mother waved her hands. "Davis can help me."

Angie gave me an amused look. "Even your mother calls you Davis?"

Mom made a face. "He throws such a fit. There's nothing wrong with his name."

"Not if you're a dog or a donkey," I muttered. "And, I do not 'throw a fit'."

It was my opinion that guys like Bob, Fred, George, and Charles became tailors, weavers, shepherds, and farmers. All the Travelers in the stories had names like Xavier, Luke, and Donovan. I had read about them in the myriad books crammed into my room on the third floor. Some were novels, some travelogues, and others diaries. They had always fascinated me. My favorites had all studied under commissioned Trainers in their hometowns. Each one had gone into the world, bringing back exciting stories of his adventures.

I had decided early on that my given name was more indicative of a life as a gardener or sheepherder than an adventurer. As soon as I began studying with the Trainer of Jonesboro, I had dropped it and started going by my surname Davis.

She sniffed, turning back to her batter. "Well, you never answer to it."

I unbuckled my shotgun holster and hung it on a hook beside the front door, then picked up the mixing bowl and began dropping large spoonfuls onto the hot griddle. She was making polenta pancakes – my favorite. Roman soldiers used to eat them when in the field, my father said. I bet they ate them at home, too. I hoped there was honey or syrup for them.

Mom took Angie to the bathroom so she could clean up. Why, I don't know. Angie was always miraculously clean. So was I these days, courtesy of her sensitive nose. Perhaps not as miraculously, though.

"She's a lovely girl," Mom said, bustling back into the room.

I had to agree. "She is."

"I'm glad to see you moving on, after that business with–"

"It's not like that."

100

"So you're traveling with her for convenience?" Her tone threatened to turn acid.

I flipped over the cakes. "No, for safety."

"Then you two aren't...?"

"No."

I could tell she couldn't decide whether to be pleased or disappointed that she'd raised such a fine, upstanding son. I scooped up the cakes and put them on a plate for Angie, dabbing them with a little butter.

"Then you're still upset."

"I'm not upset." I dropped more batter on the sizzling skillet.

"It still bothers you, then."

I sighed. What was it about mothers thinking they needed to pick you apart so they could dredge through all the bad feelings and display them to the light? Maybe it was only my mother who tried to heal all my boo-boos even after I had passed puberty and killed my first man.

Angie came back just in time, proving her a true druid. It was magic indeed, making my mother quit pestering me. My mother pulled a large roasting pan out of the oven. The smell of herbs and roast chicken filled the room as she tested it for doneness.

"Are there onions in there?" I asked hopefully.

"Potatoes, carrots, onions, and green beans," she answered, replacing the lid. "Your father should be home shortly."

"Is there something I can do?" Angie asked.

"You can set the table," I said. "Plates are in that cabinet." I pointed to the correct one.

"Son, she is a guest!"

"It's okay, I want to help," said Angie. She took four plates from the cabinet and smiled at me over her shoulder before carrying them to the table and setting them in their respective places. The druid also collected napkins and silverware, and made sure there was salt and pepper available. Finished, she came back to me and leaned close.

"Is there molasses?" she whispered.

I opened the cabinet door and grabbed a jar filled with

golden liquid. "Is honey okay?"

"Oh, wonderful." She fairly danced to the table and placed it in the center like the precious commodity it was. Bee keeping was one of my father's hobbies, in addition to the thrilling work of designing optimal soil mixes. I didn't mind tilling, planting, and harvesting, because I knew that's where we got the food to fill our bellies. The more esoteric parts of soil mixtures, worms, and beneficial nematodes, however, were enough to put me to sleep.

As I flipped the last polenta cake on the griddle, the door opened and my father entered. He was a big man, about a foot taller than my five-foot-five frame. Thankfully, even though I had not taken after him in height, I had inherited his burly, muscular build. From the looks of him, I surmised he had been up before dawn, either working in his garden or on Mr. Farmer's land. He removed his large-brimmed hat and ran his fingers through his dark hair, shot through with silver at the temples. His skin was tanned from the many hours he spent in the sun every day.

"Son," he said, smiling broadly. "Welcome home."

I could always count on Father to be happy to see me. I knew Mother was glad to see me as well, but we had exchanged so many hurtful words of late that it was difficult to get past the pile of bad feelings they had created. He hung up his straw hat, kissed my mother's cheek, and proceeded to wash his hands in the sink. Drying them, he looked Angie over with a pleasant expression on his face.

"And, who might you be?" he asked, smiling at Angie.

That was when I realized that he just might be making the same assumption my mother had. I wondered if he would be happier if his prodigal son came home for good, bringing a woman with whom to settle down, raise children, and happily dig in the dirt.

"I'm Angie." She looked intently at him, then at me, then back.

"Charles," he said, taking her hand with almost exaggerated delicacy.

"Davis has your eyes," she said happily. "Such an attractive shade of gold."

Angie thought my eyes were attractive?

"So, how long have you two been together?" my father asked, giving me the look for making her call me by my last name. I sighed inwardly. I'd rather have faced bandits than have this conversation around my mother.

"A few weeks," Angie said. Somehow, she had picked up on the unspoken thoughts and the slight tension between my mother and me. With the delicacy of a fairy amongst the flowers, she navigated the conversation and deflected it away from any awkward assumptions.

"I've been Traveling, and Davis was kind enough to escort me here," she continued.

"Did you now?" His eyebrows rose.

Angie answered for me. "We met on the road, and he's such a gentleman that he couldn't allow a woman to travel all alone. Said it was much too dangerous. And do you know he was right? It was my first trip, and I had no idea!"

I waited for my mother to begin her usual diatribe about how it was ridiculous for young people to spend their most productive years wandering around in the wilderness instead of settling in a career that contributed to society, but she didn't. I helped her carry the food to the table, and we heaped our plates with chicken and vegetables. The polenta pancakes I placed in a stone basket, wrapped in cloth to keep them warm. They went on the table, closest to Angie. My mother poured everyone a glass of cool tea, and added a slice of lemon to her own.

Angie took a sip and her eyes grew huge.

"Is this sweet tea?" Angie asked, an incredulous look on her face. "I haven't had this in years. No one knows how to grow it anymore at home and it all died out."

My father smiled broadly. "Growing tea is one of my passions. Nita loves it so." He sent a warm look her way. My mother smiled and lowered her dark eyes modestly.

If there was one thing I cherished most about my parents, it was their enduring love for one another. He grew tea because she loved it. She made polenta cakes because they were his favorite. He helped the neighbors with their farms because he knew it was important to her that they be part of the community. She made sure he had a warm seat by the fire in wintertime after working all day in the cold. They appreciated each other, and they showed it to one another every single day.

Maybe that was the heart of truth, the real reason why I had left Jonesboro. Deep inside, I knew there was no one in the entire town that would love and cherish me the way my mother loved my father.

We ate in relative silence for several minutes, until Mother engaged Angie in conversation. I was grateful to be left out of it. I knew it was only temporary, but any reprieve was welcome. Angie kept it simple, describing our activities in Kingston, including how we had met in the bar and excluding our adventure at the stream. She mentioned the various people of the caravan, leaving out her abduction. She also left out her magical abilities, unicorns, dragons, or the fifteen people I'd had to slaughter keeping her safe.

I realized that while it would seem insane to most people, it had been an interesting trip. After all, who in the world but me could say he was Traveling with a druid? I sat and shoveled food into my mouth while they talked. During a lull, I poured myself some more tea and asked my mother if anything interesting had been going on since I left. I didn't really care about the town or its folk anymore, but if she were talking about them, she would leave off talking about me.

"The Meyers' built an addition onto their house." She smiled at Angie. "Gotta have someplace to put all those kids, you know." She turned back to me. "Mr. Farmer fell and broke his leg, so your father has been putting in more hours in the greenhouse and the fields."

Since the Fracture, some people had adopted their professions as surnames. I idly wondered if our family name would have changed to Gardner, had I followed in my father's footsteps. My mother continued on, dropping various tidbits, skipping from family to family while I half listened to her as she continued her singsong ballad of gossip – until she dropped that all-important name.

"…Just last week we had a baby shower for Sarah. She's

due in December."

"That's nice," I said, barely paying attention. Then I realized what she was saying and lifted my head from my plate.

"Oh, I'm so sorry..." my mother's hand fluttered to her mouth in distress.

I waved her away. "Don't worry about it. It's ancient history."

Angie raised an eyebrow.

"Who's Sarah?"

"That would be the person who showed me just how unimportant I am in the world, and why it's important to be respected in a town."

She mouthed a silent "ohhh" and nodded. "Is that the reason for the whole Hardy thing?"

"Pretty much."

"Now, son," said my father. "She was a silly girl who played a foolish game in order to get what she wanted."

"Yeah, and it worked. She married the man she really wanted, and I got the shit kicked out of me."

"Davis!" my mother said. "Watch your language!"

"I'm sure she didn't realize that you would be hurt," said Father.

"I'm sure she didn't give it a moment's thought," I replied.

"Excuse me, I'm sorry..." Angie interrupted. "What happened, exactly?"

The room fell quiet. My parents didn't answer, allowing me to choose whether or not I wanted to explain the situation.

"It's fine," I said. "I don't care if she knows."

My mother sighed. "It's a silly game of manipulation as old as the world. A girl wants a certain man to commit to her, but he won't. So she pretends an interest in another man to make him jealous."

"Only, I was stupid enough to think she was serious," I muttered.

"You weren't stupid." Angie's green eyes were bright with anger. "She deceived you."

"Unfortunately, Trainer was jealous," Mother said.

"More like homicidal," I said.

105

"He tried to kill you?" The druid was incensed. "And nobody did anything about it?"

"Dad pulled him off me."

"He should have been horsewhipped," she seethed.

"Well, I think having the town gardener beat him to a bloody pulp in front of the whole town was justice enough," said my mother, her eyes glowing with admiration for my father.

Angie turned to him curiously. "Did you really?"

"It's what any man would do for his son."

"Well, once again we have had a fabulously uplifting dinner conversation," I said, then turned to Angie. "Want to go for a walk?"

She practically bounced out of her chair. "I'd love to."

"Oh, good," said my mother. "Take my shopping basket and run down to the general store. I'm out of cornmeal and flour." She demurely lowered her eyes as she sipped her tea, but not before I caught the sly look in the dark depths. Damned if she hadn't found a way to get me to go into town. I couldn't refuse in front of Angie without looking like a selfish creep.

"Fine," I said, and grabbed my holster.

"You do not need to take that, Davis! Leave it here!" My mother shook her head in disgust. "And leave the machete and those tomahawks, too. You look like you're going to war."

I felt like I was going to war. Unbuckling the belts with a sigh, I hung them on additional hooks beside the shotgun. I felt naked and vulnerable. I had a strong compulsion to grab the shotgun holster and dart out the door before she could say anything more, but that wouldn't have looked very dignified in front of Angie.

"It'll be okay. We'll have fun," said Angie. I turned to see the druid, who already had the basket in hand. She was such a striking figure, with her whimsical beads and feathers, gold earrings, and embroidered garb. I doubted anyone would even notice my presence, and I told her so.

She laughed softly, blushing, and I closed the door behind us.

* * *

"Sorry about my mother," I said when we were out the gate and headed toward the center of town.

"Why are you apologizing?"

"She kind of put you in the middle of our family feud. You must have felt awkward."

Angie laughed. "That's nothing compared to the politics back home. Besides, I can tell she just wants you to be happy."

"She wants me to be happy, so long as it involves settling down and giving her grandchildren."

"Sounds like a typical mother to me."

"I wouldn't know," I said wryly. "She's the only one I've ever been around."

"What about your friends' mothers? Don't they worry about their sons over the same things?"

I was silent, not knowing how to respond. It's a hard thing to admit that you have no friends, because an entire town holds your faith against you. It had been a long, lonely existence, and I had been desperate to belong to something. Perhaps it was the real reason why I had put up with Trainer's harsh teaching methods. He had been mean long before he thought I was trying to take Sarah from him.

"Was it something I said?" she asked, her smile gone.

"Remember what Kam said about how her sister was treated in Hardy?"

"Yes."

"Everybody here knows that we aren't Triune. My parents never hid it. They don't advertise it, either, but the fact that they've never set foot in the church has been noted."

"But your parents are respected here, aren't they?"

"They are, yes. But apparently none of the other parents wanted their children corrupted by spending time with me." I couldn't keep the bitterness out of my voice. At that instant, I hated the town and everyone in it. Here I was, spending time with a beautiful young woman who had expressed admiration for me, and I was having to admit that it was undeserved. Until that moment, I had not realized how important her opinion had become.

I felt her fingers curl around mine. She never said a word, never expressed empty platitudes of sorrow or understanding. That simple touch conveyed compassion, comfort, and a reassurance that my deep revelations had not changed how she felt about me. I let my own hand close about hers, and we walked hand-in-hand the rest of the way.

"Sarah's family owns the general store," I said. I did not want to go in, for I would surely not be welcome.

"Would you mind if I went in and did your mother's shopping for her?" she asked, as though I had not spoken at all. "I want to look around a little bit, and I know how men hate to shop."

"Sure."

She gave my hand a little squeeze before releasing it, then trotted up the stairs with the basket swinging on her arm. I moved to a nearby bench and leaned back against the porch. Closing my eyes and tipping back my head, I felt the muscles in my neck and back relax as I soaked up the sun. I was just starting to think that I might be able to survive this trip to my parents' town, and idly wondered if that might be more of Angie's magic.

I felt one side of my mouth curl upward. So far, I hadn't seen much magic of the sparkly, flaming, electric kind, but she had certainly brought the magic of warmth and light. I hadn't realized how dark and grim life had become for me. As we had traveled, there had still been harsh times, and difficult problems to overcome, but being with her had brought me back up when I descended to the depths of fear and anger.

It was then that a female voice called my name. My first name. Who the hell was using my given name? My eyes snapped open, and I fixed a glare on the woman standing before me.

It was Sarah. She stood before me in the sunshine with her honey blond hair done up in braids and an uncertain smile on her face. I had once fantasized about taking down each braid, one by one, until I could plunge my fingers deep into the thick mane. I felt my gut twist, and my heart start to pound. I was careful not to move a single muscle, for fear of either running away or starting a fight with someone.

"It's Davis," I said. My tone was so cold that I barely recognized my own voice.

Her smile faltered. "I didn't think you'd mind. Before, you always let me call you–"

"That might have had something to do with the fact that we were courting. At least, I thought we were."

She swallowed hard. "I'm sorry you were disappointed."

I wasn't interested in anything she had to say. She had deceived me and then betrayed me. It was just one more affront added to the list of indignities I had suffered because I was different.

"That's not much of an apology," I heard myself say. "Not only did you lie to me, but you let everybody in town think I was guilty of something I wasn't."

What had gotten into me? Why was I even bothering? It's not as if anyone cared.

"You're right." She tried to smile again, and failed miserably. I looked her square in the face and realized that I no longer found her beautiful. Compared to Angie, she was merely attractive.

The bell on the door of the general store jangled, and footsteps sounded on the porch behind me. "Davis, darling, who are you talking to?"

Darling? I turned my head to look up at her, leaning over the rail, lovely dark brown curls framing her face. She gave me a quick smile that never touched her glittering green eyes. She lightly trotted down the stairs, sashaying over to me. She offered me her arm. Bewildered as I was, politeness dictated that I rise to my feet to take it.

"This is Sarah, Trainer's wife." It wasn't quite as galling to say as I had once thought it would be.

"Oh, Trainer's wife? I've heard so much about your husband."

I had never heard Angie tell a lie before, and really hoped my face wasn't betraying me. I had never breathed a word about him before lunch with my parents today.

"Oh… how nice." I began to get the feeling that Sarah had expected Angie to say that I had talked so much about her.

Angie looked sideways at me, as though confused. "I thought she'd be prettier." Sarah's jaw dropped. "Then again, I suppose that a true beauty wouldn't have had to play a nasty trick on two men to get one of them to marry her." Angie's claws sank deep and the blonde girl paled.

"I repented of my sin," she said, tears springing into her eyes.

"Oh? Did you 'repent' to the one you hurt the most?"

A tear slid down Sarah's cheek, and she looked down at her feet. Then, at the worst possible moment, her husband appeared. I hadn't seen him in better than four years, and I could have happily spent the rest of my life without seeing him ever again. He rounded the corner of the general store, took one look at his tearful wife, and stopped in his tracks.

"Great," I muttered. "Come on, Angie."

I took her arm, but she resisted. I wasn't the kind of man to force a woman to do anything, so I let her go. I also wasn't about to leave her alone with these two, as much as I wanted to run back to my parents' house with my tail between my legs. I stepped as far away from Sarah as I could without moving too far from Angie. I think I moved about three whole inches.

"You," said Larry Trainer, recognizing me. His voice carried all the disdain and contempt he was capable of mustering, which was more than just about everybody in the world combined. "Just what the hell do you think you're doing talking to my wife?"

I glanced at Angie, to see if she was paying attention to him, and caught sight of Sarah's bloodless face. She looked terrified. It hit me that perhaps Trainer was just as harsh to his wife as he was to his students. No matter what humiliation I had suffered at her hands, it was not a pleasant thought.

"Get over here, Sarah!" he snapped. She practically tripped over herself in her haste to comply, and then stood before him trembling with her head bowed. Angie stared at them open-mouthed. I guess druids didn't beat their wives. Not that they had wives. Even so, a man would have to be a fool to hit a woman who could defend herself with magic.

"I told you not to talk to him! Didn't I tell you never to talk to him ever again?" he barked. She nodded mutely, looking like a whipped dog. "You get yourself back to the house!" he shouted, and she lifted her skirts and walked quickly away.

Until then, the streets had been relatively clear. With his shouting and the rapid departure of his obviously upset wife, however, people were starting to notice. They were coming out on their porches to watch.

"This is how people here treat women?" Angie asked incredulously. I groaned. It was the worst possible thing she could have said. Realizing it a split second later, she gave me an apologetic look.

"What? Who do you think you are? I'll not have some wild woman criticizing the way I run my household! I have half a mind to teach you some respect." He took a threatening step toward the druid. Without thinking, I stepped in front of her.

"No, you won't," I said. I reached my hand over my right shoulder, grasping only air. Belatedly I remembered that the Ithaca was hanging in its holster in my mother's kitchen.

He gave a harsh laugh. "What's got into you, boy? Tired of hiding on your daddy's farm? I bet you think you're some kind of tough guy now. Why don't you come show me what an almighty Traveler you think you are."

"You mean you'd like to see if you can beat my ass again to make you feel better about your sorry existence in this shithole town."

Gods, what was I thinking? Obviously, I wasn't; the words had come out of my mouth of their own accord. I had never spoken to Trainer like that in my entire life. The fact that I had said it in front of witnesses was guaranteed to make him that much angrier. His face reddened, and a vein rose to prominence in his forehead above his left eye.

"I don't have to see if I can whip you again," he growled. "You have yet to stand up to me in a fair fight."

"There was nothing fair about that fight," I growled.

Out of the corner of my eye, I saw a couple of boys in their late teens jump off the porch of the barbershop and swagger in our direction. They were obviously two of his current crop of sycophants. They stopped, flanking their instructor and trying to look tough with their arms folded across their chests. Both of them were bigger than me, but I wasn't impressed.

"Watch your mouth, boy. Your words dishonor me."

"You don't need any help from me in that regard. You're doing just fine on your own."

Since when did I have so little control over my own tongue? If I didn't know any better, I'd say that I wanted to fight him. I didn't. Did I? After all, my whole life's experience was him kicking my ass and me limping away to lick my wounds until the next time.

"Are you going to fight him?" asked Angie, looking worried.

I turned my head to look at her. "I think it's better if we leave," I said. The next thing I knew, Trainer's fist was speeding toward my face. I staggered under the blow, putting my arms up defensively. I should never have taken my eyes off him, but I really hadn't thought he would attack me in front of all those people. It was just like when I was sixteen; I hadn't thought he would hurt me then, either.

He followed his initial punch with a flurry of blows that kept me busy blocking and dodging while I looked for a chance to hit him back. I took couple of hits to the ribs, and he relaxed his stance, thinking perhaps that I was not going to fight back.

He was wrong.

I feinted with a jab, then hit him in the cheek with a left cross. Regrettably for me, married life had not made him fat and lazy. His head snapped to the side, and then back toward me as though I hadn't hit him at all. All it did was piss him off. I didn't wait, but simply blocked the wild haymaker that followed and jabbed him twice in the nose. He knocked the breath out of me with meaty fist to my gut, followed by powerful jab to the face. I tried to regain my wind as blood poured into my eye.

At the sight of my own blood, something snapped inside me. I had a sudden, excruciatingly vivid flashback of when he had beaten me in the street before, when the whole town stood and watched a grown man nearly kill a sixteen-year-old boy. From that second on, I was no longer in a safe and familiar hometown. I was a Traveler, a stranger to these people, fighting for my life.

Red-hot rage boiled over from my chest and into my head.

112

A rush of adrenaline coursed through my body and gifted me with increased strength. I tucked in tightly to block his attempts to hit me again in the midsection, then jabbed him twice in the face, sharp and hard, followed by a thunderous right hook. Blood gushed from his split lips, and I took advantage of his momentary weakness to slam my fist into his gut.

Trainer bent over with a wheeze, arms wrapped around his middle. More blood sprayed from his nose and mouth with every labored exhalation. Seeing their master incapacitated, his students took the opportunity to come after me. I snapped a kick into the first one's knee before he could come within arm's reach. He bent to grab it and I kicked him in the face. Another one jumped me from behind and wrapped his arms around my chest. I crouched, throwing him off balance and making him support my weight. His hold on me loosened; I twisted right and left, slamming my elbows into his head. Once he'd released me, I spun and grabbed him behind the neck, kneed him in the gut a couple of times, then kicked him in the crotch. He collapsed in a heap.

I came about just in time to see Trainer upright and moving again, sporting a black eye, split lips, and a swollen jaw. From the way he moved, I could tell he was hurting. He was more dangerous than ever, because I had just downed two of his students, making him look bad. That would hurt his reputation, but it would be nothing compared to how he would look if he lost a fight in the middle of his own town.

"I'm not finished with you," he said, and spat a gob of blood into the street.

"Fine by me," I growled. "I haven't knocked any of your teeth out yet."

I saw him hesitate, a flicker of uncertainty in his eyes. I took the opportunity to feint a shot at his face, but my follow-through was interrupted when he tackled me. He grabbed me about the waist in an attempt to take me down. He was bigger than I, outweighing me by probably fifty pounds, and if he got me on the ground, I would be finished. I kicked both legs out, jumping backwards to stop his head-long rush. Forced to support my weight in addition to his own, he struggled to retain his hold. I took advantage of his distraction, striking him viciously in the face with my knee. He roared in pain, and clutched harder at my shirt. I slammed my knee into his face again, feeling the bones in his nose crunch. He bellowed in pain and began struggling to get away, instead of trying to hold on. Keeping control of his right arm, I rolled him over on his back so I could safely get out of his reach. He tried to punch me with his free hand, so I hammered him twice more with my fist – once in the mouth, and once again in the nose – before he collapsed in defeat.

I backed off, chest heaving as I tried to catch my breath. I sidestepped the blood pooled in the dirt. Mother would not be pleased if I tracked it all over her kitchen floor. Trainer curled up in a fetal position clutching his face. Turning away from his prone figure, I looked over the previously cheering and now-silent crowd.

"Anybody else?" I shouted. "I'm still fresh. Now's your opportunity, you cowards."

I wanted them to come at me, so I could vent my rage upon them. I wanted them to feel what it was like to feel hurt and humiliated. I wanted them to slink away to their homes, nursing wounded spirits and hearts like I had done so many times.

"Davis." Angie grabbed my arm. The look I gave her would have melted anyone else. She swallowed but stood firm.

"That's enough," she said. "You won. It's over."

Chapter 9 – Home Fires

Rules of Gunfighting #6:
Proximity negates skill. Distance is your friend.

I sat at the kitchen table with Angie fussing over me as if I was mortally wounded, rather than having relatively superficial injuries. I had a rapidly swelling black eye, a bloody nose, and a sore jaw. I ran my tongue over my teeth. None of them were loose, but my lips were split in a couple of places. My ribs ached a bit, and so did my upper abdomen, but those were easily tolerated. A little willow bark tea would cure most of what ailed me. The worst injury was the laceration to my left eyebrow, which was still bleeding. Angie made me hold pressure to it while she cleaned my face with a damp cloth. She was now holding the dressing herself, so that I could tilt my head back and pinch my nostrils to stop the nosebleed. She might have been going a bit overboard, but a deep, dark part of me enjoyed the attention.

We were alone in the house. My mother had left a note saying she was taking soup to a sick neighbor and would not be back until suppertime. I thanked the gods for that small blessing.

"I think you need stitches," the druid said.

I groaned and made a face. "First aid stuff is in the bathroom."

She was gone a few moments before returning with the first

aid kit. It was stuffed full of cotton bandages, suture, needles, antiseptic, and all those other things that were cruel to be kind. She threaded the tiny needle and bent close.

"Wait. Have you done this before?"

"I can sew clothes."

"Maybe I should wait until my mother gets home."

Angie rolled her eyes. "Really, how different from sewing can it be? Hold still."

I grit my teeth did as instructed while she closed the wound. Her face displayed a variety of painful expressions, as though she were the one pierced by needle and thread. It was a little distracting and would have been entertaining, had she been suturing someone else's head wound. She tied off the thread and snipped the excess. I closed my eyes as she cleaned the wound and washed my face with gentle fingers. Having her touch me like that was almost worth getting punched in the face.

"How do you feel?" Angie asked.

"Sore." It would be worse tomorrow.

"I imagine you are. However, what I really want to know is how you feel about, you know, beating him."

I shrugged. "It just means everybody will hate me more than they already do."

She sighed. "Forget everyone else." She knelt by my chair and looked up at me. "I just want to know... Do you feel better now?"

Part of me wanted to groan, because not only did my mother want to know all my deep thoughts and feelings, now Angie did, too. I thought about it for a minute and decided that wasn't so bad. If she didn't care, she wouldn't ask, right?

It wasn't something you were supposed to admit, but I felt vindicated. I felt like I had shown everyone who needed showing that I was no whipping boy, someone to be abused and cast aside like trash. She placed her hand on my knee, as if to remind me of her presence.

"I do. Not... not because I wanted revenge," I said. "But because... Maybe now people will see him for what he is – a bully."

"Good." She smiled softly. "I'm glad."

She washed her hands in the sink and began repacking the first aid kit. I thought about the time we had spent together, and how she had consistently been supportive, understanding, generous, and brave. She was an incredible woman, kind and gentle, resilient as leather, and committed to her calling in life.

"Angie?"

"Yes?" She halted in the doorway, on her way to replace the kit in the bathroom.

"Why are you here?" I asked. She raised an eyebrow and I tried again. "I mean... Why do you care about me at all?"

"Other than the fact that you've saved my life repeatedly?" she replied lightly.

I shook my head. "I have walked away from you. I have refused to be what you want me to be. I haven't really done anything you've asked of me. So why do you still care?"

She looked away, uncertain. When she faced me again, her expression was resolute. "Actions speak louder than words," she replied. "So, while you have been consistently saying 'no,' your actions have repeatedly said 'yes'."

After thinking about it for just a little longer, I decided she was right.

* * *

My mother was in a fury when she came home.

"All I asked is for you to go to the general store and pick up a few things for me, and all you managed to do is pick a fight!"

"If you had let me take my shotgun, there would have been no fight at all," I retorted.

"Why, so you could kill him?"

"I wouldn't have had to. As soon as I pointed the barrel at his face, and he would have found someone else to harass."

"How on earth do you get yourself into these messes?"

"You sent me to the general store, which is owned by Sarah's family. So guess who showed up? Sarah! And then he showed up!"

"What did you do to make him angry?"

"Why do you always have to assume that I did anything?"

"Because you have a smart mouth!"

"Whose side are you on, anyway?" I said.

"I'm not on anybody's side," she snapped. "I just don't understand why you can't get along with people!"

I jumped to my feet. "Why should I?" I shouted. "I'm not the one who decided I wasn't good enough for this town! Just for once I'd like it if you backed me up, instead of worrying about how much people like you."

"You have no idea what we sacrificed to bring you here and raise you!" Her hands shook with anger.

"Oh, yes, I do. You sacrificed me." I jerked the kitchen door, fully intending to stomp outside, but my father stood on the other side of it, blocking my way. He stepped over the threshold, calm eyes taking in the tense scene. Unmovable as a mountain and solid as stone, he brought the calm and quiet with him in the face of turmoil.

"I take it you've heard," he said to Mother, his quiet voice bringing the tension level down a notch.

"Of course I heard!" she snapped. "Everyone in town is talking about how our son jumped Larry Trainer in the middle of the street, when the man was merely defending his wife!"

"That's not true," my father interrupted.

My mother looked at him irritably. "What?"

"Mrs. Farmer saw the whole thing. She said that Larry threw the first punch and then two of his students ganged up on him. Our son was defending himself."

She looked at me, and the fire in her eyes died to a smoulder. "Three of them jumped you?"

"The disciples didn't like seeing me whip their master."

She rounded on Father. "This is your fault, teaching him to fight!"

"A man needs to know how to fight."

"No, he doesn't," she said angrily. "We agreed on that."

"You decided that. Not me."

"It was for the best!"

"It's best for him to be defenseless against them?"

"They aren't them, Charles! They're us! We are a part of this community!" She threw up her hands. "If you hadn't taught

118

him to fight, he would have been forced to stay here and work out his differences with people. Instead, you just made it easier for him to run away!"

My father rubbed his chin thoughtfully. He shook his head and said, "I don't think that made a difference. He was going to leave anyway. I just wanted to make sure that he survived. I told him I'd teach him everything I could, if he would only wait a couple years before he went."

"How dare you do that behind my back!"

"It was hardly behind your back," I said. They both ignored me.

"Because I disagreed with your opinion on how things should be done," said my father. "You were wrong."

Mother was incensed. "He is my son! You have no right!"

He raised an eyebrow. "Don't I?"

They stared at each other for several long moments. I had never heard them argue like this. I wondered if it was because my father had always bowed to my mother's wishes where I was concerned. Where anything was concerned, actually.

"I'm sorry," said Angie, interjecting herself into the conversation. "Nita, I don't understand why you're so upset. Davis is strong, he's smart, and he's self-sufficient. He's brave. As far as I can tell, being a Traveler helped him develop all those attributes."

"Traveling is a useless waste of time," Mother snapped. "There is no point to it."

Angie didn't back down. "How can you say that? The world is so big and beautiful, and there is so much to discover."

"It will gain him nothing."

"You don't know that."

"Young lady, relative to joining a community, becoming a contributing member, and raising a family, it's nothing."

"But that's not going to make him happy."

I thought my mother was going to choke. "Some things are more important than personal wants, like the needs of all of humankind," my mother said. I wondered how Angie was going to counter that. I had never been able to without sounding like a selfish bastard.

"Humankind has gotten along just fine for millennia without the help of the entire race. Not everybody contributes in the same way." She held up a finger. "Just because Davis contributes in a different way, does not necessarily mean he's wrong, or that he's denying humankind his particular talents. Maybe he's meant for other things. Maybe even greater things."

She was getting dangerously close to admitting to being a druid in possession of vast magical abilities that for reasons of economy could be unleashed only in times of greatest need. I halfway hoped she would tell my parents, just so I could see their faces.

"So you two are up to 'great things'." Mother's voice dripped with sarcasm.

"Yes, we are."

My mother waved her words away. "I cannot think of any greater thing than raising a family and bettering mankind."

Angie leaned forward, meeting her intense gaze. "Just because you can't think of it, doesn't mean that it doesn't exist."

The expression on my mother's face was priceless.

"Besides," said Angie. "What happened this afternoon was as much my fault as anyone's."

"Is that true?" my father asked quietly.

"Yes," she said. "I insulted Trainer's wife."

"And why would you do that?" Mother seemed torn between anger and exasperation.

"Because she hurt Davis." Her lips were pressed tightly together, eyes once again alight with anger. "No one hurts my warrior."

"Your what?"

I immediately tensed; when my mother used that tone, it meant bad things. She was as volatile as my father was even-tempered, and had no compunction at all about raising her voice – and the roof – when she was upset.

"Yes."

"Would you care to explain that, please?" It was not a request. Her calm voice was a lie; the quieter she became, the more dramatic the outburst of temper. I had always thought of it as bundling up dynamite for the explosion to follow. All of a

120

sudden, I wanted to be out of the kitchen, because staying between these two would probably be dangerous. Battlegrounds usually are.

Angie looked my mother in the eye. "I am a druid, and Davis is my chosen warrior." I liked that she hadn't spoken for me. Not exactly. I mean, she hadn't told them I had agreed.

Which I hadn't.

Yet.

"The hell he will!" my mother snapped.

"You have nothing to say about it."

"I'll not have it!" My mother clenched her jaw and her face turned deep red. I wondered whether she had known about the existence of druids, or if she was just objecting on general terms. None of this seemed terribly surprising to her.

"You have no choice in the matter," she responded quietly. "The gods have decided."

Quakes! I wanted to crawl under the table, or maybe under the house. Yes, definitely under the house. There was a space down there where I used to go hide when I was in trouble as a kid. I figured I might still fit, if only I could get out the door. My mother pinned me with her furious gaze.

"Why would you agree to this?!"

"I don't have anything else going on at the moment." It didn't matter if I had agreed or not. I was going to back Angie up the same way she had supported me.

"Do you know what you've agreed to?!" she demanded. "Do you realize this is your life?"

I most certainly did. It was she who had never realized that it was, in fact, my life.

Her attention snapped back to Angie. "Realize that he won't be any good to you," she said, an edge of triumph in her voice. "He's taken a vow of celibacy."

Why was it that every private thing in my life had to be screamed about over the kitchen table? I had made that proclamation four years ago! I hadn't even meant it. I had just been angry about Sarah and had sworn off women forever. I suppose my reasoning had been that being alone was more bearable if it was my choice, rather than feeling rejected.

Angie looked at me with wide eyes. I made a face and shook my head, waving my hand to show it was irrelevant. Fortunately, she got the message. There was silence for a moment, then she turned back to my mother.

"And of course that had absolutely nothing to do with that Sarah girl."

Mother crossed her arms over her chest.

"Sometimes when people are hurt, they make foolish decisions, and foolish vows. When they heal, they move on." Angie was one hell of a politician; I had to give her that. She was holding her own against my mother, who could drive anyone into the ground with her arguments.

"Foolish vows like becoming warrior to a druid."

Angie bristled. "And what would you know about it?"

"More than you know."

"Perhaps you'd care to enlighten me."

Mother just stood there, glaring silently at her for a long moment before turning back to me.

"Son... Don't do this. Travel if you want, go where you please. Come home whenever you want, I'll stop giving you grief over how you live your life... But please, do not go with this girl."

"Why not?" I asked, leaning forward and resting my folded hands on the table. Ow, my ribs.

She licked her lips. "I can't tell you. You must trust me in this. If you go with her, your life will no longer be your own, and you will be in danger every moment."

"I'm in danger every time I step out on the road."

"Not like this."

A heavy silence reigned in the kitchen, as I looked from my mother, to Angie, then Father. I could tell he knew her big secret. He remained still and silent, as solid as the earth he worked, but he radiated strength to me. There was also no small measure of approval in his eyes; in fact, he looked delighted. Why would he be so happy about this decision? He should have been as opposed to it as my mother was.

"If this is so important to you, and such a risk to my life and independence, I think I deserve an explanation."

122

"Please just trust me." It was then that I saw something I rarely if ever saw in my mother's eyes – fear. Fear for my life? Fear that I would achieve greatness on my own? Fear of losing control over her only child?

Taking into consideration all the times she had tried to make me quit training, quit playing with tomahawks and knives, and quit the road, trying to convince me that I was wasting my life, it seemed glaringly obvious that she had some ulterior motive for keeping me here under her thumb. There was something in her past, something she regretted about her life choices, and she needed me to give up my life in order to make her feel better about her decision.

That was the moment when I made mine.

* * *

Angie and I left the next morning. I don't know that either of us got much sleep, because my parents argued about me far into the night. The conflict in and of itself was a rare occurrence, because my parents were in agreement about most things. In fact, it seemed that the only thing they ever fought about was me. Listening to their raised voices, I wondered what was so important to my father, and why my mother was so dead set against it. I had never heard him insist on something so vehemently, and I departed Jonesboro without discovering what their disagreement had been about.44

I had never before set out on a journey feeling as badly as I did that time. I had to admit it was emotional more than physical. Mother alternated between hot anger and cold silence until we actually left. Sometimes she seemed to be fighting tears. Father saw us off, and gave me an ancient map on a well-tanned animal skin. I recognized his handwriting on the map; he had made it himself. It showed an area of about twenty thousand square miles.

"I didn't know you had Traveled so far," I said, unable to keep the awe out of my voice.

He smiled. "Your mother was with me for most of it."

"Then why is she so hell-bent on keeping me from it?"

"Like all mothers, she's afraid for her child. She was only able to have one – you. It's made her over-protective."

"You're not afraid."

"I worry sometimes, but I know you are in the hands of the gods. I remember what it was like to struggle for my freedom as a young man. We've given you roots. Now it's time to let you have your wings." He placed a hand on my shoulder. "I trust your judgement, son. I know you'll do well."

I felt my throat tighten at his words. He handed each of us a large bag of travel food, with extra canteens for water. I didn't tell him the extra canteens were unnecessary. That would involve explaining about Angie's water magic, something I didn't want to get into. It was a lot of weight, and I wasn't sure why he thought we needed so much.

"Your mother packed them," he said when I looked askance at him with my one good eye. "Be sure to stop by Grandmother's on the way."

"I will." He hugged me, and then surprised me by hugging Angie, too. Tears were in her eyes when she smiled up at him.

"Try to keep him out of trouble," he said to her. Then, to me: "Keep her safe."

We had started toward the western pasture when my mother came running out of the house, calling for me to wait. I stopped and allowed her to cling to me for a long time. I told her I loved her, and kissed her on the cheek.

"Come back safe to us," she whispered tearfully. "May Lugh and Brighid, and all of the Tuatha de Dannan guide and protect you."

She stood at the gate, watching until we were out of sight. When I looked back, my father was standing beside her with his arm around her shoulders. Angie and I waved farewell and passed beyond their sight.

"I'm so sorry we're leaving like this," she said.

"It's always like this," I replied.

* * *

I was hoping to avoid meeting anyone along our departure

route, but Trainer was on the southern road with Sarah and a group of his followers. Her face paled when she saw mine. I looked her straight in the eye, wanting her to know what a mean bastard her husband was. Then again, maybe she already knew. She looked away, and I thought I saw a tear slide down her cheek. It was probably my imagination.

"Leaving so soon, Davis?" Trainer asked. The derision in his voice was significantly reduced by the fact that his fat lips and missing teeth had given him a lisp. His latest batch of apprentices snickered and elbowed each other behind him.

"Time to go," I said, nodding to Angie to precede me.

"I'm talking to you, boy–" He made a grab for my arm. I evaded, spun on my heel, and drew my shotgun in one fluid motion. I pointed it straight at his chest. He raised his hands and backed away. I walked backwards for several steps before I turned and followed Angie.

"You're a failure, Davis!" he yelled. "Worse, you're a disappointment to your family!"

Over my shoulder, I sent him the universal finger gesture of disrespect, and continued on without saying a word. We walked in silence for a good long while, maybe an hour. I was feeling all my aches and pains more acutely by that time, and knew we wouldn't be able to go far. I supposed I should have been grateful; the last time Trainer had beaten me, I had been laid up for three weeks.

My swollen black eye was affecting my depth perception, so judging distances was difficult. When using the shotgun, which had a definite range limitation, that could be the difference between a hit and a miss; hence Father's suggestion that we stop and see Grandmother.

"You know, Davis," Angie began. "I don't expect you to commit to me. I was just saying all that stuff to get your mother off your back."

"That's all right. It was true."

She looked at me sidelong. "Which part?"

I thought about what Angie had said when she had pointed out that my actions had made my refusals a lie. Again I considered how willing I was to take off for parts unknown with

Kam, with no thought of settling. I realized that looking for a place to be respected was nothing more than the wish of a boy who wanted to be accepted and appreciated, egged on by a town's rejection and a mother's nagging. Seeing the pride in my father's eyes when Angie announced that I was to be her protector was a huge factor in my final decision. He approved of my choice. I couldn't tell if he knew what this life would hold in store for me, but he believed in me.

The events of the past few weeks Traveling with Angie rolled through my mind. It had been exciting, and I could no longer deny the feeling that I had been doing the work I was meant to do in the world. I finally felt like I belonged somewhere. More than that, I could not help but be drawn to her. It was more than her lively green eyes, bouncy dark curls, and curvy feminine shape. There was something more there, in the way she looked into my eyes, and the way I sometimes caught her watching me when she thought I wasn't looking. It was worth exploring.

"Davis?"

"All of it," I replied. "If you still want me, I'm yours."

She shook her head, as if unwilling to believe.

"You can't make this decision just because you're angry at your mother," she said.

"Rule number one, Angie. Never tell me what I can't do."

"There are rules?"

"There are always rules," I replied with a chuckle. "Don't worry, I'm not running away from my problems. I am embracing my destiny." I grinned at her. Angie bit her lip, seeming to fight off tears. I took her hand in mine, gave it a quick squeeze. She smiled at me, and I watched the uncertainty that had dogged her for weeks drain from her demeanor. She relaxed into the idea that her quest was not a loss, and that she would not return home a failure.

"Thank you," she whispered. "I know it wasn't an easy decision for you."

"It wasn't so hard, once I stopped fighting the idea and really considered it."

"What do you mean?"

126

"Remember asking me how I found you in the woods?"

She nodded.

"The only conclusion I could come up with is that we're linked somehow. All I could think of was that I couldn't let you get hurt. I didn't run blindly into the woods, Angie. There were no wrong turns or backtracking. I followed an instinct that led me straight to you."

"The magic bond really does exist," she murmured, sounding awed.

"What?"

"It's something recorded in the histories," she said, with a hesitant glance at me to see if I was going to criticize her books. When I didn't, she continued. "Partners are supposed to be able to locate each other, just based on a feeling."

"That's a useful ability to be able to draw on."

"The books say it has limitations," she said. "It's latent and can't be directed, for one thing. Distance is another limitation. Also, the strength of it increases or diminishes based on either person's emotional state."

"I assume that means that if you want me to find you, or if you're scared, I will?"

She nodded.

"I bet that's going to come in handy," I said wryly.

"Gods forbid!" Angie said. "That would mean we were separated!"

"It's bound to happen eventually." I shrugged casually, but on the inside, my ego was puffing up its chest at her dismay over the thought of being away from me.

"Couldn't you find me the way you did the first time? That works over long distances."

"With a fetch?" She looked surprised. "Maybe. Fully trained druids rarely use fetches, though. It really is an extension of someone's spirit. The more powerful the druid, the more magical substance in the fetch. I've read that if a fetch is killed by magic, the druid will also die." She glanced shyly at me. "I was fifteen when I first sent mine out, so there was little risk."

"Wait, how old are you now?" It was a little embarrassing to be asking the question at this point in time, but it hadn't come up.

"I turned twenty in January."

She was most definitely a woman grown. Even if she had been younger, things were different now than they had been in before the Fracture. People tended to grow up quite a bit faster; anyone who did an adult's work was considered an adult.

"It took five years to find me? I thought you said you looked for three months."

"The journey took three months," she said. "Finding you the first time only took a few weeks. Spirit animals always know where they are going, or what they are seeking. So it was just a matter of travel time."

"You sent a spirit cat up the road, to travel for weeks to find me?"

"It's called a fetch. It just looks like a cat, but it's part of my spirit. Because it is a creature of spirit, it doesn't have to eat or sleep. Once set on a path, it will continue without much guidance."

I cast my mind back five years. I would have been fifteen, just starting my time with Trainer. My mother was constantly disapproving; my father seemed to have a continual expression of concern when he looked at me. It might have had something to do with the fact that I came home with black eyes and bruises all the time. I never told them that Trainer often beat me just for the heck of it. I knew they would make me quit, and that was a fate infinitely worse than beatings.

"Did you ever have a pet when you were a child?" Angie asked, pulling me out of my reverie.

"We had a family dog. It hunted with us, herded sheep, things like that."

"How about a cat?"

"Can't say that we…" I paused. "Wait, I did have a cat once. Sort of. It just sort of appeared one day, and I fed it. Wasn't around all the time, came and went as it pleased. Every once in a while I'd sneak it into the house and let it sleep in my bed at night. When I started Traveling, it stayed behind. My mother said it disappeared whenever I left, and always came back when I did. She didn't like it, said it was bad luck."

"Was it light brown, with stripes on its legs and chest, and spots on its back?" Angie asked.

"Yeah, how did you – that was you?"

She smiled. "That was me. Well, part of me, anyway." Her smile widened. "I was really proud of that. Not easy for your average fifteen-year-old elementalist."

An uncomfortable thought came to the fore. "Can you see what your spirit animal sees? Or hear? Feel?"

Her smile faded. "A little. I could see more as time went on and my magic grew. It can act autonomously, but if you want to directly command it, that takes more time and energy."

Another memory surfaced, this one less pleasant. "You were with me when I... stopped courting Sarah." She nodded reluctantly. "And, during what happened after." Angie nodded again, chewing on her lip.

I had been so messed up that I could barely get out of bed to take a piss. That cat had stayed with me night and day, often as not curled up purring beside my head, or on my chest. Mother hadn't liked the cat being in the house, but had tolerated it because it had made me feel better.

"Is that why you were so rude to her when you met?"

Angie looked at me, eyes flashing. "She's a selfish little bitch, and she doesn't deserve you."

I stifled a grin. "Especially since you had already laid claim."

"I did no such thing." Angie sniffed.

"Okay." I had to chuckle.

"I didn't!"

"Whatever you say, my lovely druid."

She rolled her eyes and let out a humph, but I could tell by the set of her mouth that she had liked the compliment, wrapped in a tease as it was.

Chapter 10 – Grandmother

Rules of Gunfighting #24:
Your number one option for Personal Security is a lifelong
commitment to avoidance, deterrence, and de-escalation.

After walking for a couple of hours, we turned off the main road. Making sure we were unseen, I headed for a solid wall with thick ivy covering its stones. Angie looked askance at me until I lifted the vines and pulled them aside, revealing a narrow archway. She smiled in appreciation and stepped inside. I led the way through an orchard full of beautifully blooming fruit trees. She looked as though she were about to speak, but I put my finger to my lips. We had to be quiet here, lest someone outside the wall hear, and start looking for a way inside.

The trees toward the front of the orchard had been allowed to grow more or less wild, to avoid attracting notice; the cultivated ones were toward the back. We walked through the wildwood, with Angie touching each trunk we passed, an expression of delight on her face. She breathed in deeply of the orchard's fresh scents, her footsteps silent as her body moved effortlessly between the trunks of the trees.

A small, rundown cabin appeared at the back of the orchard. I stopped and whistled a birdcall. There was an answering call, and the cabin door opened. A little old woman stepped out gingerly, using a cane for support.

"Davis? Is that you?"

"Yes, Grandmother," I answered, smiling. She wasn't really my grandmother. In fact, she wasn't anyone's grandmother any more. When she had outlived the rest of her family, the town had adopted her, the townspeople taking turns providing for her and ensuring her safety.

"Why are you walking so funny, boy?" she asked, peering at me. Her eyesight was growing poor in her later years. When she was close enough, she spied the bruises.

"Pissed off Larry Trainer again, did you?"

"Something like that."

"You headed out again?"

"Yes, ma'am." I always stopped by her house before leaving. Sometimes I came to visit when I was on the way in, but usually I was low on supplies – or out altogether – and unwilling to burden her with feeding me.

"Well, you can't go like that. I bet you can't see for shit. You'll get yourself killed for sure." She took my arm and started for the house. "Best if you stay here until you're better."

"Mother gave us a lot of food," I said. "So we wouldn't be a burden."

"She knew you'd come here. Smart woman, your mother," she cackled. "Who do you have here, eh?" She peered closer. "Druid, eh?"

Angie's eyes widened. "How did you know?"

Grandmother cackled again. "I have my ways. You're not the first druid I've met."

"Really?" I asked. How had I missed that bit of information? With the extensive education my parents had provided me, how was it even possible that I had reached adulthood without even hearing the word druid?

"I haven't always been a bent old woman, boy." She peered at me again. What're you doing with a druid?"

"Davis has agreed to be my protector, and my warrior," Angie said candidly, with no small amount of pride.

Grandmother grunted. "Bet that pissed your mother off. How did your father take it?"

"Surprisingly well," I said. "I think he was happy about it."

"As I might expect." She nodded sagely.

Angie and I exchanged a look. Grandmother was privy to information that I was not. Before I could open my mouth to ask, she said, "Don't ask me about it, Davis. It's your parents' business, and if they wanted you to know, they'd have told you. I'll not disrespect them. They've done well by the town, not to mention my own family."

She ushered us into the cabin, which was larger and in better repair than it appeared from the outside. When she had refused to move into the town proper, the residents had built the walls around her land, planted the ivy, and added on to the cabin. There were two main rooms and one smaller one. The first room was the sitting room, the second one the sleeping room, and the third a bolt-hole. It had a secret door, in case she needed to hide from bandits or thieves. As the story went, there were a few unwelcome guests in the early days – before the ivy had grown up – but the young men of the town had chased them off, guarding her until her farm could do the job.

She bade us sit, and we made ourselves home at the small table while she put water on to boil.

"You're a mess, Davis," she said. "Hurt much?"

"It looks worse than it is." I had brought my injuries to her many times before. Grandmother knew a thing or two about potions, poultices, and brews.

"What was it you did, again?"

Why did everyone assume I was at fault here? Glowering, I slumped down in my chair and crossed my arms over my chest.

"Don't pout, boy, it's unmanly."

Angie interceded for me. "It was my fault," she said. "I was rude to Trainer's wife."

Thankfully, Grandmother didn't ask why. I didn't think I could bear having my personal business aired a second time. Instead, she let out a little cackle and said, "Already getting you into trouble, is she? Better get used to that."

Angie looked uncomfortable, so I let the matter drop. The road was dangerous; there were bandits, thieves, and wild animals. I was traveling with a girl, which was bound to attract attention. Trouble was to be expected, because there were always people who wanted what you had and who were more than happy to take it from you however they could.

"The man's an unbearable asshole, anyway. So full of himself, like he's the prize stallion of the herd. He deserves to have that manipulative little tart for a wife," Grandmother concluded, taking the teakettle from the fire. She poured most of the water into a cracked blue teapot, and the remainder into a mug, then dropped a large tea strainer into the pot, and a small bag of herbs into the mug. Next, she pulled out a loaf of bread, cut us each a slice, spread butter over each one, and warmed them over the fire. The smell of Grandmother's tea and toast filled the cabin, bringing a sense of comfort and peace.

"Anybody with half a brain could see that your father is ten times the man Larry Trainer is, and a better fighter, to boot. A better teacher, too. Has patience as well as knowledge. He should have been Trainer, instead."

I had heard this from her before, usually when she was patching up injuries that his cruel training methods had inflicted on me. Obviously, my father was capable. He had traveled the roads with my mother and had survived with all his body parts intact. I had also seen the myriad scars on his naked torso when he worked shirtless in the summertime. When I was a child, I thought that he must have been the most powerful man in the world.

"Shame that he had to give it up. He was good at it."

I wondered if this had anything to do with a druid, and if my grandmother was giving me a hint. However, after living a life of travel and war on the road, and losing the coveted spot of Trainer to another man, I had never known him to be bitter. It made me wonder if my mother had encouraged him to try for the position, or had discouraged him from it. He had seemed to enjoy teaching me, but his true love was the rich soil and healthy growing plants.

"I've always thought it had to have been difficult for him to watch his son train under that piss-poor monkey-handed donk. Especially when he knocked you about for no good reason."

"You think he was harder on me because Father used to be his rival?"

"Looks like that smack you took on the head knocked some smarts into you, boy." She said it with a wink, and a smile that wreathed her face in kindly old wrinkles.

When the tea had steeped long enough, she poured it into cups for herself and Angie, and then passed out the bread. She pushed the mug over to me. It would probably make me feel much better and taste horrible.

"Don't make faces at good medicine," Grandmother scolded. "Eat your bread and drink your tea. You'll need to lie down and rest afterward; it's strong medicine."

She always said everything was strong medicine.

I quaffed the tea as quickly as possible. The horrible taste made me shudder.

Grandmother rolled her eyes. "Go lie down, Davis."

I stood up and staggered slightly. Strong medicine indeed; my legs felt wobbly and my head swollen. I stumbled to the bedroom and sank to my knees on a pallet there. I lay down, feeling my muscles relax from head to toe; tingly warmth spread through my body.

"Now, girl," I heard Grandmother say, as I slipped away into a dreamless sleep. "You and I are going to have a little chat."

* * *

Angie and I remained at Grandmother's for two weeks, until I was completely healed. Mostly I had to wait for the swelling in my eye to diminish. I was outside and moving around the day after our arrival. I spent quite a bit of time scaling ladders and picking the newly ripened fruit, with Angie assisting. I also split several cords of firewood, both to make sure I was up to full strength and to make sure Grandmother would have enough to last a good while. She was old and tended to chill easily, so she had a fire laid nearly year round.

At last, we were ready to leave. My eye was still a rainbow of colors, but my vision was unimpaired. I kissed Grandmother goodbye.

"Thank you for everything," Angie said, also giving her a kiss on the cheek.

"That's what old people are for," said Grandmother with a smile. "To teach young people the things they should know."

Angie touched her fingertips to forehead and heart, then extended her hand toward the elder woman. I guessed it was some sign of honor and respect among druids.

We departed through the orchard, exiting around the back. No one ever left from the front, because there was no way of knowing who might be out there to observe. We walked along the back wall, then along the south wall until we reached the road. I paused and looked around, wary of strangers, then started down the road to continue our journey. We walked until noon without seeing another soul, which made me happy. As we walked, I quizzed her about magic.

Angie considered. "It's easier to explain if I give a little history," she said.

"Here we go with the stories again."

She stuck out her tongue at me. "My father is a druid, and so was my mother, and my grandmother, and all of their ancestors back to the time of the Rebirth. That was when magic first came upon us. Those who gave worship and sacrifice to the gods were blessed with their favor and elemental power. It started gradually at first, each person given only one blessing, but as they intermarried, the children began displaying two elemental powers, or even three."

"So, if everybody has all these great magical powers, why do they need protectors?"

"True druids channel their magic directly from the gods, but an elementalist will run out of magic, eventually."

"You lost me. Isn't everyone a druid?"

"Everyone who worships the gods is considered druidic, but not necessarily a druid. We try to make the distinction by saying 'druidic people' or 'the druidic', but if someone refers to everyone as 'druids,' it's understood that they are one of us, and not necessarily druids."

"So are you a druid, or just a druid?"

"I'm an elementalist."

"Ye gods."

"It really isn't that complicated, Davis."

"That's easy for you to say."

"Look, an elementalist uses the same type of magic that a druid can, but to a lesser degree. Where a druid has virtually limitless magic, an elementalist is limited to the magic that springs from within. Once an elementalist's magic is depleted, that's it until she rests. So if an elementalist uses magic to defend herself..."

"She'd be easy to kill afterward." I eyed her. "I thought druids were for healing the earth, not combat."

"Ideally, the warrior fights the battles, so that the druid can use her magic for the good of the mother. I suppose that all our magic could be used to destroy, but our true purpose is healing the earth. Traditionally, men are the protectors, while the women are healers.

"The old world was a terrible place, Davis. These roads that we travel, the cities, the vehicles they used for transportation – they all were slowly poisoning and destroying the world. She is now trying to heal herself, but it is occurring very slowly. We work to speed that up, or make reparations by cleansing the poisons."

"How can magic do that?" It seemed an impossible task.

"We have five elements: air, earth, fire, water, and spirit. Spirit is the life force within all things. It also can be wielded in other forms, such as electricity or lightning."

"Lightning." I shook my head. "You have got to be kidding me. If somebody can throw lightning, they definitely don't need anyone else to protect them."

Angie's mouth twisted to the side, and I wondered what I had said wrong. "Even a spirit elementalist will eventually run out of magic," she said.

"So, what, do they just call them down out of the sky?"

"No. Usually it's brought forth from within. If you want to call lightning from the sky, you have to bring up a storm. In order to do that, you have to possess air, water, and spirit."

I was feeling overwhelmed at that point. These people could whip up storms? I wondered if they could also create tornadoes or floods. Did having control over the earth mean that a druid could cause earthquakes? The thought was unsettling.

"Raising a storm just to get lightning is a little bit of overkill," Angie said. "Most people direct their magic with their hands. It's not really necessary, but it's sort of human nature to make gestures when trying to accomplish something."

"So, a fire elementalist just aims his hands at something and, poof, there's fire."

"Typically they make fireballs, because they are easier to direct and control. It's like your shotgun. Point and shoot." She grinned, and I had to chuckle.

"And, so you just control water?"

Some of her good mood seemed to evaporate. "Yes."

"That's a good element to have," I said. She looked rather astonished. "Think about it," I continued. "There's always fresh water to drink. You can bring moisture to dry earth and make things grow. And then that stream you cleaned... I can't think of a better way to heal the world."

She smiled again, and it seemed to be one of gratitude. "Thanks," she said. "People don't think very much of water elementalists. No good in combat."

"You're here to heal the world, not bring war to it," I said. "So why would that matter?"

"It has to do with the current politics of the grove. Some people are more concerned about power than duty."

I nodded. It was like that everywhere, it seemed.

"Well, I'm glad you just have water," I told her. "If you could make storms or throw lightning bolts, I think I might feel a little extraneous after a while." This did not seem to reassure her. I tried a different tack. "So basically, my job is pretty much what I thought it was – keeping you safe so you can do your druid thing."

"Yes. There has never been a warrior in all of history who regretted making the decision." She sounded like she was quoting from a class, or a textbook.

"Were they all asked?"

She gave me a look of puzzlement. "Why would anyone ask?"

"Miserable people rarely complain to those who are the cause of the misery," I said. "Not that I expect to be miserable with you. Just… thinking out loud." I chuckled. "I sound like my father."

We walked onward, toward the setting sun. It was tempting to stop at sunset, as we usually did, but we had lost so much time because of my recuperation, I wanted to go a few more miles.

"Are you tired?" I asked.

"A little."

"There's a crossroads ahead," I said. "It's not a good place to stop. Think you can go another hour, until we're well past it?"

"Sure."

The crossroads was as I had predicted. I always hated coming through here, but if we were going south, it was impossible to avoid. The area surrounding it was a swampy bog with sinkholes that would suck a person down in seconds. I figured that the people who lived here probably knew a safe way through it, but I didn't, so I stuck to the road and the less risky town. It was a small, open town and the people who lived there were rough. In my opinion, they were little better than bandits.

We stopped so I could take a long look around. I saw no one, but there were buildings on three of the four corners, and I could hear music from one and voices in another. I felt it was an acceptable risk, and we moved on. As we reached the opposite side of the streets, a voice called behind us.

"Hey, how much for the girl?"

I stifled a sigh and turned around. A lone man stood in the road, with his left hand at his side, and his right hand behind his thigh. Hiding a pistol, I guessed. It was no match for my shotgun at this range.

"She's not for sale."

"This is Cash," he said with a twisted grin. "Everything here is for sale."

"We're just passing through. I don't want any trouble." It was the only warning he would get.

"Too bad, man," he said. "We like trouble, here." He snapped his fingers and I heard the sound of blades being drawn behind us.

I shoved Angie down, spun around, and whipped out the shotgun, firing before I had even stopped. I fired twice more in

138

quick succession, then looked over my shoulder. The first man was almost on me, having charged while my back was turned. I rolled away from him, came up on one knee, and fired. He was too close to miss, and he fell dead on his face in the street.

Grabbing Angie, I pulled her to her feet and started to run. I hadn't seen anyone come out of the buildings, but the shotgun blasts would have been audible from one end of the town to the next. Anybody – or everybody – could be gearing up to come after us.

Angie let go my hand, lifted her skirts, and sprinted ahead of me, running like a deer. I matched her pace and followed slightly behind, checking our back trail. After a half-mile or so, we slowed to catch our breath. We walked another half hour, checking our back trail in the fading light, just to be sure.

We set up camp quite a distance from the road, hiding it as well as possible within a stand of trees. Most townies couldn't find their way through a forest with a map and a torch. The pines would easily conceal us so that we could sleep, safe and secure. I even felt confident enough to light a small fire. It was then that I noticed Angie's knees, scraped raw from the broken road. I winced and apologized.

"I'll live," she said, pulling out a cloth to wipe her knees clean. After rubbing on a salve, she wrapped thin bandages around her knees and tucked in the ends. We heated bathwater over our tiny fire, and took turns slipping into the darkness to get clean. I put out the fire and smothered the ashes before lying on my blanket beside her.

"I don't think I've ever run so fast in my life," she whispered in the darkness. "And I've never seen you run before."

"I don't, usually," I said. "It's a good way to get shot in the back, but it seemed like the right thing to do at the time."

She giggled – giggled!

"What's so funny?"

"You're just so… blasé… about the whole thing. You just always take everything in stride."

"Is that a compliment?"

"Absolutely."

And so began the second leg of our journey.

Chapter 11 – The Gunsmith of Searcy

Rules of Gunfighting #11:
Someday someone may kill you with your own gun, but they
should have to beat you to death with it because it is empty.

Most of my trips into the wilderness were quiet and uneventful, when I never saw another living soul except for birds and animals. During other trips, I would occasionally come across fellow Travelers. These were usually pleasant experiences. Sometimes we followed the same path, hunting and sharing goods, as well as swapping tales and advice about which places were best for trading, where the hunting was optimal, and what areas should be avoided. Other times, it would be a shared meal and campground, with farewells spoken in the morning.

This trip was like none of those. The only other people we saw were the thieves and thugs that dogged us every step of the way. More often than not, we were plagued by three or more. Maybe it was the unfamiliar territory; perhaps it was generic to this locale.

Grandmother's comment returned to haunt me, and I began to wonder if it had something to do with my little druid. I began to set snares for small game every night for meat. Then I started to worry about running out of shotgun shells. After a few weeks, I began to wonder if I would be able to keep us alive. Traveling south was far more dangerous than anything I had previously experienced. I really wanted to get off the road and cut across the countryside, but wasn't sure if it would be any safer.

The roads and highways were cracked and falling apart. Bridges were dangerous to cross; I never knew when one would collapse under our feet. The darkness of ivy-covered overpasses often hid the presence of those we did not want to encounter. I had heard stories from other Travelers about the kinds of people who dwelled in the darkness and had no desire to see if they were true.

I fought for our camp space nearly every night. Sometimes the shotgun scared them off. Sometimes it didn't. I wasn't sleeping well – if at all – and fatigue was starting to affect my judgement. We were going to have to stop at a town soon, for ammunition if nothing else. The extra ammo I had packed before leaving Jonesboro wasn't going to be nearly enough. I always collected my spent casings, of course, but they were useless without gunpowder and shot. Obtaining more was becoming imperative. I hoped that wherever we stopped had a press I could borrow to reload the shells. I kept reloading machines and supplies at my parents' house, but that was in the wrong direction.

We came to what appeared to be a rather large town, with twenty-foot walls, guard towers, and people with guns manning the towers. I had never been here before, but it looked like the kind of place that shot first and asked questions later. It also might be the kind of place that made you give up your weapons at the door, which I was understandably loathe to do.

"What do you think?" Angie asked quietly.

I puffed my cheeks, letting out a breath. "I don't know. Could be really good or really bad. Could be a place that's dedicated to protecting the freedom and security of its citizens, or..."

"Or?"

"Or, a place dedicated to making other people provide freedom and security for its citizens." I rose and stretched. Today might be a good day to die, but it was a never a good day to become a slave. "There's only one way to find out."

We shouldered our gear and returned to the road, heading for

141

the main gate. It was inconsiderate of them to have built their front gate right in the middle of the road, on the only intact bridge for miles around spanning the turbulent river. We stopped right before the gate, just before they predictably yelled:

"HALT!"

I really wanted to point out that we had already halted, but figured that would only get me into trouble. "Yes, sir," I said, instead. Sometimes having parents that raised you "the right way" came in handy.

"State your business, Traveler."

At least they had recognized me as a Traveler and not a bandit.

"Just passing through," I said, tucking my thumbs in my belt. "Looking to do some trading."

"What you got?"

"Meat, skins, knives. Need to reload my shells, too."

"How about her?"

"She's with me."

"And I suppose she's a Traveler, too?" The skepticism in his voice was evident, and I was tired of talking.

"No, sir," I said. "She's a druid."

Angie's head snapped around and she glared at me.

"You never said it was a secret," I said. "Might get them to shut up and open the door."

"Wait there," said the guard, and disappeared. A few moments later, the doors began to swing inward.

"See?" I said. "It worked." The cocky grin slipped right off my face when five men on horses rode out, guns at the ready. So maybe telling them she was a druid hadn't been such a good idea. I left my weapons where they were. Even if I could kill them all – which I doubted – there were probably twenty more behind the gate. To my surprise, they trained the weapons on Angie. This made me a little uncomfortable, seeing as how I had sworn to protect her. My father had raised me to keep my word, and I had every intention of doing just that.

The other reason I was uneasy was that while I had never met a druid before, these people obviously had. In addition, they thought a druid was dangerous enough that it would take five gunmen to bring her down. I glanced at the guard towers, noting the glint of scopes there. Make that nine.

One man had a black patch over his right eye and a big shiny star on his left chest. I figured that made him the leader.

"Druid, eh?" he drawled.

Angie shot me a final look of disapproval, then faced him calmly. "Yes. I am a druid."

"What are you doing here?"

"I came for my chosen warrior."

He spat. "Didn't think that was done anymore."

"I follow the old ways," Angie said, lifting her chin.

"You're a young'un, then." He nodded, as if that statement made sense. He grunted to himself, and didn't seem to be impressed. That was okay with me; if they didn't think Angie was a threat, all the better. "All right. You can come in. No magic, girl. Not even for healing."

Angie nodded seriously. "Yes, sir."

I was dumbfounded by the entire situation. It seemed that everyone in the world had heard of druids except me. Maybe they would feel less threatened if they knew she was only a water elementalist. I glanced sidelong at Angie, considering whether or not I should tell him.

The sheriff spat in the dirt, and fixed me with his one dark eye. "You can keep your weapons, too, so long as they stay put up. Pull a gun or knife in there and the best that'll happen is it'll be taken away. You actually hurt somebody with one of those weapons, and you'll be one sorry son of a bitch, get me?"

"Yes, sir."

He made a sharp gesture with his arm; the riflemen wheeled their horses around and trotted back to the gate. We followed at a jog, in case they were in the habit of closing the gates quickly. Once inside, I approached the sheriff.

"I appreciate you letting us in, sir," I said.

He looked me up and down. "There are more of us than you, and I'm betting your girl there isn't fully trained. If you act up, we can take you down faster than a man drops his pants to take a shit."

I let the insult slip. "If it's not an inconvenience, sir, would you please tell me if there is anyone with a press where I could reload?" If the head honcho was seen helping me, then other members of the community might be inclined to follow suit. It had worked for me many times before, in many different places, and I was counting on it to work here. He eyed me some more. I stood there and let him. Finally, he nodded.

"You'll be wanting Sinclair. He's the gunsmith here in Searcy. Take the off-ramp, go left on Race Street, then take a right after you go under the bridge. He's down a-ways, in the old Wammart building."

"Thank you, sir. I appreciate the help." I gestured to Angie, and started across the bridge.

"And son…"

I turned back. "Sir?"

"Keep an eye on your girl. There are mostly good people here, but there are also some as don't hold with them pagan ways."

I nodded once to him. "I'll do that." I would also have to watch myself, but I was used to that. Angie wasn't. I knew exactly what sorts of problems the bigotry of others could cause. Once they got a posse or a riot going, there was no telling what people might do.

Angie waited until we were at the bottom of the off-ramp to take me to task for telling them she was a druid. Her restraint was admirable; I'd expected her to start yelling at me as soon as we turned our backs on the sheriff.

"You didn't have to tell them I'm a druid!" she hissed.

"Got us in, didn't it?"

"I'm not supposed to tell. It puts me in danger."

I didn't see how not telling had kept us out of danger so far, but didn't argue the point.

"You didn't tell them, I did."

She huffed in exasperation.

We took a left on Race Street, and found ourselves looking beneath the overpass. Having to go beneath an overpass made me uneasy, even though this one was in the middle of a protected and seemingly law-abiding town. I relaxed when I saw that this one was lined with open stalls that served as shops. Goods of every sort were on display: cloth, clothing, leather, wool, food, flowers and even jewelry. A good bit of foot traffic was moving through the underpass, but we had plenty of room to traverse the middle of the road. I glanced around at the goods, making a mental note to come back when we were finished at the gunsmith.

Angie stuck close to me, even taking my hand. She seemed to avoid the touch of anyone else. I chalked her timidity up to being the object of the curious glances cast our way. I was used to this, having frequently been the stranger in various places for the past few years. We would have to be careful. The fact that we were not worshipers of the Triune God would spread through town like wildfire if we weren't.

I had experienced a few places that were intolerant of those with differing beliefs. In one town, I had witnessed a woman burning at the stake. At the time, I had just wandered in to see where the smoke had originated. After seeing the smouldering corpse and hearing the hate-maddened screaming of the people, I had made a rapid departure.

We arrived at the gunsmith in short order. Angie's eyes widened at the sight of the huge building. Not many buildings like this had survived the earthquakes. It also seemed to house not only the gunsmith, but also the blacksmith, farrier, and welder. I supposed that made sense, as the building was made of concrete blocks that were unlikely to burn. There was a guard at the door; I told him our business and he waved us on. Angie's jaw dropped as she took in the interior height. I figured they couldn't have found a better place for the work done here. There was lots of space, fireproof walls, and a high ceiling to help vent the smoke away. Pure genius.

Sinclair's shop was at the back of the giant structure. He was sitting in a chair, tipped back against the wall, with his hat over his face and a shotgun in his lap. I stopped a respectful distance away and cleared my throat. The chair legs came down with a thunk, the hat was pushed back, and the sawed-off shotgun leveled at my chest.

I wasn't allowed to draw weapons in Searcy, but evidently that law did not apply to its citizens. I glanced at Angie, who seemed to be concentrating on remaining unnoticed.

"Who are you, and what do you want?" said the old man.

I tore my eyes away from the shotgun and looked at his weathered and tanned face with its blind eyes. Blue-white cataracts nearly glowed in the dim light.

"My name is Davis. I'd like to borrow your press to reload my shotgun shells."

"Traveler?"

"Yes."

"I might could work you a deal."

"I brought trade items."

He snorted. "Nothing I can't get myself, or buy around here."

"I see. You said something about a deal?"

"Aye. You can borrow my press, and have gunpowder to boot."

"And you want what in return?"

"My shells reloaded, and those of my customers. Four to one of yours."

I did some mental math, calculating how many shells I could make per day if I really hustled. We'd be here for days if I took that deal. "Two to one," I countered.

"Three to one."

"Deal." We shook on it, sealing the agreement. I figured that was the best I could get. After all, if he were the only gunsmith in Searcy, he could charge me whatever he liked, and I would have to take it.

"Know anywhere we might find a room?"

"We? You got someone with you?"

I looked pointedly at Angie. She gave me the barest shake of her head. I gave her my best glare. She glared back.

"I have a girl with me. She's shy. Doesn't like to talk to strangers."

"Funny how I can't hear her breathe. And even when I can't hear breathing, I can still sense someone's presence," the old man mused. "Knew you were here even before you made a sound."

I had hardly been trying to sneak in, but decided not to mention it. "She's a druid," I said.

146

"Davis!" she protested.

"Don't be so rude next time," I said.

"It's all right, boy," said Sinclair. "She's right. Can't be too careful, the holy rollers might get wind of her and decide to have a bonfire, if you get my meaning."

"She's not a witch, she's a druid."

He shrugged. "There are those who won't bother to differentiate, son. To them, pagan is devil worship, and all that quaking crap. As for a place to stay, I have an extra room, if you don't mind those idiot blacksmiths hammering away all day and night."

Sinclair showed me his workshop. I let out a low whistle in admiration. At my parents' house, I had only what I needed to fill the 12-gauge shells that the Ithaca required. This man had more equipment for reloading than I had ever seen. He even had a setup to mold his own bullets and shell casings. It was obviously convenient to live by a blacksmith, no matter how annoying the noise might be. Next, he showed us to the room, which had a small fireplace, table with two chairs, and a single small cot.

"Sorry about the bed, don't host many couples. Don't put much of anybody up, anymore. Not many Travelers lately."

"That's fine," I said, looking around. "I have my own blankets."

He looked at me, and for a long moment seemed to see my soul. Then he turned back to Angie.

"That's new and different," he said.

I had no idea what he was talking about.

She frowned at him and crossed her arms over her chest. "We've only just met," she said.

"I've never known that to matter to your people before," he said.

"The older generation may have done things a certain way," she replied archly. "I do things my way."

Sinclair shrugged. "I didn't get to be this old interfering in other people's business. The room's yours if you want it."

"We do," I said, before Angie could reply. "Thank you."

Chapter 12 – Bonfire

Rules of Gunfighting #12:
Always cheat, always win.
The only unfair fight is the one you lose.

Angie stayed in our little room to unpack and set it up for our hopefully brief stay. I also thought she might be avoiding me until I forgot about her brief exchange with Sinclair. She would find me not so forgetful on that score. I make a point of remembering to ask about things I don't understand, because in general, it helps me stay alive. Knowledge is power, as my father was fond of saying.

I immediately set to work reloading shotgun shells. I set up a bucket beside the press and kept a mental count of the shells that would be mine. I figured Sinclair would want to divvy them up later. I worked quickly throughout the afternoon, not wanting to stay long in Searcy. It's not that I don't like towns; I just like the wilderness better. Forests and grasslands are so much nicer to look at than decaying roads and heaps of rubble.

The old man came by after a couple of hours to check on me. "Some people in the past have thought to cheat the old blind man," he said, weighing the bucket in his hand.

"My parents raised me better than that," I said, having expected to have this conversation with him at some point. He was well within his rights, and I didn't blame him for being cautions. He was blind.

"I've heard that before."

"All the shells are in that bucket. You can divide them up later as you see fit."

He smiled, wreathing his face in wrinkles. "That's just what I was going to suggest."

"This is not my first rodeo," I said, turning back to the press. "I've been Traveling a while."

"That don't mean nothin'." He snorted. "Travelers lie, cheat, and steal just as much as anyone."

"I don't."

"And, I suppose your folks taught you that, too?"

I shook my head. "Saw a man horsewhipped for stealing when I was younger. It made an impression."

"Ah." He set the bucket down. "I invited some of my best customers to bring by their spent shells. You'll have all the work you could want for."

"Thanks," I said, appreciating the gesture. The more shells I made for Sinclair and his clients, the more I could make for myself.

He clapped me on the shoulder. "I figure you're going to need 'em."

* * *

The next few days passed swiftly, filled with the shells, gunpowder, and the curiously relaxing process of reloading with a press. Sinclair really did have fine equipment. More and more people came by the shop and dropped off their empties. Sinclair told me that word was getting around, that people knew I was making a quality product.

Of course I was making a quality product – a third of the shells were going to be mine. Anyway, I only knew one way to make a shell – the right way. The old man hinted a few times that people spoke well of me, that I was a hard worker, that such dedication was rare in a young man, that he could use a good hand like mine, that I was welcome to stay. The thought of doing this day after day for the rest of my life made me want to run for

149

the city gates.

Angie made herself scarce most of the time. She prepared our meals and baths, washed clothes, and cleaned the gunsmith's shop. I didn't know what else she was up to until our third day. Upon arriving home from the market, she slipped away into the room we shared. After a few moments, the clinking of bottles and rustling of leaves caught my attention. I took a break, straightening to stretch my neck and back. I went to our little room, lifting the privacy curtain and letting it fall closed behind me.

"What are you doing?" I asked.

"Making oils," she said, with the expression I had begun privately referring to as the mysterious druid look. I took a chair, turned it backwards at the table, and straddled it. She gave me a look like she wasn't sure if she wanted me watching her or not.

"I don't have to watch if you'd rather I didn't," I said, starting to rise.

"It's fine. Really." She proceeded to uncork a large bottle of light golden oil and pour it into several smaller bottles of different sizes and shapes, each capable of holding about an ounce or two. "It took a while to collect all the materials," she said. She then took out four dark brown bottles with rubber stoppers. She opened each of them and added a few drops from each to the oil. Carefully recapping the tiny bottles, she picked up the crystal vial in both hands and closed her eyes. Her lips moved silently; then swirled the oils gently; clockwise, I noted. Holding the bottle to her nose, she took a deep breath and murmured silently again.

She gazed at me then, green eyes intent. "This is an oil of protection," she said, her voice barely above a whisper. "With your permission, I would like to anoint you with it and cast a spell of protection over you."

While I was concerned about the citizens of Searcy discovering our true nature, it stood to reason that we were safe enough. Secreted in our little room in Sinclair's shop, no one would see us. It was unlikely that we would be overheard because of all the blacksmith's hammering. If it would make her feel better, I was agreeable. It certainly couldn't hurt.

150

"Sure," I told her.

"You don't have to believe for it to work," she said, dipping her finger in the oil. "It protects against magical and psychic attacks."

"I believe in your magic," I said, then grinned. "You don't happen to have an oil that wards blades and bullets, do you?"

"No, sorry. I'm still a... a beginner, you might say." She nearly choked on the admission. There was something galling for her about her magical status, or whatever it was called.

I closed my eyes, listening to her whisper what I could only guess were magic words, feeling her finger trace symbols across my forehead, temples, and throat. She took each of my hands and anointed the palms. I didn't know if it was her touch or her magic, but a feeling of warmth and peace flowed through my body, starting at my head and flowing down to my hands. I opened my eyes to see her satisfied expression.

"I would like to repeat this occasionally, if you don't mind," she said, corking the crystal bottle and putting it away. "After you bathe would be best, and I can touch more of your skin."

So far in our journey, I had been careful to avoid showing too much skin, and now she was asking me to show her more. I certainly had not seen her in any stage of undress.

"You don't have to be naked or anything," she hastened to add. "I just need the major parts: your head, back, chest, arms, abdomen, and legs."

I raised an eyebrow. "Is that all?"

She blushed. "Um... and your feet?"

"We can do that tonight," I said, rising from the chair. "I have to get back to work."

The afternoon continued as had the three before it. Angie went out again, presumably for something with which to make supper. Out of my portion of the shotgun shells, she used some to trade with the owners of the booths beneath the bridge, buying food, herbs, salt, and other items that we would need.

Sinclair was taking a turn at the press while I sorted out shells for his customers, his stock, and myself. It was a sign of trust that he was allowing me to do so. I had started keeping notes as to what person had brought what type of shells and how

151

many. The old man had taught me to reload several different types of ammunition, and I'd gotten a lot of practice at making them.

After finishing the tally, I walked outside to get some fresh air. We could leave any time now, and I felt a sense of relief. I was grateful to the old man, but eager to be back on the road. Having lost track of time, I was surprised at how late it was. Angie should have been back by now.

A cold chill raced down my spine.

Angie should have been back by now.

All of a sudden, I felt a very deep sense that something was amiss. More than amiss. Wrong. Bad wrong. A sense of urgency came over me, and along with it the powerful feeling that Angie was in danger.

My druid was in danger and I wasn't there to protect her.

I turned on my heel and went back to the gunsmith's shop. "Something's wrong," I told him. He seemed to stare off into space a moment, then nodded.

"Storm's coming," he said. "Bad omen."

I didn't give a shit about storms or bad omens. My druid wasn't home, and she should have been a long time ago. I grabbed my shotgun.

"You can't go after her with guns blazing," Sinclair said, putting a hand on my arm. I ignored him, and he slapped me on the back of the head, just like Trainer used to do. I gave him a glare of angry disbelief.

"I know what you are, or what you're trying to be," he said. "But, if you go out there with that gun, those self-righteous idiots will shoot you dead, kill your girl, and kneel beside their beds to say a prayer for allowing them the blessed opportunity to rid the world of Satan's minions. When it's all said and done, the sheriff will shrug it off and sleep like a baby because he warned you fair."

He was right. I had forgotten the proscription against my wielding arms. I spun about the room, looking for anything I might use in place of my own weapons.

"What am I supposed to do, then?" I snarled. I could feel the adrenaline burst forth, the heated anger that always accompanied it following rapidly.

"Well, boy, it seems to me that we have a bit of time, as they'll wait until midnight for their little party."

"You can't be sure of that."

"I can't be sure of breathing in the next ten seconds, but I think I will," he said reprovingly. "Get ahold of yourself, boy. Panic doesn't look good on you."

Great, a blind man had just criticized the way I looked. It did settle me down a bit, though. "What's your idea?"

"Me being a gunsmith and all, I have a fair amount of gunpowder lying about. I suppose we might be able to put it to some productive use." He grinned and winked with one blind eye.

I've never handled explosive materials as carelessly as I did that night. In spite of Sinclair's admonitions to slow down, I made homemade bombs recklessly and fast. It was by the gods' protection that I didn't blow up the entire building. Maybe it was Angie's spell. We "borrowed" segments of pipe from the blacksmith, filled them with gunpowder, stuck in a fuse, and sealed them with candle wax. It was quick and dirty, guaranteed to make a small explosion, with the added bonus of shrapnel. We loaded the bombs in a couple of backpacks and started out of the shop. A giant appeared in the doorway, one of the blacksmith's assistants. He was so loaded with muscle that his neck was lost somewhere between his shoulders and his head.

"Going somewhere?" he asked, cracking his knuckles.

"Out for a stroll," said Sinclair. "Nothing to concern you."

"Having a Satanist in my town concerns me. He brought her in, and you put her up. We figure that makes you a devil worshipper, too."

"Nobody here is a Satanist," said Sinclair in a reasonable tone.

"'Thou shalt not suffer a witch to live –'" Thunder rumbled in the distance, low and threatening.

Anger blossomed like a deadly flower, thorns piercing my self-control. "She is not a witch!"

"Figures you'd lie about it, since you're the one bedding Satan's whore."

153

My anger got the better of me. I handed my bag to Sinclair – carefully – and stalked over to the man, who was as tall as my father and probably outweighed him by fifty pounds.

"I'm leaving whether you like it or not."

It made him mad, as I figured it would. He hauled back to throw a punch, but I snapped a kick into his solar plexus. Steel-toed boots hurt. He bent double, clutching his gut. I came up with an uppercut to the jaw, following through with a left hook. He may have been a giant, but he didn't know the first thing about fighting. I, on the other hand, had acquired a vast wealth of experience in fighting people much bigger than me.

I jabbed a punch into his nose, ducked his feeble attempt at a haymaker, then delivered two more punishing jabs and broke it. He bellowed in pain, spraying blood all over the floor. The pain only made him angrier. He charged me, driving his shoulder into me like a battering ram. I twisted before he could slam me into the wall, and his head cracked against the doorframe, knocking him out cold. He slid to the floor and flopped over, head thumping the concrete. I spun on my heel and marched back to Sinclair, taking back my sack of explosives.

"That'll teach you, you thick-skulled, self-righteous jackass," Sinclair said to the unconscious man, then turned and led me through the night, away from the heart of town until we could see the firelight glow on a hilltop. Lightning flashed, illuminating the crowd of people gathered there.

"This is as far as you go," I told him, reaching for the sack. "You need to be in a bar getting drunk as fast as possible."

"You gonna kill 'em all?"

"They've given me cause enough."

"I guess that's as good a reason to get drunk as any."

Thunder boomed, followed by another flash of lightning. Maybe the thunder would cover the sound of the explosions and preclude attracting the sheriff's attention. I ran for the hill, charging up without worrying about being seen. It was dark and peals of thunder were sounding more frequently. Fiddling with the flint and steel in my pocket, I scoped out the scene from behind thick bushes. As it was impossible to count the people present, I settled for looking for Angie. I didn't need to aim at

154

them; I just needed to avoid hitting her. It didn't take long to find her. They were leading her through the crowd, toward a pole surrounded by firewood.

Sinclair hadn't been kidding about the bonfire. It seemed to take forever for them to bring her up; by the light of their torches I could see she was fighting with everything she had. It was hopeless and a waste of energy; she was a small woman, a couple of inches shorter than I and maybe a hundred and thirty pounds. I could feel her fear and despair even at this distance. The fear I could understand; the despair left me stricken. She thought I wasn't coming to save her. She thought she was doomed. Her lips were moving frantically; I couldn't tell what she was saying, but the men closest to her brought up a strip of cloth and gagged her with it. Then they stripped her naked and tied her to the pole.

Naked.

My druid – naked – in front of those self-righteous sons of bitches.

White-hot anger lanced through me, and I watched a pipe bomb sail through the air before I even realized I had lit it. It was a long throw, toward the back of the crowd. The last thing I wanted to do was hurt Angie myself, but I was going to bring the thunder. Three more bombs launched toward the back of the crowd, and then the explosions started, one after another. I barely heard the screams, and continued pitching bombs around the perimeter of the hilltop where people were fleeing.

One group was holding fast, determined to get the bonfire lit. I tossed another pipe, praying their bodies would block any shrapnel that might come close to Angie. A savage grin stretched across my lips as I saw body parts fly and hair catch fire. The ones closest to the pole screamed; blood poured from gashes where tender flesh was ripped open by shrapnel. Those who could flee did, except for one man holding a torch and another holding a rifle beside him. I wasn't worried about either of them. The gunman would have to be a mutant from out West to aim it properly in the dark. I walked in a crouch closer to the crown of the hill, tossing a few more bombs over the sides to make sure nobody would even think of coming back. I had plenty left; I hadn't even begun to dip into the second bag. The two men at the top held their ground.

I walked up behind the rifleman and snapped his neck, dropping him like a sack of potatoes. I picked up his weapon and turned to the man with the torch, who backed up a step in terror. He was dressed all in black but for the white collar at his throat.

"Devil's tool!" he shouted, thrusting the torch at me. I sidestepped and fixed him with a scowl.

"I'm nobody's tool," I said, hitting him with the butt of the rifle and breaking his jaw. He screamed and fell to his knees. He was a lucky man that day, because I decided not to waste time killing him. Slinging the rifle's strap over my shoulder, I turned to the pole. Seeing Angie strapped there, naked and gagged, infuriated me all over again. Her eyes widened, seeing the look on my face.

I drew a knife and began slicing ropes, unleashing my rage on the offending hemp. Finally loose, she fell into my arms. I gently pulled the gag from between her lips, and picked her up. Angie buried her face in my neck, sobbing violently. I turned around and stopped dead in my tracks. Standing before me was the sheriff and what I had to assume were his nine best gunmen. I stood my ground, not bothering to hide Angie, wanting them to see her.

The rope burns on her wrists.

The tear stains on her face.

Her naked and defenseless body.

"She did nothing to deserve this," I said angrily.

The sheriff stepped forward, rifle cradled in his arms.

"Jeff," he said to someone behind him. "Take your shirt off and give it to her." A tall blond stepped forward and removed his shirt. I gently set Angie on her feet after some encouragement, blocking their view of her with my body, and dressed her in Jeff's shirt.

"Thank you," I said, still trying to tamp down the killing rage.

He bobbed his head. "It weren't right, what they were doin'."

I nodded in response, and turned back to the sheriff, arms still tight around Angie.

"Think you can be ready to leave tomorrow morning?" he asked, almost kindly.

"Yes, sir."

"I'll make sure my boys escort you."

"Thank you, sir."

In fact, four of his men escorted us back to the gunsmith's shop. Sinclair wasn't there. I sincerely hoped he had taken my advice to visit the closest establishment that served alcoholic beverages. People knew he had let us stay with him, that he had gunpowder, and that he was friends with the blacksmith. I wanted to make sure that no one suspected him in helping me rescue Angie, and that he could complain long and loud for weeks on end about the gunpowder that I had "stolen."

Shortly after our arrival, three more of the sheriff's men showed up with Angie's clothing. Even her boots were there. I guess none of them had wanted to wear clothing tainted by a "witch." I felt my anger start to rise again, and had to take deep breaths to keep it at bay. It would not help, not then.

When they had gone, I turned back to Angie, sitting in a chair by the fire, still wearing Jeff's shirt. I started to unbutton the shirt and she started shaking. I murmured soft words to calm her and covered her with a blanket. I had warmed a pot of her bathwater; after dipping a cloth into it, I gently washed her tear-stained face. Her beautiful eyes were alive with horror and the remnants of the terrifying ordeal.

I gently massaged her neck and shoulders, slipping the blanket aside to clean her back. I washed her arms and legs and the dirt off her feet. I winced over the scrapes and bruises on her skin; she never flinched. I lifted her from the chair and laid her on the pallet; she rested there limply, not really with me at all. Her bag caught my eye; I rummaged through it and found the crystal vial of oil. I knelt beside her, brushed her hair from her face.

"Help me," I said. "Tell me what to do."

"Forehead... first," she said. I traced the symbols as best I could, anointing her temples next, then her neck and shoulders, followed by her heart. After touching her palms, I slipped my hand beneath the sheet to trace a symbol on her belly, a line down each leg, symbols on the soles of her feet, whispering words of protection the entire time. She joined me in the whispered words of magic, her voice becoming stronger with each word.

With the last utterance, her entire body gave a tremendous shudder, and she relaxed completely. It was a comfortable pose, unlike the lifeless slack she had demonstrated before. I draped a blanket over her, then lay down and pulled her close with her back against my chest. I closed my eyes and said prayers of thanks to the Morrigan for guiding me in my fight, and to Brighid for keeping us safe. Her breathing evened and deepened, and she floated into a peaceful sleep.

I stayed awake all night, watching.

I swore never to let her out of my sight again.

Chapter 13 – Ambush

Rules of Gunfighting #8:
In ten years nobody will remember the details of caliber, stance,
or tactics. They will only remember who lived.

I rose with the dawn. That is, if it could be called rising when I hadn't slept all night. I quietly packed all our belongings, and began strapping weapons to my body: boot knife, then slender belt upon which the tomahawks hung, followed by the machete on its wider belt, buckled about my hips. The Ithaca 37 was in its holster on my back. I stood there with the newly acquired rifle in my hands, unsure what to do with it. I laid it on Sinclair's workbench; it added too much weight, so I decided not to take it with me.

"Glad to see you both survived," said a rusty voice.

I turned to see Sinclair standing in the doorway.

"You shouldn't be here."

He let out a snort. "Ain't nobody gonna come after a blind old man. Kinda hard to tell who's a witch or whatnot when you're blind. People think I'm senile anyway. Come on, I want to show you something." He gestured for me to follow.

With a quick glance at Angie to make sure she was still sleeping, I went with him. From a high shelf, he pulled down an object wrapped in oilskin. He unwrapped it, revealing a leather bandolier. The inside was lined with slick, polished leather. The

159

outside was studded with leather loops for holding shells. It could hold a lot of them, too, many more than my shotgun holster.

"It'll hold about twenty shells in the front and seventeen in the back" Sinclair explained, his hands sliding over the well-oiled leather. "See this?" He fingered a small toggle dangling from the strap, where it would lay over the front of someone's shoulder.

"This is my own invention." He slipped the bandolier over his head, adjusted it in place, and gripped the toggle. "Knowing you, you'll go through twenty shells in no time," he said. He gave the toggle a yank, and the smooth leather slipped over his shirt as the entire thing rotated, bringing the rear shells to the front. "This cuts a little off your reload time, 'cause you don't have to take it off to get to the shells in the back."

"Volcanic," I said. "Did you make it yourself?"

"I had it made for me." His hands ran lovingly over the leather. "I want you to take it."

It was then that I realized that this was Sinclair's Traveling gear. I looked up, astonished. "You're giving me this?"

"It's not like I can use it anymore. I want it to go to someone who will appreciate and use it."

"I can't just take this," I protested.

"You can and you will." He tilted his head, as though listening for Angie in the next room. "If you two are about what I think you are, you're going to need it." He paused, handing the bandolier to me. "Druids are a force for good in this blasted world," he added softly. "They can heal it. You're a good man, for agreeing to be her protector. Especially since it's not because you're bedding her."

Embarrassed, I didn't know what to say. Was that what he had been hinting at when we first met? No wonder Angie had gotten her skirt in a bunch over it. She had probably felt insulted. Then again, from what she had said about druidic relationship habits, maybe not. It made me wonder again about what, exactly, the extent of our relationship would be.

"However," Sinclair continued. "Know that you've chosen what will probably be the hardest road of your life. The first part is the toughest, from what I hear. So you take this belt and use it

– and your wits – and anything else you can to survive. And, if she takes you somewhere to get trained, you take advantage and give it your all, because you're going to need that, too."

"I will. Thanks for the advice. And for the bandolier."

"You're welcome. Now, get your girl and get out. I need to get some sleep after drinking all night."

* * *

Angie was dressed and ready to go when the sheriff and his men arrived to escort us out of the city. They were all mounted and armed, the same as the first day we had met. I wondered if they ever walked, or went anywhere without their guns. Maybe they slept with both guns and horses. Before I could begin speculating on the possibility of wives and children also sleeping with horses and guns, one of the group walked up leading a grulla stallion and a palomino mare.

"You're giving us horses?" I asked, still overwhelmed by Sinclair's generosity.

The sheriff spat over the side of his horse. "It gets pretty rough down south. There are places where running won't keep you out of danger. You'll need 'em."

"I can't... I don't have anything to trade for them." I ran my hand over the stallion's muscular neck and shoulder, admiring the dark grey sheen of his coat and the heavy black mane.

"Boy." I looked at him and we locked gazes. "Their owners won't be needing them anymore."

"Then they should have minded their own business."

It probably wasn't the smartest thing to say, but I was still angry over what they had tried to do before. Angie had been completely innocent of any wrongdoing.

He shifted in his saddle, a hard glint in his eye.

"Ordinarily, for what you did last night, I'd have arrested you and scheduled your hanging for noon today," he said. "However, they've been giving me some trouble for a while now. Seemed to think that this here town should be run by a preacher, and not the elected officials. So, I'll settle for having you getting the hell out of my town and never coming back."

I got his message loud and clear. I had done him a favor; by giving us horses and letting us go free, he was calling it even.

"Thank you, sir. I appreciate it."

"The horses will get you on your way quicker," he said.

"Yes, sir," I said, taking the hint. I looked over at Angie, who had been quiet and distant all morning. Her mood seemed to have lifted with the arrival of the mare. She caressed the mare's nose, and I thought I saw a small smile cross her lips. What girl doesn't like horses? I hoped she could ride.

I squatted and laced my hands together, wordlessly offering her a boost up. Her lips curved further as she placed the toe of her boot in my hands. I boosted her up effortlessly and made sure she was settled on the mare's back, assisting with stirrups and such before tying her bundle on the back of the saddle.

I walked back to the stallion. He looked at me with dark eyes from beneath his long black forelock. He seemed to be calm and cooperative, but I hadn't mounted up yet. I decided to give him a little more time to get used to me. I tucked the shotgun into a handily placed saddle holster, tied my blankets and pack behind the seat, and took up the reins.

"Not gonna ride?" the sheriff asked.

"It's been awhile," I said. "If he's going to throw me, I'd rather it wasn't on the concrete."

The sheriff let out a snort of amusement. "Better get him used to you fast. Pretty sure you're in for an ambush once you're out of sight of the city."

Of course there would be an ambush. Anything else would have been too easy, and people were always so ready to take revenge for the slightest reason. I took his warning to heart; out of sight was out of mind, as far as he was concerned.

"Thank you again," I said, deciding that the bandolier was likely to get its first use today. I slipped it over my head, feeling the reassuring weight of its thirty-seven shell loadout.

He put heels to horse and started leading his posse away. Angie followed on her palomino, looking happy and content. It was a relief. I took one last look at the gunsmith's shop, mentally thanking the old Traveler.

I led the stallion through town at the rear of the posse. He

162

was quiet and well behaved, with no head tossing or balking. I wrapped the reins around the crook of my elbow, pulled an apple out of my pack's side pocket, and cut it into slices, feeding them to him one at a time. He crunched contentedly, swishing his long black tail.

We arrived at the gate; this was the moment of truth. The gates opened and Angie rode through. I led the stallion through the gates and waved at the posse. They closed and locked the gates, and I imagined I could hear them scrambling up the steps to the guard towers, to see if the stallion threw me. I checked the cinch to make sure it was snug and jumped aboard. If he was going to throw me, I didn't want to break my leg because I couldn't get it out of a stirrup on the way to the ground. The grulla shifted slightly and pointed his ears toward the road.

I nudged him forward gently with a squeeze of my legs, and he stepped out eagerly. Angie looked back over her shoulder and grinned. We both turned around and waved at the men in the guard towers. I put my feet in the stirrups, directed my horse to the grassy strip between the broken stretches of concrete, and urged him into a trot. Angie's mare matched his stride, pretty as you please. She was beautiful, her body a deep burnished gold, pale mane and tail flowing in the breeze. Angie laughed aloud, urging her horse into a canter, moving ahead of me. I didn't like that much and neither did the grulla. He snorted, powerful muscles driving us faster to catch up with her.

I let the race go on for about a hundred yards before pulling him up. Angie followed my lead and reined in her mare. The palomino reached over and nipped my horse's neck. He arched his neck and pranced for a few strides, then settled down with a snort. They must have been stable mates, or at least from the same farm.

"Aren't they wonderful?"

"They are," I agreed. "But remember what they're for." I nodded at the road ahead, curving slightly to the right and uphill. I pulled the shotgun from the holster at my knee and mentally prepared myself for trouble. She looked worried then, which I hated, but we could relax a while after fending off the expected attack. The horses walked at a relaxed pace. Eventually we should lead them, so as not to tire them out too soon, but that could wait until we were safe. Safe being a relative term, that is. Safe was when you weren't sure if an attack was coming. Danger was when you knew something was coming or were in the thick of it.

That was all right, though. I had a plan.

It came pretty much when the sheriff said it would, as we were cresting the hill a mile from the city. The horses' ears twitched, and the mare turned her head toward the trees, giving away the ambushers' position. Angie ignored it as I had instructed, and continued onward, leading the grey stallion.

I silently crept through the forest, keeping a watchful eye on Angie while hunting the enemy. As soon as I saw one person break the tree line, I aimed the shotgun and fired. The mare whinnied and bolted as Angie clung tightly to her back, lying low over her neck and releasing the stallion's reins. He followed for a few strides before coming to a halt. Holding down the trigger, I proceeded to slam fire the next four gunmen, all dropping dead in their tracks.

I guess nobody around here had heard of a shotgun that could carry eight shells, because a second group was hot on the heels of the first. Instead of going for my horse or trying to shoot Angie, they turned on me. I slam fired twice more before they dove for cover. I killed one and wounded another, his belly spattered with dots of blood. From the sound of his screams, I doubted he'd live out the day.

There was no immediate movement, so I ducked behind a tree and quietly reloaded. Long minutes passed, with no movement or noise of any kind. The dark grey stallion was calmly grazing, ears flicking attentively. I tired of waiting and decided to draw them out.

"Best if you just let us go and nobody else gets hurt!" I shouted, pulling out four of the homemade pipe bombs, along a little box of matches that I had swiped from Sinclair.

"There are already those been hurt!"

"Next time don't go hunting trouble!" I shouted, more to pinpoint their location than for the sake of argument. He hawked loudly and spat. Spitting seemed to be an art form in Searcy. I heard the metallic slide and click of rifle bolts. That meant they knew where I was, and I got ready to move.

"Thou shalt not suffer a witch–"

I was sick and tired of hearing that particular phrase. I stood, sliding my back up the tree, then lit the first pipe bomb and threw it. The boom of exploding gunpowder cut off the speaker before he could finish. I lit another one before the match burned out and tossed it in the direction of rustling bushes and running feet. Screams met my ears and I felt a dark kind of satisfaction.

Risking a peek around the tree, I raised the shotgun and visually swept the area for threats. Taking a deep breath and steeling my nerves, I swung the barrel around the tree once more, slam firing into their flimsy cover. Two more ambushers fell. I reloaded and scanned the area, waiting longer than I had the last time.

Angie was out there by herself and it made me nervous. I jogged to the horse, swung aboard without stirrups, and urged him forward. He whinnied and shied again, crab-stepping away from the trees. I pulled on the reins and spun him about, swinging the shotgun in an arc and firing. I dropped the reins and fired three more times. Two more bodies lay sprawled in the grass.

Without waiting for more, I bent low over the grey's neck and urged him into a gallop, guiding him in an irregular zigzag pattern within the grassy strip in the middle of the road. There were no final parting shots, however, and I escaped with my skin intact.

It was then that I understood what value the sheriff saw in his mounted riflemen. I was a mobile arsenal, with the good fortune to have a mount who could alert me to danger and who didn't spook under fire. I decided then that I had to give the horse a name, because I was going to keep this guy for a long time. We raced down the grassy center of the road to catch up to Angie.

* * *

The miles passed uneventfully until we approached another

walled city around noon. Unlike Searcy, the walls of this one did not obstruct our path.

"What do you think?" I asked.

"About what?"

"Feel like trying the town?"

"Have you ever been here before?"

"No. This is the farthest south I've ever been."

She twisted her mouth to the side, studying the city walls intently.

"I think I'd rather skip it," she said at last. After what had happened in Searcy, I couldn't blame her.

"Let's mount up and ride by, just in case." She needed no further urging. Seconds later we were mounted and trotting away. We had been walking the horses for a couple of hours, so they were rested. I watched the gates of the city as we trotted past, seeing no signs of welcome. I was fine with that; I liked sleeping under the stars. Angie seemed to like it as well; maybe it had to do with being a druid in tune with nature.

A couple of hours after the sun reached its zenith, the lack of sleep began to weigh heavily on me; my attention was wandering and my senses were dull. If danger approached, I knew I wouldn't react quickly enough.

"We need someplace to stop," I said. "Can you find somewhere with water? Maybe a pond or a lake?"

"Sure," said Angie. She lifted her face and closed her eyes, as if scenting the air. "That way," she said, pointing southeast. I let her palomino mare take the lead, knowing the stallion would follow. I guided the still-unnamed horse out of the middle of the road, over the cracking pavement. After wandering across a field of grass, the horses brought us into the coolness of a sparse wood, to the bank of a small stream. It met with my approval; it was always best to camp well back from the road and amongst trees. The water was a bonus, and the stream looked deep enough to take a swim. A nap followed by an evening dip in the creek would be a welcome pleasure.

"This'll do nicely," I said. The horses whickered agreement, nostrils flaring as they smelled the water. We both dismounted and I dropped to my belly on the bank, dipping in a hand and tasting the water. It was fresh.

Angie frowned. "Did you really have to check?" she asked.

"Oh. Sorry. You can tell when it's good from a distance?"

"Obviously, or I wouldn't have led us here."

I turned my back on her and loosened the stallion's girth. I was hot and tired, had spent the last few weeks doing nothing but running and fighting. I was not going to deal with her high-handed behavior. Refusing to meet her gaze, I took her mare's reins and led both horses to the stream. They drank a few moments; then I pulled them away, not wanting them to drink too much at once. They weren't really hot, as we had been walking, but I didn't want to take chances. My parents had owned riding horses when I was younger, and now had a couple of plow horses, but it had been a long time since I had cared for one. My mother had taught me to ride, but my memories were pretty vague about what not to do with one.

I removed their bridles, suddenly wishing we had halters. They immediately lowered their heads to graze. I hesitated a bit, wondering if they would wander away. I supposed it was possible, but there was good grazing here. Unless they were spooked, they should still be there in the morning. With a mental shrug, I removed their saddles and placed them back under the trees. Out of curiosity, I opened the mare's left saddlebag, to find a comb and brush for the horse, as well as a hoof pick and some other odds and ends. The stud's held the same. It seemed that the sheriff had really had our best interests at heart... or at least that of the horses.

Angie was laying out our blankets and unwrapping food for supper. My stomach growled. We had skipped breakfast, and had eaten only dried fruit for lunch. When she was done, I tossed her the curry supplies for her horse and began tending to mine. I brushed his coat, which he loved, and combed his mane and tail, which he didn't. He tolerated me picking up his hooves reasonably well. I inspected them, noted that he wore no shoes but had sturdy, well-formed feet. I finished and patted his shoulder. He still needed a name, but nothing had come to mind.

I plopped down on my blanket, pulled off my boots and socks, and wiggled my toes, contemplating a swim. I'd eat first, then see how I felt. I considered waiting for Angie, but as she seemed to be intent on brushing the mare all afternoon, I went ahead and quieted my hungry stomach. She finally joined me and picked up her food, only to put it down again. It was beef jerky, biscuits, and dried fruit. Nothing fancy, but nothing to sneeze at, either.

"Something wrong?"

"I didn't know it was going to be like this," she said, frowning at it.

"It's travel food," I said. "Enough to keep you going, but that's about it."

"No, I meant..." she trailed off.

I raised an eyebrow, but decided to wait her out. I lay back on my blanket on the soft grass, cradling my head in my hands and feeling the muscles in my back begin to relax.

"I didn't know this was supposed to be so hard," she cried softly. "I could have been killed last night. And before that, you've had to fight off bandits and stealers, and everything else. You could have been killed a dozen times!"

I was unprepared for an emotional breakdown. If I hadn't been so weary, I might have seen it coming. A pretty horse couldn't fix everything, it seemed. I thought for a moment. "Why were you so dead set on finding me? Don't you trust them to pick someone good for you?"

She shook her head.

"You don't trust your own father?"

"You don't trust your mother to guide your life," she retorted. "Anyway, he's not the one doing the choosing."

"Look, I'm sure that whoever is doing the choosing–"

"The ArchDruid."

"Right, the ArchDruid. I'm sure he has your best interests at heart."

Again, she shook her head. "No, she doesn't. She only wants to cement her position in the grove through political alliances, and she's doing it through us."

This grove of hers sounded worse every time she spoke of it. Putting aside my misgivings on the matter, I tried to soothe her. "Look," I said. "You could have found a bodyguard anywhere.

168

So could she, for that matter."

Angie replied, sounding like she was quoting from a book: "A druid is supposed to have a warrior of guardian spirit, of impeccable loyalty, who will never leave, never run, and always fight to the–" She broke off, a look of horror crossing her features.

I turned on my side to face her, propping my head in one hand.

"To the death?" I asked softly. "No, I guess you wouldn't find that just anywhere, and certainly not for hire."

Hence the need for a spirit animal, to find the one person in the world who would sacrifice himself. This journey felt like some kind of test to see if I measured up.

"I'm so sorry, Davis," she said, tears streaking down her cheeks. "I just thought it was an ideal, not a necessity. I didn't think anyone really expected a warrior to give his life for a druid. I certainly didn't."

I had the feeling that her people had known it was a necessity, which is why they had wanted to pick someone for her. I felt like I had destroyed her innocence, although it couldn't be true. Then again, she had probably never seen another human being die until I had killed one in front of her. I wondered if she would grow to see me as some kind of soulless killing machine.

"Since meeting you, I have killed more people than I ever did in all my travels alone," I said. "I don't like it and I don't enjoy it. But, I do recognize it as being something of a necessity. And frankly, I'd rather kill than die." She sniffled in the growing darkness, wiped the tears from her face.

"My father once told me that the only thing required for evil to flourish, is for good men to do nothing." I reached out and took her hand. "If there is something I can do to help others, I'm going to do it. Especially if it's for you." I was suddenly smothered in tears and curls, when she threw her arms around me and buried her face in my neck. I expected for the tears to begin in earnest, but they didn't. I held her close and reminded myself to be patient. No matter how exhausted I was, nobody had tried to burn me alive last night.

"Since I came into my magic," she whispered, "All I have

ever wanted is for someone to be with me for me, not for what I can do."

"And nobody in the entire grove could be that for you?"

"Not that I can trust. It's like a nest of vipers – you never know who you can trust. The only way to be certain was to send out my fetch."

"I bet it came as an ugly surprise that it was me."

She sat up abruptly. "What? No!" She laid a hand on my chest. "No, Davis, not at all. I was excited that it was someone from outside, because that meant that you would be untainted."

Untainted? Hardly. "You make living in the grove sound horrible."

She sighed. "Things have changed over the past few years, for the worse. The young men have no magic of their own, so they started jockeying for positions with the elementalists with the most power."

"So what you're saying is that because you're a water elementalist, you thought you'd be scraping the bottom of the barrel? That nobody would want you?"

Angie looked at me with an unreadable expression. I was too tired to figure it out, but I did understand feeling unwanted, undervalued, and unlovable. If I had possessed magic, how far would I have gone to find someone who would appreciate me for who I was?

She traced my jawline with a gentle finger.

"There is no one in all the world who could replace you," she said. "No matter what happens, always remember that."

I eyed her skeptically. I enjoyed her touch, but her statement was unsettling. "You sound like you think I'm not going to survive this trip."

"It's a possibility."

"If I don't survive, neither will you."

"I know. But it's not really the trip I'm worried about."

"Then what is it?"

"It's the destination." She paused. "I worry that you'll be taken from me."

I snorted and lay back on my blankets with my hands behind my head. "You don't need to worry about them handing me off to

170

someone else," I said irritably. "I haven't risked my life just to be passed around at the ArchDruid's convenience. I'll either be with you or with no one at all."

The slow, sweet smile that crossed her lips made the whole tiresome conversation worthwhile. I closed my eyes and took a deep breath, inhaling the light aroma of honeysuckle that always surrounded her. Her lips brushed my temple.

"Rest now," she whispered.

Sleep beckoned with an irresistible intensity, and I gave in to it at last.

Chapter 14 – Shattered Quiet

Rules of Gunfighting #17:
Don't drop your guard.

I probably would have slept all afternoon and into the night if the caress of something cold and wet hadn't wakened me. It ran lightly over my forehead and down my cheek, coming to rest on my neck. When it pulled away, I could feel water dripping onto my chest. I thought it was Angie trying to wake me up, but when I opened my eyes all I saw was a crystalline snake-like form, waving sinuously over me. I let out a startled yell and slapped it away, rolling to one side. It burst into a water shower that soaked my shirt.

Peals of laughter came from the stream, where Angie was leaning on the bank. Her shoulders were shaking, and sparkles of water glinted in her hair.

I gave her a dirty look. "Not funny."

She hid her grin behind her hands, but her eyes danced and she snorted with laugher. I must have looked ridiculous, yelling and freaking out over a magic water snake.

"I thought you were going to sleep all day," she said, still giggling. "Come swim with me."

"I think I already have," I said, indicating my sopping shirt.

"You could use a break."

"Somebody has to keep watch."

172

"You weren't watching while you were sleeping," she said. "Besides, your shirt needs to dry."

"I have another one," I said, pulling the wet one over my head.

"Come on," she said. "You can have a little fun."

She was right, and I had wanted to go for a swim. I stood there with my wet shirt in my hands, watching her. The past few weeks had been nothing but struggle and stress. I needed to relax. I hung my shirt on a nearby tree branch to dry, as she splashed, arcing her body over the water before becoming submerged, then came up swimming toward me. The skin on her back, bottom, and rounded thighs gleamed in the setting sun. I stopped what I was doing and waited until she came up for air.

"Are you naked?"

"That's usually how people swim."

I frowned. Angie rolled her eyes.

"You've seen me naked before, Davis," she said.

"That was different. You were in danger."

"Those Triune people you grew up with sure rubbed off on you," Angie said, shaking her head ruefully.

"There's nothing wrong with being modest," I retorted, but what she had said settled it. I wasn't Triune, and we weren't anywhere that anyone would object to nudity. Obviously she didn't.

"Fine. Whatever." My hands moved to unfasten my pants, but I hesitated when I noticed Angie was still watching. I gave her a pointed look, and she grinned again and turned around. I shucked them off quickly and stepped gingerly into the cool water. It was the perfect temperature, just right for cooling off from the summer heat.

I noticed Angie looking back at me over her shoulder with a mischievous smile.

"Were you peeking?" I demanded.

"Of course not!" she said, all wide-eyed innocence.

I shook my head and laughed, giving in. Why should I care if a beautiful woman wanted to see me naked? I closed my eyes and sank under the water, coming up to find Angie floating a few feet in front of me.

173

"It feels good, doesn't it?" She smiled.

"You were right. It does." I returned her smile. "Show me that thing you did before."

"What?"

"The water snake."

With seemingly no effort at all on Angie's part, a glassy tube made entirely of water and held together by magic separated itself from the surface of the stream. It arched over our heads, weaving back and forth like a hypnotized cobra, then curled around my body and draped itself over my shoulders. There was a tiny glitter in the druid's eyes, just before the snake ruptured in an explosive splash.

I spluttered and shook my head, sending water flying everywhere. Angie laughed out loud and swam away. I gave chase and splashed her back, and the water war was on. We played and swam until the sun started to set, then dried off and dressed in clean clothing. I put on some blue jeans and decided to skip the shirt. The night was warm, with the barest of breezes ruffling the leaves on the trees around our campsite. The western sky was gradually turning from blue to a deep grey, with a myriad of orange and yellow streaks highlighting the clouds.

I was working on lighting a fire and had the tiniest flicker of flame going when Angie re-emerged from the brush where she had changed into dry clothes. I glanced at her and then took a second look. I couldn't help myself. She was wearing a thin shift that left little to the imagination. It clung to her small breasts and little waist, flaring out with the ample width of her hips. As it swirled about her thighs, I revised my opinion, deciding that the dress revealed just enough to set my mind on fire.

Thoughts of what lay beneath the thin cotton crowded into my mind, especially since I had gotten several glimpses while swimming. I reluctantly tore my eyes away from her and turned my attention back to the fire, which had died while I had been staring at the druid.

Chagrined, I shook my head and started over.

"I didn't see anything in the snares," said Angie, kneeling across from me. The fabric stretched tightly over her thighs.

"But I caught some fish in the stream, if you're interested."

"When did you do that?" I blew on the tiny flames that were growing in the kindling.

She shrugged. "I set a few water nets while you were sleeping. There's a couple of nice big trout swimming in one of them."

"You can make water solid enough to hold fish?"

She nodded. "With enough effort and concentration, I can make it as hard as a rock."

"You mean like ice?"

"Yes, except it isn't cold."

"The more I hear about your magic, the more impressed I get," I said. The tiny fire nearly went out again. I sighed in exasperation before again blowing on it gently to encourage its growth.

"What's wrong?" Angie asked. "Is the wood wet?"

"No," I said, adding a few more twigs. "I just keep getting distracted."

"Am I distracting you?"

I glanced at her, noting her expression of fond amusement. The look in her eyes was the same one that I had seen the day I bought her a beer in Kingston. I studied her face for several seconds while a glow of pleasure lit in her green eyes, as if she felt like having the ability to distract me was the greatest thing in the world.

"Yes," I admitted, peeved with myself. "Why don't you go find some sticks we can roast the fish on, and let me get this fire started?" She smiled broadly and rose to gather sticks and the fish. She didn't seem offended in the slightest by my grouchy tone.

I looked back down and saw the fire was out again.

After a delicious supper of trout roasted with Angie's herbs from Searcy, we spread our blankets beneath the night sky. The horses grazed peacefully nearby. We lay side by side on my blanket, looking up at the stars. I pointed out the different constellations to Angie.

"So that's Draco?" she asked. I had to lean closer to follow the line of sight determined by her raised arm.

"Right. And see the faint constellation that's kind of wrapped up in Draco's tail? That's Ursa Minor, the little bear. You can see it fairly well tonight, because the sky is so clear. Then to the right of the tail, there's Ursa Major, the big bear."

"My friend Irri likes bears," said Angie. "Sometimes she pets them."

"Bears are dangerous." I hoped friend Irri wasn't in the habit of dragging Angie out to pet bears. I felt her shrug against my shoulder.

"I guess she talks to them so they'll be nice to her. Kind of the way I did with Mule One and Mule Two."

"You used magic on the mules?"

"I had to get them to behave somehow. I don't have as much of a connection to other animals like I do with cats, but I can usually get my point across."

I chuckled incredulously. "I think living at the grove is going to be stranger than anything I've ever experienced."

"It's nothing like Jonesboro, that's for sure." She pointed to another star cluster. "What's that one?"

Scooting closer to her, I peered to get a better view. "Mmm... I think you're pointing to Hercules."

"It looks like Draco is about to eat him," she giggled. "How did you learn so much about the stars?"

"My mother taught me. My father is familiar enough with astronomy to navigate, but she really loves the night sky. We used to lie on the roof and stare at the stars for hours, and she'd tell me stories of the gods that went with them."

"Do you miss your parents?"

"Occasionally, but remembering how she wants to run my life usually fixes that."

"She does love you, you know."

"I just wish she'd let me be who I am. It's like she's afraid that something terrible will happen to me."

Angie sighed, resting her cheek on my shoulder. "Terrible things have happened to you."

"And yet, somehow I've survived it all," I replied, trying to lighten the mood.

"I worry about you, too," she said softly, a slight frown creasing her brow.

I wanted to reassure her and say that everything would be all right, but I wasn't in the habit of lying. There was no way of knowing what tomorrow would hold. I reached over and took her hand in mine, hoping to give her some comfort.

After a few minutes of silence, Angie spoke again.

"Irri said that if I came back with you, then she was going to seek her own chosen. So did some of the others."

"Why would they wait?"

"Because they're afraid of the ArchDruid."

"So they're letting you stick your neck out to see how it goes?"

She shook her head. "It's not really like that. It's more like... If I succeed, then maybe they'll have a chance, too."

"I didn't realize that there was so much riding on this."

"I wanted you to choose on your own," Angie replied. "Not because of the pressure I put on you." She paused. "Did you choose on your own?"

"More or less."

"I'm sorry."

"Why? I'm not."

"Because you had to choose without knowing about all the politics and obstacles we're going to face." She snuggled closer to me, her head more firmly on my shoulder and her belly pressed against my hip. I closed my eyes when she let go of my hand and slid it up my bare chest, her breast pressed lightly against my arm. My heart started to beat just a little bit faster. I hoped she wouldn't notice.

It was full night, the only light being from our small campfire, and a beautiful woman in a captivating dress was provocatively close to me. We were alone in a very private place, watched only by the nature spirits, ancestors, and the distant gods.

"Think of it this way," I said, trying to distract myself from what her nearness was doing to me. "When we make it back to the grove, after everything we've been through, wading through the politics and pressure is going to seem like a cakewalk."

"Do you really think so?"

"I doubt that fending off stern looks and sharp words will be so difficult to endure after having people try to kill us every other day for three months," I said dryly.

Angie rose up on her elbow, looking down at me.

"You always say the right thing to make me feel better," she said, lightly tracing patterns on my chest with her fingertips. My breathing quickened.

"Threatening to kill you in the middle of the road when we first met didn't seem to make you feel very good."

Angie laughed softly, and before I knew what was happening, she was kissing me. Stupefied, I hesitated for a split second, then kissed her back. She drew back for a moment, studying my face. Apparently satisfied with what she saw there, the druid bent to kiss me again.

"I'm not sure you should do that," I whispered, feeling my heart thundering in my chest.

"Why not?"

"Aren't you worried about what the ArchDruid will think?"

"I couldn't care less what she thinks. After all, if I don't think she should have a say in who my warrior is, I certainly don't care what she thinks about my love life." Her green eyes glowed darkly. "I'll be the one to choose who the father of my children is, thank you very much."

I was a little taken aback by that statement, but decided that she must have been speaking in general terms, not specifically about me.

"I thought she wanted to pair people up to give her the best political advantage."

"Would I be here if I cared about her political aspirations?"

"I just don't want you to suffer any... unpleasant consequences."

"I don't really care about that either, right at this moment." She spoke in a bare whisper. "Do you?"

The scent of honeysuckle surrounded me, as Angie leaned in close, her face just inches from mine. I stared at those full lips, hoping for another taste.

"No... not really."

"Good," she said, and kissed me again.

* * *

We left the road the next morning, deciding to travel cross-country. To my way of thinking, this would help us avoid both towns and people. Traveling through the forest seemed safer. We rode in silence for most of the morning, with occasional comments from Angie about trees, or birds, or animals. She also talked to her mare, who she had named Magic. Magic seemed happy to listen, her ears flicking back and forth.

My horse still didn't have a name yet. Angie had suggested several names, but they were all girly titles like Silver, Dancer, Wizard, stuff like that. He was a stallion, and I wanted him to have a strong name. Wizard was pretty volcanic, but I was a warrior and having a horse with a name like that didn't seem to make much sense.

I wasn't wasting time thinking of a name for him, either. My thoughts were entirely occupied with the memory of Angie's lips on mine and the feel of her supple body pressing against me. I didn't know why I was so caught up in what was, realistically, the smallest bit of intimacy last night. I had kissed girls before; Sarah may have been the first, but she most certainly was not the last.

Somehow, being with Angie was different. Maybe it had something to do with our swim yesterday. Almost of its own accord, my mind replayed how playful and uninhibited she had been in the stream. She had acted as if it was the most natural thing in the world for us to frolic naked together.

Maybe it was as simple as the fact that she had kissed me, and not the other way around. I didn't care that kissing was as far as we had gotten. It was such a pleasant surprise to have a woman display interest and affection first. I had wondered whether there was more than friendship between us on occasion, the few instances when she had given me this considering look, or that glance laden with meaning. Her advances last night had confirmed what I had not dared to believe – she liked me. Not as a friend, or a protector, but as a woman likes a man.

Angie had put her hair up, twisted into a loose bunch of curls. A few stray corkscrews draped over her slender neck. I had my eyes firmly on her backside, swaying attractively in the saddle. I was curious about how far she wanted to take her affections, and couldn't help but wonder if I should take the initiative. Maybe I should continue allowing her to take the lead, but I didn't want her to think me disinterested.

I was definitely interested. Prior to last night, I had assumed that our connection was one of friendly companionship. She had demonstrated a desire for something more, however, and it had completely shattered my understanding of what our relationship was supposed to be. I thought back to how devastated she had seemed at my initial rejection. I recalled her frank admiration of me in the beginning of our journey together, and some of the comments she had let slip in recent days. The one that sprang to mind was when she had spoken about choosing the father of her own children, spoken practically in the same breath about choosing her own warrior. At the time, it has seemed off-the-cuff, but after careful reflection, that might just be exactly what she meant. During our early arguments, she had expressed no concern at all for finding a mate and settling down. Neither had she been concerned about my ability to do so. The obvious reason should have slapped me in the face, but it was only now that it was all starting to make sense.

Druids and warriors spent their lives together, wandering in the wilderness and healing the earth, so it was only natural that they shared a partnership that included physical as well as emotional intimacy. It was the ideal situation, I supposed, with two people roaming for months or years on end with only each other for company. In addition, a warrior might protect his druid from a strong sense of duty, but how much more ferocity would he display, knowing it was his lover for whom he fought?

My attention diverted when Magic came to full alertness, ears pricked and swiveling, nose high as she whinnied in alarm. The stallion snorted, raising his head and lashing his tail in agitation. I just had enough time to whip out the shotgun when the first attacker appeared. He jumped at Angie, trying to yank her off her horse. The golden mare whinnied and reared, pulling away. Holding onto the pommel and cantle of the saddle, the druid managed to kick him in the face and knock him away.

The shotgun was useless in this situation; he was just too close to her. I pulled out a tomahawk and threw it, catching him in the lower back. He screamed and fell to his knees, trying to yank the blade free. Magic spooked and trampled him in the close space between the trees. As I turned to look, there were four others converging on the druid and her mount, and four more coming at me. At first glance, I thought it was another group of bandits but they were ill-dressed and poorly armed. It was just a group of thugs armed only with knives and clubs. With the Ithaca, I should have been able to handle them all with relative ease. However, we were in such close quarters I feared shooting Angie or her horse.

The others tried to pull the druid from her saddle, thinking that their compatriots would keep me busy. They found soon enough that I was never busy for long. While the dark grey stallion danced in circles to keep the four surrounding me from coming closer, Magic reared and spooked sideways, giving me a clean shot. Cold adrenaline pounded through my veins, and I again held the trigger and worked the pump action, slam firing and taking down two of the thugs attacking Angie. One dropped to the earth dead; scattershot peppered another's right arm and chest.

The stallion reared, lashing out with his hooves and whinnying loudly. One sharp kick thudded into the forehead of one of the thugs attacking me, dropping him instantly. The other three dodged to either side of us; I managed to shoot one and throw the tomahawk at the other. The tomahawk missed, thunking hopelessly into the leafy forest detritus. Its intended target dove away from me, giving me a clean head shot. Blood and brain matter splattered across the leaves and dirt, sprinkling the stallion's black legs. He reared again and would have bolted but for Magic blocking his way. He turned and crow-hopped sideways, snorting. I ignored the remaining attacker and turned to help Angie.

She was half out of the saddle, kicking and yelling as one rough man clung to her leg. The other was holding her mare's bridle, attempting to hold Magic still. The mare was having none of it. She squealed and reared, pulling the man off his feet. He let go and fell onto his butt and into my sights. The Ithaca's voice boomed and half his face was ripped away.

"Let her go!" I shouted to the last thug who was accosting Angie. I holstered the gun and drew the machete, urging my horse forward. I slashed at the man's arm, opening a deep gash in the meat. He cried out and released her, blood pouring from his arm. At the smell of blood, the mare screamed in terror and started bucking in panic; Angie lost her already unstable seat and went flying into a bush. I turned the stallion back to the one remaining uninjured person. I would have preferred to make sure Angie was all right, but he was still a threat and I had ignored him long enough. He stalked toward me with a snarl on his face.

"Come down off that horse and fight like a man!" he screamed, spittle flying. I was always amazed at the hypocrisy of people. He didn't like the odds now, but five minutes before, nine on two had been manly. I dismounted, machete in hand.

"You've got that big gun and you're going to hack me to death?!" He screeched. "Be a man and shoot me!"

"Waste of ammo," I said, then stepped forward and cleaved his neck, nearly separating it from his shoulders. Blood sprayed everywhere, but I stepped aside to miss most of it.

"Davis!" Angie screamed.

I spun on my heel, bringing the machete around. Standing before me with a pistol in his hand was the thug whose arm I had cut. I'd never draw the shotgun in time. I threw the machete as hard as I could; the bandit fired his pistol. His strangled cry echoed off the trees, just as something slammed into me, throwing me to the ground. I lay there for an eternity trying to breathe.

Angie dropped to her knees in the leaves beside me, tears running down her face. She placed her hands on my chest, shaking me. I struggled to get one lungful of air, and then another.

"Is he dead?" I croaked, gasping for another breath. "They're all dead?"

She nodded, unable to speak.

"How bad?" I managed another deep gasp of life-giving air.

"Y-your s-shoulder," she sobbed. There was blood all over her hands. I wanted to scream when she started to apply pressure, but didn't have the breath. A tortured groan escaped my lips.

"Time... to go," I panted.

"I have to stop the bleeding."

"Magic..."

"I can't!" she wailed. "I can't heal, I don't have the gift!"

I shook my head. "Magic's pack... bandages."

She raced away and was back seconds later with the pack, dumping it on the ground. "Left... pockets," I wheezed. She dug through our supplies and found two thick wads of cotton bandage. Fortunately she knew what to do, laying one roll over the bleeding hole in my shoulder under my shirt, then using the other as a pressure dressing, wrapping it around my arm and shoulder, then a couple of times around my neck and chest for stability.

"Up," I said. She helped me stagger to my feet. Tears still streaked her cheeks, but now there was a determined look on her face. I stumbled over to the bandit's body and almost fell over trying to pull the machete out of his upper abdomen, just below the sternum. It was a one in a million shot, and surely it had been the intervention of the Morrigan that saw me still alive while he was dead.

Of course, it might be a temporary situation.

"Machete," I wheezed. Angie set her jaw and grabbed the hilt, bracing her boot on the man's chest to gain enough leverage to release it. She lost her balance and nearly fell when it finally pulled free. She wiped it clean on his clothes and slid it into the sheath at my hip. She fetched my tomahawk from a pile of leaves, yanked the other one from a dead man's back, and strapped them to my saddle. Next, she helped me hobble over to the stallion, where I let go of her and clung to the stirrup. Even though breathing had become a little easier, from that perspective the saddle looked to be about ten feet up.

"Down," Angie said quietly. I saw her place her hand on my horse's forehead, then watched as the stallion knelt before me. I

183

put my foot in the stirrup and clumsily swung aboard. Angie helped me get my right leg over the rest of the way and tucked that foot into the other stirrup. I swayed unsteadily in the saddle as the stallion gracefully rose to his feet. He snorted and shook his head, as if to say, What have I gotten myself into?

"Me too, buddy, me too," I muttered, patting his shoulder. I held my wounded left arm tight to my chest and gripped the saddle horn with the right. Angie was back on her horse with the stallion's reins in her hand. She set the horses to a fast walk, heading out of the woods and back to the road. I concentrated on staying in the saddle. My head eventually cleared, which was both a good and a bad thing. It was good, because I could finally focus and ride my horse; bad, because my shoulder started to really hurt.

Once we were clear of the trees, I squeezed my legs around the stallion, urging him alongside Angie's mare. I reached over and took his reins from her, ignoring her look of wide-eyed disbelief. It was all I could do not to grimace, grunt, and groan. Trotting hurt. Every step the stallion took caused another bolt of pain to my shoulder. The passing thought that it might be broken ran through my mind and was dismissed as irrelevant. Even if it was broken, there was nothing I could do about it.

"Time to go," I said again, and urged the stallion into a canter. The palomino mare followed quickly. I didn't think I could handle a gallop; anyway, I wanted to save the horses' stamina for when we really needed it. Every time I looked behind me it was like being stabbed by a knife; thankfully, no one was following us. I let the horses go for about fifteen minutes and then backed them to a trot.

I gritted my teeth for another fifteen minutes, unable to prevent small sounds of pain from escaping. It felt like a hot poker jabbed into my shoulder with every step the stallion took. Angie glanced at me every time I made a noise. Maybe she thought I was going to fall off? Or maybe she thought I wasn't being a man? Quakes, I'd been shot, and I'd never been shot before. It hurt worse than anything I'd ever experienced.

We cantered again for another fifteen minutes, until I just couldn't stand it anymore, and slowed the stallion to a walk. In the quiet, broken only by hoof beats, I could hear my breathing. I was grunting with every breath; a short breath in, then grunting on the exhale. That didn't sound good, and I wondered if it was due only to pain, or if the bullet had nicked my lung. If that were the case, I was as good as dead. I didn't feel too terribly short of breath, though, so we could keep riding till sundown, or until I fell off my horse, whichever came first.

Davis?"

I grunted in response.

"Are you okay?"

"I'll live."

Her face was pale and scared. "I'm really worried about your shoulder. We should stop so I can clean it and put on a fresh bandage." For some reason she wasn't looking me in the eye, staring at my chest instead.

"No," I said. "We'll stop at sunset." It seemed to be getting darker all the time. Weird. Shouldn't it be daylight for a few more hours in the summer?

"Davis, I don't think–"

"When it's dark we can hide. You can take care of it then and not before."

Her face crumpled, and she started to cry again. I hadn't meant to sound harsh. It wasn't her fault they had sent her out half-trained and mostly helpless.

"I'm sorry, Ang," I said. "I didn't mean that the way it sounded."

"Davis–"

I shook my head. "It's not your fault, sweetheart."

A wave of dizziness washed over me, and I closed my eyes to let it pass. After a few moments, I awakened to the sensation of the stallion's black mane was tickling my nose. Cracking my eyes open, I realized that I was slumped over the saddle with my head resting on the horse's neck. Blood coated his withers and dripped down his shoulder. When had he been hurt? I didn't remember him bleeding before I had mounted. Surely I'd have noticed. I pulled myself upright with a groan of effort, in order to examine him. That was when I caught sight of my arm. My white shirt was turned scarlet, my hand coated in bright red blood that dripped from my fingers. Oh, good, it wasn't the stallion's blood.

That meant it had to be mine. The world spun crazily a moment, and I felt myself slide sideways from the saddle and hit the ground with a thud. Good thing my feet had fallen out of the stirrups a while back. Like the excellent mount he was, the grulla stallion stopped and stood obediently still, shining like dark steel in the sun.

Steel. Now there was a good name for a horse. I became aware of Angie by my side, and I gazed up at her worried face.

"Steel," I said, hearing the word slur.

"What?"

"You... have Magic. So... I have... Steel." The world greyed a little around the edges, until I could only see her face. The golden sun caused her skin to glow, and her hair gleamed in its warming rays. I reached up and touched her cheek, feeling its fragile softness.

"You're so beautiful," I whispered, before the world went dark. I'd made it to sunset after all.

Chapter 15 – The Witches of Ward

Rules of Gunfighting #9:
If you are not shooting, you should be
communicating, reloading, and running.

When I woke up, it was in a place unknown to me. So, I did what I always do when I wake up in a strange place – I leapt to my feet, hands groping for weapons. There were no weapons at hand, but I did find the floor.

It was hard wood, and it hurt.

The door was flung open and a man in a long robe strode through the door, heading right for me. I'd never seen anyone dressed like him: the long grey robe had buttons to the waist, revealing black trousers and boots with each stride.

"Where's Angie?" I snarled, feeling the welcome rise of anger and heat to empower me as I climbed to my feet. I didn't need weapons to fight. They just saved time.

"Peace," said the man, stopping in his tracks. "This is a peaceful household."

I hesitated, fighting off a wave of dizziness.

"Please, Davis. You are wounded and need to rest. You lost a lot of blood." My shoulder throbbed painfully, bringing back memories of the attack... and the gunshot.

"How do you know me?" Adrenaline began to subside.

"Angie told us."

"Where is she?"

Just at that moment, she burst through the door. "Davis!" she cried, then ran to throw her arms about me. It killed my shoulder, but I stifled the grunt of pain, and slipped my good arm around her shoulders. I just stood there, holding her in silence, breathing in her scent. She felt so good, so warm in my arms. I told myself I was just glad to find her safe.

"I'm okay," I murmured. "Don't cry."

"You almost died," she sobbed. "You almost *died*."

I pulled away a little, so I could see her face. "But I didn't."

"You almost–"

"Almost only counts in horseshoes and shotgun shells," I said with a smile. I didn't feel like it, but I hated to see her cry. Angie stared at me for a moment before a tremulous smile crossed her lips. I wiped away her tears with gentle fingers.

"Are you sure you're okay?" her voice trembled.

"Unless I starve to death, which I think I might."

She rolled her eyes. "Oh, you–" she slapped my arm lightly. I clenched my teeth against the pain and saw the grey-robed man suppress a smile.

"We have food prepared," said the man, gesturing to the open door. "If you would care to join us."

I looked questioningly at Angie; she smiled and nodded, leading me by the hand – my right hand, thankfully. My left arm was bound in a sling. I stopped before the man in grey, turning loose Angie's hand.

"You know my name, but I have not yet had the pleasure of learning yours," I said, holding out my hand.

He took it, with a firm, friendly grip. "Brennan."

"Thank you," I said. "For helping me, and for keeping Angie safe."

He inclined his head graciously. "It is our way."

I let Angie reclaim my hand and lead me to the next room. "It's an uncommon way," I said.

He smiled. "That it is. As is yours."

That gave me pause, but the thought was forgotten as I stepped into the large, rectangular room. It had a high, open ceiling with hundreds of bunches of herbs drying in the rafters.

Mixed scents wafted in the air, blending together to give the room a warm, woodsy, cozy feel. A long table ran down the middle of the hall, with multiple benches on each side. There was a large fireplace on the closer end, with heavy double doors on the opposite end.

"Welcome, Davis. It is good to see you on your feet."

I turned to see a woman, perhaps in her late twenties or early thirties, with long red hair tied in a tail with bright blue ribbon. Brennan walked over to her and slipped an arm around her waist. She smiled and handed him the spoon. He laughed silently, as if sharing a private joke, and took over stirring the pot. Whatever was in it smelled wonderful. My stomach rumbled noisily.

"This is Rhiannon," Angie said. "She's the leader of..." She broke off as though unsure.

"It's all right, dear," Rhiannon said with a warm smile. "We do not hide what we are."

"Which is?"

"A coven. I am High Priestess here. Brennan is our High Priest."

"Witches?"

"Witches," she confirmed with a smile.

I took her hand. "It's a pleasure," I said. "Thank you for helping us."

Her eyes sparkled. "You are welcome to that, and to anything else you need. Please, sit and eat."

I was more than happy to oblige, putting away three bowls of stew and half a loaf of crusty bread. I ate the first two because I was starving; I ate the third because it was the best stew I'd ever eaten in my life. I sent my mother a mental apology.

Other members of the coven entered, busying themselves with chores. They were polite and didn't stare at me too much. By the time I finished my second bowl, the members of the coven had all introduced themselves to me (Angie knew them already), and were sitting and eating. A feeling of warmth and family permeated the room.

Angie sat quietly beside me, eating little. I kept tearing off small hunks of bread and putting them in front of her so she would eat more. The food was as tasty as it was plentiful. She needed to eat as much as possible while we were here; we still had a long way to go.

When most were finished eating, I faced Rhiannon. "Would you mind filling me in on what's happened while I've been down?"

"We brought you here to recuperate," she said. "You'd lost a lot of blood. We cleaned up your wound, cast spells of strength over you, and fed you broth whenever you woke. Angie has been with you night and day, except when we made her take some fresh air and exercise."

"Of course you'd wake up when I was outside," Angie grumbled. I patted her knee under the table. I felt her fingers close over mine and decided to leave my hand where it was.

"How did you find us?"

"That would be your druid's doing." Rhiannon did not seem pleased. I looked at Angie, who blushed. It was startling; I had never seen her cheeks so pink. It was also charming, setting off her delicate features. Memories flooded back to me, of swimming and stargazing, of how I had been devouring her with my eyes when the attack had occurred. Suddenly aware that my inattention had nearly cost us both our lives, I let go of her hand.

I could not allow myself to love her, to care more than I already did. It had already affected how well I protected her. Remembering how easily we were caught unawares, I felt a deep sense of shame. When it came to the fight, I needed to be cold and calculating, not thinking about a pair of exotic green eyes or lusting after a well-rounded rear end.

She murmured something, too low to hear.

"What?"

Her cheeks darkened further. I had a feeling it was due to the presence of fellow magic users, rather than any embarrassment over telling me. She looked like a student ashamed at being caught out by a teacher.

"I went faring forth to find help."

"Faring forth?" Angie did not explain, so I looked to the High Priestess.

Rhiannon raised an eyebrow. "It means she sent her spirit out of her body. It left the both of you unprotected. It was a foolish thing to do, leaving your body on the side of the road where anyone could have come along. You could have been killed."

"Davis was dying!" Angie said, the blush suddenly gone. Her eyes snapped green fire.

"He is expendable. You are not." This didn't really come as a surprise to me, but it still stung.

"Not to me!"

"Perhaps not to you or me, but most definitely in the eyes of your grove. Young woman, do not make the mistakes that others have made. With your bloodline, you have the potential to be a most powerful druid," Rhiannon said. Then, in a softer tone, she added: "This world needs you."

"And I need Davis." Angie met Rhiannon's eyes unwaveringly. There were long moments of silence, until the coven leader looked away with a sigh.

"What's done is done," she said, with a wave of her hand. "I cannot say I agree with your grove's method of raising its druids. You are all too precious to risk for foolish reasons."

"That makes two of us," I said, running my fingers through my hair to brush it out of my face. I needed a haircut.

"It makes us strong and our warriors loyal." Once again, she seemed to be quoting from the druid handbook.

"It makes you dead, loyal warriors along with you. Neither of which is good for anything."

Angie swallowed hard and looked down. I met Rhiannon's eyes and gave her an ironic smile. She was smart and tough, and I liked her no-nonsense attitude.

"We'll try not to do any other stupid things while we're here," I said. "I'd hate to put you out further."

She smiled back at me, grey eyes dancing. "You're both welcome to stay as long as you like."

"In fact," Brennan said, "Midsummer is coming. We would be pleased to have you both stay and celebrate with us."

Recovering from her shame, Angie seemed pleased by the invitation. "Thank you," she said. "We would be honored."

I didn't know what a Midsummer festival with witches might involve, as my family's celebrations of the High Holy Days had tended to be quiet affairs. We were certain to find out, however, because I didn't think I was going to be ready for travel for a while. I would have to baby my arm for several days, maybe weeks. The thought made me uneasy, but these people had proven themselves trustworthy. They had treated my wound, and had kept Angie safe when I couldn't. I figured that was worth some trust on my part.

I discovered that it was lunch I had eaten, when Angie laced her fingers with mine and led me outside into the early afternoon sun. As had become usual that summer, it was already hot. I didn't mind, though. I turned my face to the sun, letting its light and heat soak into my skin. I breathed deeply of the warm air laden with the scent of ripened fruit, green growing things, and rich earth. I didn't know where we were going, but it didn't matter. I needed to get out and stretch my legs. I followed her through the orchard and into a barn. The darkness was cool silk on my skin after the heat of the sun.

"Hey," I said. "You brought the horses!"

"We had to tie you on Steel to get you here."

"Steel?"

"That's what you named your horse."

"I did?"

"It was after… after you fell off."

Leave it to me to find a name for a horse after falling off it. The stallion left off his feed and came to the door, poking his head over it. I considered his shining grey coat and decided that I had picked a good name, no matter how impaired I had been at the time.

"How long have we been here?" I asked.

"Three days." Her eyes were haunted. "They found us the night after you were—" Her voice broke on the last.

I put a hand on her arm. "It's okay. I'm okay."

"Oh, Davis, I was so scared." She took my hand from her arm and held it to her cheek. I just stood there, emotions warring within me. "I thought I'd lost you," she finished in a whisper. I could feel a tear slip over my finger. I pulled her close and put my good arm around her, telling myself it was only to make her feel better. Angie laid her head on my shoulder and slipped her arms about my waist. She had bottled up all the fear and worry

192

for the three days I had been sleeping. Now that I was awake, she could finally relax and let it all out.

I just held her while she cried; if my mother had taught me nothing else, she had at least hammered into my head that sometimes all a woman needed was to have a good cry. She grew quiet after a few minutes, but never moved away. "I wish we could stay here forever," she whispered into my chest. She spoke so quietly that I thought maybe she hadn't intended for me to hear.

I stepped back and broke the embrace, then gently wiped the tears from her cheeks. "I will be with you, no matter where you go," I said softly. She nodded and tried to compose herself. I changed the subject.

"How long has it been since they've been out?" I asked.

"They've been stabled since we arrived," she said.

"Is there anywhere we can turn them out?"

"There's a corral."

"All right, then." I found a halter and lead, opened the stall door, and slipped it over the stallion's head. Angie opened the mare's door and let her out. Steel's ears perked up, and he eagerly followed me to the nearby corral. I opened the gate, unsnapped the lead rope, and he trotted outside, snorting happily.

Someone had taken good care of him. He looked rested and his muscles rippled like liquid metal beneath his coat. The palomino danced after him, her coat glimmering gold under the shining light of the sun. She nipped at him, and he wheeled about to chase her. She trotted away, with her head turned as though watching him, waving her tail like a white flag.

I chuckled, sitting on a hay bale and leaning back against the corral fence. Even after such a short time on my feet, I was weary. Angie seated herself beside me and we sat together without speaking, watching the horses play. When they had settled down and had begun to graze, I broke the silence.

"Everyone here seems nice."

"They've been wonderful," Angie said. "Especially Maeve. She's the one who healed you."

"I don't think I could have done it, even if I had the gift of healing," she admitted. "After faring forth, I was too drained to do anything else. I was as weak as a kitten for two days. All I could do was sit at your bedside and pray."

I didn't like the way that sounded. "Is that why the High Priestess was angry with you?"

"Yes." She looked down at her boots. "She said I over-extended myself, and that I could have been lost on the astral plane forever." Her admission sent a chill down my spine.

"What would happen then?"

"Without its spirit, the body dies."

"And the High Priestess brought you back?"

"Yes."

I thought about it for a moment or two.

"I guess we were both lucky," I said. "But Angie... the High Priestess is right. You shouldn't have done that. Don't risk your life for me again."

"Davis, you were dying!" she protested. "I had to sit there and watch you try to ride your horse while you passed in and out of consciousness! You spent half the time slumped over Steel's neck and you were bleeding so badly! I couldn't make you stop, you were so determined to–" She broke off, biting her lip and fighting tears. "I had to watch you die a drop at a time, and couldn't do a thing about it!"

It sounded heroic the way she described it, but I didn't think I'd care to give a repeat performance.

"It's what I swore to do," I told her quietly. "Your life will always come before mine."

"It's not right," she said between clenched teeth.

"It's the way it is."

"Then I don't know if I can do this."

I put my arm around her again. It was understandable that her faith in her mission had been shaken, but she had to get over her fear and face reality one way or another. She either needed to quit, or be committed to returning to the druid grove. I was not so great a fool as to accompany her back on the road if she was lukewarm about the whole thing. That would only get us both killed.

"It's very simple, Angie. Either it's important to return to the grove and carry out your mission to become a full druid, or it's not." I stifled that newborn part of me that had discovered some very raw emotions where she was concerned, not wanting to influence her decision.

"I want to be a druid, but I don't want you to get hurt."

She sounded like a pouty child.

"We've both seen how likely that is. I don't run from fights."

"I think you like fighting," she said sulkily.

"Sometimes it can't be avoided."

"I don't know what to do," she said, eyes closed in pained distress.

"That's okay," I said. "We have some time before you have to decide."

I wanted to kiss her, but I settled for patting her on the shoulder. Seeking some distance, I wandered into the barn to look for a brush and comb for Steel. He didn't need to be brushed, but I felt like brushing him. It was something to do so that Angie could have some space to think, but still close enough that I could keep an eye on her.

"Can I help you?"

It was then that I noticed a young man up in the hayloft, peering down at me. "Do you have a horse brush?" I asked.

He smiled. "Of course!" he said, setting aside the pitchfork and sliding down the ladder with practiced ease. He was about my height, but more slenderly built, with deep blue eyes and dark red hair. It was difficult to tell his age; he could have been as young as sixteen, but was perhaps older with a young-looking complexion.

"You must be Davis."

"Guilty as charged."

"That stallion is a fine animal," he said.

"You've been caring for him?"

"It's been a pleasure. They are both very well-behaved. Easy to groom, willing to pick up their feet, even stand cross-tied." I suppose even pagan-haters liked to have well-trained horses. Those folks from Searcy were probably rolling in their graves.

"Here are your grooming supplies," he said, gesturing to a

195

couple of small wooden boxes hanging from the stall walls. I hadn't noticed them earlier. "Angie told us you had your own, so I took the liberty of borrowing them."

"Thanks for looking after them," I said. "Is there any way I could repay you?"

"No payment is necessary," he replied. "However, I do have a mare or two coming into season, if you wouldn't mind him standing stud?"

"Not at all," I said. One of us might as well have some fun.

"My name is Ruadh, but everyone calls me Ahearn," he said, holding out his hand.

I took his hand, noting the calluses and firm grip as we shook. "Why is that?"

"Ruadh is the name my mother gave me, but Ahearn means 'master of the horse'."

"I never use the name my mother gave me, either" I said. "So everyone is stuck with calling me Davis." We shared a grin, instantly bonding over having mothers who had given us names we didn't like. I collected the brushes and took them out to Steel; Ahearn followed with Magic's supplies. I could feel Angie's eyes on me as I walked out to the horses. I gave her a quick glance, scanning the surrounding area out of habit. As my father often said, a habit can either save your life or get you killed. Mine had saved me on many occasions.

I whistled and Steel's head came up; he trotted over to me, snuffling at my pockets. Ahearn nudged me and handed me an apple. I cut it up and gave it to the horse, who munched happily while I combed his long forelock. Then he rubbed his face against my chest, getting it all messed up again. I laughed and shoved his head away. He snorted and nosed at the pile of hay in the center of the corral before settling down to eat. Ahearn began grooming Magic, speaking to her in a language I'd never heard before.

"It's Gaelic," he explained with a quick smile. "My mother says it's the language of witches and horses. I hear you and Angie are staying for the Solstice."

"That's the plan." I wiggled my arm in its sling.

"Bum luck," he said, closing his fist except for his index and pinky fingers, with the thumb holding down the others. I recognized it as sign to ward away evil. Grandmother had used it frequently; I had also seen Angie make it, usually right before things got hairy and the bullets started flying.

"Is she really a druid?" he whispered, taking a quick peek at her around Magic's shoulder.

"Yes, she is."

"Wow." He took another quick glance. "Wow."

I raised an eyebrow. "First time you've met a druid?"

"No, of course not." He ran the brush over Magic's back with long, firm strokes. "It's just that she's... really something." He glanced at me, then, as though concerned that I might take offense.

"Speak your mind, Ahearn. I don't bite."

"She's beautiful," he admitted quietly. "You are *so* lucky."

I wasn't feeling so lucky, at the moment. I was bruised, beaten, sore, and wounded; I also was depending on the charity of others, which was somewhat hurtful to my male pride. In addition, I was trying to get used to the idea that I would be forced to continue our platonic relationship when I wanted something more. Of course, if she changed her mind about wanting to be a powerful druid who traveled around healing the world, I might start feeling considerably more blessed.

I grunted. "It's not as glamorous as it looks."

"Oh, don't get me wrong," he said. "Everyone knows how difficult it is to be warrior to a druid. But I bet sharing the bed of a gorgeous woman puts everything back in balance."

I blinked.

Seeing my expression, he backtracked. "Forgive me, Davis. I forget not everyone discusses things as openly as we do."

"No offense taken," I said. "But it's not like that. Between Angie and me, I mean."

He looked at me with an unbelieving expression. "You've got to be kidding me."

I wish I was. I managed to bite back the words before they escaped my lips.

"Would you mind if I..." he trailed off. "What I mean to say is, Solstice will be here soon, and we celebrate with food, and

197

dancing, and fire... and other things. And if you two aren't 'together' in that way, I feel that just about every man in the coven will be interested in... Well, in seeing if *she* is interested."

I got his meaning loud and clear. It was plain as day that he himself was "interested." Well, who wouldn't be? He was right; she was stunning.

I couldn't afford to think of her in that way anymore. It was better to think of her as the druid who needed me only for protection – and the sooner, the better. I could never again allow myself to become so engrossed that an enemy could sneak up on us again.

"So... People are going to wonder if you mind."

I kept my face carefully neutral. "Angie is her own person," I said. "She's free to do as she pleases."

"You *do* mind." Ahearn laughed. "I suppose that's just as well. She's quite dedicated to you."

I didn't answer, just kept brushing Steel's coat.

"I heard she risked her life to save yours," he continued. "I didn't think female druids were supposed to risk themselves like that."

"They're not," I said shortly, then added in a growl: "If she does it again, I'm going to kill her."

He laughed.

"I like you, Davis."

* * *

At the end of the day, I was going through my pack and taking stock of its contents when Angie came to the door. It felt very strange to be alone after so many weeks in the company of another. Part of me relished the quiet. The rest was wishing for Angie's company, and that was a bad thing. I needed some space, as well as some time to alter my thinking back to the way it was before. I had ended up nearly dying because I had been paying more attention to the way Angie's hips swayed in the saddle, instead of the world around me. If I had died, she would have been horribly abused and possibly killed, and I simply could not let that happen.

She stopped and looked at me, frowning.

"What are you doing?"

"Just taking stock."

"Oh. You're not thinking of leaving, are you?"

"No."

"So why are you doing that now?" She closed the door behind her.

"Something to do. I have only one arm to work with, and I'm bored."

When she sat on the pallet beside me, my awareness of her closeness spiked. We had camped alone for weeks on end, but this was different. Everything about her, the soft brush of her skirt, the timbre of her voice, one dark curl against her cheek, the fullness of her lips, and the soft glow of her green eyes all hit me with a special kind of intensity. We were alone, in a room, with the door closed. It sorely tested my new resolve.

"What's everyone else doing?" I asked, pulling out the items in the side pockets of my pack. I had already unpacked, reorganized, and repacked them before Angie had come in. She didn't know that, though, and it gave me an excuse to do something with my hands while she was here.

"Gone to bed."

Something in my chest tightened. "You're not tired?"

"No."

Sigh. I was going to have to kick her out. Or...

"Would you help me with something?"

Her eyes glowed in the candlelight. "Not at all."

I rubbed my shoulder, pretending it was hurting. It wasn't much of a pretense. "Do you think you could make some tea to help me sleep?"

Her face fell somewhat, but she recovered quickly. I stuffed things into pockets, pretending not to notice. This was not good. We had only shared a few kisses, but it was clear that wasn't all she wanted. I felt the same, and hated that I might cause Angie pain by refusing her. I told myself that it was for the best, and that it was better for her to have hurt feelings than physical pain and mental anguish.

"Of course," she responded. "I'd be happy to."

I breathed a sigh of relief when she left.

Moments later, Rhiannon walked in the door. My quick glance at her was followed by a double take. She was a fine-looking woman. It might have been my imagination, but it seemed that she had brushed her hair and painted her lips. She wore a flowing gown that clung to her breasts and flowed about her legs. I quickly looked away, not wanting to seem disrespectful.

"Are you well, Davis?"

"Quite," I said, randomly stuffing more things into pockets. I would have to repack the whole thing before we left, so I would know where everything was. "Thank you for asking."

"Is there anything I can provide that would make you more comfortable?"

Grey eyes turned blue in the darkness gazed down at me. I wasn't sure how to read her expression, but I made sure to keep my eyes on her face only.

"I'm fine, really."

From behind her came Angie's voice, with a decidedly acid tone to it. "I'm sure I can meet all of my warrior's needs, High Priestess." She slipped into the room with my cup of tea.

"Thank you," I said. Then to Rhiannon: "Angie made me something to help me sleep."

"Of course," she said demurely. "That's very fine of her."

There was an uncomfortable silence, during which Angie's eyes attempted to burn holes in Rhiannon's skull, the High Priestess ignoring her all the while.

"Very well," she said. "I'm sure you're tired. If there is anything at all you desire, you have but to ask."

"I appreciate it," I answered. "Thank you."

She left without closing the door. Angie stood there staring out the doorway with her lips compressed.

"Ang?" She startled, as though she had forgotten I was there. Seeming to remember why she was in my room in the first place, she knelt and handed me my tea. I immediately took a sip, suppressing a shudder at its awful taste. The witches must have the same recipe as Grandmother. Blech. There was something wrong with me, that I would choose to drink this dreadful concoction rather than explore just what sort of feelings my druid might have been having.

"There seems to be some tension between you and the High Priestess," I said, careful to keep my voice neutral.

"She talks to me like she's my mother." She rose, staring again at the door with her arms folded over her chest. "I don't like it, and I certainly don't appreciate her interfering just now."

I finished the tea in two huge gulps, wishing for some dirt to wash the taste from my mouth. Recognizing that I had yet another problem before me, I was going to have to handle this very carefully. Angie may have been my age, but lacked my experience with the ways of the world. It was possible that she would let her feelings overcome her good sense and erode our welcome status with the coven.

"Seems to me she's looking out for our well-being."

She said nothing.

"Sit here," I said, patting the pallet beside me. She hesitated a moment, then complied.

"As much as I hate to admit it, we need them right now."

"We're fine alone, just me and you," she said, jumping to her feet. "We don't need anyone else."

I gently took her fingers in my hand, caressed them with my thumb. She swallowed and looked down at her feet. Something in this coven disturbed her, and I didn't think it was being yelled at like a kid.

"Angie, look at me..." Her eyes met mine, glanced away, and flickered back. I pulled her back down on the pallet beside me. "I cannot use my arm. I can't even ride. It would be agony to fire the shotgun. My balance is off for using the machete. With my arm in a sling, I can't defend either of us. Do you understand what I'm saying?"

"Yes," she whispered, looking down.

"I need to stay here. I need time to heal." I paused, touching her cheek. "Do you know how it would tear me up to know that bandits were coming, and be powerless to protect you?"

A slow tear trickled down her cheek. I hated doing it, but offending the High Priestess of a coven of witches was a much worse alternative. I didn't think that she would ever turn her magic to evil, but Angie's anger toward someone who had shown such generosity was unacceptable.

"I need to be in a place where I know you'll be protected, until I'm well enough to do the job."

More tears flowed over the contours of her face. They dripped from her chin, and I tenderly wiped them away. I kept my voice to a whisper, the whole world down to just us two. She was hurting and I felt guilty for causing it, but I had little choice. Contrary to what my druid had claimed, we were not fine on our own just then, and we did need other people. Maybe that was a part of her fear, that other people would be admitted to our little world.

Little did I realize it was more.

Much, much more.

Chapter 16 – The Coven

Rules of Gunfighting #15:
Use cover or concealment as much as possible.

I joined Ahearn in the stable several days later. I liked the red-haired witch. He was good with horses and a hard worker, as well as being intelligent and quick witted. The whole time I spent at the coven, I never once saw him use a halter, whip, or even a lead rope. He controlled the horses through voice and hands – and by whistling. All the horses were trained to obey different whistle patterns. I picked up a few of them, like the one that called them to me and the one that said they should follow. I never saw one of his horses balk at a command. I suspected that his magic augmented his skill.

It was warm in the barn and we worked shirtless. It hadn't rained in weeks; the summer was the hottest I could remember and the drought showed no signs of abating. Before long, we were both dripping with sweat. It was unbelievable how good I felt, after losing so much blood only a week before. If nothing else made me believe in the witches' magic, that did.

I should have been flat on my back for weeks after an injury like that, yet here I was, acting as if I'd suffered nothing more than a sprained arm. True, I couldn't toss hay bales or muck stalls, but I could brush and feed horses and clean tack. I even gave Steel a bath, after which he promptly rolled in the dirt.

Ahearn laughed himself silly over it, almost falling out of the hayloft.

I glared up at him. "If I didn't know better, I'd think you told him to do that, O Master of the Horse."

"Maybe I did," he teased, sliding down the ladder. "Want to go riding?"

"Hmm..." I worked my shoulder, testing out my pain threshold. The sling was gone, but it was still bandaged and sore. Angie had warned me sternly not to use it until Maeve said I could. I probably shouldn't have laid a hand on the pitchfork, but it felt good to be doing something.

"I'm not sure if that's a good idea."

"She worries about you, eh?" he said, nodding his head in Angie's direction. I glanced over to where she was sitting on the corral fence feeding carrots to Magic.

"She'd probably break both my legs for even thinking about getting on a horse."

His blue eyes sparkled with mischief. "We could sneak away tomorrow, while the girls are all busy working on their dresses for the Solstice."

I couldn't help smiling at the thought. "We'll see."

"It'll be good exercise," he said. "There's nothing wrong with your legs, is there?"

"Not yet." I gave Angie another quick look. Ahearn laughed. Finished with the barn work, we turned the rest of the horses out into the pasture adjacent to the corral.

"Come on, old man," I said to Steel. Might as well brush the dirt off him and get the hay out of his mane. I didn't want anyone to think I neglected my mount. Steel didn't want to be brushed, however. He wanted to play. I started to wipe some of the dust off with a rag, and he grabbed it in his teeth and trotted away with a whinny.

Oh, for all that was green and good! I walked over and tried to grab the end of it, but he danced away. It made me laugh, so I joined his game and chased him around the corral. It was a lot like playing with a dog. I lunged for the rag, missed, and gave his tail a gentle yank instead. He whinnied and cantered across the corral. Then he ran right for me, stopping just short of running me down. I held still, knowing he wouldn't run over me.

He slid to a stop, kicking up a cloud of dust. Dangling the rag in front of me, he snorted and shook his entire body. Dust and hay flew everywhere, coating my skin and making me sneeze. I cursed him good-naturedly, patted his shoulder, and walked to the water trough. I could hear his hooves thudding on the dusty ground as he followed me.

When I bent to duck my head in the water, he butted me with his head, sending me head over heels into the trough with a loud splash. Coming up, I heard Ahearn's roar of laughter and the thump as he fell off the fence. I jumped to my feet, straddled the trough, and splashed water at Steel. He squealed and reared, backing up a stride or two before bucking and kicking up his heels.

"You got another bath anyway, how do you like that?" I said. Laughter from beyond the corral informed me that we had an audience. Leaning on the fence beside Angie were three young women, all smiling and laughing. I also noticed that Angie was *not* laughing. I knew what was wrong with her, but I couldn't fix it. For the past few days, she had tried to rekindle that spark between us, not knowing that I had decided to let it die.

I wasn't any happier than she was, but I hadn't had a chance to discuss it with her. We were hardly ever alone, because even when I was in my room, the witches were always dropping by to say hello. It was starting to get to her, I could tell. At first, she had been grateful and pleasant to everyone; now she was moody and taciturn. It wasn't like her at all.

I did my best to ignore her – and the girls – and whistled up my stallion. I opened the corral and led him to the pasture. Steel trotted after me, still carrying the rag in his mouth. When I opened the gate, he started through and stopped. He turned his head toward me and dropped the rag on my shoulder, then rubbed his nose on my chest, spreading lots of gooey horse slobber there.

"Nice," I said. "Go on. Have fun with the ladies."

He leapt forward with a whinny, powerful haunches churning as he built up speed. He was beautiful to watch, and I wasn't at all sorry that a whole bunch of intolerant sons of bitches had died to make him mine.

Ahearn walked up, wiping tears from his eyes.

"Amazing. Where did you get him, anyway?"

"Long story," I said. "Remind me to tell it to you when we go riding."

He closed the pasture gate, and we walked back to the corral.

"I need a bath," I said.

He eyed me skeptically. "In the middle of the day?"

"A certain someone is going to tell me how bad I stink," I said. "Just you wait."

"Women." Ahearn shook his head. "I suppose the hay and dirt are bound to make you itch, anyway. Here," he said when we had arrived at the barn. He handed me a clean bucket. "Get some water out of the rain barrel and rinse off."

I took his advice, dipped the bucket in the barrel, and drew it out carefully. I poured it over my head, feeling the wonderfully cool fingers of water running over my shoulders, chest, and back. I shook my head, sending water spraying in all directions, then ran my fingers through my hair to get it out of my face. It was getting long and shaggy; soon it'd be in my eyes. I usually had my mother clip it short when I was home, but had forgotten on the last visit. We'd been too busy yelling at each other. Since then, Angie and I had been too busy trying to stay alive. It's hard to remember things like haircuts when you're dodging bullets, blades, and angry parents.

The noon bell rang for lunch, a metal triangle, pounded with delightful ferocity by a small girl.

"I'm too dirty to go in, and you're too wet," said Ahearn. "Want to eat here?"

"Sure." In the heat of the afternoon, the barn was one of the coolest places in Ward. It was also a great place for an afternoon nap. After he had gone, I glanced at the fence where Angie had been perched, but she was gone. The alarm that I always felt when she was out of sight clenched my heart. I made myself breathe evenly and calm down. She had probably gone in to lunch.

The three girls still lingered by the fence, smiling. One gestured for me to come over. At least I assumed it was me, as no one else was in the barn. As I moved closer, I noted that they all wore identical expressions – a blend of curiosity, mischief, and fun. They were all very different in appearance: a redhead with pale skin, a blonde with a rich tan, and an ebony-skinned girl with her hair in cornrows.

"I'm Rowena," said the redhead.

"Bébhinn," said the blonde.

"And I am Ianna," said the dark one. "You must be Davis."

"Nice to meet you." I smiled at each of them. "I'd shake hands, but I don't want to get you dirty."

Bébhinn looked me up and down in a most provocative manner. "Oh, we don't mind getting a little dirty."

"Mm-mmm," said Rowena, sharing a look with Ianna, who said, "Girl, you know it."

I wondered how I had walked into this particular mess. These girls couldn't have been more than sixteen or seventeen, and they possessing all the subtlety of trio of tornados. I decided to change the subject.

"So are you all looking forward to the Solstice?"

"We've been waiting months," said Ianna. "Some of us took a little longer than others to develop."

"Hey," pouted Rowena. "It's not my fault I was late being Goddess-blessed."

"Of course not," purred Bébhinn. "We're just glad we'll be able to be together at Solstice."

"Are you planning something special?" I asked. It was an innocent enough question, or so I thought.

"Just experiencing the pleasures of the flesh," said Bébhinn with a wink.

"On the same night," said Rowena.

"With the same man," finished Ianna.

I knew that someday my insatiable curiosity about people and the world was going to get me in trouble. Today was that day.

"Really," I said. "Good luck with that." I just about tripped over myself in my haste to retreat to the sanctuary of the barn. Their hysterical laughter followed me. I glanced back at them once, over my shoulder, to see them pointing and giggling. I felt a sense of immediate relief when I was back in the barn and out of their sight. Ahearn came in from the front with two plates loaded with food. I took one from him, straddled a hay bale, and started eating.

"I see you've met the Weird Sisters."

I stopped with my fork halfway to my mouth. The only Weird Sisters I knew of were from an archaic text by a man named Shakespeare.

"What?"

"They're not really sisters," Ahearn said. "But they were all born on the same day, and rumor has it that the same man fathered all three."

"Busy guy," I muttered, taking my first bite. The randiness of the father seemed to have been passed to the daughters. Maybe all the women here were like that, and the older women were just more reserved. The thought gave me pause, remembering when Rhiannon had come to my room. I brushed aside the thought. There was no way the lovely High Priestess would be interested in me, when she could have any man in the coven.

"They've been inseparable since they learned to walk," he continued. "They even had a secret language of baby babble, and didn't learn to speak real words until they were three or four."

"That explains a lot."

He raised an eyebrow. "Oh, they told you, did they?"

"Yes, after looking me over like a prize bull."

He chuckled. "What I wouldn't give…"

I snorted. "Seems like a lot of work."

"Oh, but this would be the best kind of work."

"There's bound to be some jealousy." After all, how would a man decide which one would get to be first? Wouldn't that offend the other two? I couldn't believe I was even wondering about this stuff.

"Oh, we don't get jealous." He shrugged and shook his head.

"With a bunch of women living in close quarters, I'd have thought it would be inevitable."

"They all say that just because you don't have a certain man tonight, doesn't mean you won't have him tomorrow night."

"And just how do the men feel about this?"

208

"We are woefully outnumbered," he said with a grin. "There are more of them than us."

"Sounds like their chances of sharing a man for the night are pretty good, then."

He laughed. "Pretty good? I bet every man in Ward would give his right arm to share that night."

I wasn't sure that wooing three virgins sounded like much fun. But then again, those three didn't seem like they would need much wooing. More like they'd need restraints.

Seeing my expression, Ahearn said, "Oh, come on, Davis. That doesn't sound like a great night to you?"

"It's not exactly my cup of tea," I said.

"Oh. Sorry, I didn't realize."

"Realize?"

"It's okay if you like men. We're pretty open with that sort of thing, here. After all, the Weird Sisters may be virgin to men, but Lord and Lady know they aren't virgins to each other."

"Okay, whoa, whoa, *whoa*," I said, holding up a hand. "I don't like men. I like women just fine. I'm just not ready to settle down and have a family right now."

"Oh, they won't care if you go or stay. They'd be thrilled if you made them pregnant, though."

"They're kind of young, don't you think?"

He shrugged. "We raise the children together. I mean, they sleep with their mothers, but all the fathers share in the parenting." He elbowed me. "We kind of have to, man. I mean, you never know, it might actually be your own kid you're carrying on your shoulders."

I didn't know what to think about that. I tried to imagine having ten or twelve men standing around looking stern and yelling at me when I did something stupid. It made me grateful that I only had one father.

"So, you don't know who your father is?"

He shrugged. "I'm pretty sure it's Brennan, because Mother often says I favor him."

This was strange beyond anything I had experienced. Then again, all the settlements north of Jonesboro were alike... or seemed to be.

209

"Are all covens like this?"

"I haven't met many people from other covens, but I don't think so. Most others seem to live fairly monogamous lives, marrying and raising children in households. I don't know why we do it this way. It's all I've ever known, so I never thought to ask."

When we had finished eating, we returned the plates to a wide bucket on the front porch of the house. A slender young woman, a little older than Angie, came out to collect the bucket. She was curvaceous, with dusky skin, round apple cheeks, and a slender waist. Her dark eyes met mine, and she tucked a lock of thick, black hair behind her ear.

"Blessings, Maeve," said Ahearn.

I looked at her with new interest. "You're Maeve."

"So I am." Her full lips pursed with amusement. She stopped and struck a pose with her hip cocked and the bucket resting on her hip.

"I haven't had a chance to thank you for healing me yet."

"I don't mind, Davis," she said. "And, you can thank me as you please." She tipped a wink at Ahearn, and went back inside. I stood there with my jaw hanging open. Ahearn reached over and shut it for me.

"That's four," he said. "Seems the ladies are quite taken with you, my friend." He slapped me on the shoulder. "Just try to save some for the rest of us, eh?"

*　*　*

At supper that night, preparations for the Midsummer festival – that I knew as the High Day of Litha – were discussed around the table. Like the women of Jonesboro when preparing for a holiday, the witches mostly discussed what dishes they would prepare, what they would wear, or how they would do their hair. Unlike Jonesboro, they also discussed the pairings they hoped for during the week prior to the festival with disconcerting frankness, and the night of the feast itself in particular. The men smiled good-naturedly as the women and girls teased them mercilessly. I buried my attention in my food, and tried to tune it all out.

I noticed Angie did not. She barely touched her food.

"Why aren't you eating?" I asked.

"I'm not hungry."

It made me concerned... and a little guilty. I'd seen my druid eat like a starving wolf after watching me blow away the Searcy ambushers with my shotgun. I'd seen her devour food like there was no tomorrow after I had rather messily slit the throat of a bandit who had snuck up on our campsite. I had seen her ask for seconds after watching me take down some tough guy with a shotgun blast to the chest.

But here, in this safe place, surrounded by people we could trust, who had helped us and taken us in without question, sharing what they had without expecting anything in return, and she wasn't hungry. I didn't have to wonder what was wrong with her. My continued rebuffs at her attempts to be close to me were taking their toll. I felt like a cad, but I was resolved to keep my distance, at least emotionally. I couldn't afford to make another disastrous slip. I comforted myself with the thought that at least it had been only a few kisses.

It wasn't much consolation.

"How are you feeling, Davis?" asked the High Priestess, derailing my train of thought. She was sitting at the head of the table, so I had to crane my neck forward to see her.

"Much better than I expected," I said. "I can't believe how fast I've healed."

"Maeve?" she turned her head. "Have you checked his shoulder lately?"

"I haven't, Priestess," I heard Maeve reply. "I will be sure to after dinner."

"I'm finished," I said, carrying my dishes to the sink and washing them. "I'm ready anytime you are."

"Very well, then," she said with the barest of smiles. She rose gracefully from the table, took an oil lamp, and stood waiting for me. Something made me stop and look at Angie. Her eyes were a glittering green.

"I think here will be fine, Davis, don't you?" Angie said tersely.

It wasn't a question, not really.

"I'd rather not take off my shirt at the dinner table." I turned and started to lead Maeve to my room, but not before I heard her mutter:

"It didn't seem to bother you in the barnyard."

I started to turn and respond, but Maeve had her hand on my back, and she applied light pressure to indicate that I should go on. I wasn't about to argue with a healer, much less a witch, so I walked through the doorway to my cubicle. I sat on my sleeping pallet, as there was nowhere else to sit. Maeve closed the door behind her.

"Do you mind?" she asked, indicating the pallet.

"Please do." I gestured that she should sit. She sank to her knees just as gracefully as she had risen from the table, gave a gentle toss of her head to swing her long hair back over her shoulder, then set the lamp on a small table, and turned up the flame. I stripped off my shirt and she bent forward to examine the wound.

"Ahh," she said, sounding pleased. She probed my shoulder with gentle fingertips, asking occasionally if this hurt, or that.

"So how bad was it when they brought me in?" I had asked Angie, but she had refused to answer.

"You'd lost blood, but not a critical amount," Maeve said. "I removed the bullet and cleaned the wound, then applied pressure until the bleeding stopped. After that, all it needed was some healing herbs and bandage to keep out any infection." She raised my arm up over my head, then had me perform active range of motion, starting with lifting it forward, then to the side, and then to the back. It was a little stiff, but it only hurt when I moved the arm backwards, or in large circles.

"I don't usually sleep for three days," I said. "How did you manage that?"

"Magic," she said with a wink. "Even so, you're a hard man to keep down."

I grinned. "So I'm told."

"The wound has healed nicely. Be sure to build your strength back slowly, carrying light objects before you start tossing hay bales with Ahearn. You should be right as rain by

Solstice." She paused. "Your shoulders seem tense. Would you mind if I worked them a little?"

"Not at all," I said. Hey, she was the healer. If she thought my muscles were too tense, then they probably were. She brought out a small vial, poured out a viscous liquid, and warmed it between her hands. She bade me turn around, and when I complied, knelt behind me, and slid her hands across my shoulders. Her hands massaged my neck and shoulders for long minutes, strong fingers sliding over my skin.

"This would be especially helpful at the end of the day, if you had to use your firearm," Maeve murmured, her breath warm on my neck. "It seems to me that the recoil would made your muscles tight."

"It does," I agreed. At that point, I think I might have agreed to anything just to keep her massaging my shoulders. I felt all the stress of the last few weeks falling away, as well as my worries about Angie. Maybe it was true that people carried their worries like a burden on their shoulders.

"Lie on your stomach, Davis."

I complied with her request, flopping down full length on my pallet. Her hands worked magic on my back, running the length of it, working alongside the spine. I yawned. It was warm, my belly was full, and I still tired easily. Her hands traveled further to my lower back, massaging there. Ahh, bliss.

"I've treated pistol shots before," Maeve said thoughtfully. "This wasn't at point blank range."

"No." I blinked slowly, mesmerized by the dancing shadows cast by the flame in the oil lamp. My eyes were growing heavy, as every muscle in my body began to loosen up and uncoil. I had trouble focusing on her words, because her hands were volcanic.

"Davis?"

"Mm-hmm?"

"I'd like to hear that story, how you were injured?"

"Eh… He tried to kill me and I killed him first." I yawned hugely again. "Thanks, Maeve," I mumbled. "That was great. I'll sleep like a baby tonight."

Her hands froze in place a moment, and then withdrew.

"You're welcome. Sleep well, Davis."

213

"You too," I mumbled, drifting off to sleep.

Chapter 17 – Manipulated

Rules of Gunfighting #4:
Only hits count.
The only thing worse than a miss is a slow miss.

True to his word, Ahearn was ready and raring to go riding as soon as the women were holed up in the hall to work on their outfits for Litha. There were four horses in the corral plus Steel. He looked frisky and energetic after his night with the mares. I patted his shoulder and stroked his muscular neck.

"I heard Maeve gave you a massage last night," Ahearn said with a sly smile.

"Lord and Lady," sighed the blond boy beside him. "Her massages are the best."

"This is Weylin," Ahearn said. He gestured to the other two, who appeared to be identical twins. "Riordan and Tiernan. Don't bother trying to tell them apart, they spend all day being each other anyway."

"It drives us crazy." Weylin rolled his eyes, and the twins merely grinned.

"So, how did you like your massage, Davis?" Ahearn asked, swinging aboard his white mare bareback. The others did likewise. I trusted Steel not to dump me, so I mounted him bareback as well. He snorted and danced in a circle, ready to run.

"It was great," I replied. "Really relaxing. It put me right to sleep."

The four boys stared at me in stunned silence for a moment. When they burst out laughing, I thought they were going to fall off their horses. Was it something I said?

"Oh, man," said Ahearn, wiping tears from his eyes. "No wonder Maeve was so cranky this morning."

"I thought she was going to hit me with a wooden spoon for stealing biscuits," chuckled Weylin.

"Why would she be upset?" I asked.

"Probably because you feel asleep on her."

"More like because you didn't fall asleep on her," said Weylin, which set them all to howling with laughter again.

I felt like an idiot. Angie must have known what Maeve was about. Obviously, Rhiannon had as well, since she had assisted in setting the whole thing up. My druid's comments from the day before started to make sense; that had been jealousy glittering in her green eyes. I had been trying to be sensitive to her feelings, while keeping her at arm's length, but instead had managed the exact opposite.

"What's the deal? Are you holding out for someone special, Davis?"

"Not… not really."

"You've gotta be kidding me," said Weylin. "Nobody has caught your eye?"

I remembered Rhiannon, the first night she had come to my room. That had definitely caught my eye, and I said so, only not in such explicit terms.

Weylin nodded knowingly. "That figures. High Priestess gets first pick."

Ahearn agreed. "True. Mom does take advantage of that particular perk of the job."

Mom? Oh, dear gods.

"The High Priestess is your mother?"

"Yup." He ruffled his red hair as if to emphasize the relationship.

"I'm sorry. I hope I didn't offend you."

"Not at all. Why would it?"

"Yeah," put in Weylin. "You're not a baby at the tit

216

anymore, you can share them."

Ahearn laughed and punched him in the arm.

"I just can't believe no one minds the attention I'm getting," I said at last, turning to look at the others.

"Hey," said Ahearn. "Somebody will have to comfort all the sad ladies mourning your departure."

"Yep," agreed Weylin. "Just because she's not with me tonight, doesn't mean she won't be with me tomorrow night." He and Ahearn reached across the space between their horses and bumped knuckles.

I followed them, riding easily, lost in thought. They never seemed to notice, joking amongst themselves as we rode. I decided that maybe I needed to talk to the High Priestess. She seemed worldly and wise, and perhaps could give me some advice on handling my druid.

* * *

After our little talk several days ago, Angie had been considerably more respectful of the High Priestess. While it was obvious that being polite was an effort on Angie's part, I could tell Rhiannon was satisfied. For my part, after talking with Ahearn yesterday, I was quite curious about the workings of the coven, as well as the organizational structure. In addition, the whole partner sharing without jealousy thing was unbelievable. I wasn't sure if I was comfortable discussing the issue overtly with her, but perhaps would learn something about it anyway.

Jonesboro had been a rather loosely run democracy, with everybody able to voice an opinion and vote on matters. At least, that's the way it was supposed to work. In reality, there was a council of people that made the rules and ran the town. In comparison, the Ward Coven was something between a democracy and a theocracy. Ahearn had told me that everyone had a voice, and votes were taken, but the High Priest and Priestess could override everyone and make a ruling decision at any time.

Unlike druids, I had heard of witches before. I had to endure a lot of flirting and innuendo, but I spent a lot of time with the

217

various coven members, asking questions and poking my nose into their business. They seemed not to mind. They had only one law, calling it their Rede: "As long as you do no harm, do as you will."

I tracked Rhiannon down several days later.

"It seems like a good rule to me," I told Rhiannon, as we strolled about the coven grounds. "There's plenty of wiggle room."

She laughed and took my arm. "It's not as roomy as you think. It is all encompassing, applying to the self, as well as others."

"Meaning?"

"Name something you do that harms you."

I snorted. "I take on nine thugs and get myself shot in the process."

Again, she laughed. I liked her laugh; it was lusty and unrestrained. "That was not your doing. Seriously, Davis, think about it and then answer me."

I did think about it, while we walked through the coven's orchard. The other members were standing on ladders scattered about the trees, tying ribbons and flowers in the boughs, and talking happily to one another.

"I go home," I said at last.

She looked sideways at me, curiosity sparking in her grey eyes. "I'd like to hear about that, if you don't mind."

"I don't usually talk about it," I said. Then, I considered what kind of life I'd led so far, and what kind I was going to be leading as the protector of a druid. There were times, I had to admit, when being alone was too much of a good thing.

"Is it a girl?"

"Is it that obvious?"

"No, but it was the obvious question," she replied with a sly grin.

"There was a girl."

"Ah… was. Do tell me more."

"She had dark brown eyes and golden hair. And she let me court her, for a while."

"And, did you allow her to call you by your first name?"

I was taken aback, both by her question and her knowing eyes.

"Yes," I admitted.

"But your druid does not."

"No."

"She doesn't even know your name, does she?"

"No." I had been going by my surname for so long that it hadn't occurred to me.

She was silent a moment. Then she asked, "And then what happened to your golden-haired beauty?"

"She married someone else."

"I'm sorry to hear that."

I shrugged. Life goes on. The bruises and broken bones had healed. Only bad memories remained, and those had been replaced by my new, happy memories of Angie. All of a sudden, giving up what I thought would be a wonderful life with her hurt terribly. I would never leave her, but it would be a misery to be so close, yet so far away.

Was that really what I wanted my life to be like?

"So… you hurt yourself by going home, where you see this girl you cared for in the arms of another man."

That wasn't exactly it, but I nodded, to bring this discussion to an end.

"Is that all there is to it, Davis?"

"I'd rather not discuss it, after all," I said. "I really don't think I do anything to hurt myself."

"That takes a remarkable person," said Rhiannon. "Everyone I know seems to self-sabotage in some way or another."

After a statement like that, I just had to ask. "And, what is your self-sabotage?"

"I'm attracted to men I can't have."

"I didn't think anyone here was monogamous."

"That's true," she said. "Early on, our founders decided that if our coven was to survive, we couldn't limit the breeding to mated pairs, so to speak. Some people still jump the broom, though. Some still tie the knot."

"Sounds like the perfect solution for you, especially since

jealousy doesn't seem to be a problem here. If none of the men are in committed relationships, then technically you're not breaking wedding vows."

She chuckled. "Oh, Davis, I've shared my bed with almost every man here. I have children by three of them."

"Then what–?" I was confused, but only for a split second. I released her arm and stepped to the side. "You don't mean–?" I was sure she was talking about me, unbelievably enough, but I wanted a verbal confirmation. With women, sometimes that is very important.

Rhiannon looked me dead in the eye. "You're a handsome man, Davis. You're young, strong, and confident."

"Don't forget the part where I belong to someone else," I said, not feeling particularly flattered, if she truly considered this my most attractive attribute. At first, I wondered how in the world I had gotten myself into this mess. I seemed to be getting in a lot of messes lately. I had intended to talk over my situation with Angie with the High Priestess, but after a proposition like that, I couldn't. My druid had realized what I hadn't. Again, I was left feeling like an idiot. At the same time that the witches had been hinting their interest, I had been pulling away from her. I could only imagine what she has been thinking. I needed to talk to her, and soon.

"I see I've made you uncomfortable. I'm sorry, that was not my intention."

"No offense taken," I said. "It's irrelevant, anyway."

"You love Angie."

"I can't afford to do that," I replied, shaking my head.

"Why is that?"

"After what happened, with Angie risking herself for me, I can't risk letting my guard down again. She could have been killed."

She raised an eyebrow. "What does she think of this?"

"We haven't discussed it," I replied darkly.

"You have other options, should you feel the need."

I shook my head. "I won't make her feel worse by doing that."

"That's too bad," Rhiannon said. "The others will be

disappointed. We will, of course, respect your wishes."

Wait, what? "Others?"

"The other women. We all cycle around the same time, along with the phases of the moon. The others were also hoping you would be interested in… participating in the festivities."

I stopped in my tracks. I knew about Maeve and the Weird Sisters, but this… "You were all hoping I would want to bed twenty women in one night?"

"Of course not. We were hoping you'd have made the rounds already now. Most men would have happily provided fresh seed to our soil by now." She laughed merrily.

More like fresh meat, if you asked me. I sounded like a Triune. I felt my face flush. Angie was right; I had lived too long among them.

"I see." We walked on in silence.

"Angie will be disappointed as well."

I didn't answer. I didn't want to hear what she had to say about Angie's disappointment, Rhiannon blithely continued.

"Her eyes shine so when she looks at you. You have no idea, Davis. I think she's in love with you, too." She smiled ruefully. "She's not a virgin, and she cannot for the life of her figure out why you haven't come to her yet. She's surely hoping you'll come to her at the solstice. But you and I know something she doesn't."

"What's that?" My mind was spinning, trying not to think of Angie in terms of virginity or the lack thereof. It wasn't something I had even considered.

"That you've never been intimate with a woman, Davis."

Oh. That. Here I was thinking that she was going to make some huge, important revelation about myself. I looked frankly at her.

"And that's important because…?"

She stepped close again. "Let me help you, Davis. Angie is a beautiful young woman, and I know you care for her deeply. You'd do anything for her, anyone can see that." She paused, licking her lips. "Druids and witches rarely make it out of puberty without tasting the pleasures of the flesh," she continued in her breathy voice. "It would only be natural to be concerned about what she would think–" Her fingers brushed my cheek, traced my neck and shoulder.

I grabbed her hand – gently but firmly – and stepped away. I took a couple of deep breaths, waiting for my heart to stop pounding. Rhiannon was seductive; my body wanted her even before I had made up my mind. Confusion crossed Rhiannon's face, her brow furrowing a moment. Her expression hardened, as she seemed to arrive at some understanding.

"She won't be allowed to keep you," said the High Priestess. "So you're quite right to give her up now."

"What?" I wanted nothing more than to be away from this verbal battle. I was tired of the endless innuendo and wanted nothing more than to get away from everyone and be alone.

"You won't be allowed to stay with Angie." She looked sad for a moment. "From what I hear, the current ArchDruid is very involved in the partnering of warriors and druids. I'm surprised she was even allowed to seek you out."

The ArchDruid's manipulative behavior was old news to me. Angie had spoken of it before.

"She's just a water elementalist," I said. "She came to find me because she wanted someone who would appreciate her, and water elementalists aren't valued."

"She hasn't told you." Rhiannon frowned. "I told her that if she didn't tell you the truth, I would."

"The truth about what?" Something in the High Priestess's tone made me ask, when I should have gone straight to Angie for the answer. Rhiannon the seductress was completely gone. Only the regretful High Priestess remained.

"Angie isn't who you think she is. I was the one who found her when she was faring forth. I've seen her spirit, her astral form, where she could hide nothing from me. She's not some poor pitiful water druid that nobody wants. She's a very powerful elementalist who possesses the magic of air, water, and spirit. She's what the druids like to call a 'triple threat,' and I assure you, she is very highly valued in the grove. Whether intentionally or unintentionally, she has misled you, Davis. They will never accept you as her warrior."

"I told Angie I'd take her home. I gave her my word that I

would stay with her." I felt my heart sink. Angie had lied to me?

"If you feel it necessary, go ahead and escort her there," Rhiannon said. "But do not stay. You can come back here afterward and decide where you want to go from there. We would be happy to have you."

"I can't abandon her."

"You have no future with her. You have no idea what a godless place that grove is now. The young ones are no longer allowed to choose their own partners. They are pressured into accepting those chosen by the ArchDruid and her sycophants. They are permitted no freedom. They no longer travel the world, healing it. They exist solely for the purpose of consolidating her power. Mothers are pressured into blocking their sons from magic while still in the womb. The boys are neutered, their magic taken away forever. The girls are sequestered when they turn fourteen so they can be indoctrinated to the ArchDruid's mad ideas.

"Those mothers of honor and love who allow their sons to keep their magic are scorned, and their sons are abused by the rest of the grove until they either agree to be blocked or forever exiled from the grove. Sometimes they lie and raise their sons to hide their magic, which cannot be done forever. When the truth comes out, the young men are expelled from the grove. Some of them have made their way here. The tales they tell of the cruelty they have suffered are blood-chilling. Please don't go. I fear for your very life."

If everything she said was true, Angie had indeed lied to me. At the very least, she had withheld important information, which was very nearly the same thing. I stared at Rhiannon in shock. Overwhelmed by the deluge of information, I stumbled backwards, away from her. Then I turned and walked away, back through the orchard, toward the cornfield.

"Davis? Davis, wait!"

I ignored her and started running, disregarding the pain in my shoulder and in my heart. It was just as my mother had once said: you never knew you really wanted something, until it was taken away.

She was right about that.

She was right about a lot of things.

Throughout the night I walked the rows of corn, my mind agitated and my spirit in turmoil. When I was too exhausted to walk any more, I knelt in the dirt and wept. Beneath the moon and the stars, among the cornrows, I vented my sorrow. I wept for the soul mate I thought I would never have; the unconditional love I would never experience. I would never have the joy of seeing a woman become my wife, discover the joy of learning to please her and enjoy being pleased in return.

As soon as Rhiannon's words had sunk into my soul, it had hit me with a frightening ferocity that I wanted all those things and more, and I wanted them with Angie. I didn't want to give her up; nor did I want to merely be her companion and protector. The cry of my heart was for her as a lover, someone with whom I could share everything.

All this time I had told myself that none of this was important to me, that nothing mattered to me but the freedom of the road. I never realized how much of my mother was in me, the deep desire for home and family.

I no longer wanted to be merely a warrior to a druid, but how could I break my vow? Angie would be alone and defenseless if I let her return to her grove alone. I had risked my life before, and would do so again, even if it meant certain death. Rhiannon was right about one thing – I cared deeply for my druid, and would do anything for her.

Dawn was breaking when I finally made my decision, and so was my heart. It's like my father always said: A man is only as good as his word.

Chapter 18 – Summer Solstice

Rules of Gunfighting #14:
A – Have a plan.
B – Have a back-up plan,
because the first one won't work.

I came back to the hall dirty and tired. Angie jumped up with a wordless cry and ran toward me, but I held up a hand. I tried not to see her green eyes alive with worry, or the meaningful glances around the table. I especially ignored the look of concern given me by Rhiannon. I couldn't let Angie touch me, couldn't even speak to her.

Not yet.

I went to my room and shut the door, stripped naked and collapsed on my pallet. I was so tired but unable to sleep; my brain just wanted to spin around in circles like a rat in a wheel.

There was a knock on the door; I ignored it. I caught sight of a cup, half-full of the witches' nasty sleeping potion. I tossed it back in a single gulp, savoring the flavor. The taste was bitter and sour, like my heart. I closed my eyes as voices raised in the great hall.

"Leave him be, Angie." It was Rhiannon.

"You don't tell me what to do with my chosen!" Angie shouted.

So glad I was worth fighting over. I suppose I deserved to

be treated like an object, since I was stupid enough to let myself get led around by the nose, and for being pigheaded enough to believe my mother had her own interests at heart, rather than mine.

"This is my hall," Rhiannon stated firmly. "And, when you are a guest in my hall, you will respect the wishes of my guests. All of my guests. Leave Davis be."

"You dare meddle with a druid, witch?"

"You're no druid, little girl. A real druid would have told him the truth about the choices he was making, rather than leading him blindly onward to his doom. I've heard how the warriors of your grove are treated. He deserves better than that."

Angie said something in a low voice that I could not make out. Rhiannon gave a sharp laugh.

"You're not capable of keeping such a promise. A real woman would have told him the truth. A real woman would also have bedded him successfully and well by now."

Angie hissed something that I didn't hear. I was floating on a sea of tea. It seemed stronger than usual. I wondered if it got stronger the longer it sat?

"Foolish girl, you know nothing about men, and even less about your own warrior."

Angie's voice rose. "You don't know what you're talking about."

"What's his name?"

"Wouldn't you like to know?" my druid spat.

"You won't say, because you don't know. Do you?"

"It's none of your business."

"He's never told you, has he?" asked the High Priestess in cold tones. I pulled the blanket around my shoulders. It was getting downright chilly in here. "He told that girl he courted. Did you know that?"

"That's not fair, she knew him from childhood."

"He gave her permission to call him by his given name, Angie."

Silence.

"If he truly thought you cared about him, don't you think he would have told you his name?"

"I respect him enough not to pry," said the druid in an arrogant tone.

"Respect? Respect?" Rhiannon barked a laugh. "You respect Davis about as much as a pet poodle."

"How can you say that?" Angie screamed. "I love him!"

So nice to be loved. Like a favorite toy. Or maybe a favorite tool. Yeah, definitely a tool. Maybe it was good that I had been given a name suitable for dogs and donkeys.

"Little girl, you don't know the first thing about love. Or trust." Rhiannon's voice had a venomous tone. "I cannot believe you would betray the trust of your own warrior, a man who has protected you time and again, who nearly gave his life for you. I told him the truth about your magic, something you should have done long ago."

"How dare you pry into my personal–"

Rhiannon said something in a low voice.

There was a deafening silence, followed by Angie's loud wail of anguish. It was a long, drawn-out thing, a howl to comfort dreaming demons as they slept in hell. Her tortured utterance turned into a wordless scream of rage followed by an angry tirade.

"How could you?" she was screeching. "You don't know what you've done! The ArchDruid promised me! She promised–"

Her voice was cut off by the sound of a loud slap. I didn't know if she had hit Rhiannon, or if the High Priestess had struck her, but there was a deep silence afterward. Good, now maybe I could sleep.

* * *

I spent the next few days helping the coven members finish decorating the orchard that surrounded the hall. The branches were festooned with yellow flowers tied with red and blue ribbons. Soft bowers had been built, scattered around in relatively private places throughout the orchard. Wild roses were twined in the canopies, with holly leaves tied to the posts. They looked comfortable, but I doubted I would find out personally. I had done the work out of a since of duty; if not for the people of Ward, I would not be alive. It was worth some discomfort to give something back to them.

I had never before participated in a High Holy Day with a large group of people. I had wanted to share all this with Angie. Not necessarily a bower, although it would have been nice, but definitely the dancing and feasting. She had often talked about how much fun it would be to join the festivities, and to dance around the bonfire. I knew she had been planning something when I was not around, and had kept it a secret. Now I would never know.

Brennan had loaned me a soft robe of coal black, along with some cream-colored trousers that I had tucked into my boots. Rhiannon had tied a silky red sash about my waist, telling me it was for good luck. I thought I looked rather dashing. I swallowed some more honey mead and watched the dancing for a little while, observing how people paired up, separated, and made new pairs. Occasionally a couple would disappear for a while, to the bowers I assumed. It made me envious, and I had never envied anyone that I could recall.

When they lit the bonfire, I couldn't help but be pulled out of my personal darkness into the light. It must have been the witches' magic. Rhiannon had told me that their magic was very powerful at this time of year. As I understood her explanation, it was a time to further one's goals, or to cast spells for increase. Perhaps that was why some of them wanted to be impregnated around this time. I tried not to think about that as I helped toss more oak logs on the fire. Soon it was a roaring blaze, and everyone was drinking and dancing.

Everyone except Angie, that is. She had stayed in her room for the past few days. Feeling lost and alone without her, I was pretty sure that things between us were finished. We hadn't spoken since her fight with Rhiannon. I was just waiting for her to tell me the bad news.

I couldn't understand how I could feel so hurt but yet still want her by my side. It was ridiculous to feel so badly, since I had spent just about every waking moment at the coven trying to push her away. I missed Angie's company, which was stupid since I knew she had lied to me. Then again, I had been so busy keeping my distance that I hadn't exactly given her a chance to come clean.

"Come on, Davis!" called Rhiannon, as she grabbed my hand and pulled me into the circle. I wasn't drunk at all by this time – well, not much anyway – and I managed to join the dancing without tripping over my feet. Surprisingly, the mere act of dancing started to lift my mood.

"Burn off your bad luck!" She thrust bunches of lemon balm into my hands, and we danced around the bonfire, tossing sprigs into the fire. When everyone had thrown in their herbs, a sweet fragrant smoke drifted upward and circled around us all. She took my hand and led me through the smoke – the healing smoke that would cure sickness and bring good fortune. I certainly needed a lot of both. I was heartsick and my luck so far had been terrible.

We laughed and ran through the smoke, the witches chanting their spells as they went. Praises were sung to the Lord and Lady, the gods and goddesses of nature and fertility and the hunt. There were a variety of folk dances, some that I knew, and some that I learned. Out of breath, I took a break to eat and have another mug of mead. Food was laid out on blankets beneath the trees, where we ate and drank our fill. There was roast goose and sausage-stuffed peppers, huge bowls of mashed potatoes, sautéed squash, sweet potatoes, and turnips, and pies made with the fruit of every tree in the orchard… and polenta pancakes. I found that I actually had an appetite. Rhiannon sent me an approving look.

The hall door slammed. Out of habit, I sent a quick glance in that direction. What I saw there made me take a long, hungry look. It was Angie, clad in a dress of flowing pale yellow. It had thin straps that showed off her shoulders, and was short enough to reveal her calves. Her hair was piled in curls atop her head, adorned with yellow flowers; matching yellow ribbons trailed down her neck. I climbed to my feet when she walked up to me and those lovely green eyes met mine, everything else faded into the background.

"Davis, I–"

I reached out and took her into my arms. I couldn't help

myself.

"Dance with me," I said. "Don't talk. Just dance with me."

I led her by the hand to the bonfire, and we joined the others, spinning and laughing. I tried never to let go of her hands. We switched partners, came back together, switched again. Her skirts swirled up around her thighs when her other partner spun her around. I drank in the sight of her, wanting to see more.

"Having second thoughts, Davis?" said a breathy voice in my ear. It was Rhiannon. We had switched partners, and my eyes were so full of Angie that I hadn't noticed.

"How could you tell?"

"I *am* a witch, you know." She gave a throaty laugh.

I looked into her laughing grey eyes. "Did you cast a spell on me?"

"No, but I think *she* did." She nodded at my druid, twirling around in thin yellow cotton with a smile on her face. We switched partners, circled twice around the bonfire, and then I came back together with Rhiannon.

"It's time to decide, Davis," said the High Priestess. "She's determined to keep you. Maybe she'll be strong enough to resist the ArchDruid."

"What will I have to do?"

"Fight for her," she said.

I gave her a look that said *You've got to be kidding.* "That's all?"

"You'll be up against the best warriors in the grove, I'm afraid," she said, grey eyes twinkling. "All of them will want to be partnered with her."

"I don't know why she would still want to be with me," I said.

"Love makes people do crazy things."

I looked again at Angie, dancing now with Brennan. He was the perfect gentleman, guiding her through the steps of the dance.

"Crazy like risking death to be with someone?"

"That is exactly what I mean. You should expect them to try and kill you during training. It will look like an accident, of course."

"They'll find me quite a bit harder to kill than that," I said.

"You can still change your mind," she said. "We'd love to have you here. I would love to have you here."

I shook my head and gave her an ironic smile. "Ah, but then I wouldn't be unavailable any more, would I?"

She threw her head back and laughed, swirling away, and I found Angie once again in my arms. The music slowed, a gentle tune with a slow beat, and I pulled her against me. I breathed in the scent of wild honeysuckle, relishing the feel of her soft body against mine. I just wanted to savor her essence, my beautiful druid who had proclaimed her love for me to the entire coven at the top of her lungs. Maybe this was her magic, that I could not turn away from her.

"Davis, I'm sorry I wasn't more honest with you–"

"Shhhh…"

"I never wanted to hurt you–"

"I know."

"H-How?"

"Because you love me." I felt her jerk slightly.

"You heard that?" Her voice sounded weak.

"My lovely druid, everyone in Ward heard that."

I closed my eyes and buried my nose in her hair, slipping my arms more tightly about her slender waist. She was silent for a few moments, and we moved gracefully as one in time to the music. I held her closely, so she couldn't get away, lips close to her ear.

"Davis, I need to tell you–"

"Call me Charlie. That's my name." I whispered it into her ear.

She fell instantly silent, freezing in place.

I moved back slightly so I could see her face. "Forgive me for not telling you sooner. I don't like it, so I didn't even think of telling you."

"Y-you don't… don't n-need to apologize to me." Her eyes were full of tears, but none spilled onto her cheeks. She did, however, clutch my neck more tightly. I didn't mind that at all.

"This makes us even," I said, once again holding her close. "No more secrets from now on."

"Davis–"

231

"Charlie. Give me your oath. Make me this most solemn vow. Promise me, because if we're going to stay together, there can be no secrets between us."

I couldn't keep the desire from my voice any longer, if indeed I ever had been able to. Without saying a word, she took me by the hand and led me to a dark corner of the orchard. To my disappointment, we passed several bowers on the way. Strangely, she scooped up a small handful of tilled earth when we stopped at the edge of the cornfield.

"Give me your knife. The one in your boot."

I hadn't realized that she knew about the knife I kept secreted in my boot. I pulled it free and handed it to her hilt first. Before I realized what she was doing, she had sliced open the palm of her left hand. She hissed in pain, and then sliced open my left palm. I barely noticed. She sprinkled the rich earth on each of our palms, then took my hand in hers, letting our blood mingle with the earth. A soft, bright blue glow insinuated itself around our joined hands, and I could feel a strange tingling move from my palm, up my arm, through my shoulder, and across my chest to rest in my heart.

"Among the druids, a blood oath sealed with earth and spirit is the most powerful vow one can make," she said. "I make my most solemn vow to always be honest with you, and to never keep hidden any secret from you, no matter the cost. I will be loyal to you always, first and foremost, before everything and everyone."

I squeezed her hand. "I make my most solemn vow to stay by your side always, my druid, and to love you to the exclusion of all others. I promise to protect you always, even if it means my death. So I do swear, and may the sky fall on my head, the sea rise up to drown me, and the earth swallow me whole if I break this vow."

I raised her hand to my lips and kissed it tenderly. She pulled her bloodied and dirty hand from mine. She used her water magic to wash both our hands clean, staring at me incredulously.

"You can't… you can't make an oath like that, Davis."

"Charlie. And don't tell me what I can't do." I said it

lightly, tipping her a wink. She looked away, frowning. I was not about to let her good mood vanish.

"Do you want to dance again?" To be perfectly honest, I wasn't all that interested in dancing. I was giving Angie the option, if visiting a bower was not something she had intended this night.

"No," she said softly, moving up close to me. "I don't want to dance anymore."

"What do you want?" I asked, lips brushing her ear. I inhaled the scent of honeysuckle until I was nearly drunk with it.

"Rhiannon told me that you're–"

"A virgin," I murmured. "And she told me you're not. It doesn't matter."

"She told you what?" She pulled away, looking distressed. I didn't let her get far.

"Angie, I don't care–"

"That's not true. She's wrong." Her mouth drew a stubborn line.

"She said that the druid tradition usually included some... experimentation." I was trying to be delicate, but quakes it was hard to think. My hands had started to shake; I kept them pressed against her back to steady them.

"It does. I didn't." She paused, chewing on her lip. "My fetch told me–"

"The kitty that led you to me?" I teased.

"I'm serious!" she protested, slapping my chest. It wasn't much of a slap. There wasn't enough room between us for that.

"Sorry," I said with a chuckle. I was intoxicated on spirit, fire, and the sweet scent of her skin. My blood heated with the desire to taste her mouth.

"I knew that my warrior would be untouched by any woman." She looked me in the eye. "So I decided to meet him on the same terms."

No wonder she had been so jealous.

I bent my head, breathing in her ear. "Tell me what you want," I whispered. She grabbed my hand and led me deeper into the orchard, to a bower decorated with red roses and yellow ribbons, with holly sprigs and oak leaves woven into the canopy.

She started to sit, but I stopped her, holding her in my arms and kissing her gently. I sat down and settled her on my lap with my hands about her waist. She looked nervous, her body trembling slightly. Had I been possessed of anything resembling normal human reasoning, I would have been, too. Rationality had long passed, brushed away by her swirling skirt during the dance.

We took it slow, carefully exploring each other's likes and dislikes. There were lots of likes, and pleasingly few dislikes. I let her unfasten the laces of my borrowed robe, delicate hands slipping it back off my shoulders. She made a sound of dismay over the gunshot wound in my shoulder. I pulled her hand away from it, brushing my lips lightly along the inside of her wrist, to her forearm. I kissed her neck and shoulder until she forgot about mine.

Angie rose and unbuttoned her dress, never taking her eyes from mine as she did so. I watched the dress slip down her lithe body and drank in every curve. She came to me when I held out my hands, allowed me to touch her. By the gods, she was the most beautiful thing I'd ever seen. I ran my fingers appreciatively up the wide expanse of her hips, dipping in to her slender waist and slipping them over her ribs. She was a goddess in the flesh, deigning to grace me with her holy presence.

I quickly stripped the rest of the way, sat back on the bower, and pulled her onto my lap with her back to my chest. My hands roamed over her lush body, cupping her breasts in my hands and stroking her dark nipples, feeling them peak beneath my fingertips. My tongue ran lightly over the back of her sensitive neck, following it with tender kisses.

Further exploration of her body revealed her secret places, soft hair and delicate flesh, all open for me to touch. Angie was so sweet, and her breath came in quick little pants with each stroke of my fingers. She rocked her hips, giving a little cry of protest when I stopped, but I had other ideas and would not be rushed. Satisfied myself that I had touched every soft inch of her skin, I laid her back in the bower and kissed her mouth. She clung to my shoulders with a kind of desperation while I kissed my way down her body, not wanting to miss a single part. I licked and suckled her nipples, caressing her breasts until she was panting with desire. I traced the curve of her belly with my tongue, ran my hands on the silken insides of her rounded thighs. I tasted and teased her until she was slick and quivering, my lips and tongue tracing where my fingers had been just moments before. She tasted as sweet as she smelled. She plunged her fingers into my hair and arched her back, moaning. Only the greatest restraint kept me from plunging deep inside her at that moment.

Easing away, I sat up and helped her over to me, pulling her onto my lap, this time facing me. Staring into her wide green eyes brightly lit with lust and eager anticipation, I whispered her name, sliding inside her slowly, so slowly, pulling her closer with my hands on her wide hips. Her hands gripped my shoulders, nails digging in hard as her whole body shuddered. We stayed that way for a minute, an hour, an eternity, joining together as one. Angie's body was taut as wire until I found her mouth with mine, kissing and tasting her lips again. She tilted her head back, allowing me to place tender kisses along her jaw and down her neck, feeling her start to relax as I did so. I closed my eyes, feeling her silken heat slip down all around me as my tongue traced the delicate skin at the base of her throat. As much as I wanted to take over and speed things up, I made myself be patient. It was her first time and mine, so I let her set the pace. She began moving against me in a maddingly slow rhythm that took my breath away.

I bent my head to taste her nipples once more, hearing Angie moan as I lightly scraped them with my teeth. She gripped my shoulders more tightly, thrusting her hips faster and faster, her breath coming in ragged gasps that erupted into wild cries of passion. Hearing her helpless whimpers and feeling the surges of her body around me, I lost all control, pulling her hard against me, driving ever deeper, growling into her neck.

The first time she spoke my name, Angie didn't merely say it. She uttered it in a breathless whisper.

Chapter 19 – Unified

Rules of Gunfighting #3:
Bring ammo. The right ammo. Lots of it.

I awoke with the dawn. The sky was beginning to lighten in the east, and I quietly watched Angie sleeping, curled up in the crook of my arm with her head on my chest. Dawn's first rays began to illuminate the sky, bringing with it all the possibilities of my new life. The sun broke over the horizon and the world brightened dramatically, awash in color. I turned my gaze upon Angie, taking in how the light slipped up her legs, then her hips and torso, revealing flesh previously hidden in shadow. I drank in the sight, feeling myself stir again. When the newly brilliant light slipped over her delicate features, her eyelids fluttered open, and I found myself staring into her glowing green eyes.

"Good morning," I murmured, and kissed her tenderly on the lips. She smiled and stifled a yawn. I kissed her again, harder this time, my hands beginning to roam lightly over all the places I now knew she enjoyed being touched.

"Charlie, it's light out," she whispered, tensing slightly.

"The light of the dawn serves to show me how beautiful you truly are," I murmured against her neck. I traced the path my hands had made with lips and tongue, until she no longer had the breath or the desire to protest. I could not get enough of watching how she reacted to my touch. Seeing her expressions of passionate delight made me even more eager to complete her, and to seek my own pleasure in her body. The golden light of the sun made her skin shimmer in elegantly dark contrast to the soft, white linens of the bower. We made love until the sun was full in the sky, greeting the day united in body, completing each other in heart and soul.

Angie sighed softly and sank back against the linens, slowing running her fingers up and down my arm. Occasionally she traced a path around the gunshot wound in my shoulder with her fingertips. I took her hand in my own and kissed it.

"Hungry?" I asked. My own stomach had started to growl. One appetite had been sated – one volcanic appetite, at that – and now it was time to settle the other.

"Starved," she said, slipping off the bower to dress. I threw on my clothes, stamped into my boots, and slipped my arm around her waist as we walked back to the hall. As we came closer, I noticed that we were not the only late risers. I saw a thatch of red hair among a tangle of limbs, and noticed Ahearn, snoring.

"Oh, my," said Angie, eyes wide.

Ahearn was entwined with all three Weird Sisters, somehow having managed to cuddle with all three. They looked like a pile of puppies that had fallen asleep while playing together.

"It looks like we're not the only ones who had a good night," I said, giving Angie a wink. We continued on to the hall and entered the busy sanctuary holding hands.

"Good morning!" Rhiannon greeted us with a wave. Maeve looked over, then turned away, mouth set in a thin line. The High Priestess noticed and scowled at her. So, there was envy sometimes, but it was quite literally frowned upon. I didn't think Angie noticed and I pretended not to.

Brennan looked us over with a wry smile. "I see you two had a good time last night."

I looked down at my rumpled clothes, then at Angie's wrinkled dress and mussed hair. Much of it was still pinned up, with long ringlets framing her face. Most of the ribbons and flowers had fallen out, left in the bower where we had spent the night. We were a mess.

Angie blushed and hid her face in my shoulder, but I could feel her smile. I hugged her close and kissed her temple, then guided her to the nearest bench. I then fixed us plates laden with ham, scrambled eggs, biscuits, and polenta cakes, making sure to drizzle the cakes with plenty of honey. I slid Angie's plate in front of her, and sat beside her with my own, immediately wolfing it down.

"Looks like someone worked up an appetite," said Weylin, taking some ham off his own plate and thumping it down on mine. I thanked him with a quick smile.

Rhiannon slid onto the bench beside Brennan. "We're all going to the bathhouse after breakfast, would you like to join?"

My eyes came up, saw hers sparkling at me. "Um…"

"Sure," said Angie, never looking up.

"What?" I looked at her. I couldn't believe she had agreed. There was no separation between men and women in the bathhouse – everyone bathed together in one or another of two huge tubs. For all of the days we had been in Ward, I had waited until after dark to bathe in order to have some privacy.

"You don't want to take a bath?" she said. "It's really nice. You can soak all the way up to your shoulders."

I was at a loss for words. Angie had been bathing communally?

"Oh, come on, Davis," said Maeve drily. "It's not like we haven't seen all of you already."

"What?" Angie and I said at the same time.

"You're not the only one who stays awake past dark," she said with a smirk.

Oh, my gods. My face was positively on fire.

"You've all been watching him *bathe*?" Angie asked, as though she thought they had all gone insane.

"He's so shy," said one of the other witches, her face the picture of innocence. "How else were we supposed to get a look at him?"

* * *

I somehow managed to get through the communal bath

238

without dying of embarrassment. Actually, it wasn't that bad once I was in the water. Having Angie wash my back was pretty awesome. Not to mention that she let me wash her hair. Afterwards I helped her move her belongings into my little cubicle behind the fireplace in the great hall. I lay down to take a nap, but my little druid had other ideas. Once the door closed, she stripped bare and shoved me back on our pallet.

"I want you, Charlie," she said, slipping the drawstring of my pants loose. Her voice was husky, her green eyes glinting golden in the candlelight.

"Oh, my," was all I could say, closing my eyes and relishing the feel over her hands on my body.

"I waited such a long time for you, my warrior," she purred, nibbling my ear lobe. I started to lift my hands to touch her, but she pinned my wrists. Her soft lips traced down the left side of my neck. I inhaled deeply of her scent – warmth and light and summer flowers.

"...traveled the Road months with you, sleeping beside you..." Teeth lightly scraped my skin, traveled over one taut nipple. My arms tensed, muscles flexing, but she applied more pressure to my wrists, making it clear that I was not to move. Gods. I groaned helplessly; I didn't know if I could stand it.

"...desperately wanting to see your flesh... to touch you..." She left a trail of wet kisses down my belly. "...aching for your touch... "

My body was on fire, my muscles shaking and tense with the effort to keep still. Her tongue darted out, hot and wet, tasting me. My skin tingled with every touch of her fingers. Sweat beaded my forehead, slid down my temple. Soft breezes cooled me, wisping through my hair. In mere moments, I could take it no longer, and had reversed my hands to grip her wrists and flip her over onto our sleeping mat. Angie gasped in surprise, eyes widening. Moments later, she was gasping for another reason. She buried her face in my shoulder to stifle her cries, but there was no way I could be silent after what she had done to me. Our ardor sated, we curled up on the pallet with her back to my chest, breathing in the cool air.

"Did you do something?" I asked, realizing that it should be sweltering in here.

"I did a lot of 'something'," she said, with a chuckle that sounded positively smug.

"What happened to my innocent little druid?" I teased.

"Just because I waited for you, it doesn't mean I was ignorant." Her tone was light, but I could tell she meant it.

Okay, I had to ask. "And, how long have you been waiting?"

"Since the moment I saw you," she said softly. "I watched you for a long time through the eyes of my spirit animal. I felt like I knew you before we even met." As she finished, there was a note of uncertainty in her voice, and her body tensed.

"You had quite a head start on me, then. Why didn't you say something?" I ran my hand from her shoulder to her hip, then slipped it around her waist, feeling her relax. I didn't want her to be afraid of what I might think or say.

"I didn't want to just throw myself at you. I wanted to wait until you were ready." She paused. "Then we came here, and I saw how all the other women looked at you, Charlie... You never even seemed to notice them, like you were used to being stared at by pretty women. I started thinking maybe that's why you never really noticed me, either."

"I noticed."

"You don't sound happy about that." The worried tone was back.

"I never really knew what you expected of me. Then, when we started to get close, there was the attack..." I shook my head slightly. "I was so full of thinking about you, that I wasn't paying attention to anything else. I promise, I will never allow that to happen again. I almost got us both killed."

"Is that why you pulled away from me?" she asked.

I nodded. "I thought that if we weren't romantically involved, then it would keep me from making the same mistake twice. Except..."

"Except?"

"Except I couldn't stop thinking about you then, either."

"I don't mind that at all." She leaned over and gave me a kiss on the cheek. "I was afraid that you had seen the witches and decided you wanted one of them instead. Especially considering how aggressive they are. My goodness."

"Believe it or not, I wasn't particularly flattered."

"Most men wouldn't care one way or another."

"Guess I'm not cut out to be a stud," I said with a grunt.

Angie hesitated a moment, then said. "Maeve wasn't interested in that. She can't have children."

"That's too bad."

"She wanted you for *you*, Charlie."

"Hm." I wasn't so sure about that. This place was full of cooperation, but also competition. The women may not have been jealous, but they were competitive, just like people everywhere.

"You don't believe me."

"I'm a little skeptical."

"Why?"

"She never talked to me."

Angie obviously thought I was crazy. "Charlie, she got the High Priestess to fend me off, and came in here to give you a massage. And everybody knows that she doesn't just give simple massages."

"Apparently they forgot to tell me," I said drily. I didn't know why Angie was hung up on the whole massage thing, but I could tell it was bothering her. "Look, she rubbed my back with oil and asked me a bunch of questions about how I was shot."

"You said she didn't talk to you."

I shrugged. "She's a healer. It's logical for a healer to ask how an injury occurred. It didn't occur to me that she was concerned with anything other than my health."

"It never occurred to you."

"No."

"Never crossed your mind."

"No."

"Weren't you tempted at all?"

"I fell asleep!"

"You were not tempted in the least by any of the witches here?"

"No."

"No?"

Then I remembered. I sighed, because it could cause problems. "Well, once."

"I knew it. Who was it?"

"Rhiannon."

"I knew it!" She rolled over to face me.

My father had often said that a woman often liked nothing more than to be Right, with a capital R.

"Can I ask what it was about her that tempted you?"

I took a deep breath, thinking back to the day when I had walked in the orchard with the High Priestess.

"We were walking in the orchard and talking, and she was asking me questions about myself. That was when she told me about it's the norm for witches and the druid to engage in some… experimentation… upon reaching sexual maturity. She offered to…" I trailed off, not wanting to talk about it anymore.

"… to teach you," Angie finished softly. "Why would that be tempting?"

I closed my eyes and took a deep breath. She stroked my cheek.

"So you wouldn't be disappointed."

"Oh, Charlie," she whispered. "I could never be disappointed in you."

"It's water under the bridge," I said, pulling her close. "We're together now, and that's what counts. Besides, we'll be gone soon."

"How soon is soon?"

"Litha has passed and my shoulder is healed. We just need to take stock, see what needs to be replaced or repaired, collect the horses, and go. Then you can fill me in on everything else I need to know on the way."

She was silent.

"Do you still want to go?" I asked.

There was a long silence before she answered me, during which she stared at the ceiling and avoided my eyes. It was several seconds before she answered.

"Yes."

Chapter 20 – Truth Revealed

Rules of Gunfighting #5:
If your shooting stance is good, you're probably not moving fast
enough or using cover correctly.

We took leave of the witches of Ward several days later. In truth, we hadn't needed to make any real preparations during that time. I could just tell that Angie wasn't ready. I waited until she was committed; there was no way I would step out on the Road with someone who wasn't ready to face it.

There was also the small favor that Rhiannon asked of us, which entailed joining the coven members in blessing the fields in a way that only druids and witches could. Though it was a bit awkward and the very request made Angie blush, we felt it was only right to oblige her, considering the coven's generosity.

Suffice to say that I was happy to help, and even though we got really dirty, it was quite fun. Afterward we took a couple of days to rest, because, frankly, we were both exhausted. I'm not sure Angie would have been able to ride, in any case. For that matter, I wasn't sure I could, either.

Ahearn and the Weird Sisters rode with us as far as the boundaries of Ward. After he had told us about a parallel path to the main road that led to a safe town, I had made the decision to go that way. Rhiannon had mentioned bandit towns that occurred with unpleasant frequency from here to the big river. The one that worried me in particular was called the 'Ville; it was located near a pre-Fracture military base, and there was no telling what type of lethal weaponry they had. I wanted to stay as far from the place as possible.

"Thanks, Ahearn." We shook hands across the gap between horses. "I hope to see you again."

"With the Goddess' blessing, so mote it be." He placed his hand over his heart. Together he, Ianna, Rowena, and Bébhinn, chanted: "Merry meet, and merry part, and merry meet again."

"So be it," Angie and I answered, waving goodbye. We started down the road, allowing the horses to walk for a while to warm up, and then urged them into a trot. Every thirty minutes or so, we switched the horses' gaits, from walk to trot and back again. We did this only for a couple of hours, as Steel and Magic had spent most of their time being lazy, rolling in the dirt, and eating. They had put on some weight and had plenty of energy. Steel's time with the mares had made him a little feisty, but he still responded well. I figured maybe we could have a nice gallop after lunch to settle him down a little. Magic was the perfect mount, obeying Angie's every command with willingness and precision.

When we stopped to have lunch and rest the horses, I started asking Angie questions. I figured it would be easier than expecting her to tell me all of it at once.

"So when we get to the grove, what's the first thing that will happen?"

Her face instantly closed up. Apparently, I had picked a bad question with which to start. I took her left hand in mine, letting our palms touch. A tingle of warmth grew between them, moving up my arm and to my heart, the way it had when we had originally made the vow.

"I love you," I said. "Whatever happens, I will never leave you." It seemed to make things worse. Angie was fighting tears.

"You can't promise me that." She sounded miserable.

"Don't tell me what I can't–"

"They'll separate us."

"Excuse me?"

She collected herself and stepped back, but still holding on to

244

my hand. "We'll be separated. For training. I'll go to mine and you'll go to yours. That's not the way it was done in the past. In the traditional way, once two people were partnered, they were allowed to live together while they trained. It was a way to build a solid relationship and work out any potential problems well before they were out in the world and exposed to danger."

I frowned. "How am I supposed to protect you, if I'm not with you?"

"We'll be in the grove," she said, as if that explained everything. For me, of course, it didn't.

"And?"

"I won't need protection in the grove, Charlie. It's the safest place in the world." From some of the things Rhiannon had told me, I wasn't so sure of that. However, if Angie really was the ArchDruid's golden child, as the High Priestess had said, she was probably right.

"Well, you got your way about coming to find me," I said. "Maybe you can convince them to let us stay together."

"I doubt she'll allow that. I fully expect her to do everything in her power to keep us apart. We'll be able to see each other, but beyond that, I don't know."

"How often?" A bad feeling crept over me.

"During the Holy Days, at least."

"Are you serious?" I felt my temper start to rise. "The High Days are two months apart!"

"Most of them are only six weeks," she said defensively.

In the face of my growing anger, Angie had put on her mystical druid expression. I hadn't seen that look in weeks, and it was disturbing. In fact, it irritated me even more.

"Oh, yeah, that's much better. You couldn't tell me this before?" We had been intimate for less than a month of the three we had spent together, but I had rapidly become accustomed to the joys of Angie's company. I certainly didn't want to give them up.

"Your training will be grueling, Charlie. I doubt you'll have the energy."

"I'll believe that when I see it."

Unexpectedly, Angie laughed, then slipped her arm about

my waist and hugged me. I frowned at her.

"There's nothing funny about this," I grumped.

"I know you better than that, my loyal warrior. As soon as the masters start giving you tasks, you'll throw yourself into it with everything you have."

"Only because we can leave as soon as I finish."

"Exactly. And if I'm around to… distract you…"

"Trust me, it'll be more motivation than distraction."

She laughed again. I decided that I could endure a year of separation, if I got to see her on the High Days. Maybe there would be full moon rituals, too.

"So… how long is this going to take, again?"

Her smile vanished.

"That depends."

"On what?"

"It depends on how fast you learn. How quickly and how well you master the skills they teach." She spat out the words as though they had left a foul taste in her mouth. It seemed that she thought I was going to be the weak link here, and that she was confident in her ability to learn quickly and graduate from training, but not in mine.

"I've already been trained," I said. "You do realize that this is how we've stayed alive so far?"

"This is different."

"How?"

"For one thing, you won't have your shotgun."

I took a deep breath and let it out, trying to release the anger. She was right; I could use the tomahawks and the machete, but I did rely primarily on the Ithaca for defense. Self-righteous indignation reared its ugly head.

"If you doubt me that much, you never should have brought me south," I retorted, rising and stomping several yards away. I couldn't go far, because then she would be unprotected. This knowledge brought forth a deep resentment, which only fed the flames of my anger. Ignoring her when she called my name, I dropped to my knees with my back to her. I needed some space, but I couldn't have it.

I didn't want to be angry with Angie. This trip had been just as hard on her as it had been for me. I had been shot, but she had nearly been burned at the stake. I had wrestled with whether to accompany her or not; she had endured waiting for me to make up my mind. Remembering a calming technique my mother had taught me, I placed my hands on my thighs, closed my eyes, and took several deep breaths. I had been quick to anger as a child and she had insisted that I learn to control my temper. I hadn't used it in years, but right now, I needed some control. I concentrated on just breathing until I could think rationally.

Angie had followed me on the Road, sometimes blindly trusting as we navigated into and out of dangers. She had sometimes questioned me, but had always given me her absolute trust and confidence that I would get us through whatever happened. The very idea that Angie could doubt me after all we had been through shook me to the core. I sat with that thought for long moments, just breathing, waiting for all the negative energy to subside. The possibility that Rhiannon had been right drifted across my mind. It was possible that they would try to kill me. Even if I managed to avoid any "accidents," they might still find me unsuitable, no matter how hard I worked, no matter how many martial skills I mastered.

If I failed the training, then I would lose Angie. If she wanted to continue being a part of the grove, my druid would have to choose a new warrior and I would lose her. That old fear from childhood, of being unimportant, forgotten, and an outcast, clawed its way up out of my gut again.

I breathed.

The negative energy subsided once again. I considered again the possibility that Angie doubted me. I reminded myself that she had undertaken her quest with something of a flight of fancy in her mind, expecting me to be a bold and daring warrior who would fall in love with her at first sight. Instead, I had been a cunning and ruthless Traveler who had first rejected and then abandoned her.

Logic would suggest that Angie would not have chosen to remain with me if she didn't think I would make it through the required training. She most certainly had chosen to be with me. She had chosen again and again. I finally had to admit that the part that bothered me the most was being separated from her. My anger had sprung from selfishness. Before, I had only a small idea of what I was giving up. I hadn't experienced what it was to love a woman and be with her completely – body, mind, and spirit. Now I knew exactly what I was giving up, and it would be a tremendous sacrifice.

Opening my eyes, I looked over my shoulder at Angie's distressed expression and realized that she felt the same way. Just because she had accepted the probability that we would be apart, it didn't mean she was happy about it.

I went back to Angie and sat beside her. She didn't look at me.

"Are you leaving?" she asked quietly.

"No."

She swallowed hard, once again fighting tears.

"Did you really expect me to?"

She bit her lips, nodding tightly. A single tear slipped free, rolling down her cheek.

"Why? I said I wouldn't leave you, and I meant it."

"I've fought this battle by myself for so long," she said, angrily brushing the tear away. "I can't expect anyone else to help, or even to understand. Especially you."

"What? Why wouldn't I?"

"Because you're not from the grove. You're going to be fighting for something you don't even believe in. You don't know the traditions or the lore. You weren't raised like the rest of us."

"I haven't spent my entire life being afraid of a tyrannical ArchDruid, either," I said, putting my arm around her. She leaned over and laid her head on my shoulder.

"If I didn't know better, I'd think you were trying to make me leave."

"Maybe I was. I'm just too selfish to let you go."

I hugged her more tightly. "That makes two of us. Don't be afraid; we'll be all right."

"I just don't want you to be hurt."

"You're afraid I'm going to die during some training accident."

"No, I'm afraid someone will kill you deliberately."

So Angie wasn't as naïve as Rhiannon had believed. She had known all along how dangerous this would be. Her drive to heal the world and live a true druid life must have been intense, to risk both our lives like that.

"Why would they do that?"

"To take your place. With me, I mean."

"Is it common to commit murder over a woman where we're going?"

"I'm serious, Charlie! I'm already one of the most powerful elementalists in the grove."

"And here I was, thinking that you sought me out because you were a poor little water druid that no one wanted."

Angie bit her lip.

"It's the opposite, isn't it?"

"It shouldn't matter whether I'm unwanted because of being a lesser elementalist, or greatly desired for being a powerful triple threat. I still sought you out because I wanted someone to want me just for being me, not for what I can or can't do."

"It matters because Rhiannon was right. I'll have to fight tooth and nail to keep you."

Her face twisted sourly. "This wouldn't be so bad if they had let me come find you when I wanted to. Then we'd be ready at the same time, instead of you starting to train when I'm almost finished."

"Really." I paused. "Then why haven't you been able to use magic?"

Her mouth twisted in distaste. "The ArchDruid blocked me."

"Come again?"

"If you're only an elementalist, you can be blocked from your magic. The ArchDruid wouldn't let me seek you unless my magic was blocked. I am too strong for her to block against my will, so I had to submit to it. I do have command over three elements. She said I could choose one to keep for the journey."

"I bet she didn't think you would be willing to give up your magic at all."

"All the magic in the world isn't worth anything if you can't be with your soul mate," Angie said, twining her fingers with mine. "Ideally, we would have been training at the same time. If you had come to the grove when you were fifteen or sixteen – when I originally asked for you, by the way – we would both almost be finished."

I thought back to when I was nearly sixteen, when my father had started teaching me to fight. It would have been the perfect time for her to seek me out, as I had been thoroughly disgusted by my hometown and its people.

"I don't understand why she would send you out defenseless. Did she not know it would put you more at risk?"

"She was angry that I wanted to choose my own warrior. She punished me for sending out a spirit animal to find you." Bitterly, she added: "She's already picked out a partner for me."

"Nice."

"I don't think she expected my father to let me go," Angie continued. "But I never told him about the block, and apparently she didn't think to inform him. I seriously doubt he would have allowed me to go if he had known. Especially since I chose to keep water and be blocked from spirit and air."

It was good to know that she had at least one parent with sense.

"Why did you choose water?"

"So that when we made it back, everyone would know it was because of you, and not my magic."

"Come again?"

"Everybody knows that water isn't good for offense or defense," she said. "I can defend myself with air and attack with spirit. Water is only good for healing or sustenance. And, since I haven't learned to heal, it meant that you would be solely responsible for getting me home safely."

I realized that I was just as much a pawn in the game as Angie herself was. It was an uncomfortable feeling, as it was my lovely druid herself who had placed me on the board, without either my knowledge or my consent.

"It was supposed to convince her that you are worthy of being my partner. It's a moot point now, since Rhiannon removed the block and restored my magic. I'm sorry now for all of it. It wasn't right for me to put you at risk like that. I just assumed that you'd be a warrior. Mother Oya, you could have been a farmer."

"I almost was," I said wryly, thinking of my father's attempts to interest me in the earth and growing things.

"I'm sorry, Charlie. You've been hurt for no good reason at all."

"Don't worry about it," I said.

"But, I feel so guilty," she replied morosely. "You didn't ask for any of this, and I'm expecting too much from you."

"Do you love me?"

"Yes," she said, looking at me as if I was crazy for even asking.

"Then it's all been worth it."

Her expression melted into loving gratitude, and I smiled at her.

"I think my father will back me up on this," Angie said softly. "It's hard for him, though. He's caught between a rock and a hard place. Even if he can't openly say it, I know in his heart he will support me."

"You're his only child," I said. "There should be no question of how he chooses."

"It's complicated."

"Nothing is so complicated that a father chooses against his own daughter."

"Even if he's First Warrior to the ArchDruid?"

"You have got to be kidding me."

"I wish I was."

"In the name of all that is green and good, why would he have made a decision like that?"

"Because after my mother died, I was the first child that she adopted. Her own protector was gone, and my father offered his service to stay close to me."

"The ArchDruid stole you from your own father?"

"Children belong to the mothers," said Angie. "And since I had no mother…" She shrugged.

I thought about that for a while, wondering what it would be like to grow up without a mother who loved me unconditionally or a father who protected me fearlessly.

Just as I had read books on the old world, the changed world, science, and dreams of Traveling, Angie had grown up with books of druid lore, hallowed traditions, magic, and dreams of healing the world. How difficult it must have been for her to hold onto those desires, all the while watching her role models go against everything she knew to be true. She had believed in those traditions so much that she had given up nearly all of her magic, embarking on a dangerous journey to find what she believed would be the one person in all the world who would support her in her endeavors.

Her chosen warrior.

Her soul mate.

Me.

I was humbled and proud all at the same time. I was humbled because it was me the gods had chosen to receive her fetch. My heart swelled with pride in Angie, because she had never given up, had never given in to the incredible pressures that must have been put upon her. She had never given up on me, even when I had rejected her out of hand.

True, she hadn't been entirely honest with me in the beginning, but I couldn't hold it against her. Seeing as how she had been raised by someone who viewed other people as merely a means to an end, it was actually surprising that she hadn't been more manipulative. I might have done the same thing, had I been in her position. Becoming a full-fledged druid devoted to healing the earth was her calling, her duty, the cry of her heart. What was more, I wanted to be with her, supporting and protecting her in her quest. I truly believed it was our calling, put in our hearts by the gods. I would have to trust them to see us through it.

I rose to my feet and helped her stand. I put my hands on her shoulders and looked deep into her eyes. "You are going to be the most renowned druid the world has ever seen," I said. "People will sing songs about your deeds, and your fame will precede you wherever you go."

"What about you?" she whispered.

"Me? I am going to be a living legend," I said with a wry smile, then kissed her forehead. That kiss led to another, then another, and we made love beneath the sun's golden light. After that, we ate and made love again. After all, if I was going to have to give this up, I wanted to get all I could now.

Chapter 21 – The Road South

Rules of Gunfighting #22:
Be polite. Be professional.
But… have a plan to kill everyone you meet

Late that afternoon, our path brought us to a place that had been destroyed in the Fracture, its broken buildings covered over in ivy and broken streets shot through with weeds. I reined Steel to a halt so that I could take a good look around. Rhiannon had said that they sometimes traded with the people nearby and that they could be trusted. Their community was to the southeast, however, and we would have to get through the ruins first.

"What is it?" Angie said.

"I don't like it here," I said. I disliked city ruins even more than bridges. Even though the buildings were too hazardous to enter, a desperate person might do it anyway. A clever thief or thug could hide between them and launch an attack from some cubbyhole. In the buildings that had stood the test of time – thankfully, there were blessed few – a sniper could shoot us through the broken windows. I wasn't the only person in the world with a functioning firearm. Even if I was, a bow and arrow could be just as deadly – often more so, because they were silent.

If we needed to get away quickly, it would put the horses at risk of falling or breaking a leg. The earth had heaved and buckled beneath the ancient streets, making them cracked and uneven. Piles of rubble from fallen structures made a twisty path with chunks of rock scattered about. It reminded me somewhat of Jonesboro, in the old, uninhabited sector. There were no bandits in the old city, as any who tried to set up a permanent residence there were quickly run off by the militia. In those parts, the criminal element was never likely to band together for long, tending to break up rapidly over petty squabbles. Here, however, the situation could be entirely different.

I looked at the sun's position, estimating that we had about four hours until sundown. We needed to be through this place and well away from it before dark. Holding the reins in my left hand, I drew the shotgun and let it rest in the crook of my left elbow. I nudged Steel and we started forward again. The winding path brought us past several buildings that had weathered the earthquakes better than most. To my relief, the remnants of humanity's past were not extensive here. We passed through it quickly, finding ourselves once again in an open area bordered by trees.

It was true that an attack could come from the woods, but the birds would give us ample warning that something was amiss. At the moment, they were all singing and chirping, filling the air with a lively cacophony. Angie began whistling various bird calls to amuse herself. A mockingbird swooped down and landed on Magic's head. The mare tossed her head, and Angie laughed when the bird flapped away.

"That wasn't a bad bird call," I said.

"It was good enough to fool the mockingbird," she said with a grin.

We traveled onward at a comfortably lazy walk for about an hour until we came to a small lake. The sleepy, relaxed posture of both horses changed to one of alert interest. Their heads came up, ears swiveling about. Steel settled back to his sleepy plod a moment later, but Magic turned her head in the direction of the lake.

"I think someone is over there," said Angie. "Want to go see?"

I had already been contemplating the idea of stopping here

for the night. Fresh fish for supper would be a welcome change. I was leery of approaching people, but since the High Priestess had assured me that folks in these parts could be trusted, I was willing to take the risk.

"Sure." I still held the shotgun at the ready. Steel was a good horse; if I dropped the reins to fire, he wouldn't go anywhere. We turned the horses toward the lake, and once again the stallion started paying attention to whatever it was that he and Magic could hear and we could not. After a few minutes, I could hear the cheerful sound of human voices, calling to one another. Soon we came upon a small group of about a dozen people fishing. Two children were playing in the water. I looked them over carefully. The fact that they had children with them engaged in play put me at ease.

The moment they caught sight of us, the people became quiet. The children ran to their mothers. The rest put down their poles, I assumed to pick up weapons. I raised a hand and gave the traditional greeting of the Traveler:

"Heya!"

They relaxed somewhat, but were still on alert. I would be, too, were our situations reversed. Even a thug was smart enough to use a Traveler greeting to get close to his prey.

Angie dismounted and began leading her mare over to the group. "How's the fishing?"

I dismounted and followed her, the shotgun propped on my right shoulder. Steel eagerly moved to the edge of the lake for a drink. I let him pull me along, because it gave me a clear shot at the people with little risk to Angie. Noticing the waterline on the dock supports, it was apparent that the drought had affected this area, too. The surface of the water was three feet lower than the waterline indicated.

The fishers relaxed when she greeted them. Several made the sign of respect that I had seen Angie give Grandmother, recognizing her as a druid. I gave her a quick glance, remembering how unique she had seemed to me when we had first met, with the feathers and beads woven into her curly hair. Now it was all just a part of her looks, but to other people, it set her apart as something special. I holstered the Ithaca.

"Eh, so-so," said one of the men. He looked to be the eldest of the bunch, skinny and bony. His dark skin contrasted sharply with the wispy white hair that clung to his balding head. He spoke with a rather bizarre accent. Strange dialects occurred in places where the people kept mostly to themselves, with little outside contact.

"We been here since dis morning, and don't even have enough fish for supper yet," said a younger man. He too was quite thin. None of them looked as well fed as the people in Jonesboro and Searcy.

"Maybe I can help with that," Angie said, handing Magic's reins to me. Smiling at the people, she rolled up one sleeve and knelt to plunge her hand into the water. She stayed there for a couple of minutes before rising again.

"Try again," she said. "You might have better luck now." She came and took back Magic's reins.

"What did you do?"

Her green eyes sparkled. "Magic."

"Of course."

"Really."

"I believe you."

"You don't sound like you believe me."

"If you say you're doing magic, then you're doing magic. Even if I can't see anything," I said. Still, I was curious. "What did you do?"

"I told the fish that there was lots of food over here, and it would all be attached to shiny things."

I didn't think that was quite fair, but didn't want to sound stupid, so I said, "Won't that unbalance the lake?"

"There are plenty," she said. "Even if we catch a lot, there will still be many. Besides, I only called the older fish, the ones that are fully grown."

"Can all druids speak to animals?"

"All druids can speak to animals, but animals don't listen to every druid," she replied, a mischievous glint in her eyes.

We stood there a few moments, watching each person with a pole reel in a good-sized fish. The children grabbed filleting knives and began carefully dressing the fish. Angie smiled in satisfaction. I understood how she felt. None of these people looked like they could afford to miss a meal.

"The earth mother is rich in her bounty," she said softly. "No one should ever have to go hungry."

I nodded agreement. In fact, if I didn't get busy, we weren't going to have any supper either. I passed both sets of reins to Angie and walked over to the fisher-folk.

"Mind if I join you?" I asked.

The old man looked at me like I was crazy. "Of course not! Dey's plenty of fish in de lake." He cackled like he had made the funniest joke in the world.

Satisfied that my presence would not be unwelcome, I returned to the horses and began removing their tack. I dug through my own pack and pulled out my fishing gear. On first inspection, it looked like nothing more than a collection of sticks and some string. A talented woman in Green Country, a few days northwest of Jonesboro, had crafted the fishing rod. I assembled it by screwing the pieces together, then tied the string to the end of it. To the other end of the string, I fastened a hook.

"You fish?" my druid asked, raising an eyebrow.

"Doesn't everybody?"

She cocked her head to one side. "It just seems strange. I rather pictured you as more of a hunter."

"I do that, too. A man's gotta eat." I cast my line into the lake. "I'd better catch the biggest one!" I called over my shoulder as she lead the horses away. She laughed and began setting up our camp a short distance from the lake, under cover of the trees. I went back to join the fishermen, who were now catching their second round. They offered me the use of their bait, which I gladly accepted. When Angie returned to our company, the fisher folk introduced themselves and began telling us about their lives and their town.

They called their home Pickthorne. Like most people that had survived the earthquakes, floods, and fires, they had endured by leaving the old civilization and retreating back into nature. The forest where they lived had a stream running through it, as well as plenty of places to hide from enemies.

"Dis be a peaceful place a long time, since I be a small boy," said the Old Joe, the wrinkled and balding black-skinned man. "Not anymore." He shook his head ruefully.

"What happened?" I asked, guessing it was bandits.

Young Joe, who had turned out to be the old man's grandson, confirmed my suspicion. "We can't let the women and children go out of de woods alone," he said. "Too many times dey never come back."

Young Joe's wife, Mollie, nodded in agreement. "Even if we just fishing, we go in a large group."

"It did be different, when dey druids be roamin' all over," said Old Joe.

"Was it?"

"Yeah, man. Dey women do be healin' and fixin' and cleanin', and dey men be killing dem bandits." He shook his head. "No more."

I looked at Angie for confirmation.

"It's true," Angie said, looking chagrined. "When the ArchDruid came into power, she decided it was too dangerous to let us go far from the grove. We became very isolated."

Apparently the druids had isolated themselves so much that it had allowed an increase in bandit activity that had put the surrounding communities in danger.

"Do you have weapons?" I asked, thinking that the knives and clubs I had seen so far would not be very effective against bandits who possessed firearms.

"No guns, no more," came the reply. "We have bows for hunting."

"Everybody learns how to shoot dey bows, even when a tiny child," said Mollie.

"Heya, Traveler, you wanna see?" asked the older of the two children, a girl about thirteen.

"Sure," I said. It was impossible to miss the eagerness in her eyes. She and her younger brother scrambled to get their bows and slung matching quivers over their shoulders. They used a scrap of cloth as a target, pinning it to a tree. I noted that they were careful to ensure that no one would be in their line of fire. They took turns firing from slender recurve bows. Neither of them missed the target, which could not have been more than five inches square. More often than not, they hit in its center. Each child demonstrated an amazing ability and superior targeting skills. I was impressed, and told them so. They beamed with pride and returned to their chore with the fish.

Angie smiled at me. "You're good with children."

I shrugged. I had been around very few children, but after having been treated like a virtual pariah during my teen years, I was always careful to treat them with kindness.

After we had caught enough fish for supper, we all set to work cleaning and dressing the fish. Angie contributed salt and herbs from her pack. As twilight fell, they lit a small fire, banking it with ashes. Delicious smells rose from the fish, wrapped in thick leaves and placed upon the hot coals. Before we ate, Old Joe looked at Angie. "You mind if we pray?"

She smiled. "Not at all."

"Well, I be wantin' to know, with you havin' so many gods and all."

She chuckled. "We druids pray to so many different gods, that surely we share at least one in common."

He nodded agreement at her wisdom and bowed his head to pray. "Father, make people have enough respect for ee 'n dem. Make your rulership come. Give we food we need every day. Forgive sin dem who forgive dem others. No let we see temptation, and keep dem evil ones from us."

"So be it," Angie and I murmured, while the others answered: "Amen."

After supper, the fishermen took out pipes and began to smoke. Mollie told their people's stories of the Fracture, when the earthquakes shook the world to its core, raising up mountains and sending volcanoes bursting through its crust. She told of the First Forest People, who settled their village of Pickthorne in an agreement of peace and trust, and worship of the One God, who had protected them ever since. The only time they had ever come under attack was when they had strayed from His Way, becoming selfish and greedy. Half of the population had died in a plague, leading them to repent and change their ways. Ever since then, they had walked the Path of God, and He had blessed them.

I was fascinated by the stories, as they were so similar to the two-thousand-year-old texts embraced by the people of Jonesboro. These people were not Triune, though they seemed to share the same Father God.

The fisher-folk settled into a comfortable quietude, gathered around the campfire preparing for bed. Steel and Magic grazed contentedly beside the lake, swishing their tails to keep the flies off each other. The rising moon cast silver ripples on the surface of the water, and I silently acknowledged her presence. Angie leaned over and touched my chin, beckoning me to look at her.

"Want to go for a swim?" There was no small amount of seduction in her voice and eyes. I glanced over at the fisher-folk, most of whom were settling into their blankets to sleep. I kicked off my boots and eagerly climbed to my feet, tossing aside my shirt. Angie giggled and danced away barefoot in the grass. When we were a suitable distance from the others, we stripped bare and slipped into the lake. I reached for her, but she swam away, laughing softly. I dove after her, and a few powerful strokes later caught her up in my arms. She squirmed in an attempt to get away, her lush body rubbing against mine in all sorts of delightful ways. I pulled her to the shallow end, where I could stand and hold her against me, then kissed her into playful submission. Her arms encircled my neck for a few kisses; her legs wrapped around my waist after a few more.

I carried Angie from the water and sat in the soft grasses with her straddling my lap. She plunged her fingers into my hair and kissed me deeply. I ran my hands down her back, feeling a breeze kick up around us, drawing off the moisture. She tipped her head back, allowing me access to her supple neck and sculpted shoulders. My hands on her buttocks, I pulled her closer to me. As she rose onto her knees, I bent my head to lick each erect nipple. She ground her hips against me, her breath coming in little pants as I nipped and sucked, feeling her fingers grip my shoulders tightly.

As the breeze died away, I lay back in the grass, running my hands over her hips and waist, moving them upward to caress her breasts. Angie leaned forward, kissing me, and guided me inside. A little moan escaped her lips, while I sucked my breath in sharply at the sudden heat. With a guttural growl, I arched my

261

back, lifting my hips to drive in deeper, and was rewarded by hearing Angie gasp.

When I lowered my hips again, she began rocking steadily against me, slowly at first, while I gently pinched and stroked her dark nipples. I closed my eyes, reveling in the lusty sounds, the feel of her taut body beneath my hands, and the hot, wet sensations where we joined as one. The pace of our joined rhythm increased, and her little pants turned into soft moans with every exhalation. I opened my eyes to watch as she moved against me ever faster, before throwing back her head and giving voice to her ecstasy.

The sounds she made when was lost in passion sharpened my own desire. With a growl, I rolled her over and thrust deeply, eliciting yet more of the wonderful noises. She gripped my forearms, nails digging in hard. I fought to hold back, just a few moments more, until she wrapped her legs around me. There was no denying her intensity and I gave in to carnal need, driving ever harder and faster. When the moment came, I lost myself in her eyes and in her loving whispers. We held one another, murmuring the kinds of secrets that only lovers share, bathed in the glow of the goddess overhead.

Chapter 22 – Thunderstorm

Rules of Gunfighting #18:
Always perform a tactical reload
and then threat scan 360 degrees.

In the morning, we broke our fast with the people of Pickthorne, enjoying leftover fish along with some nuts and fresh berries.

"You goin' back to you people?" said Old Joe.

"We are," Angie replied.

"Dis road here–" he gestured to the path beside the lake, which we had been following the day before. "Dis would be de fastest way."

"'Would be'?" I asked.

He nodded. "It's most dangerous, though. You probably will die."

"Bandits?" I asked.

"Biggest bandit city you ever see," he said. "Is called de 'Ville. Dey people go in and dey don't come back out."

"Is there a better way to go?"

"Yeah, man, but it be takin' you longer. You got to go t'rough our forest. See dat creek?" He pointed to a small stream, which ran beside the lake for a short way before veering into the woods. "What you be wantin' to do is follow dat creek through de trees. It do fork sometime, but if you keep right, you be headin' south. Dey's a town dere, too. Dey don't got no gods, but dey be nice folks, and be welcomin' you."

I nodded, considering his words. It sounded simple enough.

It wasn't.

It took over half the day before Angie and I arrived at the first fork in the creek. If we could have ridden in a straight line, it would have taken a third of the time. Sometimes the trees were so dense that we had to walk the horses in shallow water or sticky mud. Steel didn't mind much, but Magic consistently balked with much head tossing and tail swishing.

Thankfully, the trees were thinner after we turned right, so that we could ride alongside the stream. I rather thought that it would be quicker and perhaps easier if we just headed south, but stayed with the old man's directions. An easier route might only take us more quickly into danger. It was late afternoon when we arrived at the next division in the creek. This one split not two, but three separate ways. One clearly angled to the left, but the other two went right and ran parallel for a bit. I sighed in frustration.

"Do you think we should take the right right fork, or the left right fork?" I said, unable to keep the irritation from my voice. My patience had long since worn thin. I swore that it would be the last time I took directions from some old dude who probably hadn't been more than a mile from his house in forty years.

"He meant well," Angie said, trying to soothe my nerves. I rolled my eyes. The horses were irritable and the gnats and mosquitos had nearly driven us all to insanity. She looked down both streams. "Let's take the middle one," she said. "It seems to be going more in the direction we want, and the trees aren't so thick there."

I followed her lead and by early evening, we had escaped the dank forest. We were hot, tired, and itchy. Every time we had dry ground we had walked the horses, but they were still tired from slogging through muddy, half-dry creeks with uneven footing. Across the field was the town that Old Joe had described to us. I sincerely hoped it was more welcoming than the forest had been. The sight of thin columns of smoke rising from several chimneys and the odor of freshly grilled meat that hung in the air

264

was encouraging. It also made my stomach rumble.

"Oh, thank the gods," Angie said.

"Hungry?" I asked.

Filthy," she replied. "I'm hungry, too, but I can't wait to have a real bath."

A bath sounded good to me, too. So did sleeping beneath a roof in a real bed. Feeling our raised spirits, or perhaps renewed by the open air about them, the horses broke into a trot that carried us to the town in minutes. We slowed them to a walk and entered the open gates. There was a catwalk around the top of the wall, but no one was patrolling it. It spoke volumes about how confident the inhabitants were about security. It meant I could relax.

Maybe.

"Hey, there."

I turned to see a young man just a couple of years younger than Angie and I, holding a sack of grain slung over one shoulder. A pistol hung low from his belt, strapped to his leg for a quick draw. He wore a surprised expression, as if he had not expected to see unfamiliar faces. I think that if I lived this close to a huge bandit city, I'd be well armed and surprised to see strangers, too. I doubted they got many visitors. Most people wouldn't be crazy enough to venture so close to danger.

"Heya," I said. "We're looking for a place to stay for the night. Preferably with supper."

"Oh, um... there ain't no inn in Lone Oak, mister, but Miss Chasity has a boarding house where folks can stay. You can get supper there, too."

The presence of a boarding house meant that the town of Lone Oak was off the beaten path enough so that it didn't need an inn, but not so far distant that people didn't come through occasionally.

I asked, "And, where would I find Miss Chasity's boarding house?"

"It's right there across the street," said the boy, indicating the direction with a nod of his head. "Um... you're not bandits, are you?"

The difficult trek from Pickthorne had shortened my temper

265

considerably, reducing any patience I might have had in dealing with such a foolish question.

"Do bandits often stop here for supper?" I asked, raising an eyebrow.

The youth flushed, his neck turning red. "No, usually they just come by to rape and pillage."

"I guess we're not bandits, then, are we?"

He dropped his sack and put his hand on the butt of his pistol. "Mister, I don't like your tone."

"I'm a Traveler," I shot back. "I don't like it when people suggest I might be a bandit."

His belligerent expression was replaced by a look of derision. "A Traveler? Now I know you're lyin', because there ain't no more Travelers. Nobody travels anymore, the bandits done seen to that."

"Spoken like a true townie," I said derisively. His flush spread upward from his neck, darkening his face, and he drew his pistol, freezing when he saw my shotgun pointed squarely at his chest. His jaw dropped in disbelief that I had beaten him to the draw.

"Learn to draw your pistol without looking," I said. "If I was a bandit, you'd be dead."

The boy was about to retort when a man appeared out of a nearby building. I slipped the Ithaca back into its holster.

"Peter! Boy, I told you to get back with that grain quick! I told you I'd better not find you dilly-dallying in the street! Quit pesterin' them people and get your rear in gear!"

"Coming, pa!" Peter yelled back. He holstered his pistol, sneered at me, and hurried away.

"Well!" Angie said, watching him go. She turned Magic about and walked her to the other side of the street. I followed and we both dismounted and tied the horses to the hitching post in front of the boarding house.

"That wasn't very polite," she said softly, tugging the reins into a firm knot.

"He had it coming, with a stupid question like that."

"You can't blame the people here for being suspicious."

I didn't argue with her. For one thing, she was right; for

another, I was too hot to care. It was the most blistering summer I could remember, with very little rain to ease the parched earth. If not for Angie's magical ability to find and obtain water, we would have died of dehydration long ago. The farther south we traveled, the drier it had become. Pickthorne's lake and streams had been low, but they still had some water. This place looked dry as a desert.

Following her up the whitewashed steps, I looked the house over. Like most structures since the Fracture, it was a single story construction. The exterior was whitewashed, with well-maintained flowerbeds surrounding the front porch. Someone must have been watering them regularly, or they never would have survived the drought. I knocked on the door, noting its heavy design.

The house was not only pretty, but sturdy as well. The windows were too high for anyone to climb through them. A quick glance at other nearby buildings confirmed that it was a typical design. In addition, several homes had iron bars covering the windows, a further deterrent to entry. These people meant business when it came to securing their homes. No wonder they had survived living in the shadow of a bandit city.

I kept Angie behind me, in case whoever was inside decided to shoot first and ask questions later. The door opened and a middle-aged woman stood in the doorway looking me over. Her black eyes were hard like flint, her nut-brown skin weathered from years of hard work outdoors.

"Good evening, ma'am," I said. "We're looking for Chasity. Heard she might have a room to rent for the night."

"I'm Chasity. I might have a room, and I might not. Depends on who wants to rent it."

"Just two Travelers, ma'am."

She squinted at me. "There ain't no more Travelers."

"We've come from the northeast."

"Hmm." Her eyes betrayed nothing of her thoughts.

"Never mind," said Angie, taking my hand. "We'll just sleep in the forest again. Sorry to bother you."

I reluctantly let her lead me away, giving the woman a nod before I stepped off the porch.

"Wait a minute."

Chasity squinted at Angie, standing on her porch looking like a thing from the wild, beads and feathers in her hair. "You said you were Travelers," she said.

"I am."

"But she's not. That there girl is a druid. Haven't seen one of them in fifteen years or more, but I'd recognize one with my eyes closed. Never saw one running about with a Traveler, though."

I laid my hand on the butt of my shotgun, in case she made the wrong move. She waved her hand dismissively.

"Don't need to worry about her safety here, boy. We welcome druids. Used to, anyway, when they were still wandering about. Come on in."

She stepped back through the doorway and gestured that we should follow. Angie and I exchanged a glance, then followed her inside. The house was a typical log-style, its floor laid with smooth wood planks. I skirted the woven rugs that covered the flooring, not wanting to track dirt on them. We entered a large kitchen with stone floors and a large, open fieldstone fireplace on one end. In the center of the room stood a long table with several chairs, with a row of cupboards on the other end. Chasity gestured for us to sit, picking up a stone pitcher and pouring each of us a cup of water. I nodded my thanks and took a sip. It was a gesture of hospitality and great generosity in this time of drought.

"Sorry there isn't more," our hostess said. "The wells have been dry for two weeks and the stream is so shallow you can hardly get a bucket in it."

Angie and I exchanged a glance; I was pretty sure she shared my thought that perhaps we could barter her water magic in exchange for a room, board, and baths. Of course, there would be no bath until she produced some water, but that could wait.

"It's been a long time since one of your kind paid us a visit. Ain't nobody round here got any use for even one god, much less a hundred of 'em. We rely on the accuracy of our rifles and the speed of our bullets. Of course, if you want to do a little magic to help out our water situation, we'd be much obliged."

"Perhaps I can help with that," said Angie.

"You a water druid?"

"I am."

"We'd appreciate that," she said. "Want to have a look at my well?"

"Sure." Angie and I downed the remaining water in our cups and followed Chasity out the kitchen door.

"Wasn't even sure druids still existed," she said.

"We're still here," Angie said, looking uncomfortable. "Just keeping to ourselves, is all."

"Seems like there's been nothing but trouble since ya'll stopped your wandering. The weather gets worse every year, with less rain than the year before. In all my fifty years, I've never seen a draught like this. It hasn't rained since early summer, and even then it wasn't much. Then there's the bandits." Chasity shrugged. "I'm not saying it's anybody's job to round up bandits, but it seems that your menfolk sure kept them under control."

Angie leaned over the well, looking into its depths. She closed her eyes, seeming to draw into herself. Her head slowly bowed forward, then her shoulders. Her arms relaxed so suddenly that would have fallen into the well if I hadn't been standing right there to catch her.

"What happened?" Her eyes were dilated, black nearly blocking out the green.

"You almost fell in."

"Oh." She shook herself, as though waking up to the here and now. "The water table is very deep," she told Chasity, frowning at the dry well. "It's no wonder your well is dry."

"Can you bring it up?"

"I think I can." Angie paused. "I'm just not sure if I should."

"I beg your pardon?" Chasity said.

"The world exists in a delicate state of balance..." Angie began.

"If that's the case, girl, somebody already done unbalanced it powerful hard," said Chasity. "Don't see how a little more unbalancing could hurt."

"It's dry everywhere," I said. "Maybe you could draw it from the southwest."

269

"I was really thinking of filling up everyone's well." Angie looked off to the west. "Seeing as how we're on the east side of town, I might be able to draw from the west."

"The bandits' loss could be our gain," said Chasity.

"Can you do that?" I asked.

"I'll have to walk around and check things out," she answered. "But yes, I think I can."

"We'd owe you one big debt of gratitude," said Chasity.

"It's no trouble," said Angie. "This is what we're here for. To help."

"We wouldn't say no to a bed while we're here, though," I put in helpfully.

Chasity regarded the both of us with her hands on her hips. "If you two manage to fill our wells, you'll get more than that. Room and board from me, for starters. The others in town, well, I imagine they'll have their own ways of expressing their thanks."

"Deal," I said, and shook her hand.

"I'll go put your horses in the barn and tell the others to be watching out for you. Can't have anybody thinking you're bandits and shooting you on accident." She gave me a sharp nod and departed.

I turned and smiled at Angie. She crossed her arms over her chest, frowning at me.

"So you're bargaining with my magic now?"

"You did offer."

"I would help these people for nothing at all in return."

"And I'm all for that. But if they want to let us sleep in a bed and eat for free, I'm all for that, too."

Angie rolled her eyes. "Come on, let's get started."

We walked the perimeter of the village and I examined the layout further. The streets were laid out in a grid pattern, which made it well organized. The wells were evenly spaced, each located where the paths intersected between four houses. The paths between these structures were too close together to allow horses or wagons, so there were streets behind the houses for moving about with beasts and burdens. I decided that it not only would it be a nightmare to attack, it would also be difficult to defend. As far as I could tell, the townspeople only had one advantage over attackers, and that would be an intimate knowledge of the town's layout. Still, if a large enough group of bandits attacked, they would be fighting house to house, never knowing if it was friend or foe coming around the corner. I imagined that there was plenty of friendly fire and hoped I'd never be called upon to defend it.

As Angie continued to study the town's well system, I studied the shops, houses, sheds, and barns, revising my opinion of its defensibility. These people would never fight the way I did, using cover and moving between buildings. They could do it all from the safety of their own homes.

The thick logs were their best protection against gunfire, as were the high windows. Every single house had a wraparound porch, just like the one at Chasity's place. Unlike the decorative and flimsy wood slats placed in a crisscross pattern I had seen on porches in other towns I had visited, these were logs laid lengthwise like the house walls. They were constructed from smaller trees than the walls were, but I reckoned they were thick enough to stop a bullet. Cuts were spaced at regular intervals in the wood, just large enough to poke a rifle barrel through and peek out without exposing a defender to gunfire. My eyes traveled upward, to the roofs. Their steep pitch and rough shingle construction would make any invader hard-pressed to keep his footing.

My consideration of the houses caused me to study the layout of the town in general. With the houses laid out in their careful grid pattern, any unwanted visitors would be caught in a deadly crossfire. There was no place an enemy could hide. The buildings were virtually indestructible - resistant to gunfire, arrows and earthquakes. They might even resist tornados. Fire was the one thing they would not resist, but that was a small thing. Any bandit foolish enough to burn the structures would see his loot go up in smoke as well.

Periodically the inhabitants of the houses would come take a gander at us. Occasionally one would exchange a few words, commenting on the strangeness of seeing not only a druid, but a Traveler as well. Mostly they just looked us over carefully; it was something to which I was accustomed, so I paid it scant attention. By the time we finished, everyone in town would know us by sight. In the event of a bandit attack, I imagined that just might keep me from being a casualty of friendly fire.

"I don't know which of us they consider more unusual, you or me," Angie observed between wells. We were coming to the end of our examination and I was glad. Except for the few times when I had caught a glimpse of her cleavage as she bent over a well, standing around watching Angie "feel for water" wasn't very interesting.

"What do you mean?"

"If they haven't seen a druid in over fifteen years, I wonder how long it's been since they've seen a Traveler?"

I grunted. We did seem to have a following. The village children flitted in and out of sight like ghosts at midnight. Two boys with dirty faces peered at us from around the corner of nearby house, ducking away when they saw me watching. It had happened at each house. Either there were a lot of kids around here or they were following us. I didn't mind. Better that the children be curious than not. I just hoped they weren't going to beg me for any Travel stories, because I didn't have any that were suitable.

"I think it's going to rain," she said, peering down into the last well.

"You can tell that by looking down a well?"

"No. I can feel it in the air."

The sun was blazing in a near-cloudless sky. The air felt oppressively sweltering, the way it had felt for most of the summer, and I told her so. She straightened and looked me in the eye.

"It will rain," she insisted.

"You gonna make it rain?" I smirked.

She lifted her chin. "I just might."

"Be my guest"

Angie squinted at the sky, then closed her eyes for several seconds. "I think I could do it, but it would take everything in me."

"Seriously?"

272

She nodded, leaning back against the well and propping herself on her elbows. "I'd hate to create a rainstorm, only to have it turn into an uncontrollable thunderstorm."

"Volcanic," I said, impressed. "You would really do that? Call up a storm?"

Angie frowned. "Do you not believe me?"

"No, I believe you. It's just that..." I shook my head. The idea of anyone having the ability to summon even a light rain was unbelievable. The concept of drawing water from a distant source made sense to me. The concept of weaving together water, air, and electricity was unfathomable.

"I don't see the need in using magic to bring what is already coming," Angie said defensively. "Just because you can, doesn't mean you should."

"Quoting from textbooks again?"

"No, my father."

"Ah."

"Didn't your father say things like that to you?"

"Sometimes, but it all had to do with gardening. Stuff like 'Bloom where you're planted' and 'There's no need to fear the wind if your haystacks are tied down'."

Angie laughed. "Sounds like an earth druid."

"Earth druids must be a lot like farmers, then." I gestured to the well to remind her of our original purpose. "So, what do you think?"

"I think it'll take nearly as much magic to draw water through the earth as it would to raise a storm. Of course, a good rainfall would help the whole area and not just the town." Her full lips twisted into a pout. As dirty, sweaty, and smelly as we both were, it made me want to kiss her.

"We can stay here until you're rested," I said. "If you're worried about controlling a storm, then draw the water."

Angie made a face. "Water is my weakest element. I'm not sure if I could draw enough to matter for more than a few wells."

"So making it rain would be pretty tough, too."

"Not necessarily. It's already primed to rain. Just look at those clouds." She paused, thinking. "Besides, I could use all three elements if I made it rain."

273

"If I lived here, I'd be more impressed if you made it rain."

"You just want to see me do some big magic." She tried to sound petulant, but I could see the glint of mischief in her eye.

I grinned. "I wouldn't mind."

"All right, then," she said, standing up and rubbing her hands together. She pulled her hands apart slightly, sparks dancing between her fingers.

"Whoa!" I jumped back. Angie threw her head back and laughed. We walked briskly toward the center of town, where the largest well plunged deeply into the earth. She straightened her shoulders, smoothed her skirts, and faced southwest, where the majority of the rain clouds were gathered. She began taking big, deep breaths, her chest heaving with every inhalation. She spread her arms wide, palms to the sky, and raised her face to the sky.

"Mother Oya and Father Shango, hear me now!" the druid began. "In your name, I summon the wind, to bring the clouds. I summon the rain, to quench the thirst of the parched earth. I summon spirit, to charge it all with your power, without which all life would fail. Hear my prayer!"

As soon as the words had left her lips, a strong wind whipped up, blowing dust in all directions. Several dust devils spun crazily about Angie before blowing away. I looked up at the sky and saw that the clouds were indeed moving closer, slowly at first and then tumbling over each other as if in haste to reach she who had summoned them.

She snapped her fingers three times, creating a cascade of blue-white sparks to fall from her hands. There were cries of awe (and maybe a little alarm) from the children who had been following us. A few ran away, returning moments later with adults in tow. They whispered amongst themselves, alternately watching Angie and the now fast-approaching clouds. In a matter of minutes, what seemed to be the entire population of Lone Oak village gathered on the covered porches of the few houses surrounding the large well. Some stood in the yards, but kept a respectful distance from Angie. Chasity herself came out, stepping off her porch. I watched them all, turning in a slow circle to make sure no one intended her any harm. No angry or distressed faces met my gaze; all expressions were ones of wonder and hope.

I turned my attention back to Angie, breathing hard with her arms outstretched toward the approaching storm, fists clenched as though physically pulling it toward her. The wind picked up, blowing her hair straight behind her. Her blouse came untucked and her skirt pressed tightly against her legs. The metallic scent of rain, carried upon the fierce winds, enveloped the whole town. The sky darkened overhead as the thick mass roiled overhead with the first rumblings of thunder.

Raindrops spattered in the dust at my feet and I stared at them in wonder. I hadn't seen rain since the days when Angie and I had first met. I lifted my palm to catch the cool droplets, seeing them fall faster and more frequently. The druid's face was intense with concentration and effort as she summoned the rainstorm. A bolt of lightning shot across the sky, briefly illuminating the upturned faces of the townspeople. Immediately afterward, the rain came falling down; it started as a light drizzle and rapidly advanced to a heavy downpour.

The townsfolk cheered and left their protective porches, to dance about in the pouring rain. I smiled and closed my eyes for a few moments, feeling the drops pattering on my face. Angie thrust her arms high into the air; the rain came down ever harder than before. She whipped the wind into a large funnel that rose into the clouds and tucked its tail into the mouth of the well closest to her. The funnel captured the precious moisture falling directly overhead, shunting it into the well while all around it soaked into the parched earth.

The rain that fell upon the roofs of the village dripped down into rainspouts that drained into fifty-gallon barrels. Thunder boomed overhead, and several of the children screamed and ran for their homes. The adults laughed and followed, most of them drenched before they made it indoors. Chasity smiled, her dark face wreathed in wrinkles, then waved to me and went back to her house. The rain was beautiful, bringing life and sustenance to those who needed it. I could almost hear the earth sigh in blessed relief.

The afternoon grew shadier as more and more clouds rolled

in over the town. Lightning forked across the sky, the strikes accented with peals of thunder that vibrated the very air. The cloudburst was rapidly turning into a thunderstorm; Angie seemed to be focused almost entirely upon funneling water into the large well. She glanced occasionally at the sky, as if reminding it that it was she who was in control.

I peered into the large well and was astounded to find it nearly full. I waved to Angie and splashed the water around with my hand so she would know. She gave me a terse nod and moved the funnel to the next closest well. Her face was serious as she focused her magic upon the rain funnel. Shortly thereafter, the rain began coming down in sheets, with only a small area exempt from the downpour. We were damp but not soaked, as we were still standing where the funnel was siphoning all the rain directly from the clouds.

The wind was still all around, except that which Angie had whipped into the rain funnel. In mere minutes, the next well was full, and the next. We moved among the houses, tromping through the mud, filling wells in a circular pattern, moving ever outward toward the stockade walls. She had filled three-fourths of the wells when I noticed that her hands had begun to tremble. At the next-to-the-last well, her arms were shaking; at the last well, she stumbled and went to her knees. I barely kept her from falling face down in the mud.

"It's almost finished," she gasped, breathless. Hard rigors began shaking her small body.

"It's good enough, Ang," I said, alarmed. "Let it go."

She shook her head. "No… not yet."

"They have enough now," I said. "Stop."

Again, she refused. In the next moment, water poured over the wall and spilled down upon the ground.

"Let it go, Angie," I said. She nodded and began releasing the funnel. Her control broke and water sprayed everywhere as the funnel thrashed apart, soaking us to the skin. I shook the rain out of my eyes and tried to help her stand, but her legs wouldn't hold her. I scooped her into my arms and carried her back to Chasity's place. The trembling in Angie's body turned into violent rigors, her teeth chattering noisily.

Released from Angie's control, the clouds above roared with thunder and streaked with brilliant lightning as rain pelted down so hard that it needled our skin. Storm winds buffeted us, making it hard going. The thunderstorm raged out of control; I only hoped that it would spend its fury in thunder and lightning and skip the tornados.

Chasity was waiting for us on her porch.

"Get her inside so you can take care of her." She thrust the door open and urgently pointed me inside. "Never mind the floor. Your girl needs something hot to drink and food in her belly."

I carried her inside, into the kitchen, and set her in a chair. Chasity tossed me a blanket and I wrapped it about Angie's shoulders. Violent shudders wracked her small body. I could only brush her hair out of her face and rub her arms.

"Don't you know how to take care of her when she's like this?" Chasity demanded.

I shook my head, bewildered.

"We haven't... been together... very long," Angie stammered through chattering teeth.

"Well, then." The mistress of the house tromped over to the stove to pour her some tea, then brought back a thick slice of bread slathered with butter and drizzled with honey. "Eat."

Angie tried, but her hands were shaking so badly that she couldn't guide the food to her mouth. I took the bread, broke it into small pieces, and fed it to her. Once she had finished, the shaking had subsided somewhat but the druid was still weak and trembly.

"You over-extended yourself, little one," said Chasity, setting a mug of hot tea and a bowl of soup onto the table.

"It was tough," said Angie. "Maybe I'm just out of practice." She smiled wearily at me. The dullness of her eyes was alarming.

"Here," I said, holding out a spoonful of soup.

"I can feed myself," said Angie. She reached for the spoon, her hand shaking too hard to grab it. Even if she had taken it, the soup would have spilled in her lap.

"Please," I said. "Let me do this." She exhaled sharply and let me feed her, letting go of her pride. After eating most of the

277

soup, her hands had stopped shaking and were only trembling slightly. She picked up the bowl and drank straight from it. Chasity gave her more bread and butter, which Angie managed to eat successfully on her own. From somewhere in the pantry, our hostess rustled up a couple of pieces of cherry pie, which she placed before us.

"You need to eat, too," she told me, placing a cup of hot tea before me along with the pie. "I made it with dried cherries, but it's still the best cherry pie you'll ever eat." I acknowledged her statement with a nod and dug in. Angie wasn't eating, so I pushed her plate closer to her.

"I'm full," she protested.

"Nobody is ever too full for pie," I said. She rolled her eyes, but still took a tiny bite to taste it. She polished it off, finishing before I did and proving me right. Nobody is ever too full for pic.

"Feel better?" I asked, while she sipped her tea.

Angie nodded. "All I need now is a bath and some sleep."

"Well, we have plenty of water for that, now," Chasity said, gesturing to the two large kettles steaming on the stove. "I'll help the little one here. You get out of those wet things."

I started to protest, but Chasity gave me a stern look. "You're covered in mud, boy, and you're dripping everywhere. If you're not careful, you'll catch your death of cold. Take those boots outside and clean them off. You can leave them on the back porch. Stand out in the rain and let it rinse the mud off your clothes. Skinny out of them, rinse off again, and then come back for your bath, hear?"

I looked to Angie, who nodded. Frowning, I gave a sharp nod to the mistress of the house and left the kitchen. I seriously doubted that I would fall ill from being wet in the middle of the hottest summer in living memory, but I did as she instructed. I felt self-conscious stripping to the skin on someone's back porch, even if it did face the stockade wall surrounding the town. When I opened the door to go back inside, I found a towel draped over the coat rack. I quickly dried off and wrapped the towel around my hips, padding to the kitchen in my bare feet.

Angie was sitting in a chair dressed in a robe, while Chasity washed her feet and dried them. Chasity pointed to a screen set up in the middle of the kitchen.

"Your tub is back there," she said, in a tone that would brook no argument. Obediently I ducked behind the screen, finding a tub that was large enough to stand in and wash, but not deep enough to soak. It was enough, and more than I had been accustomed to as of late. I rinsed with the warm water and lathered with the soap, scrubbing every last bit of mud from my skin. Another rinse and I was clean. While I was washing, Chasity had tossed a clean towel over the screen. I dried myself, once again wrapping the towel around me and stepped back into the kitchen proper.

"There," said the woman, sitting back on her heels. "Now, Davis, you come pick her up and get her tucked into bed."

"I'm fine now," Angie said, rising from the chair. "I can walk."

"I'm sure you can," I responded, lifting her. I expected a protest, but she merely put her arms around my neck and laid her head on my shoulder. Chasity showed us to a small, cozy room with a bed big enough for two, closing the door behind her as she departed. I set Angie on the bed and slipped the robe from her shoulders. She was wearing a thin cotton nightdress, doubtless borrowed from the older woman.

The druid burrowed beneath the crisp, sweet-smelling sheets and heaved a contented sigh. I dropped the towel and slid in beside her, wrapping my arms about her. Angie snuggled up against me and slipped into a peaceful sleep, her breaths deep and even. I listened to her soft breathing and the rain pattering on the roof for several minutes, until the sounds lulled me to sleep as well.

Chapter 23 – Bandits

Rules of Gunfighting #21:
The faster you finish the fight,
the less shot you will get.

The rain continued throughout the night, all the next day, and the next. I wondered if perhaps Angie hadn't needed to expend so much of her magic in filling the wells, but at the time, neither of us had known the rain would keep falling. It was as if the world had been deprived of moisture for so long that it was reluctant to give it up.

It took Angie nearly two days to recuperate and regain most of her magic stores. Most of her time was spent sleeping or napping, and when she wasn't doing either of those things, our hostess was stuffing her with food. I didn't mind that at all; she was an excellent cook.

Our fourth day in Lone Oak, Angie pronounced herself sufficiently recovered. Chasity commented that people were wondering if the whole town was going to float away. Angie went out into the rain again, with me by her side, to redirect the precipitation. With seemingly minimal effort, she pushed the weather system northeast.

Over the next hour, the rain turned to drizzle and then stopped completely. From Chasity's back porch, I could see the clouds scudding across the sky, heading northward to bring their gift to other places. From Pickthorne to Kingston, I hoped people enjoyed it. Ward had been doing all right in spite of the drought, but I chalked that up to the witches' magic. I hoped that Sinclair in Searcy was doing well, and that Kam Stone and her dog Tuiren were staying dry. I thought of Mrs. Hayworth and her sons; the rain would help their spring river run clean and strong. My father's land and Mr. Farmer's fields certainly could use the rain. I sent a prayer to the gods that they would bring blessings to my parents along with the weather.

"Much better," Chasity said from her porch. "Now we might actually have a harvest, and some nice weather to bring it in."

"Speaking of nice weather," I said. "We should be on our way."

Chasity looked surprised. "So soon?"

I looked at Angie, who twisted her mouth in that way that showed she wasn't happy.

"You get so antsy when there's nothing to do," she said. "Can't you just relax?"

"I've spent two days relaxing. It's time to get going. Aren't we almost there?"

"Yes."

"You don't sound excited about going home."

"It's not that. It's just... I really enjoy traveling with you."

"So do I. And, the sooner we get there, the sooner we'll finish training, and the sooner we can be off again."

Chasity raised an eyebrow. "'Finish training'?"

Angie winced and said nothing, leaving it for me to explain.

"She left off training to come get me," I said. "Some old druid tradition, seeking out a protector."

"Well, I could tell you weren't from around here," said Chasity. "No druid I ever saw ever carried a shotgun."

"I'm not a druid, and I'm from up north."

"How long have you two been on the road?"

"Since about April."

"Four months?"

"We had some setbacks. Scavs poisoning a river, bandits attacking our caravan, thugs and toughs trying to steal from us. The usual."

"Don't forget the part where you got shot," said Chasity. "Oh, yeah, hon. I saw that fresh scar on your shoulder the other night."

"He's lucky to be alive," Angie glowered.

Chasity smiled wryly. "A man like that will never be happy just sittin' around," she said.

She was right. I was ready for some action.

You know what they say, be careful what you ask for.

You just might get it.

* * *

After we turned in, Angie fell asleep almost immediately. I tossed and turned, unable to relax. She would never get any rest if I continued to squirm about. I put on my jeans and quietly left the room. Thinking that some fresh air might help, I went out the back door. I stayed out there for several minutes, breathing in the sweet night air. It should have been the best kind of calm to ease me to sleepiness, but it wasn't. I was wide-awake and I didn't know why.

"What is it?" Angie stood in the doorway, wearing my shirt.

"Sorry, I tried not to wake you."

"You didn't," she replied. "When I rolled over and reached for you, you were gone."

"Go back to bed," I said. "It's okay."

"Come with me." She held out her hand and her green eyes glowed with desire. I was momentarily tempted, but my restlessness pushed it away. I turned slowly about, using all my senses. "It's quiet."

"It's town."

"Town's not quiet. Town's noisy. And even when it's quiet, it's noisy."

"It's the middle of the night, Charlie. Come back to bed."

I shook my head, still looking and listening. Angie sighed and put her hand on her hip. The long shirt rode up above her thigh, but even that could not distract me. My sixth sense was trying to tell me something, but this was town and there were so many people that it was a struggle to hear what it had to say. I slowly went down on one knee, placing my palm upon the ground, and closed my eyes to listen.

"Charlie?"

"Shh..."

There was something wrong. I could feel it to the core of my being. I tried to relax, breathing deeply and giving myself over to this most unusual and unpredictable of all my senses. The rain had stopped. There should be night birds, but none sang. The barn should have been quiet, but Steel snorted and Magic whickered uneasily in return. My nostrils flared, taking in the scents of dust and hay, leather and old wood smoke. Beneath the familiar smells were other scents, sharp and pungent. Gunpowder. Iron. Leather. Metal. Wool. Soft steps of several unknown persons moving down the main road in the village. I couldn't hear them, not with the gently rumbling thunder and chirping of the crickets, but I knew they were there. I could feel them.

Bandits.

I opened my eyes, quickly rising and ushering Angie back through the door, barring it behind us.

"Get dressed. Now."

Her eyes widened in the dimness, but she hastened to comply. I went to the front of the house and knocked gently on Chasity's bedroom door. There was no answer, so I entered and approached the bed.

"Don't even think about it, Traveler," Chasity said, rolling over to face me with a pistol.

"Good, you have a gun. You're going to need it."

"Bandits?" she asked. She threw back the covers and exited the bed in her nightgown without bothering to put on her robe.

"I think so."

"Usually they come in hootin', hollerin', and shootin'," she said, carefully opening the lid of the trunk at the foot of her bed. "But since we live a little bit precarious-like..."

From the trunk, she retrieved a rifle and a bandolier of shells. "Can't be too careful," she said. She worked the bolt action of the rifle with a metallic clack and followed me out of her room.

Angie came down the hall fully dressed, holding my shirt

and weapons. I slipped the shirt over my head, hastily tucked it in, and buckled the shotgun holster around my chest. Leaving the heavy leather belt behind, I buckled on my tomahawks. Last, I grabbed Sinclair's bandolier and slipped it over my head. It was fully loaded in preparation for a situation such as this.

"I know your kind frowns on women fighting," Chasity said to Angie. "Best you hide in the cellar."

"That won't be necessary. We've done just fine together on our journey. We'll be fine now, too."

"We've never been attacked by bandits before," I said.

"I'll not hide like a coward," said Angie.

The first shot rang out, shattering the quiet. A horse whinnied in the barn; accustomed to gunfire, Magic and Steel stayed quiet. A raucous bell began to clang, the call to wake people in times of danger. A roll of thunder from the sky met the clamor of the alarm. Chasity headed for the front door and kicked aside one of the pretty rugs, revealing a trap door.

"I'll be under the porch, if anyone needs me," she announced.

"Why don't you go with her?" I said.

"I want to come with you," Angie protested.

"This isn't like when we were in the woods or camping by the road," I said. "I'll be moving fast and quiet."

Angie nodded reluctantly and stepped gingerly into the opening in the floor.

"What are you going to do?" Chasity asked.

"I'll try and get the drop on them." In a low voice, I added: "Bar the door behind me."

I left out the back door, creeping along the side of the house. The fighting was beginning to intensify as the townspeople readied themselves for defense and began to return fire.

There came a shrill whinny and I could just make out Steel's grey form in the darkness. Magic was more visible with her white mane and tail. There were two or three ropes around her neck and she was whinnying, digging in her heels, and protesting enough to make a mule proud. The bandits had gone straight for the barn to steal horses.

In spite of the rope around his neck, my stallion tried to bite one of the bandits, then lashed out with his front hooves before dancing back out of reach. He reared and kicked, catching another bandit unawares. The man flew backward and crashed to the ground. He rolled to one side and came up with a pistol in his hand, aiming it at my horse as he was trying to regain his feet. I unslung the Ithaca and fired, knocking him down for good.

Steel crow-hopped, giving me a perfect shot at another bandit. The remaining man dropped the rope and the stallion bolted over to Magic. He bucked and kicked around her until they dropped the ropes holding her fast. Nipping at her hindquarters, Steel herded her back to the barn. That left three total standing in the street without cover. I doubted these bandits had ever seen a shotgun that could fire as rapidly as mine. It would be the last thing they ever saw.

I took no chances. If something moved in the shadows, I shot at it. I fired my last round and started to reload when a lone bandit stepped into the street and stood there with a pistol in his hand. I dropped to one knee as a bullet whizzed overhead. He had marked me by the muzzle flash of my shotgun. There came an answering crack of a rifle, and the bandit fell back with a bloody hole in his chest.

Chasity wasn't a bad shot, it seemed. Angie would be safe with the older lady for now. I finished reloading and started in the direction the bandits had gone, running in a crouch across the street through the slick mud. Hugging the walls, I rounded the corner of the general store, nearly running into the middle of a large group of mean-looking men.

I backpedaled, slam-firing the shotgun. They began to disperse, but when I slipped in a mud puddle and landed on my backside, they returned to the business of trying to kill me. I cocked the Ithaca, expecting to be riddled with bullets at any moment, yet unwilling to give up without a fight. The bandits raised their pistols and fired several shots before I could pull the trigger. Cringing from the sound of rapidly approaching death, I ducked my head and scrambled backwards through the mud. There was no way they were going to miss me.

The ricochet of a dozen bullets striking a solid object and then zinging away with a whine reached my ears. I flinched, expecting to take a hit at any moment. When it didn't happen, I raised my head to look around.

Angie stood over me in a wide-legged stance, her arms held out in front of her, palms toward the bandits. I looked up at her in shock. Her face was grim and her hair was wild, the dark curls tossed by the gale winds. I stared up at her, dumbfounded. It was rapidly becoming my usual reaction to her magic.

"It's an air shield! Get up and reload already!"

I realized that the odd sound had been bullets striking against a wall of air, generated by Angie's magic. I jumped to my feet just as they fired another volley, somehow managing not to dive back onto the ground like a coward.

"I told you to stay in the house!" Pulling shells from the bandolier, I started reloading.

"You don't tell me what to do." Her tone was icy.

"You're going to get killed out here!"

"If I wasn't out here, Charlie, you'd be dead now!" Angie shouted. "I am not going to watch you bleed half to death again. There aren't any witches around to heal you this time."

Our argument would have continued but for the loud cry of one of the bandits:

"DRUIDS!!!"

As soon as the word left his mouth, the others panicked and ran. I raised the shotgun and stepped around the invisible barrier, catching a few of them as they scrambled backwards, presumably to get away from Angie. I fired a few more times, taking two more men down, then stepped back behind the barrier... or at least where I thought it was. The few who had made it out of range of my weapon disappeared behind the corner of a nearby house.

"Why do I think this is going to be bad?"

"Probably because it is," Angie huffed. "Just like everything else that happens to us."

"Not everything has been bad," I smirked, finished the reload and cocked the Ithaca.

A burst of gunfire came from somewhere in the center of the village. I guessed that the bandits were still running away and that the townsfolk were taking them down. Seconds later, a group of fifteen to twenty bandits proved me wrong by showing up and brandishing pistols, shotguns, and rifles. As soon as they came into view, I began slam firing the shotgun. Their shots went wild, thunking into the ground around us, as well as the stockade wall. Twelve-gauge scattershot flew into the group, killing some and wounding more. Close-range firing into a crowd was exactly the kind of tactic that made the Ithaca so deadly. Even when it didn't kill immediately, the pellets punched holes that punctured lungs and ripped flesh to shreds. It was nasty.

On the eighth shot, Angie raised her air shield again, deflecting their answering fire. I couldn't see it, but I could feel it somehow. It was like the feeling you get when static electricity raises the hair on your arm.

"Nice timing."

She rolled her eyes. "I know how many shells you can fire before reloading. Hurry up. I'll keep their heads down." She held the shield steady with her left hand, moved her arm beyond the narrow barrier, and sent a forking bolt of lightning zipping toward them. They dove for the ground just as several more of their kind raced around the building. Two of these ran straight into the blue bolts, jerked as though being shaken by a giant, and dropped to the ground. I stepped to the left of the barrier, feeling my way with the barrel of the shotgun, then fired rapidly, taking the rest down.

"They've stopped," said Angie, breathless from the excitement.

"For the moment," I said. There were still shouts from all over the town. Occasionally there would be a rifle shot and a scream. Sometimes there was a shot and no scream.

"They'll try to flank us," I said, trying to figure out the best position for us to be. Ideally, it would be somewhere that we could easily defend, and where the townsfolk could pick off the bandits one at a time.

"How do you know?"

"That's what I would do, if I was up against somebody with an impenetrable barrier."

"It's not impenetrable," Angie said. "It can be destroyed.

It's already damaged."

I didn't like the sound of that. "Can you fix it?"

"I think it would be easier to drop it and raise a new one."

That got me to thinking. "How many air shields can you hold at once?"

"Two, maybe three. Or one big bubble."

I wouldn't be able to shoot out of a bubble. "What if you just put one up, and then when it's damaged, throw up another one inside of it. Then you can drop the first one."

"This isn't exactly easy, Charlie."

"Just do your best. Let me know when you start to get low on magic and we'll run for it."

She snorted. "You'll run out of ammo long before I run out of magic."

"I don't know, Ang. I brought a lot of shells." I grinned at her. "Let's go have a look at the front gate, see if anybody is outside."

"The front gate?" she said, following me. "Won't they have reinforcements out there?"

"These are bandits, not an army," I said and peered around the corner. I nearly got my head blown off for my trouble. A couple of bullets whined by my head, striking the wooden stockade that made up the village wall.

"You were saying?" Angie said drily.

"Plan B?" I said.

"Whatever that is."

"Hey, have a little faith." I trotted over to the building across from Chasity's where we had met the rude teenage boy and kicked over a small wagon. I knelt behind it, Angie following suit. If they came up the middle again, they would be caught in a crossfire. If they came up behind us, Angie could shield us with her magic and give me time to react.

What I didn't count on was them coming at us from two sides simultaneously. Luckily, none of them were behind us. Three came through the front gate, and four more were running away from the sudden gunfire from nearby houses. The ones at the front gate weren't running for their lives, so I targeted them first. Seeing the gate guards drop dead before their eyes, the four trying to escape turned and ran away from us – toward Chasity's place. I took two more down and Chasity got the other two with her rifle.

It was like shooting fish in a barrel.

Lasting only a few minutes more, the attack ceased, followed by an unnatural quiet. Rising from behind our turned-over wagon, I looked around for any signs of movement, and then stepped into the street. This was one thing I could do that the townsfolk could not from the safety of their houses – check for bandits who were still alive and lying low. Angie followed me and together we checked the perimeter of the village, walking along the stockade wall.

I had to admire the resilience and ingenuity of this village, from its basic design to the speed with which they had responded to the incursion. As soon as the alarm had sounded, they had rapidly moved into position and readied themselves to fight. We returned without seeing a single living soul and approached the front gate once again.

"Wait a second," said Angie. She put up an air shield and then we stepped through the gate. I was impressed that she could move it along with us. I brought the shotgun up and scanned one hundred eighty degrees, standing in the gap. There was no movement. Without really thinking about it, I knelt and touched the ground with my left hand, still holding the Ithaca with my right. I took a deep breath and closed my eyes, willing my sixth sense to go to work for me, looking outward.

Soft thunder rumbled off in the distance. The insects and the night birds began to pick up their song once more, hesitantly at first, then with more confidence. I felt their footsteps, fading away into the west. The smells of leather, wool and fear went with them. What remained of the bandits were the odors of gunpowder and the sharp tang of blood. The fight was well and truly over.

"They're gone." I rose and noticed Angie looking at me askance. "What?"

"It's just... interesting to see you use your... 'sixth sense'. Do you always touch the ground like that?"

I shook my head. "No. It just helps when there are a lot of

people around. When it's just us, out in the forest, I can just feel it."

"Even when you're riding?"

"Even when I'm riding. Who knows, maybe the horse helps." I grinned at her.

"Maybe it does." She smiled. "How do you suppose they got in?"

Looking around, we found a ladder leaning on the stockade wall, with a knotted rope tied to the end of it.

"Effective," I said, pulling at the ladder. The knots caught between the sharpened points of the logs at the top of the wall. Angie commanded a gust of air to toss them over to the outside. Sheathing the shotgun, I twined the rope through the ladder rungs for ease of transport and carried it inside. She followed, again using air to close the gates and replace the heavy wooden bar that held them closed at night.

The villagers had begun to stir, coming outside of their houses armed to the teeth with shotguns and rifles. A few carried knives and machetes, in case there were any living enemies to finish off. Chasity met us outside her house, rifle cradled in her arms.

"The menfolk will be startin' to clean up," she said. "It wouldn't do to leave the mess until morning. It frightens the children."

"I'll help," I said.

Chasity shook her head. "You two have done enough good deeds for us, and we sure appreciate it. I'll be out here keeping an eye on things until they're finished with the dirty work. Go on inside and get cleaned up," she said. "You're welcome to stay, but if you're still planning on leavin' in the morning, you'll need your rest."

I nodded. "Thanks, we'll do that." I took Angie's hand and led her to the back door of Chasity's house. I left my boots outside. Angie led the way into the kitchen.

"Looks like you'll need another bath," she said, setting the large kettle on to boil. When she turned back around, I smeared a dab of mud across her cheek, then dabbed a bit on her nose.

"Looks like I'm not the only one," I said.

Angie laughed, her green eyes sparkling. We helped one another strip down to the skin, taking our time. The water was hot by the time we both were bare. Angie pinned her hair up, piling dark curls atop her head with only wisps drifting down her neck. I let her go first, pouring water over her voluptuous body as she stood in the large tub. Skipping the washcloth, I soaped my hands and began to massage her neck and shoulders, moving down to the small of her back and buttocks. I rinsed the soap away thoroughly, then lathered up again.

Standing so close that my chest was against her back, I wrapped my arms around to wash her belly and breasts, sliding my hands down over her hips to stroke her thighs. Angie sighed, leaning into me and tilting her head back against my shoulder. As my hands found their way back up to her peaking nipples, she turned her head and kissed me lasciviously, her tongue seeking mine.

"Get in here," Angie murmured. "You're much dirtier than I am." She placed one hand on my chest and stole the soap. Warm water rose up from the tub and up my legs, sliding over my abdomen and chest, then over my shoulders. Angie smiled mischievously at me.

"Volcanic," I breathed. Working the bar of soap in her hands, she spread the creamy froth over my back and shoulders, warm fingers copying mine in their downward motion. I drew in a sharp breath when I felt her slippery hands slide up the inside of my thighs. Impishly she persisted in teasing me; her fingertips slipped upward, moving out to my hips. Soft breasts pressed against my back when she moved in close to wash my chest and arms. When she moved on to my belly and beyond, I couldn't suppress a moan, an almost guttural noise from deep in my chest.

I slipped from her grasp and turned about, pulling her tightly to me. Her hard nipples brushed my chest as we kissed deeply, and I gripped her hips, jerking them roughly against mine. A growl escaped my lips as our slippery bodies rubbed together urgently. The soap dropped onto the floor, forgotten. Water ran over both our bodies, directed by her magic, rinsing away the suds. Every time a portion of her flesh was rinsed clean, I tasted it with lips and tongue. Angie gasped as I scraped my teeth over each taut peak, arching her back and offering herself to me. As more water sluiced over her glowing flesh, I kissed my way down her belly. She buried her hands in my hair and drew me to the junction of her legs, allowing me to taste her sweetness. I slipped one finger inside, delicately stroking the silken flesh. She whimpered and begged for more, but I withdrew.

"Not here," I murmured, wrapping a towel around my hips before drying her softly, brushing the rough cloth against her skin. I carried her to our room and laid her on the bed, then tossed the towels on the floor at my feet. I knelt beside the bed, pushing her round thighs apart as her belly quivered in anticipation. My hands slipped up her inner thighs, caught her behind the knees, and pushed them upward, opening her secret places wide. Angie uttered my name with a whispered plea as I tasted her once, then again lightly around the swollen mound before tasting the honey inside. She gasped, the muscles in her thighs tightening. I held them apart firmly, flicking my tongue once, twice, three times, escalating her desire with sweet torture. I teased her with lips and tongue until her legs quivered uncontrollably. Angie writhed beneath my hands, her sensual moans and breaths reaching my ears. Her rapid breathing changed to gasps, then soft cries of pleasure.

"Oh gods, Charlie, now!" she cried, gripping my forearms. I climbed onto the bed, suckling one luscious nipple as I slid inside, meaning to go slow and enjoy myself. She was having none of it, bucking her hips beneath me, demanding deeper and more. Her frenzy jacked my excitement to a fever pitch, and I could not stop myself from giving in to her. Our heated movements became faster and more frenzied, culminating in my own uncontrollable release.

We came down from the high, movements slowing, caressing one another and engaging in long, tender kisses. Finally parting, I pulled Angie close to me, her back against my chest, our legs entangled. I buried my face in her hair, breathing deeply until I was engulfed in honeysuckle, carried away to sleep on the breath of the wild.

Chapter 24 – The End of the Road

Rules of Gunfighting #19:
Watch their hands. Hands kill.
In the gods we trust.
Everyone else, keep your hands where I can see them.

It was several days later when we came to the end of our journey. There was no sign of bandits, even after we turned west, so I actually enjoyed myself. The townspeople of Lone Oak had generously given us enough provisions for the remainder of the journey, so any game we caught was welcome, but not necessary. Angie and I spent our days walking, talking, and riding the horses. Our nights and mornings (and sometimes afternoons) had been devoted to making love. I couldn't have asked for a better trip.

We got a late start that particular morning, because I just couldn't get Angie to do anything productive. Meaning I couldn't get her to put her clothes on.

Not entirely a bad thing.

Sometime after noon, we crested a rise and stopped, gazing out at a fast-moving river that separated us from a gigantic pre-Fracture city. It must have spanned for miles and miles.

Two bridges still soared over the river, visually joining the city to the wilderness. The concrete bridge had been almost completely destroyed; where before it had arced over the water, now there was only space between its sides. Though twisted and warped, the metal bridge still stretched across the span. They were the biggest bridges I had ever seen, and for long moments I marveled at these antique feats of human engineering.

Angie didn't seem to notice our environment. I followed her gaze, down in the river valley, spying a settlement. It was huge; I estimated that it was at least five times the size of Jonesboro. There were several large buildings on its south side. To the west were several structures that rather resembled the training arena of my youth. On its northeast side, there were hundreds of small houses, each with its own garden and orchard. Between the druid city and the magnificent river were fields as far as the eye could see, rich with crops nearly ready for harvest. In the middle of it all, there stood a stately grove of giant oak trees, arrayed in a circle.

It was then that I realized her reluctance to leave our camp that morning. She had known our journey would soon come to an end. Maybe it was her way of saying goodbye. Maybe it was just taking advantage of the time we had together as best she could. In either case, she had not mentioned that we were so close. Maybe she had been unable to bring herself to say it. Sometimes spoken words make reality a little too real.

"Ang?"

"How will I live without seeing you every day?" she whispered, tears beginning to fall.

I pulled her into my arms, let her rest her head on my chest. I took her left hand in mine, feeling the magic flow between us, knowing she felt it too.

"Time to go," I murmured, releasing her. I gave her a leg up onto Magic. She composed herself, drying her face and settling it into that most unwelcome, impassive mask that she seemed to reserve for all things involving her home. It seemed to be inappropriately grim for entering a place dedicated to repairing the earth and healing all living things.

I mounted Steel and we started down the cliff face, taking the narrow road with multiple switchbacks that brought us ever closer to the druid grove. I figured that someone must have seen us traversing the trail and was surprised that no one came out to greet us. It wasn't a good feeling. It made me feel unwelcome.

No Traveler liked feeling unwelcome.

When we arrived at the outer perimeter of the druid community, Angie took the lead. I followed, taking it all in without actually taking my eyes off her. There were no walls, no gates, and no watchtowers. These people were supremely confident in their ability to defend themselves at any and all times. Considering their relatively close proximity to the 'Ville, it was a sobering thought.

Once inside the boundaries, I could see people moving about. There were women going about their daily business, most dressed in skirts and blouses like Angie. A few were minding children. Some of the men wore blue jeans and work shirts, carrying implements of farming or blacksmithing, or simply carting harvested crops. The rest were dressed in leather armor, bristling with weapons. They seemed to be the majority, but perhaps the others were out in the fields. I noted swords, spears, pikes, axes and maces. Each of them was menacingly lethal; each ready to fight at the slightest provocation. I kept my hands away from my weapons.

Dismounting, I walked over to Magic and helped Angie down. I kept one hand on the small of her back, trying to be reassuring. It was a difficult task, as my own guts were busy trying to make me sick with their nervous flip-flops.

"Angelina!" shouted a voice.

She turned her head and gave the man a slight smile. He was about my father's age, roughly six feet tall, with what appeared to be a trim, muscular build. It was a little hard to see his body for the armor and weapons. I looked at his face, noting the similar caramel color, maybe a little darker, framed by curly black hair, cropped short. Then I saw his eyes. They were green, just like Angie's.

"Father!" she cried, waving.

Her father.

Quakes.

He looked me over appraisingly. His expression remained neutral, except for the faint shadow of a frown that crossed his face and was gone an instant later, leaving me to wonder if I had actually seen it.

"So, this is the man you had to have, who is so much better than all the ones we have raised here."

Oh, *ouch*. Score one for the man with the mustache.

"That's not what this is about," she replied calmly.

"You should know that better than anyone."

The corner of his mouth quirked upward in what might have been a smile. "That I do," he said. "Welcome home." She went to embrace him and he wrapped his arms tightly about her. It was then that I saw warmth and affection for her in his face. They parted and he kissed her forehead before he turned back to me, green eyes penetrating.

"I hope you're worth the trouble that your presence is going to cause," he said. There was nothing accusatory in his voice, but it was difficult not to take it personally.

"Even if I am, I doubt anyone will admit it," I heard myself say. Quakes and volcanoes… that was not a smart thing to say.

He snorted. "You're right about that. Be sure to remember it. You're the first outsider we've had in years," he said. "The ArchDruid prefers that warriors raised here be matched to our young elementalists."

"So Angie has told me," I said, uncertain about her father's feelings on the matter.

"Well, *this* druid prefers the traditional way," Angie sniffed.

Her father nodded, then turned back to me. "I am Liam Everlight," he said, offering me his hand. "What's your name, son?"

"Davis." I shook, noting that his handshake was firm but not challenging.

"Davis what?"

"Just Davis."

He looked at me more closely, as though trying to figure something out. At last, he nodded to himself and turned back to Angie.

"I'll inform the ArchDruid of your return." He had just turned to walk back the way he had come when a striking woman stalked through a nearby doorway. She moved with a queenly air, her long, golden hair trailing in loose curls down her back.

Her eyes were narrowed in suspicion, and where Angie's full lips showed her pleasant and smiling demeanor, it seemed that this woman continually wore hers pursed in disapproval.

I gave her father a quick glance, remembering their family story. This was the woman who had "adopted" Angie after her natural mother had died, thereby securing for herself not only a child, but also a devoted protector. It still seemed odd that he hadn't fought to keep his daughter exclusively with him. Maybe I just did not yet understand the social structure of this place. Maybe he was trying to secure his child's position within the grove. Parents often went to extreme lengths to ensure the survival of their children.

Angie's father – Liam – bowed respectfully and stepped behind us. The woman ignored her daughter, immediately focusing on me. I didn't like that at all.

"This is what you had to travel miles and months to get?" she snapped, looking me up and down disdainfully. I was impressed. She could give Trainer lessons in scorn. Unfortunately for her, I had developed an immunity to such scrutiny and deprecating comments, seeing as how they were unaccompanied by a beating. ArchDruid Sebrina walked around me, inspecting me as if I was a horse or a bull. I ignored it. Everything she was doing was contrived to make me insecure, to doubt myself, or merely to make me give up and leave. When the ArchDruid was behind me, I gave Angie a roguish smile and a wink.

The blonde woman didn't know me at all. Her ridiculous posturing only served to strengthen my resolve and make me determined to succeed. While she paced and muttered insults under her breath, I spent some quiet moments in my head putting together the things Rhiannon had said, hints Angie had dropped, and the few things I'd seen since our arrival, coming to the conclusion that this wasn't a very nice place because its leader wasn't a very nice person.

As the saying goes, power tends to corrupt, and absolute power corrupts absolutely.

All I had to do was survive, while training to become the best of the best, and to accomplish this in less time than anyone ever had before.

It was daunting, to say the least. I had been joking when I had told Angie that I would become a living legend. Sometimes my smart-mouthed comments came back to haunt me. This just might be one of those times.

"Why are you here?" she demanded of me.

I was taken aback. Was that a rhetorical question?

"Angie said she needed me." At first, I thought I should have elaborated, but then decided that the less I said, the better.

"Of course, you weren't at all swayed by her more earthly charms."

My jaw dropped. I couldn't believe she'd say something so coarse in front of Angie's father. Angie's eyes flared bright green with a spark of magic.

"You will not speak so to my chosen warrior."

"He is no warrior," she said, in a voice dripping with venom. "You expect this outsider to train with our young men who are born and bred to fight, who are dedicated to our grove from the time they learn to walk and talk."

"He brought me here safely. He has the right."

"You risked your life foolishly, Angelina," she spat. "You have the potential to become the most powerful druid since the Rebirth."

"Traditions are worth taking risks."

"It's a foolish tradition."

"I disagree. Many fine people were brought here through that tradition."

"Your own father was not part of that tradition. I chose him myself."

"More's the pity," Angie retorted.

She lashed out to slap Angie. I caught her hand, but did nothing more because Angie's father was standing behind me with his sword drawn. He had drawn it swiftly and silently. I had already figured that if I made even the slightest misstep, he would not hesitate to separate my head from my shoulders. Vindictiveness was not a good reason to lose my life; nor did I want Angie to watch her father killing me. That wouldn't help this family dynamic much.

"Please refrain from striking my druid," I said softly. I released her wrist, and she immediately slapped me as hard as she could. I could have blocked it, but chose not to. It stung, but she wasn't particularly strong. In retrospect, perhaps I should have stopped her, because that would have prevented Angie from lunging at her, presumably to lash out at her for striking me. I wrapped an arm around my druid's waist and pulled her to me. She fought, but her strength was no match for mine.

"Angie," I murmured in her ear. "Don't give her the satisfaction." She stilled and I released her, keeping a light touch on her hand. A light tingle of the magic that bound us ran from my fingertips to hers.

"Please excuse my rudeness for presuming to touch you," I said, giving her a slight bow. One of the most useful things my father had taught me – for which I had thought him insane when I was a teenager – was that showing kindness and giving respect to rude, horrible people had a benefit all of its own. It might not have an impact on this woman, or on anyone else watching, but I would not allow her poison to invest itself within my own spirit.

The ArchDruid just stared at me, as if unable to believe her ears.

"She is my daughter, to do with as I will."

"She is a woman grown, and the druid I have sworn to keep from harm," I said evenly, returning her gaze. "I would be failing in that duty if I let anyone hurt her in my presence."

Her lips puckered more tightly, if that was possible. I wondered if she sucked sour fruit all day to help her make that face.

"You are dismissed, Angelina," she said. "Get your things and report to your hall."

Angie gathered her things from Magic's saddle and hesitated, casting a look at me.

"The sooner we get started, the sooner we finish," I said.

Breath hitching, she dropped everything and threw her arms about me, kissing me with a wild, desperate abandon. I took in one last breath of her wildflower scent.

"Be strong," I whispered. "We'll be together again."

"Angelina!"

299

I stepped back, removing myself from the embrace. Angie squatted to grab her things and then walked quickly away without looking back. I could tell by the hunch of her shoulders that she was crying. The ArchDruid stepped in front of me, deliberately blocking my view. I met her gaze evenly.

"Let me make one thing clear to you," she said. "I have chosen a protector for Angelina, just as I chose one for myself. You cannot succeed in this training, no matter how hard you try. You should spare yourself the trouble and leave this place."

Nobody would tell me what I couldn't do.

"With all due respect, ArchDruid, I have sworn an oath, and I intend to keep it."

"You do that," she hissed. "But remember, no matter what, all your blood, sweat, and tears will come to naught. Angelina does not belong with you, when there are so many others who are better than you."

"I have given my word to Angie, and I will keep it – or die trying."

She jerked her head back. "So be it," she said with a tight-lipped smile, then turned on her heel and stalked after Angie. I hoped that she would keep her hands to herself, but there was nothing I could do about it now.

"Come on, Davis," said Liam. "Let's get you settled in."

I turned my gaze to catch one more glimpse of Angie, but she was gone from my sight. I straightened my shoulders, inwardly bolstering my courage, and followed Liam Everlight, resolved to conquer the challenge ahead.

The End

Watch for the next installment of the Druid Chronicles!

WARRIOR
Book Two of the Druid Chronicles

Once he is admitted into the world of the druids, Davis realizes that at least in this place, people have not only weathered the storms of the Fracture, but have thrived because of it. With control over the elements bestowed upon them by the gods, the druids of Oak Grove live their lives in relative peace, without struggle for food, shelter, or any other necessities of life.

All is not idyllic, however, for it is a community ill at ease. For nearly twenty years, scores of young men have been denied their magical heritage by parents who have bowed to the ArchDruid's tyrannical demands. Angie continues her quest to lead her people in a return to the old ways, so that men and women can be equal once again.

While he knew his presence would not be welcomed by some, he hadn't counted on landing in a hotbed of druid politics laced with magic, through which he must carefully navigate, lest he give the inimical ArchDruid a reason to get rid of him -- permanently.

Finding himself squarely in the center of the struggle, Davis discovers that he will have to work harder than ever to keep Angie by his side. It is a test that will require all his wits and courage if he is to remain in his position as her Warrior..

Continue to read a brief excerpt.

WARRIOR
Book Two of the Druid Chronicles

Neither Niall nor Darryn had seemed happy to be riding out with me, and I didn't think it was entirely because they disliked my company. Once the grove was lost to sight, they both sat hunched in their saddles as though the sword of Damocles hung over their heads. I guess six years of combat and sword training weren't enough to prepare them to leave their safe haven to face dangers unknown.

Steel was happy enough; the little grulla stallion was marching along with his black ears swiveling in all directions, long tail lazily swatting at flies. In contrast, Darryn's bright bay mare kept trying to turn around and go back to her sunny pasture. Niall's stallion Charger, the big black that he had ridden in the joust, continually spooked at every falling leaf.

Being autumn, there were a lot of falling leaves. By the time we stopped for the night, Niall was exhausted. I almost felt sorry for him, but it was tempered by the knowledge that he had been provided with an animal of exquisite breeding, but hadn't kept up with the horse's training or his own riding skills.

I lit a fire and starting making supper. This was going to be a quick trip, so I could be more generous with our supplies.

"Why did you light a fire?" asked Niall.

"Because it's chilly and I'm hungry." I had a few small potatoes baking, as well as a couple handfuls of chestnuts. The beef jerky was rather dry, so I set it to simmer in a pot of water with some bouillon. I cut up some carrots and onions, tossed in some rosemary sprigs for flavor, and sat back to relax.

"Won't that attract attention?" His eyes darted to the darkening woods.

"That's what we're out here for, isn't it?"

Neither of them answered.

"Did you two volunteer for this?" I asked.

"No," Darryn answered, his lip curled in a snarl. "Why would I want to go anywhere with a stinking outsider?"

"Out of loyalty to the ArchDruid, of course." He glared at me and said nothing; Niall looked away.

"Honestly, I'm surprised your mothers let you come."

"They didn't want us to," Darryn growled. Niall gave him a warning look.

"Really. Hm."

Niall's eyes darted between me and the darkening forest several times, before he finally snapped: "What?"

"I'm just surprised, is all." I stirred the impromptu stew. "The First Warrior said that the members of the Tetrarch were in favor of his idea."

"What idea?" said Niall.

"The shotgun idea."

He gave Darryn a questioning look, which was answered by a surly shake of the head.

"Wait a minute," I said. "They sent you out here without explaining why?"

This time the look they exchanged was subtle and secretive.

"Just so you know, it *has* crossed my mind that she actually wants you to kill me – or just make sure I end up dead, which is pretty much the same thing." They shared another look which confirmed my suspicion. "However, if you'll both hold off on that for a few minutes, I'll let you in on Liam's plan."

"No one told us to kill you," Niall said.

"So you were maybe thinking of finishing what you started the first night you jumped me?" He looked down at his hands, but anger flared in Darryn's eyes.

Niall said, "No." but Darryn's expression said *Yes.* I reminded myself that the second time I was attacked, the dark-haired warrior had been alone.

"All right, then. Seeing as how I've suffered no lasting damage, we'll let bygones be bygones and start over fresh."

"Do you expect us to believe that?" said Darryn.

I shrugged. "I've never seen a case where taking revenge made anybody happy."

"You would die an agonizing death if you even tried," he spat.

"No doubt," I said, spooning the stew into a bowl for myself. As I stirred to let it cool, the delicious smell of beef rose into the air. As they looked at the pot with their travel rations of dried fruit, beef jerky, and nuts in their hands, I could see appetite warring with indecision.

"You're welcome to have some," I said. "I don't have another bowl, but you might make do with a cup."

"We don't need your foul food," spat Darryn. "No doubt you've poisoned it."

Slowly and deliberately, I took a bite of my stew, staring him dead in the eyes the entire time. Fool statements like that deserved no answer. Neither of them reached for the stewpot, but I left it close to the fire to keep warm. I just might have seconds, an extravagant luxury while out on the road.

"So, about Liam's plan," I began. "Believe it or not, he came to me after the jousting tournament and asked me to join him in meeting with the ArchDruid with the proposition that all the youth of the grove without magic be given firearms and the training with which to use them."

"I refuse to believe that!" said Darryn, not unexpectedly. "Our mothers would never agree to such a thing!" Niall merely stared in openmouthed shock. I ignored them both.

"As a matter of fact, the First Warrior has the full support of the Tetrarch."

"I will not stay here and listen to such lies!"

"South is that way," I said, jerking my head in that direction. "I didn't ask you to come, and I'm not going to make you stay."

"You would tell me north is south, just so I'd end up dead!"

"Don't be a fool. I think we all know that if either of you die on this little field trip, my life will be forfeit." I paused, finishing the last bite of my stew. "So, if you shut up and listen, we might all get out of this alive."

Darryn drew his sword with the swiftness of several years' experience, raised it to strike at me, and found himself staring down the barrel of the Ithaca 37.

"Like I said: I can kill you at any time." I gave him a humorless grin. "I don't even have to get up to do it."

He stood there with his blade in the air, chest heaving, his dark eyes blazing with rage. I held my position, the unwavering barrel of the shotgun pointed at his chest. I didn't want to kill him, but if he came at me with the sword, I'd shoot. Long seconds passed in which I could see the desire to kill me warring with the will to live. The very fact that it was such a difficult struggle for him was disturbing; most people had a greater sense of self-preservation.

"Enough of this," said Niall, breaking the tension. He stood up, placing himself between the two of us, effectively blocking my line of fire. I lowered the shotgun and laid it across my knees.

"Your sword," he said to Darryn. The other made no move to comply.

Niall's blue eyes grew steely. "I want to hear what he has to say. Now sheathe your steel or I'll report to the ArchDruid that you disobeyed her orders."

Darryn slammed the sword home in its scabbard, shooting his friend a look of angry resentment.

"I'm going to have some stew," said Niall, digging a bowl and spoon out of his saddlebags. I waited until he had settled with his bowl.

"I believe you were about to tell us the First Warrior's plan?" he said.

"Right. Basically, there are quite a few parents in the grove who don't think that training with swords and other weapons is going to be enough to keep their sons alive once they start leaving the grove with their elementalist partners. Having done quite a bit of wandering in the world myself, I tend to agree."

"You're not far enough in your training to make that assessment," said Niall, without heat.

"I don't need any warrior training at all 'to make that assessment'," I said. "I just have to know a little bit of history – namely, the part where swordsmanship and archery became obsolete due to the development of firearms."

He took a deep breath and let it out, obviously unhappy.

"Swords are fine for melee combat. But one bandit with a pistol will put you at an immediate disadvantage. You'll be dead or disabled before you get within melee range," I said. "As luck would have it, your wise and noble mothers agree."

"Where would they even get such an idea?" he asked with a frown.

"The ArchDruid mentioned having heard Angie's story of our trip down here. I imagine they were present at the time." I shrugged. "However it happened, Liam also seems to have some concerns as well, because they came to him asking his help to convince Sebrina to allow all the young men without magic to learn to use firearms. He wants the blacksmiths to create replicas of my shotgun, and he wants me to teach you to use them."

"A shotgun." His eyes dropped to the Ithaca lying on my lap. I had caught his interest; now I needed to reel him in. Darryn was probably a lost cause, but if Niall Ashcroft was seen training with a shotgun, others might be less reluctant to try it. It was as good a reason as any to try and bring him over to my way of thinking.

"It's a pretty good all-around ballistic weapon," I said. "It's not magic, but it'll put you on more even footing with the rest of the world."

"I don't know... It seems so unnatural."

"It *is* unnatural," I replied. "But with this baby in your hands, Niall, you can bring the thunder. And you don't even need magic to do it."

* * *

We stumbled upon a section of ancient roadway the next morning, which pleased me immensely. It felt insane, but the sooner we were attacked by bandits, the sooner we could go home. The ArchDruid had sent me out here to do murder, but I didn't have to play by her rules. I wasn't one to shoot someone in cold blood. The only way Niall and Darryn would get a demonstration of the Ithaca's usefulness was if someone attacked, for I only killed people if they tried to kill me first.

It happened the very day we found the road, when we stopped for lunch, parking among the trees. I led Steel deeper into the wood, where he would be safer but still accessible. I noticed Niall watching for a few minutes before he elbowed Darryn and tied his horse near mine. Darryn retorted in a most unfriendly manner and tied his mare to a tree in plain sight.

With someone that pigheaded, I didn't even need to try to attract attention. He did it for me.

"Just out of curiosity, what was the reason they gave for sending you with me?" I asked Niall.

He hesitated, mulling it over while rummaging in his saddlebags.

"They said you were on an assignment for the First Warrior."

"And?"

He couldn't quite meet my eyes. "And in the event that you failed in your assignment, we were to return with your weapons. And your horse."

"That's about what I expected," I said, kneeling on the ground. Touching it with my palm, I concentrated and started feeling for enemies. I hadn't used my sixth sense much since arriving at White Oak Grove, but it couldn't hurt to try.

"I don't understand why we aren't riding closer to the 'Ville," he said. "This is taking longer than it should."

"You want me to just ride up to someone and shoot them in the back?" My extra sense was indeed still working; someone was coming.

"If that's what it takes."

I whistled, counting six... no, seven. One was coming up behind, flanking us. "That's pretty cold-blooded."

"They are not druids," he said.

"Neither am I." The one behind was less of a threat; he'd probably stay hidden. It crossed my mind that my sixth sense had never been so precise before; usually I just knew that people were around. I'd never been able to put a precise number to them before.

"Angelina says you are."

"Even though I worship the gods, I am still considered an outsider."

He had nothing to say to that, so he changed the subject.

"Are we just going to stand here in the trees?"

"I don't see why not." I looked back over my shoulder to where the weasel was standing by the road in the autumn sunshine. "Since Darryn is being nice enough to offer himself as bait."

Niall's head jerked around to spot his friend; a second later he was striding purposefully in that direction. He came to a sharp halt when he saw the group of six riders standing in the street. I started moving lateral to their position and opposite the lone bandit who had hunkered down out of sight, choosing a spot where I could fire without accidentally hitting Niall or Darryn.

"You boys are awfully far from your little tree-hugger

village," said the man in the lead. A long scar ran down the left side of his face, clumped up in an ugly mass where his eye used to be, then trickled down to his chin.

"What's it to you?" Darryn said with a sneer.

"Well... Seeing as how you're breaking the treaty by encroaching on our territory, it's something to me."

Treaty? I wondered. *What treaty?*

"We are *druids*," the weasel said arrogantly. "The elements are ours to command. We go where we please."

The scarred bandit leader chuckled. "Don't be a fool, son. Everybody knows that you boys don't have magic."

There was absolutely no way anyone outside the grove could know that – unless someone inside the grove had told them. I didn't have much to go on, but it seemed that the ArchDruid had made a treaty with the bandits to keep them from harassing the druids. It certainly explained why the dyads had stopped roaming north of the grove, and why they didn't help defend the neighboring towns anymore.

Perhaps this treaty was part of her plan - to keep the young male generation from their magic. I still wondered how the druids would defend White Oak Grove if the young male population was never allowed to access magic. Once Liam's generation was too old to fight, the grove was at risk.

Remembering what Old Joe and Chasity had said about the druids having kept the bandits under control some twenty years ago, it gave more weight to the bandit leader's claim. Doubtless the people of White Oak Grove had magic enough to fight them off, but one would still expect thieves to occasionally sneak in to steal food, supplies, or horses. In fact, if the druids had remained close to home because of a treaty with the 'Ville, it would have definitely led to an increase in bandit aggression, as the towns of Lone Oak and Pickthorne had experienced. Thus, the logical conclusion was that while long ago the druid grove had protected their neighbors, now they were protected at their expense.

Niall jerked noticeably, while Darryn just growled. The man's anger completely ruled him, clouding his judgement and making him completely disregard danger.

"However... that's a real nice horse you got there," said the scarred man. "I suppose that if you were to give it to me, I'd be amenable to sending you on your way unharmed."

"She's *mine*," Darryn snarled, drawing his sword.

The members of the posse laughed. Almost lazily, the leader drew a pistol and pointed it at Darryn.

"Boy, I've been nice until now. So why don't you do the smart thing and hand over those reins?"

It was time to save the bait.

Slipping out from between the trees, I drew a bead on the leader. With a twelve-gauge shotgun, precision aiming wasn't really a priority, but I wanted to make sure they all knew who was going to get shot first.

"Actually, gentlemen," I said. "I think we'll be taking your horses instead." Several rifles were lowered and aimed at the three of us, but I shook my head at them. "Don't even think about it. Toss your guns in the grass."

There was grumbling from the bandits and clicks of hammers being cocked. We were facing rifles and pistols, in the hands of experienced men.

"You ain't one of them druids," the scarred man said.

"No, I am not," I said. "I'm a Traveler. Unless you want to die today, I suggest you drop your weapons."

"Easy, now," he said, holding up a hand. "Let's just talk about this a minute here."

"Guns down. *Now.*" The schick-schick echoed off the trees as I cocked the Ithaca 37.

The leader chuckled. "Young man, you are outnumbered six to one. Even with your scattergun, you can't hope to take all of us."

While the man was distracted, Darryn ducked into the woods and took off at a dead run. I guess he wasn't as crazy as I thought. One of the riders urged his horse after the little weasel, only to have Niall draw steel and chop off his arm with a lightning-quick strike. The man screamed and yanked convulsively on the rein held by his remaining hand; his horse wheeled sharply about, bringing it and its rider between the posse and Niall. Providence protected the idiot from being riddled with bullets.

As soon as his posse was distracted, I fired, the shotgun's voice booming loudly over the rest of the gunfire. The leader slumped over in his saddle, providing me with a decent shot at the rest. Horse and injured rider were peppered all over with bullet holes. The wounded animal screamed, rearing high in the air before falling over backwards and crushing its rider.

While the rest of the posse was hell-bent on trying to shoot Niall, I slam-fired five more times, hitting each of them at least once. I ducked behind a tree and quickly reloaded. Now mounted on his black stallion, Niall charged the riders who were still on their horses, stabbing and slicing limbs. One bandit with minor wounds spun his horse on its haunches, aiming for the blonde warrior. I took him out with a shot to the neck and chest, then finished off three more who weren't quite dead yet.

"Catch the horses!" I yelled, not wanting them to run away and alert anyone else. As far as I was concerned, this demonstration was *over*.

That's when the forgotten seventh member of the posse snuck up and shot me – or so I thought. In shock and finding myself on my knees, I looked down to see that a length of sharp steel had plunged through my back and out the right side of my chest.

Not a bandit.

Darryn.

WARRIOR

Book Two of the Druid Chronicles

Available February 2015!

~ * ~ * ~ Stay updated ~ * ~ * ~

Bookmark my website http://www.druidchronicles.com

and follow me on

Facebook: http://www.facebook.com/jpaigedunn

Twitter: @jpaigedunn

About the Author

J. Paige Dunn has dreamed of becoming a published author since the age of fourteen. In addition to writing stories, she enjoys reading, drawing, knitting, running, archery, horseback riding, and pretty much anything that would ensure survival during the zombie apocalypse.

She has one husband, two sons, a daughter and son-in-law, a darling granddaughter, four rescue cats, a ragamuffin dog, and a goldfish named Bilbo. She happily dwells in Geektopia, a little-known realm in Arkansas.

Author's Note

I would have been hard pressed to complete this novel without the assistance of some very important people, my family in particular. My husband Edward is always happy to see me writing and gives me constant encouragement to finish and publish.

My eldest son Richard was my big motivator, because I emailed a chapter at a time of the first draft to him, and he would scream for more if I took too long with the next one.

My daughter Rachel inspires me to keep writing, since she is becoming a fantastic writer herself.

Youngest child Nick thinks he has a cool mom who writes books, even if he can't read this particular one because it's too adult.

Thanks also to my parents and siblings, especially my sister Mary Claire, for her encouragement, and my mom, who lets me rave about my stories over lunch. My good friend Gabrielle taught me everything I know about horses and riding, which is a lot different than all those horse books I read as a kid. Never underestimate the power of support from those you love.

Big HUGE thanks to my critical readers, who went over the second draft and offered fabulous suggestions that made all the difference in the story:

Bacon – Without you, the character and relationship development between Angie and Davis would be stunted and the environments flat, colorless, and featureless.

Jessica – I loved your comments and insights, and I especially love having you as my very own fangirl. The fact that you love so many fantastic books and still thought mine was great really keeps me going.

Edward – Your insights on the fight scenes and firearms were critically important, because you kept me from looking stupid. You also have a great eye for continuity and helping me keep facts straight.

John – Your comments were few but relevant, and I kept them in mind during the final rewrites and edits.

Marc – Because of your observations regarding the dance between future lovers, you get credit for the swimming scene in Chapter 14.

My cover artist, Leah Kaye Suttle, deserves a round of applause for the magnificent artwork and cover design that she created. I am pretty picky about art in general and had definite ideas about what I wanted. Leah really came through for me, and I can't wait to work with her again on the next two covers. If you'd like to see more of her incredible artistry, you can find her on Facebook, and also on her site: http://www.leahsuttle.com.

The stellar Mark Francis is my incredible website designer. It just goes to show that no matter how long you know a person, they can still surprise you with how awesome they are. Check him out at: http://www.markansas.net

Credit must be given to NaNoWriMo, National Novel Writing Month, in giving me motivation to start writing again after a long hiatus – fourteen years, to be exact. On October 31, 2010, friend and fellow writer Amanda posted on Facebook that it was soon to begin – starting at midnight, in fact. I had decided to use the time to re-write my first novel. Then I read the rules, which clearly state that for NaNoWriMo, the work must be completely original. I discovered this at oh… about 9:30 at night after going trick-or-treating with Nick. By 10:00, he was tucked into bed and I was folding laundry, thinking that I was going to have a heck of a time writing a novel when I didn't have a single character, setting, or plot.

Housework has always been good for my creativity, because it's boring and my mind wanders to more interesting worlds for entertainment. Not one iota of this story existed until around 10:30, when I thought of this guy who wandered around a post-apocalyptic world. I named him Charlie Davis.

I actually won NaNoWriMo that year, earning myself the right to buy a cool t-shirt that proclaimed my awesomeness to the world, writing 50,000 words in 30 days. While wearing it one day, I even ran into a bookstore barista who knew what NaNoWriMo was, so that was pretty fun.

I figured that another few thousand words and I would be finished. 186,666 words later, it was apparent that it was going to be too big for a single volume. Thus, the "Druid Chronicles" was born. I really wanted it to be a standalone novel, but it would have been humongous. I still agonized over it for a couple of weeks before splitting it up and leaving the first two books rather short.

I'm really glad I did, because it's given me the freedom to delve more deeply into the story environment, particularly the druid's grove. I did an edit of Traveler to correct continuity errors (things evolve as a story unravels), and after the reviews from my beta readers, added several chapters onto the beginning. The second novel is titled *Warrior*, and as of this writing I'm still fleshing it out. So far I've added a whopping seventeen chapters, and will probably end up adding four or five more. The good news is that I don't think I'll have to add much to the third novel. I'm withholding its title because it's something of a spoiler.

Last but not least, I owe a debt of gratitude to Dan Speir, who allowed me to use the "Rules of Gunfighting." He didn't make up the rules, but he collected them from many contributors, some who are living, and some who have achieved immortality. Check out at: http://www.thegunzone.com/gunfighting.html.

Speaking of guns, I feel the need to talk a little about the Ithaca Model 37. The shotgun was always a shotgun, but it was a couple of other, more familiar, models first. I decided on this one after watching the movie *Aliens*, because I liked the way it looked. As Corporal Hicks says, it's good for "close encounters."

That being said, I may have messed it up. Originally in my research, I thought I had found an Ithaca 37 with a pistol grip that would hold seven shells and one more in the chamber. Much later on, after the cover was finalized, I tried to double-check for accuracy and couldn't find it. It comes in several different versions, but typically carries only five rounds if it has a pistol grip.

I really needed it to carry eight, and I think that it's within the realm of possibility for someone to modify an Ithaca 37 Defense by removing the stock and adding a pistol grip. The main issue is that the Stakeout comes with a 13-inch barrel, which would naturally hold fewer shells than the 20-inch barrel of the Defense. There might also be an issue with supporting a firearm with a 20-inch barrel without a stock, but I've had only limited experiences with guns. I imagine that the balance would be off, making it necessary to remove a portion of the barrel; i.e., making a "sawed-off shotgun." I'm chalking this one up to poetic license.

There are several other websites that I found useful while writing, and they are listed on the trilogy's web site: I probably have looked at over a hundred websites for research purposes, but have only included the ones most people might find interesting.

Where to find me on the web:

www.DruidChronicles.com

jpaigedunn@gmail.com

http://www.facebook.com/jpaigedunn

Twitter: @jpaigedunn

Blog: 365 Days of Night
http://jpaigedunn.wordpress.com

I truly hope you have enjoyed my story and will give me the chance to entertain you with the next two, so you can find out what happens to Angie and Davis.

Thank you so much for reading my book. If you enjoyed it, won't you please take the time to leave a review and share your thoughts with other readers wherever you downloaded it? I would love to hear what you think about my story. Knowing that you've enjoyed it means more to me than words can express.

December 1, 2013